The Return

to

Oliveto

The Return to Oliveto

By

Stefano A. Giovannoni

ISBN-13: 979-8-218-54781-3

Cover design by Getcovers.

Formatting by William Opperman/Keep the Voice LLC.

I would like to dedicate this book to the following people:

> To my stepfather: Thank you for loving me unconditionally and being an exceptional role model in my life. You will always be "dad" to me.

> To my nonno: You also loved me unconditionally and I'll never forget the many laughs we shared during that last trip to Italy.

> To God: Thank you for your many blessings.

To you, my dear reader: Thank you for choosing this book to be your next read. May your visit to Oliveto be a magical one; one with many happy returns.

Table of Contents

Chapter 1: A New Adventure Awaits

The last golden rays of the setting sun poured through the windows of Hornsby Manor Boarding House, bathing Nico's bedroom in a warm, amber glow. The light danced on the walls, casting long, shifting shadows as Nico and Sofia sat together on his bed, their faces illuminated in the fading brilliance of the day.

Finally, a wave of relief washed over them—they had uncovered the source of the mysterious knocking that had filled them with unease earlier. The answer had been hidden in plain sight all along: the faint, persistent sound was coming from the tiny, ornate fairy door tucked into the back of Nico's closet. It wasn't just a door—it was a summons, calling them back to Oliveto.

Nico turned to Sofia. "Are you ready to see what new adventure awaits?"

"I am," she said with a spark of excitement, "and I'm anxious to see Solomon."

Nico chuckled. "So, your costly nightly calls to each other aren't enough?"

"There's only so much you can say over the phone before you start to miss being with them," Sofia sighed. "Solomon knows I wanted to finish out the semester and not lose focus. Besides, I didn't want to pull you away from your studies just to take me back to Oliveto every night."

"True. If I had done that, my grades probably would've taken a nosedive. Thankfully, our intense study sessions paid off. Even Professor Cerveau gave us A's in our psychology class. How did you do in your other courses?" Nico asked.

"Straight A's across the board," Sofia replied with a grin. "How about you?"

"Well, I wasn't doing great in most of my classes at first," Nico admitted, "but after our spring break trip to Oliveto, I came back feeling more confident. So, I really buckled down and brought my grades up—not that they were that terrible to begin with—but I wanted to make my mother proud. I ended up with mostly A-minuses."

"I'm sure Siena would be proud of you no matter what grades you received," Sofia said, encouraging him. "You've worked so hard—it's not easy to balance everything while keeping up with Yale's coursework."

"She expects a lot from me," Nico sighed. "After college, I'm supposed to join her at the real estate office so she can mentor me. Eventually, she wants me to take over the family business."

"I'm sure you'd do well. After all, you're learning more about Oliveto than your mother probably even knows," Sofia said, then paused. "But … is that what you really want to do?"

Nico looked down, avoiding her gaze, and didn't respond. Just then Sofia's phone rang.

"That must be your nightly call from Solomon," Nico guessed. "When you're done, come back into my room—I have a plan!"

"Will do!" Sofia replied quickly, as she rushed back to her adjoining room to answer the phone.

Just as Nico was about to reach for his headphones, a knock echoed through the room.

Now able to discern where the knocking was coming from, he got up and opened his bedroom door.

"Oh, hello, Mrs. Hornsby," Nico said, surprised to see the owner of the Hornsby Manor Boarding House paying him a visit. She stood there, regal and poised, slightly taller than Nico thanks to her high heels. Her signature carmine-red lips, contrasted against her ageless porcelain skin, drew Nico's focus as she began to speak.

"Are you and Sofia planning on staying around for summer break?" she asked.

Sofia, having overheard mention of her name, ended her call with Solomon and joined Nico at the door.

Nico glanced at Sofia, who was now standing by his side, and replied, "Let's just say we'll be popping in and out."

Mrs. Hornsby smiled, almost as if she understood exactly what Nico meant.

"Oh, Mrs. Hornsby," Sofia interjected. "I promised a friend of mine that I'd ask you a question the next time I saw you."

"And what might that be, Sofia?" Mrs. Hornsby inquired, her eyes narrowing slightly with curiosity.

Sofia continued, "I know this is a longshot, but there's a couple that owns an incredible clothing store in the town of Oliveto, where Nico is from. When we were there in March, one of the owners told us how she and her husband immigrated to the area from Germany. She mentioned that it was thanks to a mysterious couple whose last name happened to be Hornsby."

"Oh, really?" Mrs. Hornsby replied, now clearly intrigued. "And what is her name?"

"Her name is Beatrice Schwartzman—" Sofia began, but Nico quickly chimed in.

"And her husband's name is Marvin."

"Hmm, the name does sound familiar," Mrs. Hornsby mused, pausing as if to search her memory. She seemed deep in thought for a moment before continuing. "When Mr. Hornsby was still alive, we traveled extensively and met many people—we were always looking for ways to bring people together. Tell me, dear, what year did your friend say they arrived?"

"1938. Or was it 1939, Nico?" Sofia asked.

Nico paused, doing some quick mental calculations. "Either year would mean that Mrs. Hornsby is in her late sixties or early—"

"Well, clearly I'm not *that* old!" Mrs. Hornsby interjected sharply. "So, it couldn't have been Mr. Hornsby and me."

"I'm truly sorry, Mrs. Hornsby. I didn't mean to upset you," Sofia said, doing her best to backpedal out of the now-awkward conversation.

Mrs. Hornsby ignored Sofia's apology and swiftly shifted the topic. "Back to the reason for my visit," she continued, her tone regaining its composure. "I wanted to inform you both that the rest of the student boarders have left for their summer break. I, myself, will be leaving tonight to make a short trip to England. Other than the household staff, who will remain to keep the place tidy, you two will be the only stragglers left here and will have the manor to yourselves."

"Thank you, Mrs. Hornsby, for checking in and letting us know," Nico said with a big smile, knowing it was his way of cutting through her sternness and hopefully diffusing any lingering tension.

"And remember, the East Wing of the manor is forbidden," she reminded them, in a firm voice, before turning and heading down the hallway.

Nico closed the door and turned to Sofia. "Apparently, that struck a nerve!"

"I know!" Sofia agreed, her eyes wide with curiosity. "She must be hiding something."

A brief moment of silence passed between them, and then they both exchanged knowing smiles.

"I bet I know what you're thinking," Sofia said.

"I'm sure it's the same thing you're thinking—we need to check out the East Wing and see what she's hiding," Nico replied.

"Exactly! Now we wait patiently for her to leave," Sofia said with a mischievous grin.

Chapter 2: Sneaking Suspicion

A few hours later, Sofia ran back into Nico's room, waving her hands in the air to catch his attention without startling him. Nico was completely absorbed, lost in the song blasting through his headphones. He sat on his bed, bobbing his head to the beat and mouthing the lyrics to an unknown tune.

Sofia approached the bed and called out, "Hello! Earth to Nico!"

Slightly embarrassed, Nico pulled off his headphones. "Sorry—I was really into this song by The Cure."

"If it's The Cure, then you're totally forgiven," Sofia said with a grin. She continued excitedly, "Anyway, I heard the front door close, so I went to the window to check. I saw Mrs. Hornsby's driver helping her into the car—they just drove away."

"Awesome! Let's give it a few more minutes, just in case they come back for some reason," Nico suggested. "We definitely don't want to get caught."

"We can finish listening to the song while we wait." Sofia sat down next to Nico on his bed and leaned in, pressing her ear against his headphones as Nico pressed play on his Walkman.

When the song finally ended, they sprang off the bed, eager to explore the mysterious and forbidden East Wing of the manor.

The hallway lighting was dim, the low wattage bulbs in the sconces casting faint light on the dark wood-paneled walls. They crept down the hallway slowly, listening carefully for any signs of the household staff moving about. A grand staircase led down to the foyer, but they cut across the upper landing, heading for a door that led to the East Wing.

"Ready?" Nico asked, his hand on the doorknob, eager to give it a turn.

"Let's do this!" Sofia answered confidently.

But the door didn't budge; it was locked.

Sofia put her hand on Nico's shoulder and spoke the Pick Lock spell, "*Resero!*"

The door clicked, unlocking, and Nico pushed it open. From what little they could see in the darkness ahead, the long hallway of the East Wing appeared to be lined with doors on either side. Various paintings hung on the walls, filling the spaces between each door.

"Great. I should've brought some dried ivy leaves—I'm usually never unprepared," Sofia sighed.

"I've got this one," Nico said, reaching into his pocket and pulling out the required spell component for the Fairy Fire spell. He crumpled the leaf and tossed the fragments into the air, invoking the spell, "*Lux Saltatio.*"

The familiar dancing lights appeared once again, illuminating about ten feet of the hallway, but still leaving a void of darkness that stretched further ahead.

"There seem to be even more doors here than in the West Wing where the students reside," Sofia remarked. "Good thing Mrs. Hornsby is gone—it might take us a while to figure out which room belongs to her."

"I'm guessing that she either chose the first door on the right or left for convenience or opted for the room at the very end of the hallway for privacy," Nico responded.

Sofia had an idea. "Nico, give me your hand, and I'll unlock the doors on the left while you unlock the ones on the right."

"A most excellent plan," Nico agreed, extending his arm across the hallway to meet Sofia's.

Together they spoke the magic word, "*Resero,*" in unison five times each as they walked along, unlocking and opening each door. They found only rooms used for storage: furniture, paintings, and other works of art. Now, they faced the final door at the end of the hallway.

Nico touched the doorknob and invoked the spell again, "*Resero,*" but there was no familiar click of a lock opening.

"*Resero!*" Nico repeated more firmly.

Sofia just laughed and turned the doorknob. "It was already unlocked, genius!"

"Hmm…maybe she forgot to lock it?" Nico wondered.

"Perhaps," Sofia replied as she stepped inside the room.

Nico followed Sofia into the room and found the light switch. He flipped it on, but even with the room now illuminated, it remained dim. A grand canopy bed loomed toward the back of the room. To their right stood a large wardrobe with a standing mirror beside it and a comfortable chair nearby. On the left was a sizeable dressing table with an elegant mirror.

"I'll search the left side of the room, and you check out the right," Nico suggested.

Sofia approached the large wardrobe, admiring its craftsmanship. It was made of rich mahogany, with a faceted crystal knob that caught the light. As she reached to turn the knob, something in the mirror's reflection caught her eye. Wispy tendrils of smoke seemed to be floating up from the room's large area rug, collecting into a hazy mass near Nico. Assuming it was just dust stirred up by their movements, she refocused on the wardrobe.

The crystal knob was cold to the touch, sending a chill through her fingers as she twisted it open. Inside, she found numerous formal gowns from different eras, three fur coats, and a luxurious mink stole.

These gowns must've cost a fortune, she thought, marveling at the intricate details of each one. "Nico, find anything over there?" she asked.

Nico was examining the items on the dressing table. There were various framed photographs, and off to the side sat a Florentine wooden tray holding a silver brush and an ivory-toothed comb. A selection of antique perfume bottles rested on the tray, but what caught his attention was a white porcelain dropper bottle, which seemed oddly out of place.

Everything in this room looks like it's from another era except this jar, which seems modern…and familiar, Nico thought.

"Just a bunch of old photos and this strange bottle," Nico replied, unscrewing the dropper lid. "Looks like some kind of facial serum—smells nice, like orange blossoms." He replaced the lid and read the jar's label: *Elixir of Youth by Stevie Cosmetics*. "Hey, what was the name of the barber's daughter? You know, the one back in Oliveto who comes from a family of shapeshifters—the one who helped us last time?"

"I think her name is Stevie," Sofia called out. "She's an aesthetician. Why?"

"Aha!" Nico exclaimed, turning the bottle around to read: *Made in Oliveto, California.* "You're right, Mrs. Hornsby was hiding something. She's been to Oliveto before!"

He quickly scanned the photos on the dressing table, searching for more clues. Each frame held images from different eras, with Mrs. Hornsby standing next to a dapper-looking man, probably Mr. Hornsby. In every photo, they were accompanied by different people.

One photograph, possibly from the mid-sixties, caught his eye. "Sofia, come look! There's a picture of your parents with the Hornsbys. I think you and Paolo are in it, too."

Intrigued, Sofia closed the wardrobe door and turned toward Nico, but suddenly froze in place. If her dark olive skin could pale from fright, it would have. "Nico get away from there!" she shouted.

Nico turned just in time to see an ethereal figure taking shape before him. The apparition was a man dressed in a sharp three-piece suit, but the side of his neck was savagely torn open, dripping with blood. As the ghost's face fully materialized, Nico recognized him; it was the man from the pictures: Mrs. Hornsby's deceased husband.

"*Get out!*" Mr. Hornsby bellowed, his voice echoing unnaturally through the room. The walls seemed to tremble with his words as he shouted again, "*Get out!*"

Nico and Sofia bolted out of the room in fear, racing down the hallway toward the upstairs landing. Their footsteps echoed as they ran, and only when they reached the landing did they stop to catch their breath. Both were panting, hearts racing.

From the distance, they heard the door to Mrs. Hornsby's room slam shut with a force that seemed to shake the walls. Then the disembodied voice of Mr. Hornsby bellowed once more, reverberating through the dark corridor, "*And stay out!*"

Chapter 3: The Return to Oliveto

The next morning, Nico woke up to the ringing of his telephone.

"Hello," he mumbled groggily.

"Nicolino, it's your mother," Siena replied. "I was wondering if you'll be coming home to celebrate your birthday with us—your father suggested we combine your birthday and mine and throw a big party at the house."

"Uh, yeah—sure!" Nico said, trying his best to sound enthusiastic about his mother's plans despite still being half asleep. "Sofia and I had planned a return visit at some point."

"That's wonderful news! I'll purchase plane tickcts for you two and let you know your flight information—I know you're on a limited budget while at college," Siena offered.

"That's generous of you, but Sofia and I will manage—besides, we're not sure yet what day we want to fly out," Nico replied quickly, knowing they could return to Oliveto in the blink of an eye via the fairy door in his closet.

"OK then. If you change your mind, please let me know—I'll even fly you out first class again!" Siena said, trying to entice Nico to reconsider her offer.

"We'll be fine—save your money for the party," Nico insisted.

"Very well," Siena said, before recalling something she meant to tell Nico. "By the way, I wanted to thank you for the lovely deep red peonies you sent me for Mother's Day."

Nico felt awkward, knowing that he had completely forgotten Mother's Day and hadn't sent her anything. "Mother, I'm sorry, but those weren't from me."

"Really?" Siena said, slightly perplexed. "You're the only one who knows that peonies are my favorite flower—and your dad isn't much into buying gifts or flowers, so I figured they weren't from him."

"I didn't even know you liked peonies—I thought yellow roses were your favorite?" Nico said, confused.

"After receiving the peonies, I suddenly remembered having a fondness for them during my late teens—not sure why. That time of my life is still a blur," Siena admitted, her voice tinged with confusion. "Well, if it wasn't you, then I wonder who knew how much I would appreciate them?"

Not wanting his mother to think poorly of him, Nico quickly blurted out, "I do have something special for you, but I was saving it to give to you in person."

"Such a thoughtful son," Siena said, her tone warming. "I'll look forward to receiving your mystery gift when you and Sofia return to Oliveto."

"OK. I need to get going—I think I hear Sofia calling me," Nico lied, needing an excuse to end the call and go back to sleep.

"All right," Siena replied. "Please tell Sofia I said hello and have a wonderful day."

"You, too!" Nico said, hanging up the phone.

Just as Nico sank back into the covers and found a comfortable position, Sofia burst into the room.

"Hey, sleepyhead, wake up!" Sofia shouted.

Nico groaned, "Argh! I guess I'm not meant to sleep in today."

"It's 10:00 a.m. already," Sofia announced. "I think you've slept in enough."

"Wow, it's that late?" Nico responded, sitting up groggily. "I guess I didn't sleep well. Last night's mini adventure kept my mind racing."

"Mine too!" Sofia agreed. "There's definitely more to Mrs. Hornsby than she's letting on."

"Well, we aren't going to find any answers here, so I think we should get ready and head to Oliveto," Nico said. "Meet me back here in a half an hour—and don't forget to get spruced up for Solomon," he chuckled.

Sofia rolled her eyes as she walked back to her room, muttering, "Sounds like a plan."

***

"Ready?" Sofia called out, entering Nico's room.

Nico was still in bed, sound asleep, with one leg hanging slightly out from under the covers.

Frustrated, Sofia marched over to his bed. She grabbed his leg with one hand and the sheets with the other. Then she invoked the magic words, "*Adtenuo!*"

The warm sheets Nico had been comfortably nestled in slowly reduced in size as the Shrink Object spell took effect.

Now barely covered, Nico was jolted awake by the cool air hitting his exposed skin. He shivered, blinking sleepily. "What—hey!" he exclaimed, trying to gather the now tiny sheets around him.

"Rise and shine!" Sofia smirked, arms crossed. "You're supposed to be up and ready!"

"Oh—I must've fallen back asleep," Nico said, slightly embarrassed. "Hey! What did you do to my sheets?"

"Desperate times call for desperate measures," Sofia said with a sly grin.

Nico touched the hand towel-sized sheets that now covered him and muttered, "*Excresco!*"

Sofia watched as the reversal spell took effect, the sheets gradually expanding back to their original size. The Enlargement Spell had worked perfectly.

"Now that that issue is resolved, if you'll excuse me, I'll actually get ready this time," Nico said, chuckling at the situation.

Sofia shook her head and headed back to her room to make a phone call to Solomon, letting him know they'd be returning to Oliveto.

Meanwhile, Nico stood in front of his mirror, surveying the damage from his restless night. His hair stuck up in all directions. His eyes wandered to the griffon tattoo on his right bicep. He turned slightly, admiring the tattooed magical mushroom beside it—inked in fairies' blood—that allowed him to use fairy doors for travel.

Focus, Nico, he thought. I've kept Sofia waiting long enough.

Deciding he could shower later when he got to his house, Nico grabbed a pair of shorts from the floor and pulled on his well-worn college sweatshirt that had been draped over his desk chair. He grabbed a baseball cap and slipped it on to tame his unruly hair.

"All set!" he called out to Sofia as he walked over to her room.

"Yes, I can't wait to see you, too!" Sofia said into the phone receiver, her face slightly blushing.

Nico hadn't realized she was on the phone, so he quietly walked in and sat down on her bed. Her room was the complete opposite of his—clean, well-organized, and filled with thriving plants, thanks to her green thumb.

Sofia continued her flirtatious conversation with Solomon, giggling softly, completely unaware of Nico's presence.

After a good five minutes, Nico's patience began to wear thin. He rose from her bed and snuck over to her desk, where she was seated. Gently grabbing the phone cord, he whispered, "*Adtenuo*."

Sofia's brow furrowed in confusion as Solomon's voice became fainter. She looked down and noticed the phone receiver shrinking in her hand. Abruptly, she spun around and glared at Nico.

Nico grinned. "Desperate times...."

Without missing a beat, Sofia reached out and grabbed his hand. "*Excresco!*" she commanded.

As the phone returned to its regular size, Sofia spoke into it, "Sol, my love, I have to go, but I'll see you soon!"

Blissfully, Sofia hung up the phone and stood up.

"I forgot how smitten you are by him," Nico said, slightly embarrassed at having overheard part of their conversation.

"How long have you been listening?" Sofia asked, raising an eyebrow.

"Long enough," Nico teased with a smirk.

"Right now, I'm too happy to be mad at you, so let's get going," Sofia responded, rolling her eyes playfully.

Sofia grabbed her purse, and they headed to Nico's room. Opening his closet door, Nico tossed some crumpled dried ivy leaf toward the back of the closet and invoked, "*Lux Saltatio!*"

The small, familiar lights danced and glowed, illuminating the space. Closing the closet door behind them, they approached the lighted area where the fairy door was placed.

Nico reached back and grabbed Sofia's hand. Kneeling, he extended his other hand toward the dusty door. Turning to Sofia, he asked, "Ready?"

"Let's do this!" Sofia affirmed, giving his hand a gentle squeeze.

Nico touched the door's carved image of a fountain, framed by two orange trees. Within seconds, they found themselves in the backyard of Nico's home—the home that his Nonna Chiara had left to him in her will.

The sun shone brightly, and Oliveto felt warmer than usual for this time of year. A light mist from the nearby garden fountain touched their faces, providing some relief from the heat as they gathered their bearings.

"Been a while since we traveled by fairy door—I totally forgot what *that* was like!" Sofia exclaimed, feeling slightly dizzy.

"I know, it takes a little getting used to," Nico responded.

Sofia gasped, "I don't think I will ever get used to those gnomes."

Nico looked around and saw what had startled her. All the garden gnomes, including Stinky, the smallest of the group, were gathered by the fairy door they had just traveled through.

"Must be the welcoming party," Nico joked, trying to lighten the mood.

"Or…maybe one of them was the one who knocked on the fairy door yesterday?" Sofia suggested.

Nico looked down at the gnomes and greeted them warmly. "Hello, guys!"

As Sofia looked around, she noticed the yard and garden were still meticulously maintained, with many of the plants now in full bloom.

"Wow, you guys have done an excellent job taking care of the yard—Nico's nonna would be proud," Sofia said, her eyes lighting up as she admired the variety of unique plant specimens around her. It was clear she was in her element.

"Sofia, look at that," Nico said, pointing to an object on the ground near the fairy door.

It was a small, tarnished, silver whistle attached to a worn leather cord.

"Someone must have dropped it," Sofia surmised. "May I see it?"

Nico picked up the whistle and handed it to Sofia.

Sofia pulled a handkerchief from her purse and carefully polished the whistle, revealing something carved into the silver beneath the tarnish.

Nico squinted, leaning closer as Sofia held up the whistle. Just then, a trio of hummingbirds zoomed in, curious about the shiny object, and hovered slightly above them.

"I can't tell if those are images, runic symbols, or just tiny words—everything is too small to make out!" Nico said, sounding frustrated. "Do you think the grimoire has a decipher spell that could help?"

"I don't recall there being one," Sofia replied confidently. "And you know I've read both the Benandanti and Malandanti sides of the book multiple times."

"Oh, trust me, I know!" Nico chuckled. "You've been a little obsessive with magic ever since we found my family's spell book!"

Sofia ignored his teasing and suggested, "Well, we can always blow the whistle and see what happens?"

"Good idea," Nico replied with a grin. "I'll let you have the honors—just in case it's cursed and turns the user into a horrible monster."

"In that case, you should do it," Sofia shot back, handing the whistle to Nico. "You've got both Benandanti and Malandanti blood running through you, so you might be better protected from any misfortune."

Nico looked at the whistle, raised an eyebrow, and then looked back at Sofia. "You're making this sound very reassuring," he said, chuckling nervously. After a brief hesitation, he took a deep breath, raised the whistle to his lips, and blew.

The three hummingbirds immediately darted away.

"I don't hear anything," Nico said, puzzled.

"Blow harder. Maybe there is some dirt stuck inside, preventing it from making a sound," Sofia suggested.

Suddenly, the sound of flapping wings echoed through the garden. A large raven, with milky white eyes and a golden band around one of its ankles descended, landing gracefully on the edge of the fountain. It let out a harsh "Kraa!" and then splashed water onto Nico and Sofia to get their attention.

They turned, startled, only to recognize their unexpected visitor—it was Simone, the undead raven who had helped them during their last adventure.

"I guess it's a silent whistle—like a dog whistle," Nico surmised. "Simone must be able to hear its frequency."

Sofia, who had once been terrified of the raven, now looked at it with a smile. "I'll bet *you're* the one who knocked on the fairy door and left this whistle for us to call you, right?"

Simone bobbed its head up and down, affirming that Sofia was correct.

"Well, now we know who beckoned us back to Oliveto," Nico said, wiping beads of sweat off his forehead. "But why? Hopefully, nothing nefarious is going on." He glanced around the sunny garden. "Hey, it's getting hot out here. Let's go inside and get settled in—we haven't even had our morning coffee yet."

"Ah, coffee," Sofia sighed in anticipation. "Iced coffee with a splash of cream sounds perfect right now."

Nico nodded. "Later, we can check the grimoire for a spell to help us communicate better with Simone. Otherwise, we'll be here all day playing twenty questions without getting any answers."

"Sounds like a solid plan," Sofia agreed, then turned to Simone. "We'll be back soon and call to you with the whistle. In the meantime, stay cool."

Simone excitedly bobbed its head up and down again. The raven then flew into the canopy of one of the nearby orange trees, finding shelter from the blazing sun.

Nico placed the whistle around his neck, and they headed to the backdoor of the house. As they approached, they heard the door unlock itself and slowly creak open, inviting them in.

"Thank you, House," Sofia said as they stepped into the cool conservatory, grateful to be out of the heat.

Nico followed behind, removing his cap and sweatshirt as he entered. *Ah, much better*, he thought, relieved to be free of the sweat-soaked fabric.

Sofia was already in the kitchen when Nico called out, "I smell coffee—wow you're quick!"

"Wasn't me," Sofia called out. "I think the house heard us and prepared everything. It knew what I wanted, but since you weren't specific, it made your regular—an espresso with a thin strip of lemon rind."

Nico entered the kitchen and sat down next to Sofia. "Iced coffee would have been a better option, but an espresso is a great start." He wiped the sweat off his upper lip and then downed his shot of espresso in one gulp.

The house, not wanting to displease its owner, took action. A cabinet door opened, and a tall glass floated down to the counter. The freezer door swung open, and about ten ice cubes marched single file through the air, gently dropping one-by-one into the glass.

"This stuff still amazes me," Sofia commented, watching the house's magic as a nearby pot of coffee poured over the glass of ice. "House, thank you. You've done enough. I'll do the rest."

With that, Sofia got up to fetch some cream from the refrigerator and added a splash to Nico's now-perfect drink.

"Here you go, Nico," Sofia said, handing him his beverage.

"Grazie!" Nico replied. "I think after this, I'm going to take a shower—I didn't have one this morning since I didn't want to keep you waiting after sleeping in."

"OK. I wanted to go to my room and change—this shirt is still sticking to me."

"But you didn't bring any clothes," Nico pointed out with a grin. "I'll guess we'll need to go back for some or…go shopping?"

He watched as Sofia's eyes lit up, knowing he had just dangled one of her favorite activities as a possibility.

"You know I'll never turn down an opportunity to buy new clothes," Sofia replied, smiling, "but I planned ahead and packed two weeks' worth of clothing in my purse. You know, because I could."

"Clever girl!" Nico commended. "That Secret Space spell I cast on your purse during our last visit really does come in handy. Looks like I'm the one who should've planned better!"

"Meet in the foyer in, say, an hour?" Sofia suggested.

"Yes, and I'll be ready this time," Nico promised, heading off toward his bedroom.

Before going to her room, Sofia cleared off the kitchen island and placed the used glasses in the sink.

Stefano A Giovannoni

Chapter 4: Hot and Cold

Nico entered his bedroom and threw his cap and sweatshirt onto the floor. He took off his Swatch and went to place it on his nightstand but paused as his eye caught sight of a folded piece of paper with a coin on top. *What's this?* he wondered.

Then it all came back to him. He remembered his last night at the house after he and Sofia had returned from their near-death encounter with Mr. Primo Cadaveri. Weary from the escape, Nico had emptied his pockets and collapsed onto his bed, exhausted.

Now I remember, he thought. This is the Coin of Favor that I took from my nonna's safe deposit box. He moved the coin aside and unfolded the note to read:

> *Call me sometime,*
> *Gino*
> *707 555-3323*

Ah, yes. The note that Gino secretly slipped to me when we were all having drinks at Moraiolo's, Nico recalled, a fleeting smile crossing his face. I never did call him...I mean, how could I after playing a part in his father's death? His thoughts darkened. But then again, he did try to kill Sofia and me. And he'd already taken so many lives from the fairy community.

Nico shook his head and opened the dresser drawer, tossing the note inside and slamming it shut. Now slightly aggravated, he walked over to the French doors leading out to the garden and opened them. A wave of hot air hit him, making him grit his teeth in annoyance—he wasn't fond of extreme heat.

19

A cold shower will snap me out of this mood, Nico decided. *But first, I need a change of clothes!* He rushed over to the fairy door to return to his room at Hornsby Manor.

***

A now refreshed Nico entered the foyer just as Sofia made her entrance.

"Ah just in time!" Sofia noted. "I see you found a change of clothes."

"I actually went back to my room at the manor and grabbed a few things," Nico explained. He pointed to the marble entry table. "Are these your keys?"

"Not mine. They weren't here earlier when I passed by," Sofia said.

Nico picked up the keys and examined them. They were attached to a keychain with a red *cornicello* hanging from it.

"I recognize these. They're to my nonna's Mercedes," Nico said. "I'm guessing the house didn't want us walking into town with these high temps."

"Driving in air-conditioned comfort is definitely a better option!" Sofia agreed. "Unless her car is like the middle bedroom—the *Stanza Naturale*—and lacks air conditioning and other modern amenities?"

"Thankfully, the car is fully loaded with features," Nico assured her. "Let's go."

As they approached the front door, it opened on its own. Nico stopped at the threshold and knelt to pick up the morning newspaper, *L'Essenziale,* whose headline read: *Oliveto Pickpocket Ring Strikes Again!*

Nico tossed the newspaper onto the entry table, and they made their way down the front steps. Chiara's tan Mercedes-Benz awaited them under the *porte-cochere*, shielded from the blazing sun.

As they got inside the vehicle, they heard the distant sound of the house locking the front door. Nico quickly started the car and turned on the air conditioning. As they sank into the comfort of the soft leather seats, the cabin began to cool, and a light scent of geranium filled the air.

"This is definitely your nonna's car," Sofia remarked. "The smell of geraniums will always remind me that she's watching over us."

Nico sighed. "The scent is so calming to me—brings back so many memories." As he put the car into drive and pulled out of the driveway, he turned to Sofia. "Do you want to get something to eat first, or are you anxious to see Solomon?"

"The coffee suppressed my appetite, so I won't need to eat for a while," Sofia replied. "Let's head to Schwartzman's."

Nico had barely pressed the gas pedal when the car seemed to take off on its own. As they reached the end of the street, the turn signal automatically engaged, indicating a right turn.

"Sofia, something's odd about this car," Nico said, puzzled by how it seemed to anticipate their desires, much like the house.

Sofia thought quietly for a few seconds before blurting out, "Car, pull over."

The steering wheel turned in Nico's hands, and the car pulled over, stopping parallel to the curb.

"Wow, this is way cool!" Nico exclaimed.

"It's perfect, since you hate driving," Sofia added. "I wonder if the car is enchanted, or if your nonna enchanted the keychain to work for any car—we might have to test that theory."

"Car, please take us to Schwartzman's Quality Clothing," Nico directed, taking his hands off the steering wheel.

The car signaled and, after waiting for a passing vehicle, pulled back into the street and drove into town. As it approached Schwartzman's, it smoothly pulled into the closest parking space, just a few doors down in front of Trattoria Moraiolo. The engine shut off, and the doors unlocked. Nico removed the key from the ignition, and they both got out.

The delicious aroma of wood-fired pizza wafting from Moraiolo's didn't stop Sofia. She quickly made her way down the sun-beaten sidewalk to her destination. She swung open the door to the clothing store, and a blast of refreshing cool air, mixed with the scent of cedar and linen, hit her exposed face and arms as she entered. Nico, trailing behind, managed to catch the door just before it closed.

"Ah, this feels good," he said, thinking Sofia was close by, but she was already halfway across the store. She had spotted Solomon near one of the display tables and immediately rushed over to him, but he didn't move.

"Are you mad at me?" Sofia asked, her voice uncertain.

A muffled voice responded, "Customer...still in...store."

"Oh, right," Sofia said, quickly appreciating the situation. She began pacing about while waiting for the customer to leave.

Mrs. Schwartzman waved to Nico from the back of the store, where she was ringing up the remaining customer. He walked over to greet her.

"Hello, Mrs. Schwartzman!" Nico said as he approached.

"My husband, Marvin, will have the alterations to your sundress completed in a few days," Mrs. Schwartzman said to the customer. "I'll give you a call. In the meantime, enjoy your new tank top." She then turned to Nico. "Come here and give me a hug."

Nico approached the counter, and Mrs. Schwartzman stepped out from behind it to embrace him. "So good to see you alive and well. After your last visit, Solomon told me about everything you and Sofia went through. I'm so relieved you two weren't harmed."

"Yeah, we barely escaped. He was going to burn us alive in the cremation oven," Nico said, a shiver running down his spine as he recalled the memory.

"Are you here for the Founders' Day Centennial Celebration?" Mrs. Schwartzman asked.

"I forgot about that. Wow, one hundred years! Quite a milestone," Nico responded. "Actually, my mother is having a joint birthday for the both of us. If my nonna were still alive, it would have been for all three of us Cancers." Nico then turned, looking for Sofia.

Mrs. Schwartzman smiled knowingly. "I see Sofia found what she was looking for," she said, noticing Sofia near a display table.

Nico turned back to Mrs. Schwartzman and chuckled. "I think they've talked every night since we left."

Just then, the bell at the door chimed as the customer exited, leaving the store empty, except for the four of them.

"I'm so glad to finally see you again," Sofia said, wrapping her arms around Solomon's wooden frame.

As his body slowly transformed into flesh, Solomon began to form a smile. Now able to move, he embraced Sofia back and kissed her forehead.

"Is that all I get?" Sofia asked, a hint of disappointment in her voice. She looked up into his piercing blue eyes, framed by two perfectly shaped eyebrows, and continued, "After all this time, I want a real kiss."

Solomon gently brushed his blond bangs to the side, briefly revealing the magical inscription on his forehead that had brought him to life as a golem. He leaned in and kissed Sofia deeply.

"You two, get a room!" Nico yelled playfully from across the store.

Slightly embarrassed, the two lovebirds pulled apart and joined Nico and Mrs. Schwartzman by the cash register.

"Mom," Solomon said, turning to Mrs. Schwartzman, "would you please bring down Sofia's birthday present?"

Beaming with excitement, Mrs. Schwartzman rushed upstairs to retrieve Solomon's special gift for Sofia.

"Oh, a present for me?" Sofia said, feigning surprise with a playful grin.

Crap, I totally forgot her birthday was on the seventeenth, and I have nothing for her! Nico thought, feeling a wave of embarrassment as his face flushed. "I just remembered I forgot something; I'll be right back," he blurted out.

"Where are you going?" Sofia demanded, a mix of curiosity and suspicion in her voice.

"Don't worry. Uh, it will be worth it," Nico replied, trying to sound confident as he rushed out of the store, back into the hot afternoon sun.

I know the perfect gift, he thought as he picked up his pace and darted off to the bank.

Stefano A Giovannoni

Chapter 5: Summoning Something

Nico crossed the street to the west side of the piazza, passing P. Cadaveri & Sons Mortuary. Even the blazing heat couldn't stop the chill of dread that ran down his spine as he walked by. But he pressed onward and arrived at his destination: Pendolino Savings & Loan.

Passing between the large, fluted Corinthian columns supporting the bank's brick and stone façade, Nico was greeted by a sharply dressed security guard who reached for the shiny brass door handle with his gloved hand and opened it for him.

Refreshing cool air rose from the highly polished marble floors, bringing welcome relief from the heat. Nico immediately spotted Mr. Rocco Pendolino, the bank's president and member of one of the town's four founding families.

Nico waved as he approached, stepping onto the carpeted area where Mr. Pendolino sat at his desk, tidying up some papers.

The banker stood up and greeted him warmly. "Ciao, Nico. Welcome back! What brings you in today?"

"Ciao, Mr. Pendolino. I'd like to access my nonna's—well, I guess I should say, *my* safe deposit box."

"Correct, it's all yours now—Chiara left it to you in her will," the banker confirmed, searching his pockets for the guard key. "Let me escort you down to the vault."

Nico followed Mr. Pendolino to the top of the marble spiral staircase that led down to the bank's secured vault. The banker stopped abruptly and turned. "Do you have your key with you?"

Nico realized he'd left it behind. "Darn! It's all the way back in Connecticut. I hid it under my mattress and didn't think to bring it with me. I'm in a hurry and don't have time to go back."

"Hmm," Mr. Pendolino mused, trying to come up with a solution. Then he had an idea. "Nico, have you learned the Summon Object spell yet?"

"I'm not familiar with that one," Nico admitted, feeling the sting of his inexperience. "I guess there are a lot of spells I still need to learn."

"Not a problem," Mr. Pendolino reassured him. "I'll teach it to you."

"But…how do you know it?" Nico asked.

"Well, my family and yours, along with the other two founding families, all shared the same basic spells when they first wrote their Grimoires," Mr. Pendolino explained. He paused to take a handkerchief out to blow his nose. "Darn allergies—now where was I? Ah, yes. When each family parted ways, they added their own spells to their grimoires."

"You mean I can create new spells?" Nico asked, his eyes lighting up at the possibilities.

"Of course, but you have to put some thought into it, or you may not get the results you're hoping for," the banker cautioned. "If Chiara were still alive, she would have made sure you were well-versed. She was the only person in town who knew all the original Benandanti and Malandanti spells."

"Cool!" Nico responded, brushing aside the caution. "So, how to cast the Summon Object spell to get my key—wait, why summon the key? Can't I just summon the object I want from my safe deposit box?"

Mr. Pendolino, slightly perturbed, explained, "Remember, the bank has many wards and strong magics in place to prevent summoning or theft from the vault."

"That's right," Nico said, recalling the challenges he and Sofia faced during their last visit. "Makes sense. OK, teach me the spell."

"First, concentrate on the object you wish to summon," Mr. Pendolino directed. "Picture it in as much detail as possible—what it looks like, where it's currently located, and so on."

Nico closed his eyes and visualized lifting his mattress to see the flat, silver key. He focused on the key, recalling every detail, including the engraving on it: *P S & L.* "OK, I'm seeing it," he confirmed.

"Good—now hold out your right hand and say these words: *Evocare Objectum,*" Mr. Pendolino instructed.

Nico held out his right hand and was about to speak the magic words when the banker interrupted.

"Impatient boy!" Mr. Pendolino scoffed. "You'll need to go outside. Remember, it won't work inside the bank."

Nico exited the bank and stood in the shaded area to avoid the intense heat. Holding out his right hand, he said, *"Evocare Objectum."*

As soon as he finished the last syllable, he felt the cold metal key materialize in his hand. Feeling victorious, Nico rushed back into the bank, waving the key in the air so Mr. Pendolino could see it from afar.

The banker escorted Nico down the slick marble stairway to the lower level of the bank, each holding onto the railing as they descended. They stood in front of the vault's entrance, its imposing steel door already open.

"Remember, follow me, stay on the carpeted path, and don't touch anything," Mr. Pendolino warned.

Nico took heed, recalling Sofia's near-mishap the last time they were here. It was about twenty degrees cooler in the vault than upstairs—almost too cold—as Nico rubbed his hands together for warmth.

Mr. Pendolino glanced back and noticed Nico shivering. "Believe me, after a few days back, you'll want to be down here all the time. This unexpected heatwave hasn't let up—it seems to get worse each week!"

"I'm surprised my mother didn't mention that when I spoke to her earlier," Nico replied.

They reached the end of the path and stood before a magnificent, shimmering door made of gold. Nico turned his head to avoid looking directly at the door, aware of its hypnotic patterns—a security measure designed to keep intruders mesmerized until security arrived.

Mr. Pendolino pulled a black fountain pen from his suit pocket, waved it in the air, and mumbled a few magic words, causing the door to open. Nico hurried to the back of the vault, remembering the location of the safe deposit box number 711.

Mr. Pendolino caught up just as Nico inserted his key. The banker reached into his pocket, pulled out his guard key, which was on a retractable silver chain, and inserted it. At the count of three, they simultaneously turned their keys, unlocking the box.

Nico pulled out the large metal drawer and placed it on the central table. Lifting the lid, he rummaged through the papers on top and found the purple satin sack containing the other twelve Coins of Favor. Beside it, he saw his nonna's ruby ring.

He held up the ring, admiring its beauty. "Perfect! She'll really love this," Nico said, certain that his present would easily outdo Solomon's.

Overhearing, Mr. Pendolino nosily asked, "Oh, are you planning to propose to someone special?"

"No, that'll never happen," Nico replied, slipping the ring into his pocket. "This is for Sofia. I forgot to get her a birthday present, and I know how much she liked this ring the last time we were here. I think my nonna would approve."

"It's yours to do with as you please—who am I to judge?" Mr. Pendolino replied.

Nico put the papers back in the drawer and closed the lid, returning it to its slot. They each turned their keys and removed them, securing the box once more.

"Thank you for teaching me the new spell and helping me retrieve the ring," Nico said. "I'm sure I'll be back at some point."

"I'm always here to help," the banker called out to Nico, who was already halfway out of the vault, eager to get back to Sofia and present his present.

Chapter 6: Presenting Presents

After leaving the refreshingly cool environment of the bank, Nico found himself back in the heat of the day. He stood at the street corner, impatiently waiting for the traffic light to turn green. Beads of sweat formed on his forehead, and as the light finally turned green, Nico stepped into the street to cross. Suddenly, a bright red Chevrolet Camaro IROC-Z28 convertible sped up to run the red light, whooshed by Nico, and swerved around him.

"Get back on the sidewalk, you moron!" the driver of the Camaro yelled, giving Nico the finger.

Nico's blood began to boil. He took a deep breath and tried to regain his composure as he watched the bright red vehicle make a right turn into a nearby driveway. A few bystanders called out from across the street to see if Nico was OK. He just nodded and continued walking back to Schwartzman's, eager to be back in a climate-controlled environment.

Mrs. Schwartzman, who had just priced some new sun hats, was displaying them in the front window. She looked up and saw Nico approaching, his face flushed and his dark, wavy hair dripping with sweat.

She rushed over to the front door and opened it. A welcoming blast of cold air hit Nico's face as he crossed the threshold. Eyeing a comfy-looking sofa near the back of the store, he staggered toward it, but collapsed on the floor before he could reach it.

Sofia left Solomon's embrace and ran over to Nico, with Solomon quickly following. They gently turned Nico over, and Sofia lifted his head off the ground. "Nico, you're going to be OK."

Mrs. Schwartzman returned with a glass of water and held it up to his lips. "Here my boy, drink this. You're probably dehydrated and not used to this heat yet."

As Nico regained consciousness, he took small sips of water. "What happened?"

"Looks like you fainted," Sofia answered.

"Heat exhaustion is probably the cause," Solomon added.

"I don't even remember getting here," Nico said, his memory slightly hazy. "All I remember is starting to cross the street and almost being hit by a car—the driver looked vaguely familiar."

"Come to think of it, we did hear a car screeching earlier, followed by some yelling—" Solomon stopped in the middle of his comment, embarrassed to admit that he and Sofia too were busy kissing to look out the window. "What kind of car was it?"

"Some red convertible," Nico replied. "A Camaro, I think."

Mrs. Schwartzman chimed in, "Sounds like Dino Cadaveri causing mischief again!"

"Ah, yes, Gino's brother," Sofia recalled. "I remember him. He wasn't too kind to Nico at Chiara's funeral."

"He's always been a bit of a jerk," Solomon said. "But ever since his father died, he's gotten worse. He's been seen spending a lot of money around town—even bought a bunch of new clothes from us the other week."

"Maybe he's just blowing through his inheritance as part of the grief process?" Sofia suggested.

"I don't know about that, Sofia. The gossip around town…" Mrs. Schwartzman started and then lowered her voice, "…is that Mr. Cadaveri didn't have much money—that the only thing left for Dino and Gino was the family business—that dreadful mortuary across the street."

Nico's body started to cool down, and his mind became clearer. "Now I remember. It had to be Dino—the car pulled into the mortuary!" Nico felt his anger rising again. "That guy is such a tool."

"Nico, drink some more water," Mrs. Schwartzman said, trying to distract him from thoughts of Dino.

"Oh, Nico, see what Solomon got me for my birthday!" Sofia said, pulling out a Tiffany box from her purse and handing it to Nico.

Nico opened the box, curious to see if Solomon's gift would be any better than his, and saw that it contained a sterling silver charm bracelet.

"Wow, this is actually nice," he said, surprised that Solomon picked out something Sofia would like.

Sofia took the opportunity to boast. "It was a very thoughtful gift, and he had each charm custom-made just for me."

Nico examined the charms: a unicorn, a wishbone, a raven, a beer stein, a golem, a star, a broom, a bouquet of roses, and a fairy door. "Solomon, nice choices. Especially the beer stein—wouldn't have thought of that one!"

Appreciative of Nico's compliment, Solomon added, "I thought a few should remind Sofia of her first visit to Oliveto—the rest are just for good luck."

"Well, I just love it!" Sofia gushed, giving Solomon a kiss on the cheek.

Nico mumbled something under his breath before carefully placing the bracelet back in its box and handing it to Sofia.

Sofia looked at Nico. "What were you mumbling? You're not jealous, are you?"

"Omigod, no," Nico said, laughing. "Actually, I was casting a spell on it—I enchanted it for you!" He smiled smugly.

Sofia assumed he was joking. "I don't recall a spell in the grimoire that can do that, smarty!"

"Oh, by the way, here's my belated birthday gift," Nico said, pulling his nonna's ruby ring from his pocket.

Sofia's eyes widened. "Wow! Nico, I can't—that was your nonna's. It's a family heirloom."

"I know my nonna would want you to have it," Nico assured her. "After all, you did save her favorite grandson's life last time we were here—that should count for something!"

Nico slipped it on her right ring finger, and she held it up to the light. Mrs. Schwartzman took Sofia's hand to view the ring up close. "Yup, that's Chiara's ruby—I'd recognize it anywhere."

Knowing that he won the fictitious gift contest, Nico turned the focus back on Solomon. "Hey, Solomon, why don't you put the bracelet on Sofia."

Sofia felt like a princess for a moment, with two handsome men adorning her with jewelry. She held out her left arm, and Solomon fastened the bracelet around her wrist.

Sofia thanked them and had an idea. "Say, Sol, is Fawn is around? Maybe we can all meet up for drinks at Moraiolo's, since it didn't happen last time."

Nico chimed in, "That's a wonderful idea—it'll be great to see her again!"

"I'll let Fawn know, and we'll meet you there around seven?" Solomon replied.

"Sounds like a plan," Sofia said, then turned to Nico. "We should get going—we have that other *thing* to attend to back at the house."

Nico nodded and walked over to give Mrs. Schwartzman a goodbye hug. "Always good to see you, and thanks for the water."

Sofia hugged Mrs. Schwartzman and went over to Solomon. As she hugged him, she whispered flirtatiously into his ear, "Be good while I'm gone."

Solomon just smiled and waved goodbye to Nico.

Once outside the store, Sofia asked Nico, "So, tell me about this enchantment you did."

"I'll tell you in a minute. First let's cross over to the piazza—it'll be cooler over there. We can find a bench under the olive tree."

Sofia agreed and followed Nico across the street into the mostly shaded piazza, where seven rather short city workers were in the midst of putting up signs and decorations.

"I guess they're really going all out for the upcoming Founder's Day Centennial Celebration!" Nico remarked.

"Well, it's not often that a town turns one hundred—I think that's a worthy cause for throwing a party," Sofia said, then joked, "Will you be enchanting a gift for it as well?"

"Come, let's sit here, and I'll tell you what happened," Nico said.

Sofia took a seat on one of the available benches. She then looked up at The Oliveto Founders' Tree that grew from the center of the piazza and marveled. "This tree still amazes me."

"Yes, it's quite spectacular—even more so now that we know the actual history behind how it was created," Nico said.

Sofia reminisced about their last visit to the town library, where they learned about how the four founding families came to settle in Oliveto. "Simply genius of the four founders to graft a branch from each of their family's olive cultivar—Ascolano, Frantoio, Moraiolo, and Pendolino—onto this ancient olive tree to create a symbol of unity."

They sat quietly for nearly a minute, enjoying the shade, when one of the city workers frantically ran by with a streamer and accidentally stepped on Nico's foot.

"Ouch!" Nico responded in pain. "Watch where you're going!"

The city worker yelled back an apology, "Sorry Mr. Frantoio."

"How does everyone know who you are?" Sofia asked.

"Don't know," Nico replied while removing his shoe and sock to check his injured foot. "Maybe we're famous after stopping The Oliveto Abductor and saving future members of the fairy population from an uncertain death?"

Sofia laughed. "Don't let it go to your head. We only did what was right and ended up saving Fawn in the process. But enough of that," she said, steering the conversation back. "You promised to tell me about the enchantment—so out with it."

Seeing no injury to his foot, Nico put his sock back on and turned to Sofia. "Well, when I left Schwartzman's, I went to the bank to get your present. I asked Mr. Pendolino to take me down to the vault so I could access my safe deposit box."

Nico stopped and slipped his foot back into his shoe. He looked up at Sofia as he laced up his shoe and continued. "So, where was I? Oh, yes—Mr. Pendolino asked if I had my key with me, and I told him it was back in Connecticut."

Sofia interrupted, "So where does the enchantment part come in?"

"I'm getting there! Geesh," Nico replied. "So, he asked if I knew the Summon Object spell—I told him I didn't. He said he could teach it to me, and that's how I got my key and retrieved your gift."

"Again, where does the enchantment part—" Sofia anxiously began.

Nico cut her off. "Mr. Pendolino said that the four founders originally had the same spells in their grimoires, but when they started their own families, they created new spells unique to each family. He basically said that I can make up my own spells."

Even with Sofia's limited knowledge of the arcane, she knew it couldn't be that simple. "There must be more to it—it can't be that cut and dry. What else did he say?"

Nico, knowing that he might be in trouble with Sofia, reluctantly told her the rest, "Uh, well—he did say that when creating new spells, 'you have to put some thought into it, or you may not get the results you're hoping for,'" Nico explained, batting his eyes at Sofia in hopes she wouldn't be angry.

"Well, my arm hasn't fallen off and I feel fine—so I guess nothing went wrong," Sofia said, still somewhat unsure. "So let me ask you this: what enchantment were you trying to cast on my charm bracelet?"

Nico got quiet. "Honestly, I don't really know," he admitted. "I just wanted to—I had the best of intentions, and then the words just came out of my mouth on their own—to be honest, I don't even know what I said."

Sofia decided to let the issue die. "Well, what's done is done. I guess we'll find out when we're meant to."

"In the mood for some macarons?" Nico asked, hoping that some treats would soothe any lingering misgivings.

"I see what you're trying to do," Sofia joked. "And I forgive you. I know you were just trying to do something nice for me."

Phew, off the hook for that one, Nico thought as he stood up from the bench.

"How's your foot?" Sofia asked. "Are you OK to walk?"

"Surprisingly well—actually I don't feel any pain at all," Nico realized while taking a few steps.

"Good to hear," Sofia said. "Let's get to Patisserie Angelique before all the good macaron flavors are sold out."

Nico and Sofia continued to the other side of the piazza. A delicious aroma, caramelized sugar and toasted pecans, wafted from the bakery, beckoning them to cross the street and enter.

As Nico went to open the door for Sofia, he noticed that she wasn't behind him; she was still back in the bakery's outdoor seating area, staring at something.

"Sofia, what are you doing?" Nico called out.

"Shhh!" Sofia answered. "Look over there."

Nico quietly approached Sofia and followed her gaze toward a café table. Three crows had landed on the table and two of them were using their beaks to collect the dollar bills and coins left as a tip. The third crow then cawed out before grabbing another dollar bill and flying off. Shortly thereafter, three more crows flew down to the same table and retrieved the remaining tip money.

An employee of Patisserie Angelique, whom Nico and Sofia remembered from their last visit, rushed past them and over to the table to shoo the crows away.

"Hello Lisette," Sofia greeted the alluring twenty-something from Martinique.

"Oh, hello, you two—welcome back!" a frustrated Lisette responded while blotting her forehead with a handkerchief. "I'm not sure which will be the death of me: this sweltering heat or these crows stealing my tips!"

"You sound like this is a regular occurrence," Nico said as the three of them headed inside the bakery.

At the front counter, Lisette continued, "Indeed, multiple times throughout the day—it's like a meticulously orchestrated theft spree. And it's not just us; many other businesses with outdoor seating are experiencing the same challenge."

"That's very odd," Sofia said. "It seemed like the patrons sitting at the other tables were completely unaware."

"Let's not let my troubles spoil your day," Lisette said. "Is there something I can get for you?"

"Actually, yes," Nico answered. "We're here for some of your delicious macarons."

Sofia, looking at the various flavors in the display case, was excited to see many of her favorites still available. "We'll take two of each flavor," Sofia said eagerly.

"Two of each coming right up," Lisette said, grabbing an empty box and a pair of silver tongs. As she began to box up the macarons, she offered, "Would you also like a couple of sticky buns? They're half-off at this time of day."

"Sure!" Nico and Sofia said in unison.

Nico paid for the items and left three dollars in the tip jar.

They waved goodbye to Lisette and headed back to the car. As they crossed the piazza, they noticed the festival decorations were now in place, and the city workers had left.

Once in the car, Nico turned on the ignition and waited for the air conditioning to kick in.

"I wonder why the crows are stealing things," Sofia said. "It doesn't seem natural. I know crows like shiny things, but why take the dollar bills as well?"

"I agree—something doesn't seem right," Nico said, then remembered Simone was still waiting for them back at the house. "We'd better get going. We need to figure out how to communicate with our friendly raven."

Nico put the car into reverse and started to back up when the car stopped moving on its own, and the blaring of a car horn was heard.

"Hey—it's you again!" a voice yelled from a car idling next to them.

Nico rolled down his window, ready to yell back, but saw it was the familiar red Camaro that had almost hit him earlier. He looked over to see who was driving and saw that it was none other than Dino Cadaveri.

"Don't you have anything better to do than pollute the world with your presence?" Nico sneered.

"At least I am not driving an old lady's car!" Dino jeered back.

"It probably has more horsepower than your piece of—" Nico hotly responded before Sofia pinched him.

"Let's not cause a scene," Sofia whispered.

"My car could beat yours any day of the week," Dino challenged.

"If we weren't in a hurry, I'd be willing to race you," Nico bluffed.

"I'll hold you to that—another day, then," Dino said. "And the loser must perform a task of the winner's choosing!"

Nico nodded in agreement and continued backing out of the parking space. Dino laid rubber as his car screeched away down the street.

"I can see why you don't like that guy," Sofia said. "Such a dipstick."

Agitated by Dino for the second time today, Nico blurted out, "Car, take us home."

And the car did just that.

Chapter 7: A Chat with a Raven

The tan Mercedes rolled under the *porte-cochere* of the Frantoio family home and shifted into park. Nico turned off the ignition and retrieved the keys. They exited the car into the covered area, which was still quite warm, and headed up the stairs to the front door. Behind them, the car doors locked with a soft click as the front door creaked open to greet them.

Sofia put her purse down on the marble entry table and touched its surface. "Ah, I wish I could take a nap on this—it's so nice and cool."

"Why don't you get the grimoire from your room and bring it back here. I'll get a couple of chairs," Nico suggested.

They both returned to the foyer. Nico placed the chairs around the table, and Sofia set the leather-bound book down, with the Malandanti side facing up. As they sat, two beverages floated into the room, presumably from the kitchen, and hovered inches above the table.

As they reached for their beverages, the glasses moved away from them. Nico and Sofia exchanged puzzled looks, about to comment on the situation, when two drink coasters floated in and gently landed on the table. The drinks then lowered onto the coasters.

Sofia laid one side of her face against the cold marble and spoke from the other side. "You look through the book while I enjoy this moment and cool off."

Nico took a sip of his drink. "Yum, lavender lemonade—so refreshing!"

He started rifling through the pages of the Malandanti side of the book. "Hmm…Ah! Nope, that's not it."

Sofia, now curious, raised her head from her marble pillow. "What did you find?"

"I found a spell regarding communication, but it's a Steal Voice spell—kind of the opposite of what we're trying to do," Nico explained.

"Turn the book around to the Benandanti side," Sofia suggested, then took a sip of her drink. "This is delicious! Anyway, I've noticed that most of the helpful spells are written there—the Malandanti side seems to focus mainly on ones that do harm."

Nico flipped the book around and then opened it. About a quarter of the way through, he turned the book toward Sofia and pointed to the spell on the page.

Sofia scooted her chair closer and leaned in to read the spell's description. "Lend Voice: Give a creature the ability to speak in the caster's voice for fifteen minutes. Touch the creature while saying the words: *Do Vocem Meam.*"

"Sounds easy enough—do you know what you want to ask Simone, since I won't be able to speak for a quarter of an hour?" Nico asked.

Sofia took the opportunity to joke. "Ah, the gift of silence! Must be a bonus of the spell."

"Very funny," Nico muttered, dreading the thought of going back outside in the heat of the day.

Leaving the grimoire on the table, they each grabbed a chair and took them back to the dining room. As they moved to the kitchen, their beverages, along with the coasters, floated through the air and landed on the kitchen island as they entered.

"House, please leave our drinks here—we're going outside for a bit," Sofia requested.

They exited the house and quickly moved to a shaded area between the fountain and one of the orange trees. Nico took the whistle from around his neck and blew into it.

The peaceful sound of the bubbling fountain was quickly interrupted by Simone's loud kraa's. The raven glided down from the canopy of the other orange tree and landed on the fountain's finial, bobbing its head in excitement that Nico and Sofia had kept their promise to return.

"I think we have a solution, Simone," Sofia offered. "Nico just needs to touch you and say a few words, and then you should be able to speak."

The raven extended its wing to Nico. He put his hand on it and invoked the magic words, "*Do Vocem Meam.*"

"Did it work?" Sofia asked. "Simone, try to say something."

The raven opened its beak and, in Nico's voice, said, "Greetings, Sofia! Firstly, I'd like to apologize for scaring you during our first few encounters. It wasn't my intention."

"I understand that now—don't worry about it," Sofia said.

Simone continued, "What originally began as an attempt to get your attention so that you could help me turned into me helping you."

Nico tried to join in the conversation, but no words came out.

Sofia chuckled and said, "I'm guessing that Nico wants to say he appreciates your bravery and is sorry, as am I, that you lost your life in the process."

"Well, I just remember waking up in the mortuary," Simone explained. "That's when I realized that Mr. Cadaveri had performed some kind of necromantic ritual to bring me back from the dead."

"Had Mr. Cadaveri known you'd end up helping me rescue Nico, I'm sure he would've left your body where he had found it," Sofia speculated.

"That's probably true," Simone acknowledged. "Thankfully, he's no longer around to harm anyone else."

Seeing Nico's discomfort from the heat, Simone splashed water from the fountain in his direction.

"Now here's what I've been waiting all this time to ask of you two," Simone continued. "My mistress is being held captive, and I need your help in rescuing her."

"We'll certainly do our best to help," Sofia said. "Who is your mistress, and where is she being held?"

"She is one of the two tree dryads who nurture and protect the forests surrounding the town. Her name is Flora, but she is commonly referred to as the Light Dryad. She helps oversee the growth of nature. She lives in the Tree of Unkindness, where a small group of us ravens roost at night after assisting her during the day."

Simone jumped down to the fountain's lower tier and hopped around in the water to cool off. Once satisfied, the raven flew back up to the top of the fountain and perched on its finial. Simone continued, "Her sister, on the other hand, is named Proserpina. She's commonly referred to as the Dark Dryad, and her home is in the hollow of the Murder Tree. She manages the death and decay of the forest to help maintain nature's balance. The entire town's crow population resides within the branches of her home and is always ready to do her bidding, day or night."

"Fascinating!" Sofia said, her eyes lighting up at the new piece of town lore. "How and why was Flora taken?"

The raven flapped its wings, shaking off excess water, then pressed its wings tightly against its body. Simone then explained, "Proserpina, unfortunately, has a terrible gambling addiction. One day, I overheard some of the crows gossiping. They mentioned that she lost so much money playing poker with those shifty satyrs that she ended up taking a loan from the efreeti to feed her addiction."

As the heat of the day increased, Sofia, now glistening with beads of sweat on her olive-toned skin, reached into her purse and pulled out a hand fan. As she fanned herself, she interrupted Simone. "When we were here last, Mr. Pendolino told us about the efreeti—that he lives inside the mountain, which is supposedly a dormant volcano. He mentioned that the efreeti is a terrible trickster and warned us to never look directly into his eyes, amongst other things."

Nico, just noticing Sofia's purse, chuckled silently as he thought to himself, *She really does take her purse everywhere! I wonder what else she has in there—a refreshing drink sure sounds good right about now.*

Sofia saw Nico's attempt at silent laughter and smiled, as if reading his thoughts. Realizing she wasn't reading his mind or pulling out a drink from her purse, Nico decided to go inside to refill their glasses of lavender lemonade.

Simone kraa'd to get Sofia's attention and continued, "The efreeti is not someone I'd want to borrow money from. Proserpina learned the hard way after failing to repay her debt."

Nico returned to the group with two refilled glasses of lavender lemonade, handing one to Sofia. They each took a sip.

Simone, slightly frustrated by the interruption, kraa'd again and continued. "Angry that Proserpina wasn't paying back her debt, the efreeti found a way to motivate her—he kidnapped her sister Flora."

"So, your mistress is being held captive inside the mountain?" Sofia asked.

"Yes," Simone replied. "Proserpina, realizing the error of her ways, took action. In an effort to repay her debt, she enlisted the help of her crows. She commanded them to steal items from inebriated tourists and take tip money from outdoor restaurant tables—but it wasn't enough. That's why I've been anxiously trying to get your attention—I need your help rescuing…." Simone suddenly stopped speaking and began kraa'ing once more.

"Looks like the spell wore off," Sofia said, turning to Nico. "Can you speak now?"

Nico cleared his throat and tested his voice. "Ah, much better."

Sofia glanced at the raven with a reassuring smile. "Simone, thank you for trusting us to rescue your mistress—you can count on us."

"We'll come up with a plan, and once we find her, we'll use the whistle to call you," Nico added confidently.

The raven hopped excitedly on the edge of the fountain at the prospect of Flora being rescued, its black feathers gleaming in the sunlight, before taking off into the sky.

"Nico, let's head back inside—it's getting too hot, even for a Calabrian girl like me," Sofia suggested with a wry smile."

With that, Nico and Sofia returned to the cool interior of the Frantoio family home, the weight of the mission now on their mind.

Stefano A Giovannoni

Chapter 8: A Friendly Reunion

S till reeling from the revelations Simone shared earlier that day, Nico and Sofia got ready for their reunion with Solomon and Fawn at Trattoria Moraiolo. They met in the foyer nearly at the same time.

"Wow, you're already here!" Sofia commented, surprised by Nico's punctuality.

"I'm trying to make it up to you—I always seem to keep you waiting," Nico replied.

Nico opened the front door, and a blast of hot air hit their faces. Feeling the intense heat, they decided against walking into town this evening. Instead, they opted to take the enchanted tan Mercedes to the restaurant.

The car parked in front of Moraiolo's, and as they exited, a voice called out to them—it was Solomon.

"Hi guys!" Solomon said as he approached them. "Right on time. Fawn should already be inside—I told her to order some appetizers and a bottle wine."

"Awesome—can't wait to see her again," Sofia said, reaching out to hold Solomon's hand.

"I'm famished," Nico said. "I think all we've eaten today is a handful of macarons. Sofia, you must be starving by now."

"I actually lose my appetite when it's hot out. Speaking of which, let's get inside," Sofia responded.

Nico held the restaurant door open for the happy couple and then followed them into the dimly lit and spacious eatery. The smell from the wood-burning pizza oven made Nico's stomach growl in anticipation.

"Ciao, *ragazzi!*" a familiar voice called out. It was the friendly waiter Matteo, who had served them on their last visit.

"Ciao, Matteo! *Come va?*" Sofia answered back.

An animated Matteo responded, "Ah, the Calabrian pizza lover has returned to our fair town!"

"Yes, we're back," Sofia said, smiling. "We're meeting up with a friend."

"Ah yes—she's over here," Matteo said and escorted them to a table with a red and white checkered tablecloth where Fawn was anxiously waiting.

Fawn jumped up from her seat when she saw them approaching and ran over to them, immediately hugging Nico. "My hero!" she gushed.

Nico froze for a second before embracing her back. "Good to see you alive and well—staying out of trouble, I hope?" Nico teased.

"Come," Fawn said, leading them back to their table. "Have a seat."

Fawn passed around the arancini she had ordered as an appetizer. Matteo hurried over with three wine glasses and poured wine for the three newcomers, finishing by topping off Fawn's glass.

"Would you like to see menus?" Matteo asked.

"I'm in the mood for more of your delicious pizza," Sofia said, turning to the group. "Are you all OK just ordering a few pizzas to share?"

"Sounds perfect," Nico replied and turned to Matteo. "How about one Margherita and…hmm…one with sausage or some kind of meat."

"Subito!" Matteo responded and zipped off to put in their order.

Solomon raised his glass to make a toast. "Here's to us being reunited once again, alive and in good health!"

"*Cin cin*!" they cried out in unison as they clinked glasses.

Sofia took a sip of her wine. "This merlot is delicious!"

"Satyr Knoll Winery is famous for their Merlots," Fawn said before taking another sip.

Nico put his glass down. "Speaking of satyrs, we heard an interesting story today."

"Yeah," Sofia added. "Apparently, one of the local dryads has been taken captive by the efreeti living deep inside the mountain."

Fawn set her glass down, leaned in, and softly spoke, "The talk amongst us fey is that Caleo, the efreeti in question, had help in abducting the Light Dryad, and he's up to no good."

Nico reached for an arancini and took a bite. "Damn, those are still hot!" he exclaimed, quickly taking a big gulp from his glass of wine.

Concerned, Sofia asked, "Are you OK?"

"I'll be fine—I always forget how much those things retain their heat," Nico replied and then turned to Fawn. "Sounds like we're in for another adventure! Do you guys remember that raven that tormented Sofia during our last visit?"

"The one that was hit by the bus and then brought back to life by Mr. Cadaveri?" Solomon asked, reaching for an arancini.

"That's the one—" Nico began to answer before Sofia interrupted.

"But get this—the raven was just trying to get our attention the whole time," Sofia said, then turned to Solomon. "Are they good?"

Solomon finished his bite. "Delicious. Here, try one," Solomon said, gently hand-feeding one to Sofia.

Nico continued, "So, we found a spell that let the raven speak, and it told us why the Light Dryad, Flora, was taken."

"Yum!" Sofia said to Solomon. "Great appetizer choice, Fawn."

"They're one of my favorites," Fawn acknowledged, returning to the main conversation. "I'm guessing the raven—does it have a name?"

"Yes," Sofia replied. "It had a gold band on its leg with the name: Simone."

"Ah, so Simone, I gather, is requesting your help in rescuing Flora?" Fawn surmised.

"Yes," Nico affirmed. "All the ravens are loyal to Flora, and now that their mistress is gone, they're desperate to have her back in their tree but helpless to rescue her on their own."

"Well, what do you need from us?" Fawn asked, enlisting Solomon's help.

"Yeah, how can we help?" Solomon added.

Their conversation was suddenly interrupted by Matteo placing two perfect wood-fired pizzas down on their table. "*Ragazzi, ecco le due pizze!*"

Sofia's eyes lit up as she inhaled the aroma of the pizza nearest her. Bubbling mozzarella di bufala covering a layer of tomato sauce made from authentic San Marzano tomatoes, topped with torn basil leaves. "I like totally forgot how much I missed your pizzas, Matteo!"

"*Grazie!*" the waiter acknowledged. "Ready for another bottle of *vino*?"

***

The group finished the second bottle and the remaining pizza slices, enjoying a lively conversation about their experiences since they'd last seen each other. They talked until Matteo kindly informed them that the restaurant was closing for the evening.

As they left the restaurant, Sofia and Solomon stayed slightly behind, saying their special goodbyes while Nico and Fawn headed toward the car.

"Fawn, I know we got distracted when the food arrived, so I want to get back to the topic of the Dark Dryad. Do you know where we can find her?" Nico asked. "Simone mentioned that she lives inside the Murder Tree."

"Let me think," Fawn responded. "By its name, I'm guessing it's a tree home to a murder of crows?"

"Correct," Nico affirmed.

"Hmm. I know of two possible trees. One is west of the piazza, just past the railroad tracks—it's a large oak tree. The other is literally as the crow flies further west from the first. It's behind the coffee shop in the strip mall near the supermarket—that one's a redwood," Fawn recalled.

"Perfect!" Nico said, excited to have a clue to follow. "Sofia and I will search for her tomorrow and see if we can get more answers."

As Nico and Fawn hugged goodbye, Sofia and Solomon rejoined the group before parting ways.

Chapter 9: A Sleepless Night

The tan Mercedes drove a slightly inebriated Nico and Sofia home safely. They staggered out of the car and made their way up the stairs to the front door, which unlocked itself and slowly creaked open.

"Man, that alcohol hit me pretty hard," Nico said as they entered the foyer.

"I know what you mean!" Sofia agreed. "Of course, we didn't drink back at school—we were too busy cramming for finals and such. So this is our first drinking excursion since our last visit."

"Right, we just need to rebuild our tolerance—" Nico began, but the sound of breaking glass from below interrupted him.

Startled, Sofia jumped and asked, "What was that?"

Nico put his finger to his lips. "Shhh!" He quietly listened for more activity, and just as he was about to speak, more glass shattered.

"I wonder if someone or something is trying to break into the house, like before?" Sofia whispered.

"I noticed earlier today, when we were in the backyard, that the garden gnomes had reattached the bars to the window, so it's probably not that," Nico said. "It sounds like it's coming from the basement—like bottles are being broken!" He cautiously made his way through the dining room to the kitchen.

"Must be from within the wine cellar," Sofia suggested, closely following Nico.

Nico approached the kitchen cabinet, which concealed the access to the basement stairs. He turned the handle ninety degrees to the right and pulled the door open. He reached for the light switch on his left and flipped it on, illuminating the thirteen steps leading down to the lower level.

47

Nico turned to Sofia. "Are you ready to do this?"

"Not sure, but do we really have a choice?" Sofia reluctantly replied.

The two crept down the stairs, holding onto the wobbly handrail for safety, and made it to the landing of the musty basement.

Five feet ahead, on the left, was their destination: the wine cellar. The iron gate to the room was slightly ajar. Nico, wanting to turn on the light before entering, cautiously reached his hand into the room and felt around on the wall. When he found the light switch, he flipped it on and pushed the gate open, rushing into the room, hoping to catch the source of the commotion in the act.

Greeted by a face full of cobwebs, he frantically wiped away the silken threads obstructing his view.

Sofia entered and exclaimed, "Omigod! Look at all those broken bottles of wine. Something must have been going on long before we got home."

Nico ventured further into the room and looked among the wine racks for clues to help them decipher what had caused the damage.

Sofia, starting to feel sleepy, sat down on one of the chairs surrounding a small table in the center of the room. An elegant crystal chandelier above the table provided dim lighting, revealing a layer of dust on the olivewood table.

Something caught Sofia's eye. As she looked closer, she saw what appeared to be small footprints among the dust.

"Nico, come take a look at this," Sofia said.

Nico walked over to the table. "Are you communing with the spirits again?" he joked, referring to their last visit when they had discovered that the table had markings to be used as a spirit board.

"No, silly," Sofia replied. "I think I found a clue. Something walked across the table and left these tiny footprints in the dust."

Nico looked quickly. "Probably just a rat, or maybe a mouse."

"Those aren't from a rodent of any kind," Sofia snapped. "Look closer. They appear to be humanoid."

"OK, Nancy Drew. Good catch," Nico said and leaned in closer to study the footprints. "Wrong!"

Surprised by Nico's comment, Sofia asked, "What do you mean, wrong?"

Nico answered smugly, enjoying the contest of observation. "While the hourglass shape of a humanoid footprint has five toes, this print only has four."

"You're right," Sofia conceded. "It has the same shape, but I guess in my weariness I missed that small detail."

"Well, whatever it was is gone now," Nico said, stretching his arms out and yawning. "We can clean up the mess tomorrow—let's go to bed."

Sofia, too tired to respond, headed back to the stairs. Nico followed her after turning off the light and closing the iron gate.

Upstairs, on the kitchen island, two cups of freshly prepared chamomile tea awaited them.

"So thoughtful of the house!" Sofia said with a yawn.

"A nice way to wind down the evening," Nico added, taking a sip.

***

Sofia was suddenly awakened by the sound of something being knocked over in the basement below her. She quickly sat up in her bed and thought, *not again.*

Turning on her nightstand lamp, she reached for her Swatch. Squinting, she made out that it was now 1:00 a.m. She got out of bed, wearing only a camisole and gym shorts, slipped her feet into her slippers, and shuffled off to the kitchen to begin her investigation.

I can do this! she thought. *Nothing to fear—probably just a rat like Nico said.*

She twisted the cabinet handle and opened it to reveal the darkened lower level.

Maybe I should wake Nico. She waffled. *No, he's tired. Let him sleep.*

Sofia reached for the light switch but froze as she heard a bloodcurdling, short-lived squeak. *That didn't sound good*, she thought.

Taking a deep breath, Sofia flipped on the light switch, gathering her wits to continue onward. Just as she was about to take her first step, two hands suddenly grasped her shoulders, startling her.

She turned to look over her shoulder.

"Did I scare you?" Nico asked.

A relieved but slightly irritated Sofia responded, "Don't ever do that again! I could have fallen down the stairs or something."

"I wouldn't have let that happen," Nico reassured her. "That's why I put my hands on your shoulders—to keep you from falling forward."

"OK, I guess I'll believe you," Sofia teased. "Hey, why are you awake, anyway?"

"I heard an odd noise and thought maybe it was you," Nico replied, then added jokingly, "I figured I might need to save you from the grasp of some horrible three-eyed creature."

"Funny," Sofia retorted. "Did you hear the first sound, too? It sounded like a box being knocked over, somewhere beneath my bedroom."

"No, didn't hear that one," Nico replied, extending his arm. "Well, ladies first—let's check it out."

Sofia cautiously descended the stairs, with Nico close behind.

"You said the first sound came from underneath your bedroom, so that should be near the secret room—about twenty feet ahead," Nico said, taking the lead.

As they neared their destination, Sofia suddenly shrieked.

Nico quickly turned around. "What is it, Sofia? Are you OK?"

"Over there," Sofia said, pointing to the barred window that had been recently repaired. "Among the boxes under the window, I saw something move."

Nico walked over to investigate and picked up a fallen box. "Found the cause of the squeaking noise you heard—looks like another mess we'll need to clean up tomorrow."

Sofia rushed over to see what Nico had found. "Oh, that's just terrible," she lamented. "The poor rat."

Before them lay a bloody rat; its neck was snapped, and its arms were missing, torn from its body.

"What could've done that?" Sofia asked. "I haven't seen any rat traps down here."

"The plot thickens!" Nico said. "Well, let's get back to bed—we're going to need our energy for the start of our search-and-rescue mission."

Nico and Sofia went back upstairs to their rooms, and it didn't take long for them to fall asleep again.

A few hours later, Nico had a lucid dream. He saw himself walking through the house, intently searching every room. He was looking behind open doors, under beds, behind shower curtains, and even in closets. Although he was aware he was dreaming, he couldn't figure out what he was looking for. Then, out of the corner of his eye, he saw something move. He thought it was some kind of dog—an affenpinscher to be exact—but it was walking on two legs. He moved toward the devilish-looking creature, but it fled, scuttling down the hallway toward his bedroom. Nico chased after it.

When he entered his bedroom, he saw the furry creature standing on his bed, its hair as black as night with eyes like glowing embers. It stood there, glaring at Nico, taunting him to make the first move.

Nico leapt onto the bed, trying to grab the baneful beast, but it vanished in a cloud of sulfurous smoke. The smell, like hard-boiled eggs being shelled, made Nico instantly nauseous.

He woke with jolt, his sheets drenched in sweat. Throwing off the covers, he got out of bed and headed to the bathroom, where a hand towel was conveniently lying by the sink. *Thanks, House*, he thought.

Nico leaned over the sink and stared into the large bathroom mirror. He ran his hands through his dark brown, wavy hair, releasing beads of sweat that trickled down his face and neck.

Nico turned on the cold water and soaked the hand towel, wringing it out before blotting his face and chest.

"What's going on?" Sofia said as she entered his bathroom. "Are you OK? You look terrible!"

"I just had a weird dream," Nico answered while rinsing the towel and once more wringing it out. "Hey, why are you up again?"

Sofia took the cold towel from Nico's hands and wiped the remaining sweat from his back. "I heard some weird noises—I think someone even entered my room! It sounded like someone was walking around the house, opening doors," she explained, rinsing the towel. "Once I mustered the courage to check things out, I eventually saw your bathroom light on—I figured it must've been you."

Nico was now confused. "I just thought I was lucid dreaming, but maybe I was actually sleepwalking—or a combination of both?"

"Tell me about the dream," Sofia prompted. "What do you remember?"

Nico turned to face Sofia. "I remember trying to find something. I went from room to room—that must be what you heard. I was searching under the beds and in every corner, and then I saw this little creature move."

Sofia folded the hand towel and laid it on the counter. "Really? What did it look like?"

"It was about two feet tall, had curly black hair, and fiery red eyes," Nico recalled.

"Yikes!" Sofia said, a shiver running down her spine. "Sounds like a walking evil teddy bear! Did it have sharp teeth and claws too?"

"I don't recall if it had claws," Nico said, trying to remember. "But I definitely saw its teeth! When I chased it into my bedroom and tried to grab it, it vanished—but just before it disappeared, it gave this menacing smile, showing a row of dagger-like teeth."

"I think I know what it might be!" Sofia said, her eyes lighting up with realization. "It's a creature in your grimoire—on the Malandanti side. Come with me, I'll show you."

Nico followed Sofia back to her bedroom. She had put the grimoire back into the cedar chest after using it earlier. Kneeling in front of it, she examined the detailed marquetry design of various flowers. Locating the image of a geranium, she pressed it until she heard a familiar clicking sound. After pressing the remaining five, the antique chest opened.

Nico retrieved the leather-bound tome and laid it across Sofia's bed. He turned it over to the Malandanti side and opened it.

"Now, where did you see this thing?" Nico asked.

Sofia climbed onto the bed and lay next to him. To her, the pages of the book were blank, so she put her hand on Nico's back. Letters began to form as the book revealed itself to her.

"I remember it somewhere near the beginning," Sofia said, quickly flipping through the pages until she found what she was looking for. "There, that's it!"

Nico read the heading on the page, "Babau." Among the writing on the yellowed pages was a hand-drawn image of the creature, closely resembling what he had seen.

He read aloud, "Commonly known throughout Italy among non-magical families as an imaginary being, similar to the Boogeyman. Parents warn their children about the Babau to encourage good behavior." Nico paused reading and turned to Sofia. "My mother never used the Babau to keep me in line, but she did tell me that she saw it when she was a kid and was terrified."

"Really?" Sofia gasped. "If it's anything like what you described, I'd be terrified, too!"

Nico continued reading, "To them, the Babau is a mischievous creature that can take many forms but is always small in stature. For us Malandanti, the Babau is a small bipedal creature with dark fur and glowing red eyes. It can be conjured to perform nefarious tasks for the summoner, but it sometimes strays from its directions, resulting in more chaos than intended."

Sofia noticed some writing in the margin, which seemed to be in Nico's nonna's handwriting. "Look here—your nonna made a note: *'Never use this spell!'*"

"Definitely some sage advice," Nico chuckled.

"Now we know what creature you faced in your dream—if it was actually a dream," Sofia said, still unsure. "Do you think it actually happened?"

"All I know is that I'm exhausted," Nico replied. "Let's try to get some sleep."

Nico gave Sofia a hug and made a stop in the kitchen before heading back to his bedroom. *Another cup of chamomile tea should help me fall back asleep*, Nico thought. He put the kettle on the burner and, as he waited for the water to heat up, searched through the cabinets for more chamomile. He was disappointed to find an empty apothecary jar labeled: *Chamaemelum Nobile*, which the house had depleted earlier.

Nico huffed. "Another trip down to the basement I guess."

He opened the cabinet door leading to the basement, turned on the light, and headed down the stairs. As he approached the area of the secret room, where his nonna kept all her herbs and magical ingredients, he glanced at the pile of boxes where they had found the deceased rat earlier. It was gone; only a pool of half-dried blood remained.

I guess that'll save me a little cleaning time, but where did it go? Nico thought. He shrugged and turned toward a small room opposite the boxes.

The room was only about four feet deep, lit solely by moonlight streaming through the barred windows of the basement. The moonlight illuminated a painting bolted to the wall above a small demilune table. Sofia had told him the painting was titled *The Search for the Alchemical Formula*, by Charles Meer Webb. Nico remembered from the last time they were here that a memento mori, represented in the picture as a skull, was the key to entering the secret room.

He inspected the painting's detailed, gilded frame. Various images were carved into it. *Now, where was the skull*, he thought. *If I only had some decaying plant matter with me, then I could cast the Fairy Fire spell—even Nonna's candelabra would've been handy right about now.*

Squinting in the dim light, he made out the image of a ladybug, then a unicorn. He remembered it was near the top-right corner of the frame and redirected his focus there. He spotted an image of a spider, followed by a shamrock, and finally, the carved wooden skull. Nico pressed the skull with his index finger, and it retracted into the frame. The wall slowly slid open, revealing the secret room.

In the darkness, Nico struggled to find the light switch. "House, please turn on the light," he called out. Within seconds, an overhead light flickered on. The room, which Nico and Sofia likened to a giant cabinet of curiosities when they first discovered it, looked just as he remembered. He brushed past a large apothecary chest, with nearly a hundred drawers filled with various spell components, and made his way to a large potting table in the left corner of the room.

Above the table, six rows of shelves lined with a variety of apothecary jars held various herbs, each labeled and in alphabetical order. "Ah, here we go," Nico mumbled, reaching for one of the jars labeled *Chamaemelum Nobile*.

He grabbed a small muslin bag from a nearby table and filled it with the dried chamomile flowers. As he was placing the jar back on the shelf, he thought he saw the shadow pass by the entrance to the secret room. With his eyes now heavy with fatigue, he decided to forgo the tea and head straight to his bed. He tossed the filled bag of chamomile onto the table, turned off the light, and closed the panel to the secret room.

As he turned to leave the smaller room, he jumped back, startled by what he saw before him.

A small, winged construct made from human flesh, a little over a foot tall, stood there looking up at him. Nico recognized the homunculus he had rescued from Mr. Cadaveri's secret laboratory.

"Hey, little buddy," Nico greeted, offering his finger for the creature to shake. "How did you get in here? Better yet, how did you find me?"

The sound of shuffling feet on the floor above them startled the homunculus, who darted to hide behind the nearby boxes.

Sofia came running down the basement stairs. "Nico, are you all right?" she called out from the bottom of the stairs.

"Over here, Sofia. By the entrance to the secret room," Nico shouted back. "I believe I found what killed the rat."

A worried Sofia rushed over to Nico, relieved to see he wasn't in danger. "I heard noises again and woke up—then talking. I thought maybe the Babau was tormenting you again. When I saw the light on in the kitchen and the basement door open, I got worried."

"I'm OK," Nico reassured her. "I came to get more chamomile since we're out upstairs, and then I ran into our little friend."

"Friend?" Sofia asked, unsure of what he meant.

Nico knelt down and motioned for Sofia to do the same. "Hey, it's OK to come out—it's just my friend Sofia," Nico said softly. "You remember her—she was with me the night I freed you."

From behind one of the boxes, the homunculus peeked its head out. When he saw who it was, he fully revealed himself, flapping his wings in excitement.

Sofia had almost forgotten about the creature she had met during their last adventure and was momentarily startled. The homunculus retreated at her reaction but stopped when he heard her voice.

"I'm sorry, please don't be scared," Sofia said gently. "Come say hello."

Nico recalled a memory and shared it. "We should've known it was you from the way that rat was killed. You finished off your former captor, Mr. Cadaveri, the same way."

"At least you didn't eat him," Sofia remarked, before noticing the dead rat was now gone.

Nico continued speaking to the winged creature. "You're welcome to stay here for as long as you want. This can be your domain—just try not to knock over any more wine bottles."

The homunculus scratched his head, puzzled by Nico's comment.

"Nico, let's get back to bed—your eyes are heavy, and I need my beauty sleep," Sofia said, tugging Nico's arm.

"We're off to bed, little guy," Nico said with a wave.

As they headed up the stairs, Sofia asked, "Are you going to give him a name? He seems to have taken a liking to you."

"Buddy," Nico answered, with a smile. "I think I'll call him Buddy."

Chapter 10: Answers Amongst the Trees

The following morning, despite his sleepless night, Nico woke up early and decided to make the most of the morning. After a quick double shot of espresso, he chose to tackle the previous night's mess in the basement so Sofia wouldn't have to deal with it.

As he flipped on the light and descended the stairs, the sound of broken glass clinking and scraping against the floor reached his ears. *Oh great, more destruction*, he thought. *Maybe I can catch the culprit in the act this time!*

The iron gate to the wine cellar was wide open. *I could have sworn I closed it last night,* he mused. Quietly, he approached the entrance and rushed in.

Nico let out a hearty laugh, relieved by what he saw. Morning light streamed through the room's barred window, revealing an animated besom sweeping broken glass. Its worn birch bristles were tightly bound around a gnarled ash-wood handle, and it diligently swept the shards into a dustpan. Amused by the house's magic, Nico stood back and watched. Each time the dustpan filled, it floated over to a nearby cardboard box and dumped in its contents. After a few repetitions, the floor was clear of debris. The besom and dustpan, followed by the box of broken glass, floated out of the wine cellar and upstairs.

"Thank you, House!" Nico called out gratefully. "If it's not too much trouble, there's a pool of blood that could use mopping up, *per favore*."

Almost as if the house anticipated his request, a tap in the laundry area opposite the wine cellar turned on, and the sound of water filling a bucket echoed through the space.

"Well, I guess my job here is done," Nico mumbled to himself. "Time to make some breakfast."

Nico returned to the kitchen. Instead of making his signature lemon ricotta pancakes with fresh lemon curd, he opted for something with more protein. He gathered some asparagus, a shallot, and some fresh herbs from the garden and prepared a *frittata* to share with Sofia.

As he finished sautéing the vegetables, he could hear Sofia's feet shuffling across the dining room floor. "House, please make a cappuccino for Sofia," Nico requested while pouring his whisked egg mixture into the heated pan.

"Wow, you're up early!" Sofia greeted him as she entered the kitchen.

"The morning sun woke me up—I should've drawn the drapes last night," Nico replied. "So, I figured I'd make the most of the morning."

Sofia approached Nico and peeked over his shoulder. "Something smells delicious—what are you making?" she asked.

"I thought I'd try something different and make us a *frittata*," Nico answered, hoping that Sofia would approve. "A healthy breakfast seems like a good idea for today's adventure."

"We should probably clean up the mess downstairs before we search for the location of the Dark Dryad," Sofia remarked as a freshly made cappuccino floated over to her usual seat at the kitchen island. "I see you already put in my drink order."

Nico, placing the frittata in the oven to broil for a few minutes, burst out laughing at Sofia's timely comment. "Nice one! And no need to worry about the mess below—I already took care of it," he said with a grin.

"You did that already *and* made breakfast?" Sofia said, astonished. "Why you're still single, I'll never know."

Nico chuckled and confessed, "Well, I had a little help…."

***

After finishing breakfast and cleaning up, Nico and Sofia met in the foyer and headed out. The morning fog hadn't yet burnt off, leaving the air cool, so they decided to walk into town.

"Oh, I forgot something," Sofia said as they stood under the *porte-cochere*.

Nico replied sarcastically, "House, unlock the door for Sofia—she's a bit of an airhead this morning."

Sofia rolled her eyes and ran up the steps and into the house to retrieve her forgotten item.

Nico took a deep breath of the cool morning air, filling his lungs to capacity. As he exhaled, the memory of his nonna's funeral crept into his mind. It had been a cool morning like this when Sofia and he left for the church to say what he thought would be his final goodbyes.

"OK, I'm back," Sofia called, startling Nico as she came up from behind. "Sorry, I didn't mean to scare you. Where were you just now? You didn't even hear me coming down the steps."

"I guess I was daydreaming about that day we went to my nonna's funeral," Nico answered. "House, lock up. We'll be back later."

"I already told the house to lock up—boy, you really were somewhere else!" Sofia said, shaking her head.

"Sorry, maybe the lack of sleep is finally catching up to me," Nico replied, starting to walk. "By the way, what did you go back to get?"

Sofia joined him. "I didn't want to forget my charm bracelet—wouldn't want Solomon to see me without it."

Nico laughed. "So you didn't forget my gift! I must have picked out the better one."

"I like them both," Sofia said, trying to keep a straight face but failing. She had fallen in love with Chiara's ruby ring the moment she first saw it last spring break, and it was a perfect fit.

They walked down Oliveto Avenue and, as they crossed the street, they noticed a familiar sight ahead.

"This is like *déjà vu*!" Sofia whispered. "Are those your parents up ahead?"

"Looks like them—it's around the time they take their morning walk," Nico whispered back, slightly embarrassed. "I don't want them to see us—I haven't even called them to let them know we're in town."

"Nico! Nicolino!" a voice called out.

"We've been made," Sofia said, giggling quietly. "You're in trouble now!"

As they approached Nico's parents, Nico called out. "Mother. Dad. Fancy running into you."

Dr. Kynigós, Nico's stepfather, spoke first on Siena's behalf, slightly irritated. "Nico, you know your mother has been anxiously awaiting your arrival—a phone call would have been prudent, don't you think?"

Nico, feeling a bit embarrassed, replied politely, "Yes, sir. I'm sorry."

Siena smiled and hugged Sofia, then turned to Nico with a look of disapproval. "When did the two of you arrive?" she asked.

Sofia jumped in to help. "We got in late yesterday. Nico hasn't been sleeping well—last night was really rough for him."

Siena's demeanor softened and she placed her hand on Nico's forehead. "Are you not feeling well? Should I make you some of your favorite soup—that Greek Lemon Chicken soup my mother-in-law taught me to make?"

"I'm fine, mother," Nico assured her. "*Avgolemono* does sound good, but it's been so hot here, I wouldn't want to trouble you with making it."

Sofia chimed in, "Yes, the weather when we arrived seemed unusually warm for this time of year."

Dr. Kynigós smiled, sensing their attempts to deflect the conversation. "It has been unseasonably warm, and it's not even summer yet."

Siena then invited them, "Come have breakfast with us."

Sofia started to speak, "Nico already made us a—"

"Sure, we'd love to," Nico interjected, remembering that he had declined a similar offer during his last visit and not wishing to be on his dad's bad side.

The four of them continued walking toward the piazza. Nico and Sofia slowed as they approached Midnight's Treasures—Fine Antiques & Curiosities.

"This is that antique store your nonna warned you about," Sofia said, recalling a memory. "I remember the creepy window display from the night we walked home from The Griffon's Claw—wow, what a night that was!"

"Ah, yes. Sure was!" Nico replied, fixated on the current window display.

The theme was a summer pool party, reimagined with thirteen antique dolls dressed in vintage bathing suits. Some lounged by the poolside, while others tossed a beach ball back and forth. But the most unsettling part was the large kiddie pool—not filled with water, but instead brimming with hundreds of blue-painted doll heads.

"That's one messed-up display," Sofia gasped. "It's even creepier than the last one."

Nico reached into his pocket to pull out his hag stone, but nearly dropped it when Sofia elbowed him to get his attention. "And look there!" she exclaimed. "I count three of those shrunken heads from Borneo—and is that a Fijian mermaid floating amongst the doll heads?"

Nico held the grayish stone up to his eye and looked through one of its many small holes.

"See anything?" Sofia asked.

Nico handed her the stone without saying a word. She held it up to her eye and peered through a hole.

"Nothing strange," Sofia said, slightly disappointed. "I don't see anything out of the ordinary."

Nico burst out laughing. "There's nothing to see. I haven't charged the stone yet, like Teresa had instructed. Remind me to set it outside in a bowl of saltwater during the next full moon."

Sofia playfully punched Nico's arm. "You totally had me going!"

"Come on, let's catch up to my parents before they think we ditched them," Nico said, smiling.

***

After a second, lighter breakfast—consisting of a croissant which Nico and Sofia split, and two cups of French press coffee—they said their goodbyes to Nico's parents, promising to visit them in the coming days.

The caffeinated duo cut across the piazza to say a quick hello to Solomon. They entered Schwartzman's Quality Clothing and looked around; the store appeared empty.

Sofia ran over to the display where Solomon was striking a pose. Today, he was modeling something more casual: a neon yellow muscle tee and electric blue board shorts, with black Ray-Ban Wayfarers covering his piercing blue eyes to complete the look.

"Sol, you're like totally hot," Sofia gushed. "No one's in the store—come on down."

The living mannequin jumped down from the display table and tightly embraced Sofia.

Nico rolled his eyes and said, "Remember, keep it short—we're on a mission!"

"Nico," a voice called out from a storage room near the dressing area; it was Mrs. Schwartzman. "Come say hello."

He left the blissful couple to greet Mrs. Schwartzman. "Good morning."

"Glad you stopped by," the proprietress said as she placed some clothing on the counter. "Come take a look at these shorts that Marvin made last night. This one's your size—go try it on and let me know what you think of the style."

Nico took the shorts and headed into the dressing room. They were longer than he usually wore, with extra pockets down the sides.

"What do you think?" Mrs. Schwartzman called out.

Nico stepped out of the dressing room and turned in front of the three-way mirror to check the fit. "They fit well," he replied. "Very comfortable!"

"We're calling them cargo shorts—I predict they'll be a hit," she said excitedly. "I want you to have a pair to model around town—help 'start a trend' as they say."

By now, Sofia and Solomon had joined Mrs. Schwartzman at the counter.

"Nice fit," Sofia called out as Nico approached and gave a quick spin. "But didn't you say we have a mission to start?" she teased with a grin.

Nico, embarrassed to be the cause of their delay, stammered, "Uh, yes, but—"

"Dear, I asked him to try on the shorts," Mrs. Schwartzman interrupted with an apologetic smile. "I'm to blame."

"Oh, it's OK, Mrs. Schwartzman. I was just teasing Nico—we tend to do that; it's our thing," Sofia said, half laughing. "I love the extra pockets—now Nico can share the burden of carrying our supplies and spell components."

"Great idea!" Nico said, touching one of the larger button-down pockets while reciting the words of the Secret Space spell, "*Fac Spatium.*"

Nico took Sofia's purse from her hand. Solomon and Mrs. Schwartzman watched in amazement as Nico slid Sofia's entire purse into his pocket.

"Tah-dah! Problem solved," Nico declared, smiling smugly.

Sofia furrowed her brows. "I said 'share the burden,' smart ass—now give me back my purse…please."

Nico turned to Solomon. "See? This is what you get when you piss off a Calabrian girl. So be on your best behavior." He retrieved Sofia's purse and handed it back to her.

"Well, now that that is settled, we should get going," Sofia suggested.

"Wait," Nico said, turning to Mrs. Schwartzman. "What do I owe you for the shorts?"

"No charge," Mrs. Schwartzman answered. "Like I said before, your family has done so much for us, we're forever in your debt."

Nico smiled, and gave Mrs. Schwartzman a big hug. "Thank you very much—I'll make sure to tell everyone where I got them from."

"Oh, and don't forget these," Mrs. Schwartzman added, handing Nico the shorts he had changed out of, which he folded and tucked into the spacious pocket of his new cargo shorts.

Sofia kissed Solomon goodbye and whispered, "Maybe we can do something later this evening?"

Solomon whispered back, "I'd like that."

Nico and Sofia waved goodbye and left the store. The morning fog had now burned off, and the air was warmer but still pleasant. They walked to the end of the block and stood across from P. Cadaveri & Sons mortuary, waiting for the traffic light to turn green.

A friendly voice called out, "Hey Nico!" It was Gino Cadaveri, standing at the mortuary's entrance, waving one of his pale white hands in the air.

Nico pretended not to hear him. When the light finally turned green, they crossed the street.

Sofia whispered to Nico, "Are you trying to avoid him?"

"It's kind of awkward—I mean, I did play a part in his father's death, after all," Nico muttered.

Sofia waved back excitedly.

"What are you doing?" Nico asked sharply, lowering his voice.

"This is a small town—you're bound to run into him sooner or later," Sofia reasoned. "Better we get this over with, don't you think?"

Gino briskly walked over to meet them. He was sharply dressed in a light blue tropical wool suit which complimented his natural ash-blond hair and fair skin.

"Oh, hello, Gino," Nico said, acting as if he had just noticed him.

Gino immediately smiled upon Nico's acknowledgement. "I heard you two were back in town."

"You did?" Sofia asked before complimenting him. "That color looks great on you, by the way."

"*Grazie*," Gino responded. "I figured I needed to step it up since I'm now in charge of the family business."

"Yes, you do look quite dapper," Nico finally acknowledged. "I'm guessing Dino told you I was back in town. He almost ran me over in his new car."

"Sorry about that," Gino said sincerely. "He's always had it out for you, whereas I—"

"We're actually in a hurry," Nico interrupted. "Maybe we'll see you at Moraiolo's or The Griffon's Claw one night?"

"I'd like that," Gino said, his cheeks flushing slightly. "You have my number, call me."

Nico hurried down the street, slightly embarrassed. Sofia quickly caught up and commented, "You sure were in a hurry to end that conversation!"

"Well, we're on a mission, right?" Nico bluffed.

"And you have his number? When did this happen? Have you been secretly using the fairy door to visit Oliveto without me?" Sofia ribbed.

"No. This is my first time back," Nico answered honestly, slightly irritated by the questioning. "And he slipped me his number months ago—that last time we were all at Moraiolo's."

Sofia decided to get one more dig in before letting it go. "Looks like we both have a thing for blonds."

Nico smiled but didn't say another word until they were near the end of the block.

"Here are the railroad tracks that Fawn mentioned," Nico said. "Look for an oak tree full of birds."

They followed the train tracks, scanning the trees as they passed. Finally, they spotted a tree larger than the rest. High up in its branches perched huge black birds.

"This must be it," Sofia said, pointing upward.

Nico looked up. "Those look like ravens to me—they're too big to be crows."

"Ah, you're right," Sofia agreed. "This must be the Tree of Unkindness, then."

Nico turned westward, facing the strip mall on the opposite side of the street. "Fawn said the Tree of Murder was a redwood tree, and that it was 'as the crow flies' from here."

Sofia pointed. "That would lead us to that row of redwood trees behind the coffee shop and other stores."

"This seems too easy," Nico remarked, checking both directions for cars. "OK, clear—let's make a run for it!"

Nico grabbed Sofia's hand, and they sprinted across the street and into the strip mall's parking lot.

"Seems busy today," Sofia observed, noting the flurry of activity.

"I think it's senior discount day at the grocery store," Nico suggested. "Plus, it's lunchtime, so a lot of businesspeople are probably eating at the various restaurants here."

"Perfect for us then—everyone should be preoccupied and won't notice us poking about," Sofia said as they made their way to the back of the buildings.

They walked down the paved accessway until they reached the midpoint of the complex.

"I smell coffee," Nico noted. "We should be close to the back entrance of the coffee shop."

Sofia noticed a garbage can by one of the backdoors, overflowing with used paper coffee cups. She ran over to it and turned to face west.

"This should be the spot," Sofia said. "One of those tall redwood trees should be the Murder Tree—we just need to climb that cyclone fence first."

They approached the fence, and Nico joked, "Too bad there isn't a levitation spell."

"I know, that would've been most helpful right about now," Sofia responded. "You'll have to be the spell—give me a boost!"

Nico knelt and laced his fingers together, creating a step for Sofia's foot. He lifted her to the top of the fence.

"See, I'm levitating," she joked, climbing over and dropping down on the other side. The ground was covered in ivy, which concealed a slight slope. As Sofia landed, she lost her balance and fell into the lush vegetation, which cushioned her fall.

"So, who's going to levitate me?" Nico joked, then noticed Sofia lying on the ground. "Are you OK?" he asked.

"Yeah, just be careful when you land," Sofia warned. "It's definitely not level ground."

Nico jumped up, grabbing the top of the fence, and pulled himself over. He gave Sofia a quick warning. "Move—I'm coming down, and I don't want to land on you."

Sofia scooted aside, and Nico landed next to her. He reached down to help her up, and she dusted herself off.

Caw, caw.

"We must be close," Nico said. "Sounds like a crow is laughing at your misfortune."

"Very funny," Sofia said dryly, opening her purse. "I need a pick-me-up. Want a macaron?"

"Sure!" Nico said, taking a lemon one. "I'll never turn one down."

Sofia bit into a lavender macaron and savored it. She looked up into the clear blue sky, noticing a group of black birds circling one of the trees.

"There, that's the tree we're looking for!" Sofia said, pointing to a tree about a hundred feet away.

They cautiously approached a massive redwood tree, deemed to be the Murder Tree. Two more crows, now aware of Nico and Sofia's presence, began to caw in unison, alerting the others. The noise of twenty or more cawing crows became almost deafening.

Agitated by the incessant cawing, Sofia grabbed Nico's arm and cried out, "*Silentium!*"

The area around them fell into silence.

"*Bravissima!*" Nico said, applauding Sofia's quick thinking. "I must've missed seeing that spell. Which side of the grimoire was it on?"

"Neither side," Sofia replied with a devilish smile. "You said you can make up your own spells, according to what Mr. Pendolino told you— just like the unknown enchantment you put on my charm bracelet." Sofia rolled the bracelet around on her wrist, admiring it before continuing. "I don't know how long this spell will last or its limitations, so let's hurry up and find the Dark Dryad."

They circled the tree, searching for a way to access its hidden interior. On the north side of the tree, amidst its thick reddish-brown bark, they discovered a small slit with a warm light shining through it.

Nico took a few steps back to get a better view and suddenly heard the cawing of the crows once more. He quickly put his hands over his ears to muffle the maddening noise.

"What are you doing?" Sofia asked.

"What?" Nico shouted. "I can't hear you! The cawing is too loud."

Sofia approached Nico and heard the irritating sound again. She quickly grabbed his hand and pulled him closer to the tree where all was silent again.

"Well, now we know the spell works in about a six-foot radius from where it was cast," Sofia deduced. "What were you trying to see?"

"There appears to be an image carved into the tree. I thought I could make it out better from a distance," Nico answered. He pulled away some of the ivy that had climbed up the tree and partially covered the image. As he removed the vines, eyeholes and nostril holes became visible, glowing with the same light that was coming out of the slit.

Sofia squinted at the image. "Ah, I see it now. It looks like a face— the slit is its mouth."

"Yeah, reminds me of the Green Man," Nico observed. "It must have something to do with how we get inside. Any ideas?"

Sofia thought for a moment, recalling a similar image in Rome. "It would make sense if it were the Green Man, since he symbolizes the cycle of life, death, and rebirth, but this reminds me more of the *Bocca della Verità*."

"I remember that—from *Roman Holiday* with Audrey Hepburn and Gregory Peck," Nico said.

Sofia's eyes lit up. "One of my favorite movies!"

"So, if it's like the Mouth of Truth from the movie, then I should insert my hand into its mouth," Nico deduced. "Hopefully, it won't bite it off!"

"Wait!" Sofia interrupted. "Let me hold your other hand in case it works like the fairy doors—I don't want to be left out here when the spell wears off, and the cawing resumes."

Nico inserted his hand into the mouth made of bark, and they were magically pulled through the narrow slit into the hollow of the tree. The interior space was confining, leaving them with barely any room to move around. They stood on a small woven plant-fiber rug and inspected the area. Behind Sofia, on a tiny round table, was a lit, verdigris copper lantern.

"Getting here was definitely a new thrill ride—and easier on the stomach than traveling by fairy door," Sofia remarked, feeling along the rounded walls for a hidden switch or lever.

Nico tapped her shoulder. "I think the answer is beneath us."

Nico knelt and pointed to a corner of the rug that wasn't lying flat. He pulled it back, revealing a trap door. Sofia moved away so she wasn't standing on it, and Nico pulled on the recessed ring to lift it open.

"Looks like a long drop into an abyss of darkness," Sofia said, reaching for the lantern to provide some light. "Reminds me of the area below the metal grate we found in your nonna's basement."

Nico took the lantern from her and lowered it into the darkness. His arm bumped against something wooden. "I think you're onto something—there's a ladder we can use to climb down."

"What a relief," Sofia sighed. "I wasn't looking forward to jumping into the unknown and hoping for a soft landing."

Nico noticed a piece of dried ivy leaf on the floor, likely tracked in on their shoes. He crumpled it up and tossed it into the darkness. "*Lux Saltatio!*" he called out.

The space below them lit up, revealing that the drop wasn't as far down as they had feared—about twelve feet to the bottom. Sofia put the lantern back on the table and followed Nico down the rickety wooden ladder. As she started to close the trapdoor behind her, the sound of the crows cawing suddenly returned. "Ah, my spell must've worn off," she noted, continuing her descent to join Nico.

The lights from the Fairy Fire spell danced around, illuminating the area. They could see only one path ahead—a long tunnel heading north.

"Hold on a second," Sofia said, opening her purse. Reaching deep inside, she found what she was looking for—her favorite sweater, which she had taken from Nico. "It's a little chilly down here," she said, pulling the sweater over her head.

Nico agreed, "Definitely a great place to return to if we need to escape the heat."

The passage was just wide enough for them to walk side by side, but they still had to be careful not to brush up against the slimy green walls. Occasionally, they moved single file to avoid random puddles formed by water dripping from above.

They eventually reached an intersection. To their left was a short passage leading to what appeared to be a wooden door, accompanied by rustling and squeaking noises. To the right was another passage that led off into the darkness.

"I'm guessing we're going for the door?" Sofia asked.

"I think so," Nico answered. "It's got to be the entrance to the Dark Dryad's home—I can't imagine she'd live too far from the tree's entrance.

Sofia joked, "Well, if she's anything like Mrs. Hornsby, she might be way down at the end of that other passage."

Nico shook his head and sighed, "Hopefully that's not the case."

Stefano A Giovannoni

Chapter 11: Knock, Knock

As they approached the door, the squeaking noises intensified, followed by the fluttering of wings. Suddenly, a swarm of screeching bats flew toward them. Nico quickly ducked to avoid their path, but Sofia wasn't so lucky—one of the bats became tangled in her hair.

"Nico, help me!" Sofia panicked, flailing her arms.

"Calm down, it won't hurt you," Nico assured her. "If you keep moving, it's just going to get more tangled."

Sofia took deep breaths, slowly counting to ten to calm herself. "One…two…three…."

Nico gently approached, attempting to free the bat. He spoke calmly to the trapped creature, "Hey, friend, stop fluttering around, or you'll just make more of a mess for yourself."

To Sofia's relief, she felt the bat stop moving. "What's going on?" she asked nervously. "Did it die?"

"I hope not," Nico replied as he carefully unwound strands of Sofia's long black hair from around the bat's clawed feet. "Oh, good, it's still alive—it just licked me."

"Eww, gross!" Sofia exclaimed. "It could have rabies or something—are you almost done?"

"Just keep counting," Nico said, huffing slightly. "Almost there."

As Nico freed the bat, it climbed onto the back of his hand and then scaled its way up his arm, resting on his shoulder. Nico gently petted the bat's head and spoke once more, "You're fine now, little guy. Time to join your family."

The bat slowly spread its wings and flew off into the darkness.

"Are you OK now?" Nico asked, watching as Sofia finger-styled her hair back into place.

"Yes, thank you," Sofia replied, then turned her attention to the door. "Do we just knock?"

Nico faced the slightly rounded wooden door, noticing the intricate carving of a pomegranate tree stretching across its length. At the base of the tree was a fallen piece of fruit, cracked open and spilling six seeds onto the ground.

"I guess it's the polite thing to do," Nico said, raising his hand to knock. But before his knuckles could touch the door, it creaked open, and a voice called out. "Well, don't keep her waiting—come in."

Nico pushed the door inward and let Sofia enter first. To their surprise, the room wasn't the cramped space they had expected. Instead, it was a large, dimly lit, and lavishly decorated entrance hall. Paintings of various flora and fauna lined one side of the room, while the other held a seating area in front of a grand, lit fireplace. In the center of the room stood a twisted iron perch, where a small owl sat. It screeched at them as they entered.

"Step forward, humans," the owl commanded, ruffling its feathers. "State your business."

To two approached cautiously, and Nico spoke, "My name is Nico Frantoio, and this is Sofia Saggio. We're here to help rescue the Dark Dryad's sister, Flora, from the efreeti known as Caleo."

"Do you have an appointment?" the owl replied, its tone flat and unamused.

"What?" Sofia said, raising her voice. "You've got to be kidding!"

"Ozvaldo, stop antagonizing our guests," a female called from outside the room.

The owl rotated its head toward the voice and screeched, as if announcing her arrival. A regal-looking woman entered the room, her skin as white as snow, contrasting with her long, formfitting black dress, which swept gracefully across the floor. Her dark hair, styled in shoulder-length ringlets, bounced with each step, and a silver tiara set with blue diamonds sparkled in the firelight.

"Welcome," she said, her voice smooth and commanding. "I'm Proserpina. Please, have a seat. Ozvaldo, tell one of the servants to bring our guests some tea and nibbly things."

The owl immediately obeyed, flying out of the room. Nico and Sofia sat down by the fireplace, and Proserpina settled into a chair across from them.

"We're sorry to intrude," Sofia began. "We were told by a raven we befriended that your sister, Flora, has been taken. We'd like to help rescue her."

Proserpina seemed distracted, her gaze fixed on Nico, who was staring into the glowing blue flames of the fire.

"Young man, what are you looking at?" Proserpina asked.

Nico turned his gaze toward the Dark Dryad. "Oh, I'm sorry. I've never seen blue fire before. I guess I was mesmerized by it—it's amazing!"

"Youth," she mumbled quietly to herself, then chuckled. "So, what brings you here? You clearly know more than most humans to have found me."

"Right, well, as my friend Sofia was saying," Nico continued, "we befriended a raven who asked us to help rescue his mistress—your sister, Flora."

Sofia leaned in. "Nico is from one of the town's founding families. His—"

"Ah, so you must be Chiara's grandson," Proserpina interrupted. "You've been quite the topic among the subterranean community."

Sofia's curiosity was piqued. "What—I mean, who else lives down here?"

Hearing the tea cart being rolled in, Proserpina took the opportunity to ignore Sofia's question. "Oh good, tea is served."

A tall, lanky, green-skinned servant in a black suit and white gloves rolled the cart over. As he poured the tea, Sofia whispered to Nico, "Do you smell that?"

Nico replied under his breath, "Do I? That thing is closer to me—it's even worse over here."

The servant placed a three-tiered tray of scones, finger sandwiches, and petit fours on the table. "Will that be all, mistress?" he groaned.

"Thank you, Barnabus," Proserpina said. "You may go."

Barnabus nodded and lumbered back to where he had come from.

Sofia picked up her teacup and inhaled the aroma of the tea. "Black tea leaves combined with red hibiscus…" Sofia paused, noticing Proserpina's gaze, and continued, "…and blue mallow flowers."

Proserpina grinned. "My boy, I think I might have underestimated your friend."

"Well, everything you've heard about me and all that I've done—I couldn't have done it without her," Nico said, looking over at Sofia. "She's very knowledgeable, can read tarot cards, tea leaves, and knows about nearly every plant in existence."

Proserpina took a sip of her tea and studied the two of them for a moment. "Very well—you two seem well-suited to be the brain and brawn to rescue my poor sister."

Before Nico could finish chewing his scone, Sofia spoke. "We'd be honored."

Nico took a sip of his tea and then asked, "Is there anything special we need to know about Caleo—other than not looking at him directly and not making any deals with him?"

"I see you've been doing your homework," Proserpina remarked, raising her brows. "Caleo is a known trickster, so you can't trust a word that he says. He's a collector and loves gifts—so if I were you, Sofia, I wouldn't let him see that lovely ruby ring you're wearing."

"Or the charm bracelet," Nico added with a smile.

"Thank you for the advice, Proserpina," Sofia said. "Do you know of another way to get into Caleo's lair besides the underwater passage?"

"That's the only way I know of, which is why I never understood how Caleo managed to take my sister—he's trapped by the water and shouldn't be able to leave the mountain," Proserpina replied. She reached forward and placed her hand on Nico's forearm. "It's going to be dangerous, and I don't want anything to happen to you…two. Calypso, the water nymph, will guide you safely—just let her know that you're on official business for the Dark Dryad."

Nico smiled warmly. "Thank you for the sound advice and hospitality—we'll rescue Flora for you."

Sofia took a final sip of her tea and said, "Yes, thank you for the tea and treats—most delicious!"

As Nico and Sofia rose to leave, Osvaldo flew back into the room and landed on Proserpina's shoulder and whispered to her, "Shouldn't you tell them they can't leave the same way they came in?"

Proserpina waited for the door to close behind Nico and Sofia before replying. "No, I'm sure they'll figure it out—if not, then I'll know they never had a chance at rescuing Flora. Though, it'd be a shame if something happened to that handsome young man."

Stefano A Giovannoni

Chapter 12: Lost and Found

As the door closed behind them, Sofia dug into her purse, pulled out a dried piece of leaf, and handed it to Nico.

"Here—I'm too tired to cast the spell," Sofia said, feigning exhaustion.

"You're too much," Nico replied with a laugh. "I think I've had less sleep than you *and* was the first one up."

Sofia looked surprised. "Omigod! You know I'm kidding, right?"

Nico snickered, "I do. So was I."

Sofia playfully slapped Nico's back. "Oh, you! What am I going to do with you?"

"If you don't know, then I'm sure the Dark Dryad will think of something," Nico teased. He crumbled the leaves and threw the pieces into the air. "*Lux Saltatio!*"

Sofia smirked, "She did seem enamored by you, so if you're ever looking for a sugar momma…."

They made their way back to the ladder and climbed back up to the small room inside the Murder Tree.

"Any idea of how to get out of here?" Nico asked.

"You could try sticking your hand back in the mouth," Sofia suggested, quickly grabbing Nico's hand so she wouldn't be left behind.

Nico reached into the mouth-shaped opening, but nothing happened.

"Well, that was a bust," Nico said, disappointed. "I guess we're going to be exploring the subterrane."

"If we head in a northeasterly direction, hopefully we'll reach the entrance to your basement," Sofia suggested. But then, a thought struck her, and panic set in. "Wait. Last time, you mentioned that kids would come down here to explore and get lost, never to be found; that most of the entrances were now closed off, and that the tunnels seemed to magically change their direction to lead everyone to the same place—the underworld!"

Nico remembered telling Sofia that chilling tale, and a sense of unease washed over him. He recalled the night he heard the story during a Boy Scout campout. *Could it really be true?* he wondered.

"We'll be fine," Nico said, trying to sound confident. "We have magic on our side—the others didn't."

"Then I'll let you lead the way," Sofia replied, remembering something. "Oh, and the servant who brought us tea—I figured out what he is! He's a troll. I wouldn't be surprised if there are more down here, so, if we smell that awful odor again, just be ready."

Nico led them back to the intersection, and this time they took the tunnel on the right. It stretched on for what felt like two city blocks before splitting again. They now faced three options: a flooded tunnel to the left, one that continued straight ahead, and one to the right, from which a warm sulfurous breeze flowed, lit by bioluminescent fungi growing along the walls.

"OK, leader," Sofia said. "Which tunnel will lead us to our freedom, and which one to our doom?"

"Such a drama queen," Nico said, shaking his head with a smile. "The flooded one on the left is probably sewer water, and I doubt you'd want to wade through that, even if it led to freedom. The one on the right seems too inviting—it's warmer and has light, so it must be a trap. That leaves the center tunnel."

"That's what I'd pick, too," Sofia agreed. She reached into her purse and pulled out two macarons. "We need to keep our energy up," she grinned, handing one to Nico.

"Yum," Nico groaned and popped the confection into his mouth.

They continued along the center path, but after about fifty feet, it split again. Nico chose the right fork, hoping this would lead them closer to their destination.

"I figure we must be somewhere beyond the piazza but close to Midnight's Treasures," Nico suggested.

Sofia shook her head. "I think we're closer to Indelible Delights than that creepy antique store."

"Well, if at least one of us is right, we're heading in the right direction," Nico said, but stopped in his tracks as the tunnel split once more, this time into four directions.

"Ugh!" Sofia exclaimed in frustration. "I think the scoutmaster's story might be right, and we're being redirected to the underworld—I have a bad feeling about this."

"Do you smell that?" Nico asked, wrinkling his nose.

"Ewww, yes!" Sofia answered. "Trolls!"

"The smell is coming from one of the two left-most tunnels," Nico observed. "The far-right tunnel would probably take us too far east, so let's try the third one."

They cautiously ventured into the third tunnel, which gradually grew darker, despite the Fairy Fire spell still in effect. Nico grabbed Sofia's hand as a precaution.

Eventually, the darkness subsided, and they arrived at an all-too-familiar intersection of three tunnels.

"For the love of all things holy!" Sofia gasped in frustration. "How can we be back here again?"

Nico shared her frustration as he saw the flooded tunnel on his left, the normal-looking tunnel ahead, and the glowing fungus tunnel on his right.

Meow. Meow.

"Sounds like a cat," Sofia said. "Come here, kitty."

Meow. Meow.

"It's coming from the left tunnel," Nico said, immediately heading in that direction.

A young black cat, struggling to stay afloat, swam anxiously toward them, its meows growing louder.

"I think it's in distress," Sofia noted, her voice laced with worry.

With hesitation, Nico stepped into the dark, murky water. With each step, the water level rose higher until it was up to his shoulders. The cat was almost within reach, but as Nico took another step, there was no ground beneath him, and he plunged into the depths of the foul water.

"Nico! Nico!" Sofia cried out, panic tightening her voice.

For a moment, Nico felt detached, as if in a dream, watching himself struggle underwater. Disoriented in the darkness, he saw his own movements from an outsider's perspective, realizing he was swimming downward instead of up. This eerie awareness allowed him to correct his mistake and head for the surface. When he broke through, he spotted the cat, barely staying above water. He grabbed it by the scruff of its neck, keeping its head above the water until he regained his footing and waded out of the flooded tunnel.

Sofia quickly pulled a large beach towel from her purse and wrapped it around the shivering cat. Nico, soaking wet, took off his shirt and wrung it out while keeping a wary eye on the feline.

"I was so worried," Sofia exclaimed. "You were underwater for almost three minutes or so!"

"Really?" Nico doubtfully replied. "It all seemed so fast. And the weird thing is that I think I had an out-of-body experience. I felt that I was actually watching as an observer—seeing myself struggle. It was so dark down there that I became disoriented, and at one point, I was swimming downward. I think by seeing what I was doing, I was able to correct my error and swim back to the surface."

Sofia handed Nico another beach towel from her purse.

"Thanks," Nico said, wrapping it around his shoulders. He grinned. "Casting the Secret Space spell on your purse was definitely the best thing I've done so far."

"It's coming in handy," Sofia agreed.

Nico gently took the towel-wrapped cat from Sofia. "Let's head over to the tunnel with the glowing fungi—the warm air there will help dry this little guy—or gal—faster."

The cat purred in Nico's arms, nuzzling against his chest as they walked to the other passage and sat down. The warm breeze felt comforting against Nico's skin, gradually drying both his damp clothes and the cat's fur.

"I wonder what the cat was doing down here?" Sofia mused.

"Do you really want to know?" Nico asked with a playful grin.

"Sure," Sofia replied, "But this time, let me cast the spell—I want to try it out."

"OK," Nico agreed, "just put one hand on the cat and the other on my shoulder. Then say: *Do Vocem Meam.*"

Sofia followed his instructions, placing her hands as directed. "*Do Vocem Meam*," she recited. She felt her throat tighten slightly as the magic took effect.

"Can you speak?" Nico asked.

Both Sofia and the cat looked at him, but only one of them answered.

"Meow—Wow, I can speak!" the cat exclaimed, using Sofia's voice. "Thank you for saving me."

Sofia spread one of the towels down on the ground and sat, pulling a baguette from her purse. She tore off a piece and silently offered it to Nico. He took some and handed the rest back to her.

"You're welcome. I couldn't just let you drown," Nico replied, offering a piece of bread to the cat. "What were you doing down here anyway?"

"One night, I was craving a midnight snack," the cat explained, taking a nibble of the bread. "While prowling the empty streets, I spotted a juicy field mouse. I chased it down the street and mistakenly followed it into a storm drain, falling into this living hell."

"How long have you been down here?" Nico asked.

"Several weeks, I think," the cat replied after finishing its piece of bread. "When I heard your voices echoing through the tunnels, I ran to investigate."

Nico's eyes lit up with an idea. "So, you must know this place pretty well by now?"

Sofia smiled, nodding her head in agreement with Nico's line of questioning.

The cat rubbed against Nico's leg, purring. "I know every inch of these tunnels and how to avoid those sewer trolls—stinky things, they are."

"Do you recall a place where a large root system blocks the way to a ladder leading up to a grate?" Nico asked.

"Yes, that's further north—I sleep there sometimes. I can squeeze past the roots so that trolls can't reach me while I'm sleeping," the cat answered. It then sauntered over to Sofia, nudging her hand with its head to encourage a pet.

"Perfect," Nico said, folding up his towel and handing it to Sofia. "Will you please take us there?"

"Certainly, but you're not going to like it," the cat warned. "You have to go through the water-filled tunnel—that's the one tunnel that doesn't change direction."

Sofia packed up the remaining heel of bread and towels. They returned to the murky pool of water, brainstorming a way to cross.

"Well, kitty, I don't want you to risk your life again," Nico said. "You can either sit on my head, or we can put you into Sofia's purse and I'll carry you across."

"I like to see where I'm going," the cat replied, leaping onto Nico's shoulders and nestling comfortably in his hair.

Nico turned to Sofia. "You don't happen to have an inflatable raft in your purse, do you?"

Sofia laughed, but no sound came out due to the spell.

"Worth a shot," Nico said with a chuckle. Once he collected himself, he outlined a plan. "OK, here's what we'll do: Start swimming as soon as the water gets deep. The tunnel's wide enough for us to swim side by side, so we can keep an eye on each other."

Sofia nodded, put her arm through her purse handle, and cautiously entered the water. The Fairy Fire lights danced above the surface, illuminating the way. After a few feet, she began to float, and Nico joined her. They swam side by side for about twenty-five feet until the water became shallow enough for them to stand.

"Ah, dry land at last," the cat sighed as it leapt off Nico's head onto the dirt floor of the tunnel.

Sofia pulled the damp beach towels from her purse and handed one to Nico. As they dried off, the cat paced nervously.

"Hurry up!" the cat urged. "I smell trolls—they must have heard us talking or smelled the bread."

Sofia quickly shoved the towels back into her purse.

"Lead the way, my feline friend," Nico said.

They followed the cat to the next intersection, where the stench of approaching trolls grew stronger. It seemed to be coming from the passage on their left.

The cat took the right passage, and Nico and Sofia quickened their pace to catch up. The tunnel stretched on for what felt like two or three city blocks. Occasionally, side passages appeared, but the cat continued forward without hesitation.

Eventually, the long passage veered to the left, leading them to a cluster of large roots descending from the ceiling and burrowing into the damp ground beneath them.

"We made it!" Sofia exclaimed in a raspy voice, the spell having worn off.

"Welcome back—did you find it frustrating not being able to speak?" Nico asked.

Sofia cleared her throat. "You know, if I didn't completely trust you, I would've gone out of my mind not being able to speak—you did well."

"Ah, thank you," Nico said, touched by her sentiments.

The cat meowed and passed through a narrow space between the roots, reaching the other side.

"OK, back to business. We need to get past this wall of roots before the trolls catch up to us," Sofia reasoned. "What was that spell we used last time when we fell into that grave and needed to get out?"

Nico thought for a good minute, trying to recall the spell. He remembered it had made nearby vines come to their aid so they could climb out of the deep grave.

"It was the Control Vegetation spell—now if I could just remember the words!" Nico said, frustrated. He began to panic as the grunting sounds of the trolls drew closer.

Sofia put her hand on Nico. "I remember! *Vinea Auxilio!*" she cried out, but nothing happened.

"Why is it not working?" Nico huffed. "I believe those were the same words I used."

"I think I know. Last time, we used it to control vines, but these are roots—I just need to use the correct Latin word for 'root' instead of '*vinea,*'" Sofia answered.

"Try '*radix.*' I believe that's the word you're looking for," Nico suggested.

Meow! Meow! The cat cried out urgently, warning them that time was running out.

With her hand still on Nico, Sofia took a deep breath and spoke the magic words, "*Radix Auxilio!*"

The large roots began to writhe like snakes and uproot from the earth. Sensing what was needed, they parted, allowing Nico and Sofia to pass to the other side.

Flickering torchlight appeared in the distance, and a nauseating smell wafted toward them.

Nico quickly turned around and called out, *"Radix Auxilio!"* The thick roots twisted back around each other, blocking the passage and burrowing back into the soil before becoming still.

Sofia began to climb the ladder but recalled that the grate above was locked and covered by a large steamer trunk.

"Now what do we do?" she moaned, climbing back down. "We can unlock the padlock with a spell, but how are we going to move that heavy steamer trunk?"

Nico moved in front of Sofia and, as he climbed the ladder, called up through the grate, "Hey, Buddy! Can you help us?"

"Who are you calling to?" Sofia asked, confused, as she backed away from the ladder. Then it dawned on her who Nico was speaking to. "Great thinking!"

The patter of small feet slapping against the cold cement could be heard above them.

"Can you move the trunk for us?" Nico asked. "It is covering the grate and blocking our way out."

Sofia suddenly screamed. One of the trolls had reached its long, lanky arm through a gap in the roots and was trying to grab her by her hair. As its clawed hand swept downward, it grazed her arm, its dirty, yellowed nail catching onto her charm bracelet. The cat immediately ran to Sofia's side, hissing and growling, to scare off the trolls. As Sofia struggled to pull her hand free, one of the charms broke off and fell near the troll's foot.

"Hurry, little guy!" Nico called to the homunculus, who was using its superhuman strength to drag the trunk away from their exit. Nico reached through the grate and touched the padlock. *"Resero!"* he incanted. The lock popped open, and the homunculus lifted the metal covering. Seeing that the cat was still focused on the trolls, Nico jumped off the ladder.

"Sofia, climb up!" Nico directed. "I need to get the cat."

Nico quickly picked up the cat just as a second troll's sharp, dirt- and blood-encrusted claws were about to strike. He used one hand to climb the ladder and the other to raise the cat up to Sofia. Then he paused to look back. The trolls had stopped trying to break through the roots and seemed to be distracted by something. Nico dropped from the ladder to get a better view. The two trolls were fighting over a metal object filled with a mysterious amber liquid, which splashed around. Satisfied that they were now safe, Nico climbed up to the surface.

The two repositioned the grate, secured it with the padlock, and moved the steamer trunk back into its place.

"Phew! That was close," Sofia sighed, patting the homunculus on the head. "Thank you for saving us, little guy!"

Nico introduced the creature to the cat, "Buddy, this is our new friend—darn, we forgot to ask his name!"

"Well, it seems this little feline is a *she*, and I'm sure *she'll* be happy with whatever name you give her," Sofia said.

The cat brushed against Sofia's leg, looking up with a single approving *meow*.

Sofia picked the cat up and cuddled her. "Say, why don't you name her after your favorite drink?"

Nico smiled. "Negroni—I like it. Buddy, meet Negroni. I hope you two will get along and know you're both welcome to live here for as long as you want."

Negroni jumped down and approached Buddy. She sat and raised her right paw. The winged construct responded by raising its hand, giving Negroni a high-five.

Nico noticed the troll's scratch on Sofia's arm. "Is your arm OK?" he asked.

"It's just a scratch—I'll live. But I lost one of the charms from my bracelet—I hope Solomon doesn't notice," Sofia replied, distracted. "Oh dear! Nico, what time is it?"

Nico looked down at his Swatch. "Its four-thirty."

"I need to get ready—I suggested to Solomon that we meet tonight. He'll be off work soon!" Sofia said, brisky walking to the basement stairs.

"Why don't you call the store and let him know you are running a little behind?" Nico called after her, but she was already out of range. He then turned to Buddy and Negroni. "Well, I guess that leaves us alone for the night."

Chapter 13: Another Rough Night

Nico, I'm heading out," Sofia called out from the foyer.

Nico left his room to see Sofia off. "Look at you—a total Betty," he complimented as he entered the room. "No one would ever guess we were almost troll food an hour ago."

Sofia stood there in a black acid-wash denim skirt and white button-down shirt with the collar popped up; a wide black belt tied the outfit together. Her hair was pulled back and secured with a black-and-white polka-dot scrunchie. Slung over her shoulder was a matching denim jacket.

"Thanks," Sofia said, blushing. "May I borrow the car?"

Nico laughed. "I feel like I'm your parent—of course, you can."

"You know, you're welcome to join Solomon and me if you want," Sofia offered.

Nico yawned. "I'd love to, but I'm exhausted. Guess my lack of sleep is catching up to me—I'd better stay in tonight and get some rest. Besides, I still need to shower."

He opened the front door, and a warm breeze blew into the foyer. "We must have missed the worst of today's heat while underground," he mused. "Here are the car keys. Have fun!"

"OK, see you in the morning," Sofia called out as she headed to the car.

Nico closed the front door and made his way to the kitchen for a glass of lavender lemonade. "House, can you make me *spaghetti aglio e olio*? I'm too tired to cook and want to shower before I eat."

A cabinet door near the stove swung open, and a large pot floated over to the sink. The faucet turned on, and water began filling the pot. Upon seeing this, Nico knew the house had acknowledged his command, so he went to take a shower.

***

After a warm shower and a delicious pasta meal, Nico wandered into the living room to see if anything worth watching was on TV. He flipped through a few channels and finally settled on a movie: *Critters*.

"I must have missed this one in the theater," he said, getting comfortable on the sofa.

About twenty minutes in, during a commercial break, Nico heard a creaking noise. He jumped up, suddenly alert. *Sounds like it is coming from the kitchen*, he thought. *I hope those trolls didn't find their way into the basement*!

Nico quietly crept to the kitchen, listening carefully. As he entered, he saw the cabinet door to the basement was slightly ajar, and Negroni was sitting there, licking her paw.

"Ah, it's just you!" Nico said, relieved. "Come watch a movie with me."

Negroni followed closely behind Nico as he shuffled back to the living room. He lay down on the sofa just in time for the movie to resume. The cat, trying to jump up onto the sofa, misjudged and landed halfway, digging her claws into Nico's leg as she struggled to pull herself up.

"Ow!" Nico shouted. Startled, Negroni released her claws and bolted out of the room. As blood flowed from the wounds, Nico pressed his palm against the deep scratches. He tried to resume watching the movie, but the pain was too distracting, so he hobbled to the bathroom to clean the wound.

Nico turned on the cold water and soaked a hand towel. As he wrung it out, Negroni crept across the cold tile floor and brushed up against his leg.

"Are you trying to show me that you're sorry?" Nico said, looking down at her. "I know it was an accident—I'm not mad at you."

Negroni licked the blood, now starting to clot. Nico knelt and gently pushed her away. "I've got it from here, Negroni," he said as he blotted the area and cleaned off the remaining traces of blood.

With the bleeding stopped, the two returned to the living room. Nico lifted Negroni onto the couch, and she nestled in his lap for the rest of the movie.

Toward the latter part of the film, Nico nodded off; he was exhausted. Every now and then, Negroni meowed to wake him, and he would raise his head and watch a little more before his eyes grew heavy again.

The movie eventually ended, and Nico looked down at his Swatch; it was now 11:00 p.m.

"You know, Negroni, I'm beat—I think I'll go to bed," Nico said as he turned off the TV. Putting the cat down, he rose from the couch and stretched. After letting out a big yawn, he looked down at the cat. "Yep—definitely bedtime. Sofia should be home in a few hours—try not to scare her when she comes in. She might be intoxicated and have forgotten that you're our guest."

Negroni let out an affirmative-sounding *meow* and seemed to nod that she understood.

Nico retired to his warm, stuffy bedroom. He opened the French doors to allow fresh air in and then jumped onto the bed, landing stomach-side down. Within minutes he was fast asleep.

***

Before long, he realized he was dreaming again, wandering through the house in search of something. *Not this dream again*, he thought, recognizing this all-too-familiar scene. Then he saw it; the short, grotesque creature scurrying though the house toward his bedroom. *Ah crap, the Babau is back!*

Nico allowed the dream to play out and followed the ungodly creature into his bedroom; it was standing on his bed, waiting for him. Nico leapt onto his bed like in the last dream, but this time, instead of the Babau disappearing into a cloud of foul-smelling smoke, he managed to grab the furry beast.

A struggle ensued, and the two wrestled about on the bed. "I've got you now!" Nico cried out, but the Babau wormed itself free from his grasp. The creature darted across the bed, climbed up one of the bedposts, and then jumped off, landing on Nico's head. With its diminutive hands, it clutched sections of Nico's hair, holding on and laughing maniacally as Nico desperately tried to swat it off.

The Babau dug the claws of its right hand into Nico's scalp and, with the other, tore free a tuft of Nico's hair, causing him to cry out in pain.

Negroni, hearing the commotion, scampered into the bedroom. Seeing the creature, she hissed and growled at it.

The Babau released its grip upon hearing the unfamiliar noises. It leered in Negroni's direction, seeing only a pair of floating eyes illuminated by the moonlight filtering into the room; the rest of Negroni was concealed in the darkness by her black fur.

Nico, still in a dream state, looked around, confused as to what was happening.

***

Meanwhile, the tan Mercedes pulled up to the front of the Frantoio home and parked. The engine turned off, and the doors unlocked. Sofia took the key out of the ignition and grabbed her purse along with a flyer she had brought back.

As she headed up the steps, she thought she heard the sound of someone yelling. The house kindly opened the door for her. She entered and stood motionless in the foyer, listening intently before taking another step.

The muffled sound of a struggle seemed to be coming from the direction of Nico's bedroom. She threw her purse onto the entry table, dropping the flyer in the process, and hurried to Nico's room.

Almost tripping over Negroni as she entered the bedroom, she stopped in front of Nico's bed. She glimpsed a small figure jumping off the bed and running out the open French doors into the garden. Negroni darted off after the creature.

Sofia turned her attention to Nico. He was sitting in the middle of his bed with his eyes closed. His T-shirt was shredded in places, and blood was dripping down his face and on one of his legs.

Sofia calmly called out to Nico, "Are you awake?"

Nico's eyes fluttered, but he looked confused. "Sofia, where are you? I can hear you, but I can't see you."

"Nico, you're lucid dreaming again—wake up," she said, climbing onto the bed. "Open your eyes."

Nico opened his eyes, relieved to see his best friend before him. He immediately reached out and hugged her.

"What happened?" Sofia asked, alarmed. "You're bleeding!"

Before he could answer, the sound of a feline screaming and howling came from the garden, followed by a struggle that quickly ended in silence.

Nico jumped off the bed and darted out into the yard. "Negroni, where are you?" he called out, looking around for signs of his new friend.

Sofia followed him to help search. She cautiously made her way toward the vegetable garden on the south side of the house. The pea gravel crunched beneath her feet as she walked between the raised beds. "Negroni, are you over here?"

Nico finished checking the area beyond the wall of potted citrus plants, where the poison garden was located, and didn't see anything. He walked over to where Sofia was searching.

Sofia heard another set of feet crunching the pea gravel and immediately turned around. "Stop, Nico! Don't come over here!" she warned, panic in her voice.

Sofia's response only added to Nico's anxiety. Ignoring her, he rushed over to where she stood. In front of a statue of the Madonna lay Negroni's lifeless body, her neck snapped.

Nico fell to his knees before the statue, bowing his head. He began to cry and picked up Negroni, holding her in his arms. "I'm so sorry! This shouldn't have happened!" Nico shouted.

Sofia stood behind Nico and put her hands on his shoulders. "She was trying to protect you—paying you back for saving her."

"I know," Nico choked out. "But it still hurts. We bonded the moment I saved her."

"It was that homunculus!" Sofia insisted. "I saw it jump off your bed. It killed her, just like it killed that rat in the basement!"

Nico shook his head. "No, it wasn't Buddy."

"Then what was it?" she demanded.

"I had the dream again—the one with the Babau," Nico said, placing Negroni gently back down in front of the statue. "I remember I was fighting it, and then something happened, causing it to stop fighting."

Sofia suggested, "I'll bet that's when Negroni entered the room. She must have made some noise when she saw it, trying to scare it away."

"That makes sense," Nico said, pulling up his T-shirt to wipe his tear-stained face.

"Come on. Let's go inside and I'll make you some chamomile tea," Sofia suggested. "We'll bury her in the morning."

They went back into the house through the French doors leading to Nico's bedroom. Nico went to the bathroom to rinse off his face and tend to his new wound.

Sofia entered the kitchen and saw that the house had already put two cups onto the island and was in the process of filling the tea kettle, which then floated over to the stove to heat up.

Well since that's taken care of, I better check on Nico, she thought.

Sofia entered Nico's bathroom. "Here, let me get that—I can see the back of your head better than you," she said, taking the damp towel from his hands. "Did the Babau pull a chunk of your hair out?"

"Yeah, I probably look like I'm going bald," Nico replied sarcastically.

Sofia didn't know if he was serious or not and tried to hold back her laughter, but ended up snorting.

Despite his mood, Nico couldn't help but laugh at the sound Sofia had made, and together they laughed for a good thirty seconds before they were able to regain composure.

On their way back to the kitchen, as they were passing through the short hallway, they heard a familiar female voice say, "Oh, dear!" followed by a giggle and a hearty masculine chuckle. They paused and looked into the enchanted mirror opposite the marble busts of Chiara and Benito Frantoio.

"Yeah, Nonna, I lost the battle," Nico said dryly.

Benito chimed in, "What was it that took a souvenir?"

Sofia spoke up in defense, not sure how Nico was taking this ribbing from his grandparents' spirits. "He made a valiant effort fighting the Babau—I wish I'd come home just a few minutes sooner—I could've helped prevent—"

Nico turned to his friend. "Sofia, it's not your fault—there was nothing you could have done. I just wish it hadn't killed Negroni."

"Oh, Nico, we're so sorry that happened to you," Chiara said, trying to comfort her grandson.

"Be careful, Nico," Benito warned. "This won't be your last encounter with the Babau. Those evil creatures are only summoned for the purposes of spying and creating mayhem."

Chiara added, "Someone has sent it on a nefarious mission, with you being its target."

Nico was becoming increasingly agitated from what he was hearing. "Is there anything I can do to protect myself, or a way that I can banish it back to where it came?"

Benito looked at his wife and then up at Nico and Sofia. "I believe your nonna put a banishing spell in the grimoire—it should be on the Benandanti side."

Chiara nodded. "Unfortunately, once the Babau is banished, whoever summoned it will know you're onto them," she advised. "You see, the spell caster must give a piece of flesh as one of the spell components; this binds the Babau to the summoner. When it is banished, the area where the flesh was taken will burn for as many days as the Babau has existed on this plane."

"That could be a good thing," Sofia interrupted. "Then we just need to look for someone who is in constant pain, and we'll know who summoned the creature."

"True," Benito responded, "but I believe my wife was about to suggest another option."

"Correct, *caro mio*," Chiara responded. "Nico, if you can trap the creature, it may buy you more time—you might even be able to coax it into giving you information on who summoned it."

Nico was about to ask another question, but both busts simultaneously closed their eyes and became silent.

Sofia reached for Nico's hand. "Well, now we know a little more about what we're dealing with—that's a good thing! Come, let's get our tea before it gets cold."

They finished their lukewarm cups of chamomile tea and retired to their bedrooms.

Nico got into bed and as his head touched the pillow, he thought, *I doubt the Babau will come back tonight....*

Stefano A Giovannoni

Chapter 14: A Disturbing Disturbance

Nico tossed and turned for the first hour, but then a raspy voice chanting startled him awake.

"By knot of one, the spell has begun. By knot of two the magic comes true...."

I must be dreaming, Nico thought, rolling onto his side and pulling the covers over his head. He tried to drift back to sleep, but after a few minutes, the voice returned.

"By knot of three, so it shall be. By knot of four, the power is stored...."

Throwing back the covers, Nico sprang out of bed. "OK, now I'm sure I heard something," he muttered, checking under the bed for signs that the Babau had returned. Only a trail of small footprints in the dust and the faint scent of sulfur remained.

Assured that he wasn't going crazy and hoping the Babau wouldn't return for a third visit, Nico went back to bed. This time he slept soundly until the rising sun woke him.

As he stretched, he heard Sofia's voice coming from the garden, "Ah, you didn't have to do that. I'm sure Nico will be grateful."

Nico slid his feet into his slippers, opened the French doors, and stepped into the warm, humid air. "Sofia, what are you doing out here?"

Sofia stood by the blood orange tree, speaking to two of the motionless garden gnomes. "Good morning. I was just thanking these little guys. I went out to grab some oranges to squeeze and noticed they'd buried Negroni."

Nico sighed with relief. "Truth be told, I was dreading having to do that. I'm still feeling pretty raw over the whole thing."

Sofia dropped one of the many oranges she was holding and shrieked as she went down to pick it up. "I hate when they do that!"

In addition to the two garden gnomes she had been speaking to, the rest of them had suddenly appeared, standing next to her.

Nico laughed. "They're a mystery, aren't they? Maybe if I remember to charge the Hag Stone like Teresa told us, we can use it to finally see them move in real time." He then looked down at the group of gnomes. "Thank you for taking care of Negroni. I really appreciate what you've done."

Sofia carefully stepped over the gnomes and headed back to the house. "I'll meet you in the kitchen for breakfast."

"Yup—I'm just going to grab a T-shirt," Nico said, returning to his room to get dressed.

The smell of bacon wafted from the kitchen, making Nico's mouth water as he entered the foyer. *What's this?* Nico thought, noticing a folded piece of paper on the floor. He picked it up and took it with him to the kitchen.

"How does scrambled eggs, crispy bacon, and fresh-squeezed orange juice sound for breakfast?" Sofia greeted him.

"What? No toast?" Nico joked. "Just playing—sounds delicious! By the way, is this paper yours?" He held up the paper.

Sofia turned to see what Nico was referring to and then remembered. "Oh, that flyer was being handed out in the piazza last night when I was with Sol."

Nico unfolded the paper and inspected it.

The Griffon's Claw Invites You to Attend Our Official Grand Opening
Date: Saturday, June 21st
Time: 6:00 p.m.—2:00 a.m.
Theme: Welcome to the Pleasuredome!
- *Half-priced drinks*
- *Appetizers, courtesy of Trattoria Moraiolo*
- *Live cover band performing all of your favorite hits from this decade!*
- *No cover charge!*

"Sounds like fun—the night before the Summer Solstice," Nico said. "Want to go? We can invite Fawn, and you can bring Solomon."

Sofia looked at Nico as she plated the bacon. "Hey, do you think Gino might want to come?"

The morning newspaper thudded against the front door, giving Nico a perfect excuse not to answer. "Going to get the paper—be right back! Oh, House, I'd like a double *cappuccino*, please."

Nico returned with the newspaper and sat down at the kitchen island, where Sofia had everything ready. She sipped her glass of orange juice, and Nico took a moment to admire the spread.

"Smells delicious, chef," Nico complimented. "But the color of the orange juice looks a little…off?"

Sofia chuckled. "I mixed in a few of the remaining blood oranges from the tree. I know how much you love them."

"Creative, I like that," Nico said, reaching for a piece of bacon. "Where's my cappuccino? I swear I asked for one."

"Yes, you certainly did." Sofia confirmed. "Are you OK? You seem a bit agitated this morning?"

Nico sighed. "I didn't sleep well. I think the Babau visited again. I heard chanting."

"House, please make Nico a double *cappuccino*," Sofia requested, then focused her attention back on Nico. "Do you remember any of the words?"

Irritated that his cappuccino was not being prepared, Nico got up to make it himself. He went to the cabinet to get a cup, and the door swung open, hitting him in the face. "Ouch! What the heck is going on?" A cup floated out, finally heading over to the espresso maker. "OK, I guess the house is having a slow start this morning," he muttered, rubbing his forehead.

Nico closed the cabinet door and noticed something was off; its knob was missing. *Hmm, that's strange*, he thought, *I wonder what happened to it?*

He returned to his seat to eat. "Oh, sorry—guess I'm a little scattered this morning. The chanting was something like, 'By knot of one,' something…something…'by knot of two'…It had to do with knots."

"That's sounds like the incantation for making a Witches' Ladder—I've seen it in the grimoire." Sofia stood up. "I'm going to get the book."

"No, sit down and eat," Nico said, then closed his eyes.

Sofia touched Nico's shoulder. "Wake up."

"I'm not asleep." Nico opened his eyes and then said, "*Evocare Objectum.*"

The leather-bound grimoire materialized before them.

Sofia lit up with excitement. "I finally get to see the Summon Object spell in action!" She wiped her hands with her napkin and reached for the book, turning it over to the Malandanti side. "Here it is," she said, pointing to a page in the open book. "This is the spell I saw. Looks like nine knots are used in the spell. How many did you hear the Babau say?"

Nico thought back. "I believe he got to the fourth knot before I jumped out of bed and scared the creature away. It didn't complete the spell, so I don't think we have anything to worry about."

"I think this is a spell you can resume at any point, since the words are said while making a knot using yarn, cord, or—" Sofia looked closer at the spell's description. "Or a lock of hair!"

Nico rubbed the bald spot on the back of his head. "So it wasn't just a casualty of our fight. It *deliberately* took a chunk of my hair."

A floating cup and saucer landed in between Nico and Sofia, slamming against the marble top.

"House, thank you for my *cappuccino*. If you were a restaurant, you wouldn't be getting a tip from me," Nico joked. "By the way, I forgot to ask, how was your night with Solomon? Did he notice the missing charm?"

"A funny thing happened," Sofia began, pausing to take a sip of her orange juice before continuing. "I was trying to keep the bracelet concealed with my sleeve, but he noticed it peeking out of its cuff. He was so delighted to see I was wearing it that he insisted I show it to him so he could explain the reasoning for each charm."

"Uh, oh, then what happened?" Nico asked anxiously.

"Well, here's the weird part," Sofia continued. "When I showed him, the missing beer stein charm had somehow reappeared."

Nico flashed back to their encounter with the trolls. "That's not as bizarre as what I'm about to tell you!"

Sofia leaned in, intrigued. "Well, out with it then."

Nico reached for his cappuccino and took a long sip, purposefully delaying his response to tease Sofia. "Remember when we were dealing with the trolls, and I suddenly jumped off the ladder?" Nico asked.

"Yes," Sofia replied, slightly puzzled. "I don't see where you're going with this."

"Well, I had noticed that the trolls were no longer trying to break through the roots—they seemed to be distracted by something. So, I went to take a closer look and saw them fighting over a silver object, which I now recognize to have been a beer stein—" Nico reached for Sofia's arm, pointing to a specific charm on her bracelet, "—a life-size version of this same charm."

Sofia burst into laughter. "I think all this lack of sleep is messing with your head."

"Only one way to find out," Nico said, yanking the charm off her bracelet and placing it before them. The two-dimensional silver charm began to stretch in all directions until it became a life-size, three-dimensional likeness of the charm, filled with beer.

Amazed, Sofia reached for the stein and took a whiff of the amber liquid. "Smells like beer," she said, then put the stein up to her lips and took a sip. "Tastes like beer too!"

"That must be the result of my enchantment spell," Nico remarked. "Not a bad upgrade, eh?"

"You got lucky—thankfully!" Sofia said, smiling at Nico.

"So, while you're in a good mood, I have a favor to ask," Nico said. "Do you mind coming with me to my parents' house today? I should go visit."

Sofia finished the last bit of her scrambled eggs and washed it down with orange juice. "Yeah, of course," Sofia said. "Hopefully, I'll finally get to meet your little brother, Remus."

"Awesome!" Nico said and took a sip of his *cappuccino*. "And speaking of siblings, how's your brother Paolo doing? We should bring him to Oliveto sometime."

"Why?" Sofia said, slightly confused at Nico's suggestion.

Nico put his cup down. "Well, he's your twin after all, and I doubt we can keep this secret from him forever."

Sofia frowned. "He's in Europe for the summer, so that won't work."

"Maybe in the fall then? The Autumn Harvest festival has an awesome carnival, and it's a lot of fun—we'll invite him into our world then."

"OK, but I think we need to focus on a plan to rescue Flora from her captor, before we decide if and when to include my twin on our adventures," Sofia said, while collecting the plates and bringing them to the sink.

Nico yawned. "Of course, you're right as usual. I think I am so sleep-deprived that I'm all over the place with my thoughts."

Sofia turned on the water and rinsed the plates. "Go get ready, and I'll meet you in the foyer in about an hour. By the way, I wanted to ask you something. When I was in the garden earlier, I noticed that the garlic are almost ready to harvest. May I cut the scapes off?" Sofia asked. "I know of a great recipe for Garlic Scape Pesto that I'd like to make. I know you'll love it tossed with some fusilli pasta!"

"Of course—that reminds me, I need to replace the garlic bulbs on the windowsills. They're getting a little funky with all this heat," Nico said. "Anyway, see you in a while!"

***

The two, perfectly in sync as always, arrived in the foyer within seconds of each other. Nico had a bouquet of sterling roses freshly cut from the yard.

"Wow, you even had time to cut roses for your mother," Sofia remarked, somewhat surprised. "I guess the patch of missing hair must have cut down on your styling time."

Nico shook his head with a smirk. "Clever! That was a good one. Shall we go?"

Sofia opened the front door, and they made their way down to the car. "House, please lock up," she called back as she opened the car door.

They pulled away from the house, unaware that something evil was happening in a shadowed, unexplored section of the basement. A low, rasping voice chanted in the darkness:

"By knot of eight, my will be fate. By knot of nine, what is done is mine...."

Evil was quietly brewing beneath the home, waiting for its moment to strike.

Stefano A Giovannoni

Chapter 15: Family Drama

Hearing the tan Mercedes pulling up to the Kynigós' home, the gardener popped his head up from behind one of the hedges. With shears in one hand, he raised the other, waving and greeting Nico with a friendly smile.

Nico waved back while exiting the car. "Juan, *mi amigo*, how have you been?"

"I am well, *gracias*!" the gardener replied. "I've been trimming the hedges for hours—you know how your mother likes them to be perfectly manicured."

"Yes, I know all too well," Nico said, inspecting the neatly trimmed greenery. "You always do such a good job—I'm sure she'll be thrilled. Can I get you something to drink? It's already a scorcher this morning!"

"*¿Qué es un* 'scorcher'?" Juan asked, his expression puzzled.

Nico quickly translated, "*¡Hace mucho calor esta mañana!*"

Juan took off his hat and fanned himself. "*¡Oh, sí, es verdad*! A drink sounds good, thank you."

At that moment, Sofia joined them. "Nico, aren't you going to introduce me to your friend?"

"Oh, sorry," Nico said, having forgotten Sofia was there. "Juan, this is my best friend from college, Sofia. Sofia, Juan."

Sofia held out her hand. "*Encantad*o."

Juan removed his gloves, extended his dark cinnamon-complected hand, and shook hers.

"It's way too hot for me out here," Nico said as he made his way toward the front door. "Juan, I'll be right back with your drink."

"Nice to meet you, Juan," Sofia said, excusing herself to follow Nico.

As Nico reached for the doorbell, the front door swung open. Siena appeared, beaming. "Nicolino! Come give me a hug."

Nico obliged, and Sofia followed, offering a warm hug of her own.

"Quick, come inside before we let in all this hot air," Siena insisted.

Nico started to head toward the kitchen. "I'll be right back! Just grabbing a drink for Juan—I can tell he's thirsty."

Siena led Sofia into the living room and motioned for her to sit. "Would you like some coffee?"

Sofia sat down. "That's very kind of you, but I've already had way too much today."

Nico zoomed past them, holding an open bottle of his favorite soda, Original New York Seltzer Vanilla Cream, and dashed back outside.

"It's so lovely of you to visit," Siena said, turning to Sofia. "My son speaks so highly of you, especially after your last visit to Oliveto."

"We've really bonded," Sofia replied, a touch of warmth in her voice. "We've been through a lot together."

Siena's smile faded slightly. "Sounds serious—is everything OK?" She lowered her voice and asked, "You aren't pregnant, are you?"

"Mother!" Nico exclaimed, having returned in time to hear his mother's remark.

Siena turned, completely unperturbed. "Well, she made it sound serious. And, between that and you going bald—"

"Relax, she's not pregnant," Nico assured her, adding under his breath, "At least not by me." Then, louder: "And I'm not going bald!"

Sofia glanced at the back of Nico's head, surprised to see no signs of trauma, with hair already beginning to grow back in.

Siena was undeterred. "When I hugged you, I noticed a thin spot. I thought maybe you were losing your hair from stress or…."

Nico sighed, realizing his mother wouldn't drop the subject. He knelt in front of her, locking eyes. "Honestly…it was the Babau. It attacked me."

Siena was silent. Nico shot Sofia a regretful look, realizing he might have said too much by being honest. His mother's lips slowly twisted into a grin before she burst out laughing.

"Nico, you know the Babau isn't real," she said, chuckling. "Sofia, please forgive him. He's always had a vivid imagination, so much so that we even sent him to therapy. Remus is just like him."

"But you told me you saw it when you were a kid!" Nico argued, frustration leaking into his voice.

Siena composed herself. "That was ages ago. I probably imagined it after my parents scared me with 'Be good, or the Babau will come get you.'" She resumed laughing.

Nico let it go, collapsing onto the couch beside Sofia.

Siena's attention shifted. "I saw you drove up in your nonna's Mercedes. How's it running?" she asked. "Your dad took it to the mechanic a few days after she passed. He had it detailed and serviced so that you could use it."

"It's running beautifully and is so comfy!" Sofia chimed in.

Siena's face softened with nostalgia. "It's a lovely car. My mother adored it. The mechanic took almost a month to get all the parts, but it was worth it."

"I had wondered where the Mercedes was the last time we were here—that explains it," Nico said, and suddenly remembered something. *Oh, crap!* he thought, *I left the flowers in the hot car—I really don't want to go back out in the heat.* He got up abruptly.

"Where are you going?" Siena asked.

"Oh, I brought you something, and realized I'd left it in the car—be right back!" Nico said, disappearing around the corner.

Sofia, sensing his intent, tried to distract Siena. "Have you ever made Garlic Scape Pesto before? I'm planning to try it with...."

Out of sight, Nico focused his mind on the bouquet of roses, envisioning their vibrant color. Whispering, *"Evocare Objectum,"* the roses materialized in his hands, warm and in need of water. He heard a quiet "Whoa!" and turned to see Remus standing about five feet from him, staring, wide-eyed.

"Hey, little bro!" Nico called out, forcing a smile. "Good to see you!"

Remus just stared at Nico, his eyebrows furrowing; he looked angry.

"What's the matter Remus?" Nico said calmly. "It's me, Nico, your big bro."

Remus ran up and punched Nico in the stomach. He then began kicking and screaming at him.

"Stop!" Nico shouted, trying to fend him off without dropping the flowers.

Siena rushed into the hallway. "Remus, stop it!"

Sofia followed, quickly assessing the chaos. When Remus noticed her, he halted, taking a step back but still glaring menacingly at Nico.

"Gigi!" Siena called out. "Come help!"

A girl, who looked to be in her late teens, dressed entirely in black, her pale skin framed by jet-black hair cut into an asymmetrical bob, rushed down the stairs. She grabbed Remus by his left wrist and pulled him away from Nico. "Young man, upstairs. Now!"

Remus immediately obeyed, following Gigi silently back to his bedroom.

Nico, catching his breath, asked, "What's gotten into him?"

Siena sighed, looking weary. "He's been like this for a while. Come. Let's go back into the living room and sit down. I'll explain further."

Nico handed her the bouquet of sterling, trying to lighten the moment. "Happy belated Mother's Day. These are for you."

Siena's face brightened. "They're beautiful!" She took them, noticing the wilting petals. "Let me put these in water."

While Siena went to the kitchen, Nico and Sofia returned to the living room.

"Does everyone want a piece of me?" Nico grumbled.

"Seems like it," Sofia said softly. "You OK?"

"I'll be fine. Just worried about Remus. We used to be so close. Maybe he's mad I didn't see him last time or that he saw me summon the roses?"

"Or it could just be teenage mood swings," Sofia suggested.

"I know. He's angry because I missed his birthday. It was last week, on June 13th," Nico mused, mentally scolding himself for another oversight. *Great. Another person I forgot to get a gift for. Way to blow it Nico!*

Siena reappeared, holding a bag of frozen peas. "Here, put this on your shin—I saw him kick you."

"Thanks," Nico said, pressing the bag against his leg. "But seriously, is something wrong with Remus? And who's that girl?"

Siena glanced at the staircase, checking for eavesdroppers. "That's Gigi Badante, his au pair. After you left for college, Pétros and I thought he needed a companion."

Puzzled, Nico asked, "'Companion'? He's an active thirteen-year-old. What about his friends from school or scouts?"

"He's been isolating ever since my mother—your nonna—died. His grades began to drop and—" Siena paused, unsure whether to continue.

"And what?" Nico asked, anxious to know all that might be troubling his brother.

"He's having bad dreams," Siena answered.

"Nightmares?" Sofia interjected gently. "He looks exhausted. I saw the dark circles under his eyes."

Siena nodded. "Like clockwork, he wakes up screaming around 1:00 a.m., claiming something with glowing red eyes is watching and waiting for him."

"Have you or dad checked outside to see if something may have actually been there?" Nico asked.

"It's just nightmares," Siena snapped. "Like I said earlier, another one of my children with an overactive imagination. Dr. Matto will figure it out and fix him—Remus is seeing him twice a week."

Nico became heated. "Oh, like you had him 'fix' me?"

"Well, he did get you to stop believing in magic and all that other nonsense, didn't he?" Siena snapped back.

Sofia gave Nico a subtle nudge to calm him.

Nico took a deep breath. "Right. Magic *is* a bunch of nonsense," he said, his voice heavy with sarcasm.

Siena seemed relieved. "I'm glad all those years of therapy did you some good. I hope it will for Remus too. And Gigi has really connected with him."

Sofia tried to steer the conversation positively. "I'm sure she's been a big help."

"She is," Siena replied. "But he'll be in summer school soon, and Gigi will keep an eye on him and help him with his studies."

"Mother," Nico interrupted, "where did you find this goth chick—I mean Gigi?"

"One of my clients recommended her," Siena said.

Nico stood up and handed his mother the now half-frozen bag of peas. "We should get going."

"It was nice seeing you again, Siena," Sofia said warmly.

"You two come by anytime. And don't forget, the joint birthday party is coming up!" Siena reminded them.

Nico mustered up a smile, giving his mother a hug goodbye. "Looking forward to it."

Sofia hugged Siena as well, and then they made their exit.

"Wow, that was brutal!" Nico exclaimed as they stepped outside. "But still not as bad as this heat!"

"Yeah, I could tell you were getting worked up a few times back there."

"Well, at least I made the visit, so I won't feel guilty for not stopping by," Nico said with a laugh. "And I got to see my brother, for whatever that's worth."

"Hey, show me where Remus's bedroom window is?" Sofia asked.

Nico led the way down the hedge-lined path alongside the house. "Follow me—it's over here."

Sofia trailed behind, noticing Juan up ahead, trimming one of the boxwood topiaries. She smiled and waved to him.

Juan lowered his shears. "Can I help you two with something?"

Sofia stepped forward. "Juan, have you noticed anything odd around the house? Maybe signs of an animal?"

Nico stopped under the window of Remus's bedroom and looked up. His brother was there, peering down at them, looking calmer and even smiling.

Juan scratched his head. "Occasionally, the deer come down from the hills and nibble on the roses. And sometimes, raccoons dig up plants looking for grubs to eat."

"Anything else?" Nico asked, studying the ground.

"Sometimes I'll find cat or fox droppings, but that's about it," Juan replied.

Nico knelt, pointing out distinct paw prints in the dirt. "What do you think left these, Juan?"

Juan squatted beside him, examining the prints. "Hmm. Looks like it might be a chupacabra."

Nico's eyes widened, and he looked up at Sofia, alarmed. The idea that an urban legend could be terrorizing his brother was unsettling.

"Nico, what if that's what I saw outside of your home last time?" Sofia said, recalling her terrifying encounter. "Remember that strange, misshapen figure I saw moving across the street toward the house?"

Juan, seeing how seriously they'd taken his joke, burst out laughing. "I'm just kidding—*un chiste*. These prints look more like a coyote's, or maybe a wolf's."

Nico and Sofia laughed, realizing how easily they had been played.

Sofia knelt beside them, taking a closer look at the paw prints. "So, Remus really might have seen something out here!"

Juan sighed, shaking his head. "Poor kid."

Nico frowned. "What do you mean?"

Juan leaned in a little. "He used to be so happy, always well-behaved. But a few months ago, he started acting out. That's when your parents hired Gigi to watch him."

"Nico, that pretty much tracks with what your mother said," Sofia observed.

"Yes, it does," Nico agreed. He turned to Juan. "Thank you for the insight, Juan."

As Nico stood, a sharp pain shot through his shin, and he stumbled back onto the ground with a thud.

Juan reached out instinctively, offering his hand with a kind smile. Nico grasped it, and Juan helped him up.

"*Gracias*, Juan," Nico said, dusting off his shorts. "Sofia, we should get going."

"It was nice to meet you, Juan," Sofia added. "Stay hydrated—I don't know how you manage working in this heat!"

Juan grinned and tipped his hat. "You get used to it."

He returned to his gardening, and Nico and Sofia walked to the car. The car started up on its own and turned on the air conditioning.

"Nico, can we stop by the grocery store before heading home?" Sofia asked. "My toothbrush went missing this morning. I had just used it last night, so I have no idea where it disappeared to."

Nico chuckled. "Don't worry about it. One of my bathroom drawers is stocked with extra toothbrushes and toiletries. My nonna always bought extras for guests."

Sofia smiled. "Crisis averted! OK then, Car, take us home."

Chapter 16: All Hell Breaks Loose

The tan Mercedes promptly returned to Nico's home and parked under the *porte*-cochere in its usual spot. Nico and Sofia reluctantly exited the cool interior and walked up the steps to the front door. Nico took the mail out of the mailbox and was about to open the door, when Sofia said, "Wait! Something's off."

Nico paused and then added, "You're right! Usually, the front door unlocks and opens by the time we're at the top of the stairs."

Sofia reached for the doorknob and found it was unlocked. "Strange—I'm sure I told the house to lock up when we left."

"You did—I remember hearing you," Nico confirmed.

"Maybe we just didn't hear it unlocking as we approached?" Sofia suggested.

"Could be. Let's not overthink it," Nico reasoned. "By the way, do you have plans with Solomon tonight? If not, maybe we can hang out here and watch a movie."

"I didn't make any plans, so a movie sounds nice."

"I'm going to the kitchen and check if there's any more lavender lemonade left. Want some?" Nico offered. "Oh, and feel free to get a new toothbrush from my bathroom; the extra toiletries are in the drawer to the right of the sink."

"Something cool to drink does sound nice—I'll meet you in the kitchen after I get the toothbrush," Sofia answered.

They went their separate ways, and as Nico entered the kitchen, he noticed that the dishes Sofia had rinsed off earlier were still in the sink. *Hmm, the house is really slacking off*, he thought as he opened the refrigerator. *Darn, no more lavender lemonade.*

Nico grabbed a basket from the counter and went out to the yard. He picked nine ripe lemons and gathered a handful of lavender from a nearby bush. When he tried to return inside, he realized the door had locked. Frustrated, he called out, "House, unlock the door—it's hot out here!" But the door remained locked.

Maybe the French doors to my room are still unlocked, he hoped. Thankfully, the doors opened, and he returned to the kitchen. As Nico placed the basket on the kitchen island, he noticed twenty knives of various shapes and sizes had been laid out before him.

"House, I only need one knife to cut the lemons, but thanks for being thoughtful—I guess," Nico said. He then searched for the citrus juicer. *Oh, it's probably still in the sink from earlier*, he thought.

As Nico checked the sink, he heard something whiz past him. He looked up to see a steak knife embedded in the cabinet nearest him. *This can't be good*, he thought, turning to face the kitchen island. The rest of the knives were now hovering in the air, all pointing in his direction.

"Nico, I hope you have my glass of lavender lemonade ready—I'm a thirsty girl," Sofia called from the dining room.

"Sofia, don't come in here!" Nico warned.

Sofia peeked her head into the kitchen and saw the source of his alarm. Cautiously, Nico stepped toward the dining room, pausing after each step. On his second step, a small paring knife flew at him. He tried to dodge it, but felt a sharp pain as it nicked his shoulder, causing blood to trickle down his arm.

Nico lowered himself to the floor and slowly crawled over to the kitchen island. "Be careful," Sofia whispered. "The knives are moving— they know where you are!"

Nico looked up and saw the knives hovering above him, like deadly stalactites. He decided to take his chances and make a run for it. As he bolted, the knives showered down, narrowly missing him as their sharp points clattered against the cold marble floor.

Sofia embraced him as he stumbled into the dining room. "You're bleeding again!"

"Yeah, one of the smaller knives got me," Nico said, pressing his hand against the wound.

Before they could relax, a rattling sound came from the built-in hutch that housed the crystal stemware and china. The doors creaked open. "This is insane!" Sofia cried. "We need to get out of here!"

The two ran into the short hallway and a disembodied voice spoke: "Nico. Sofia." It was the bust of Chiara Frantoio trying to get their attention.

They turned to listen. "You're not safe. Something's wrong with the house," the bust of his nonna warned. "Go to my bedroom—the natural room. It's the only space the house has no domain over. You'll find everything you need there. *Andate nella stanza naturale!*"

The two made haste. As they entered the foyer, the car keys rose from the entry table and flew at Nico, who ducked just in time. Unfortunately, Sofia wasn't so lucky and was struck on the head.

"Ouch!" she yelped, stumbling to the ground, slightly stunned.

Nico quickly helped her up and guided her down the frescoed hallway to the natural room. Once in the safety of Chiara's bedroom, they quickly closed the door behind them. The air was warmer in the room and Nico began to sweat.

"Are you OK, Sofia?" Nico asked. "I wouldn't have ducked if I knew you'd get hit—I'm so sorry."

"I'll be fine," Sofia sighed. "Better keys than knives. Speaking of which, are you still bleeding? Let me check."

Nico turned his shoulder, and to Sofia's amazement, the wound had already scabbed over. "You're healing faster than normal," she observed.

"I know," Nico replied. "It's odd. From Negroni's scratch to the wounds made by the Babau—not sure why."

"Even when a worker stepped on your foot in the piazza, your injury healed almost immediately," Sofia recalled. "It began the last time we were here."

Nico lay down on the bed. "Sofia, come lie down—that was a nasty hit to your head."

"I'll be fine," Sofia said, joining him. "Remember Olive Tree Hill Cemetery, when you picked that beautiful blood-red rose for me—the one growing of out of the cracked burial vault?"

Nico winced at the memory of reaching into the center of the rosebush, and the excruciating pain he felt as a large, hidden thorn pierced his hand as he grabbed it. "Oh, you bet! That thorn hurt like hell."

"That was a bloody mess," Sofia said. "I thought my application of yarrow leaves had stopped the bleeding, but the next day your hand had fully healed. Yarrow couldn't have done that so quickly."

Nico's eyes lit up. "I remember that. And my tattoo healed quickly after that, too. But none of this will get us out of our current predicament. Any thoughts on what to do next?"

Sofia looked around the room. "Your nonna said we'd find what we need here."

"But there's nothing modern here," Nico said, "not even air conditioning."

Sofia fanned herself. "It *is* warm in here."

"We can't stay and roast, but if we leave, the house will try to kill us!" Nico complained. He then thought of his mother's refrigerator. "*Evocare Objectum!*"

Sofia grinned as two bottles of Original New York Seltzer Vanilla Cream appeared in his hands. He handed one to Sofia. They simultaneously twisted off the tops, clinked their bottles, and drank.

"Ah, that was brilliant!" Sofia joked. "At least we won't die of thirst!"

Nico got up and walked to the closet. "Might be cooler in here. We can wait until sundown."

"That's it!" Sofia exclaimed, jumping off the bed. "Remember the door we found in the back of the closet?"

"Yeah, I remember unlocking it with a spell," Nico recalled. "But we never explored beyond it—I just remember a mysterious stairway leading up into the darkness and not having proper lighting to continue."

Sofia stepped into the closet's noticeably cooler space. "Crap, my purse is in my bedroom. Do you have any dried leaves for a Fairy Fire spell? It's way too dark in here."

"Hold my drink," Nico said, reaching into his pocket and pulling out a dried leaf. He crumbled it and tossed it into the closet. "*Lux Saltatio!*"

The dancing lights lit up the interior, revealing a shiny silver doorknob in the distance. Nico took the lead, and when he reached the door, he touched its doorknob and incanted, "*Resero!*" The door unlocked and he pushed the door open, revealing a long flight of wooden stairs leading upward.

"Chiara must've used a spell like Secret Space to create this area," Sofia speculated as they climbed the stairs. "One that extends beyond the roof of the house but remains invisible from the outside."

"It wouldn't surprise me. My nonna was—er, is—one sharp tack," Nico said.

At the top of the stairs was another door; this one had a red crystal doorknob. Nico tried it and it wouldn't open. "*Resero!*" he called out. Still the door would not budge.

"That's odd. Let me try," Sofia said while putting her hand on Nico's shoulder, readying herself to cast the Open Lock spell. As she touched the doorknob, it suddenly clicked, apparently unlocked.

"Hey, how did you do that?" Nico asked, surprised at what he had just witnessed. "You didn't even say the magic word!"

"I have no idea," Sofia answered as she pushed open the door to the mysterious room.

Stefano A Giovannoni

Chapter 17: The Mysterious Room

As Nico and Sofia entered the windowless room, the candled sconces lining the walls lit up one by one. They couldn't help but notice that the space was much larger than expected. Standing on a sizeable Persian rug that covered most of the hardwood floor, they looked up to find that, instead of a plaster ceiling, a clear magical dome revealed the afternoon sky while shielding them from the heat of the day.

In one corner, a cozy seating area with oversized pillows was set against a row of bookcases. Nico walked over to investigate and noticed that many of the dusty tomes looked familiar. *So, this is where Nonna kept the old books she used to read to me as kid*, Nico thought.

Meanwhile, Sofia had eyed an open roll-top desk on the opposite side of the room and rushed over. Sheets of parchment, similar to the pages of the grimoire, lay there, waiting to be written on with a nearby quill pen. Curious about what Sofia was up to, Nico turned to look but was distracted by a round table in the center of the room covered with intriguing objects.

"Hey, Sofia, check this out," Nico called as he examined the items. "There's a crystal ball, a deck of tarot cards, and an antique silver jewelry box with a note next to it."

"Cool, tarot cards! I'll be right there," Sofia replied, excited to see Chiara's personal deck. "Oh, and I think I found where your nonna wrote new spells for the grimoire! We have everything we need to add the spells we've created!"

Nico picked up the note, written on his nonna's stationery, and unfolded it. As he began to read, Sofia rushed over to join him.

My Dearest Nico,

If you're reading this note, then you've found my ruby ring and opened the door to my "work room."

Using my crystal ball, I had foreseen my own demise and had only a short time to hide my ring and some other valuable items in my safe deposit box. The rest I left in the box before you.

Nico opened the curious jewelry box, emptying its contents onto the table, and continued reading.

In this box, you'll find three items:
Your nonno's signet ring, which is for you.
My silver raven medallion, meant for the one always by your side.

"That's me!" Sofia interrupted, excited about her gift. "I remember her—well, actually her bust in the short hallway—mentioning something special for me last time we visited. This must be it!"
Nico continued:

The moon ring, which belongs to the Bound One—although the title 'Unbound One' might now be more apt. Please return it.
Love,
Nonna
P.S. The crystal ball and tarot cards must remain in this room.

Sofia picked up the medallion and examined it closely. "This looks just like the one in your nonna's portrait, the one near your bedroom."
"It does," Nico agreed. "I always wondered where it went. It wasn't buried with her, and it wasn't in the safe deposit box either."
Sofia pulled her hair away from her neck and turned around. "Help me put it on."
Nico opened the necklace's clasp, draped the medallion around her neck, and fastened it. "Turn around, let me see how it looks on you."

Sofia twirled, feeling like a princess wearing her ruby ring, charm bracelet, and the silver medallion. "How does it look?"

"Perfect," Nico complimented. "Do you think it has any special powers?"

"Good question. It probably does," Sofia answered. "At least we now know what the ruby ring can do."

Nico picked up his nonno's signet ring and held it at eye level. "So, if my nonna's ring is a magic key for this room, I wonder if my nonno's ring serves a similar purpose?"

Sofia leaned in to study the insignia on the ring. "This looks familiar—ah, yes!"

"Well, don't keep me hanging," Nico said, intrigued.

Sofia smirked. "Remember when we were at Mr. Ascolano's office for the reading of your nonna's will?"

"Yes," Nico replied, growing impatient.

"Well, the will was blank until you touched it," Sofia explained. "It had been sealed with wax, using this insignia. Your nonna must have said your name while sealing it, so the words revealed themselves only when you touched the paper."

"That makes so much sense!" Nico exclaimed. "I'm usually not this dense—guess the sleep deprivation is catching up."

Sofia picked up the moon ring and examined it. Crafted from olive wood, it was set with four distinct cuts of moonstone, each symbolizing a primary phase of the moon.

A puzzled look appeared on Sofia's face. "So, that leaves one question: who is the 'Bound One' that this moon ring belongs to? That term sounds familiar, but I just can't place my finger on it."

"We can figure that out later," Nico said. "We've got more pressing issues."

"You're right," Sofia agreed. "We can't stay cooped up in this attic forever." She picked up the Tarot cards and flipped through them. "Any ideas on how to sort things out?"

"Actually, yes," Nico said, grinning. "But I'll need your help."

"*Certo!*" Sofia replied. "What's the plan?"

Nico guzzled down the last of his soda. "OK, how familiar are you with using a crystal ball? Seems like something more in your wheelhouse of divination."

Sofia eyes lit up, excited to share her knowledge. "I've never used one myself, but I used to hide in the back of my nonna's caravan and peek out from behind a curtain to watch her tell customers their fortunes. She would wave her hands ever-so-slightly around the crystal ball, repeating the customer's question. Eventually, the ball would become cloudy, and that's when she'd start seeing things and interpreting them."

Nico sat down in front of the crystal ball, and Sofia pulled up a chair beside him. "So, like using the spirit board table in the wine cellar, but with just one person asking the questions?" he said, placing his hands over the cool crystal sphere. "I'll give it a try."

"Be specific with your question," Sofia advised.

Nico concentrated and asked, "Crystal ball, show me the cause of the house's disobedience and hostility toward us."

The crystal ball filled with swirling white smoke. Sofia leaned closer, knowing the answer was near. An image formed: a room with two cement walls and a wooden one with a barred window letting in beams of sunlight. In the center of the room, surrounded by a number of storage boxes, a furry creature lay asleep on the cement floor, clutching something in its paws.

"Does this place look familiar?" Sofia asked.

Nico squinted at the details of the room. "Hmm, the bars are like the ones in the basement, and the sunlight streaming through at this time of the day, means it's on the west side of the house."

Sofia's eyes widened. "That must be the storage area we haven't explored yet! But what is the creature?"

Anger welled up inside Nico. "As to the creature, I recognize that little troublemaker—it's the Babau!"

"Can you make out what it's holding?" Sofia asked.

Nico waved his hands around the crystal ball once more, which erased the current image like a shaken Etch A Sketch. He focused again. "Crystal ball, reveal to us what the Babau is holding."

An image began to appear, and Sofia immediately recognized the item from the grimoire. "That's a Witches' Ladder! And look—my missing toothbrush is woven into it!"

Nico clenched his fists. "That thing is behind all of this. *Evocare Objectum!*" he shouted. The Witches' Ladder appeared before them, woven with hair and various objects.

"Look. There's my missing toothbrush!" Sofia exclaimed, relieved. "I wasn't going crazy!"

Nico examined it. "It even has the hair the Babau yanked from my scalp—and look at this! It's the missing cabinet knob!"

Sofia shivered at the dark energy it radiated. "We need to destroy it to break the curse."

"How?" Nico asked, anxious.

Sofia considered. "We need to undo all nine knots and release the items woven into it. That should break the spell."

They worked together, undoing the knots and releasing the items from the Witches' Ladder. "Here's your toothbrush back," he joked as he removed it.

"Yuck! There's no way I'm using that again," Sofia said and then quipped back, "Maybe we can weave this hair back onto your head, once we untangle it?"

The two laughed, always finding a way to lighten the darkest of moods, as they continued undoing the knots, releasing the nine stolen objects the Babau had taken for the spell: Sofia's toothbrush, a cabinet knob, a demitasse spoon, a skeleton key to an unknown door, a button from Nico's shorts, a pen from Sofia's purse, a disposable razor blade, a Q-tip with eyeshadow on it, and a piece of paper with writing on it.

Sorting through the items, Sofia made an observation. "Let's see, these three items are tied to the house, and these three items are mine, so the other three must be yours—is that the mysterious note from Gino?"

Nico blushed. "Yes."

"Are you ever going to call him?" Sofia asked, then quickly backed off. "Sorry, I shouldn't meddle. It does seem like the Babau was targeting you, since your hair was the main component of the spell."

"And you got caught in the crossfire," Nico said apologetically. "I'm sorry you were put in danger."

Sofia laughed. "Ah, danger is my middle name. Besides, we make a great team. Your nonna had faith that we'd figured this out, and we did."

Nico smiled, looking at the sky through the dome ceiling. "The sun's setting—it's almost dinnertime. Maybe we should celebrate our victory and invite Fawn and Solomon over to join us for movie night?"

Sofia grinned. "Sounds great, but let's save that for another night. Remember, we're going to have a pissed-off Babau to deal with once it wakes up!"

Chapter 18: Movie Night

Nico and Sofia left the safety of Chiara's bedroom and cautiously made their way down the frescoed hallway toward the foyer. As they peeked into the foyer, they noticed that the car keys were back on the entry table.

"Well, that's a good sign," Sofia said, feeling relieved.

"Good indeed," Nico agreed. "But let me take the lead, just in case." He motioned for Sofia to get behind him.

They passed through the dining room without incident and continued into the short hallway, where the busts of both Benito and Chiara turned to greet them.

"Well done, you two!" Benito congratulated.

Chiara's bust smiled. "I knew you'd figure it out!"

"It took us a while, but we finally got a handle on things," Nico boasted.

Chiara looked at Sofia. "I see you found the gift I left for you."

Sofia placed her hand on the medallion. "Yes, thank you ever so," she said, humbled by Chiara's thoughtfulness.

"You're welcome, my dear," Chiara replied. "You'll need to be strong while wearing it."

"Nonna, can you tell us more about the 'Bound One' that you mentioned in your note?" Nico asked.

Benito's expression suddenly changed, and he appeared to be troubled by the question. Chiara immediately closed her eyes and went silent, and Benito followed suit.

Nico scratched his head. "I wonder what that was all about. I feel like we're always left with more unanswered questions."

"It's just one more thing for us to figure out," Sofia said. "Come on, let's check the kitchen and make sure everything is truly back to normal."

They entered the kitchen and saw that the knives, which had previously rained down on Nico, were now back in their proper places. To their surprise, a pitcher filled with lavender lemonade and two glasses awaited them on the kitchen island.

Sofia decided to test the house. "House, would you please pour us two glasses of the lavender lemonade?"

Without hesitation, the pitcher levitated and filled both glasses before settling back down.

"Looks like things are back to normal. That was an effortless pour," Nico noted. "Thank you, House. I hope you're feeling better."

Nico went over to the sink and pulled out a few items from his pocket, including the demitasse spoon that the Babau had taken. He rinsed it off and placed it back in the correct drawer.

Sofia called over to him, "Come have a seat and enjoy your drink with me."

"I will—just want to reattach this cabinet knob, and I'll be right there." Nico responded.

Sofia took a sip of her drink. "House, this is yummy! I think it's even better than the last batch."

Nico joined her at the island and tasted his drink. "Mmm, it really is good. I think the house feels guilty for almost killing us."

"OK, so, movie night," Sofia started to say, but Nico interrupted by summoning the TV Guide from the living room.

"Here, check out what's on tonight," Nico said, grinning. "How about Chinese takeout? I'll order while you choose the movie."

"Sounds perfect!" Sofia replied, her stomach rumbling at the mere mention of food. She flipped through the TV listings. "Ah, here we go! I've found tonight's movie selection—*Salem's Lot*. I read the book, but sadly missed the two-part miniseries when it aired almost a decade ago."

Nico looked over at the TV Guide. "And you're in luck. They're showing both parts tonight, with limited commercial interruption!"

"Awesome. I think I'm going to freshen up while you call in the order," Sofia said. "Then I can wait for the delivery while you change out of that that bloody T-shirt."

"Excellent plan," Nico agreed, finishing his drink.

Sofia put the pitcher of lavender lemonade in the refrigerator and placed their empty glasses in the sink. She noticed an item on the counter and turned to Nico. "What should we do with this skeleton key the Babau had?"

"I'm not sure what it's for," Nico replied, dialing the restaurant. "Probably a key to one of the bedrooms. Just toss it in the junk drawer for now."

Confused, Sofia asked, "And which drawer might that be?"

"Yes, I'd like to place an order for delivery—hold on for a sec," Nico said to the restaurant employee. He covered the phone receiver and instructed, "House, please show Sofia the junk drawer."

One of the kitchen drawers slid open for Sofia. She placed the key inside among various batteries, a screwdriver, a measuring tape, a box of matches, and other random items. "Thanks, House," she whispered, and the drawer slid closed.

"Food's ordered," Nico called out, hanging up the phone. "They said it should be here in about thirty minutes."

"Great, see you in the living room in a half an hour!" Sofia said, excited to finally see *Salem's Lot*.

"I'll leave some cash on the entry table, just in case you answer the door first." Nico said as he followed her out of the kitchen.

***

"Something smells delicious!" Nico announced as he entered the living room.

Sofia was opening the takeout boxes. "Looks like you ordered all my favorites: sweet and sour chicken, moo shu pork, Mongolian beef, and barbequed pork fried rice! House, please bring us two plates and napkins. Are chopsticks OK?"

"Yeah, I'm pretty good with them," Nico said, then realized something. "Shoot, I forgot to order drinks. What do you want?"

"I'm kind of hooked on that vanilla soda you like, but if you keep summoning them, your mother will notice her refrigerator is empty," Sofia said, slightly worried.

"No problem. They have a secondary refrigerator in the garage, next to my dad's workbench—it's completely stocked with all types of sodas and beer. She's always telling me to take whatever I want when I'm there, so I don't think she'll mind," Nico assured her.

As the plates and napkins floated into the room, Sofia grabbed them. "Now that you mention beer, that sounds even better—and it pairs well with Chinese food."

"Let's see what I can get for us," Nico said, and then concentrated. "*Evocare Objectum!*"

Two different brands of beer appeared. "Didn't know what she had, so I summoned random beers," Nico explained. "Do you want the Miller's Genuine Draft or the Rolling Rock?"

"Miller's, please," Sofia said, taking the chilled amber bottle. "Oh, House, one more thing please, we need a bottle opener."

Nico twisted off his cap. "Sofia, I'll get yours—House, cancel the bottle opener," he said as he removed her cap.

"To surviving the day," said Sofia.

"Surviving the day!" chimed in Nico, and they clinked bottles and each took a sip.

"Ah, now that was much needed," Sofia said, making a plate for Nico.

"What channel is the movie on?" Nico asked, turning on the television. "It should be starting at any moment."

Sofia took another sip of her beer. "It's on CBS."

Nico turned to channel five just as the announcer's voice boomed, "If you thought you could never be frightened by a television movie, watch what happens to the citizens of Salem's Lot. Is something evil killing the people in Salem's Lot or are they killing each other? The terrifying three-hour special starts now!"

***

About an hour into the movie, a commercial came on. "Want any more food?" Nico asked Sofia before boxing up the remaining food.

"I'm stuffed, thanks," Sofia said, leaning back. "Need help putting it away?"

"I've got it—should be back before the movie resumes," Nico said, taking the leftovers and empty plates to the kitchen.

As he placed the dishes in the sink, he heard Sofia cry out, "Nico, hurry!"

Nico's heart raced. *The Babau must be back*, he thought.

"House, put the food in the refrigerator," he said, rushing to Sofia. "I'm coming!"

Sofia turned, smiling. "Relax—the movie's back on."

Nico sighed in relief and sat down next to her. "Phew, for a minute, I thought something bad happened. Totally blanked that the commercial break might have ended."

"Well, hopefully, you can some rest tonight and won't be so jumpy," Sofia said as the movie resumed.

The next scene had them both tense: a young teenager was awakened by scratching at his bedroom window. "Your nonna's TV has great sound," Sofia whispered. "The scratching sound is so realistic—like it's happening right here with us."

Nico muted the TV, and they both heard a faint squeaking sound, like something scraping against glass.

"Do you hear that?" Nico asked.

Sofia jumped up. "It's coming from my bedroom."

They went to investigate, slowly raising the Venetian blinds, unsure of what might be outside the window. They peeked out but saw nothing. Suddenly, they heard a click, followed by the creaking sound of something opening. They stood there in silence, straining to hear more, until the sudden crash of a box toppling over in the basement below startled them.

Nico's face went pale. "It must be the Babau," he whispered. "I need to make sure Buddy is safe—I can't allow another death to be on my conscience."

Sofia started unlocking the hope chest, pressing the floral combination. "That'll take too long," Nico said, bolting off to the kitchen.

Nico opened the cabinet door leading to the basement and skipped multiple steps on his way down. When he reached the backmost part of the basement, he felt a warm breeze coming from one of the barred windows, which had recently been opened.

Buddy stood there, waving his hands and flapping his wings to get Nico's attention. Relieved that the construct was unharmed, Nico watched as Buddy pointed toward the raised cement area that he and Sofia had seen in the crystal ball earlier that day.

Sofia emerged from the nearby secret wall. "What's going on?" she asked.

Just as Nico was about to answer, a hissing sound, followed by high-pitched growling, echoed from the dark cement area. Nico froze, recognizing the sounds. Thinking quickly, Sofia reached into Nico's pocket, grabbed a dried leaf, and crumpled it in one hand. Placing her other hand on Nico's shoulder, she tossed the spell components into the darkness. "*Lux Saltatio!*" she cried out.

The unexplored area lit up, revealing cobwebs, recently disturbed, swaying from the wooden beams of the ceiling. Many of the once neatly stacked storage boxes lay overturned, their contents scattered across the cold cement floor. In the center of the chaos lay the Babau.

Sofia stepped onto the raised cement area to take a close look. "I wonder if it's still asleep?" she whispered back to Nico.

"Sofia, stay back," Nico cautioned. "I have a feeling there's something else nearby, probably hiding behind one of the boxes."

Sofia took a few steps back, realizing that Nico might be right. The Babau wouldn't have made all that noise, or created such a mess, if it were alone, she thought.

"Let me go first and check things out," Nico said, stepping onto the raised area. "At least if I get hurt, we know I'll heal quickly."

"Be careful!" Sofia whispered.

As Nico inched closer to the Babau, he saw it was lying on its stomach. Tufts of fur floated in a pool of blood around its lifeless body. He then noticed a set of bloody footprints leading away from the corpse, further into the darkness of the room.

Nico poked the Babau and then turned to Sofia. "I think it's dead."

"Can you tell what happened to it?" Sofia asked.

Once again, Nico froze just as he was about to answer Sofia. Something furry brushed against his bare leg. *No, it can't still be alive,* he thought.

Meow. Meow.

Nico looked down and saw Negroni, nudging her head affectionately against his leg. "But how?" he said, then called out to Sofia, "Quick, come here!"

Sofia entered the area and gasped. "But she was dead—the gnomes buried her!"

Nico reached to pick up Negroni, but she scurried over to the dead Babau and began lapping up its blood.

"Negroni, no!" Nico shouted, quickly grabbing the cat. "Bad kitty— we'll take you upstairs and give you some fresh water to drink—then we'll see about cleaning you off."

Negroni purred loudly in his arms.

Sofia knelt down to inspect Babau's furry corpse. "I never got to see this thing up close," she said, grabbing its hand and turning it over onto its back. "Eww!"

"Ugly little bugger, isn't it?" Nico added. "A face only a mother could love."

"You can almost see the evil etched into its maniacal expression," Sofia said. Then she called out, "Hey Buddy, come here for a second."

The friendly construct approached, waving.

"I have a theory," Sofia said. "Negroni must have been scratching at the window, and Buddy released the latch to let her in—that explains the noises we heard." She looked down at Buddy, who nodded in affirmation.

"Jinkies, Velma, you've solved the mystery!" Nico teased.

Sofia couldn't help but laugh at his timely joke. "Well, Negroni got her revenge, but now whoever sent the Babau knows that we're onto them."

"Not necessarily," Nico said. "My nonna said that if we banished it back to its original plane, the summoner would feel pain and know. But it wasn't banished…." He grinned.

"You're right—the body is still here," Sofia said, catching on. "If we preserve it, the summoner might never know?"

"Let's take care of Negroni first," Nico said, carrying the cat to the top of the stairs. He then turned to Sofia. "Here, you take her and clean her up. I'll deal with the Babau."

Sofia took Negroni to her bathroom while Nico grabbed a large black trash bag from under the kitchen sink. "This should work," he said, hurrying back to the Babau's corpse.

He picked it up by one of its hands, dropped it into the bag, and knotted the end. "Off to the freezer you go, you little bastard."

Nico opened the large chest freezer across from the wine cellar, near the laundry area. The sight of large glass jars filled with frozen homemade ravioli brought back memories of past holiday dinners with his nonna. Clearing a space far from those cherished reminders, he placed the foul creature inside and closed the lid.

"It's finally over," he sighed. "Now I can get a good night's sleep."

Chapter 19: Back on Track

The next morning, Nico was suddenly awakened from his restful sleep to find Negroni sitting on his chest, her face inches away from his, staring at him.

"Good morning, my little protector," Nico greeted as he gently moved his feline friend to his side.

Nico got out of bed and stretched his arms upward. *Finally, a good night's sleep!* he thought. As he shuffled over to the French doors leading to the yard, Negroni hissed.

"There's nothing to worry about. The Babau is gone," Nico said, trying to comfort Negroni as he opened the doors.

A beam of sunlight streamed into the room, illuminating the duvet cover. Negroni let out a yowl and jumped off the bed, scampering out of the room.

Hmm, I wonder what's gotten into her, he thought. *Maybe she's not looking forward to another hot day.*

Nico put on a T-shirt and headed to the kitchen. As he approached, he could hear Sofia talking on the phone, so he stayed in the short hallway to listen.

"Yes, Sol, I miss you too," Sofia said into the receiver. "A lot has been going on, but maybe we can hang out tonight?"

Nico snickered. *I wonder if Solomon is jealous of Sofia spending so much time with me,* he thought.

The bust of Chiara opened its eyes, looked up at Nico disapprovingly, and whispered, "I thought I taught you better than to snoop on your friends."

"You did, Nonna," Nico responded, slightly embarrassed. "I wasn't spying, I just didn't want to startle her."

The bust closed its eyes and Nico entered the kitchen.

"Oh, Nico's up," Sofia said to Solomon. "I should go. I'm sure I'll see you later today, if not tonight."

Sofia hung up the phone and joined Nico at the kitchen island. "House, *due cappuccini, per favore.*"

The house began preparing their cappuccinos as Nico asked, "Is everything all right between the two of you?"

"Yeah—I think he's just anxious to spend time with me while I'm here in Oliveto," Sofia said. "You know, a long-distance phone relationship can only go so far."

"Makes sense," Nico said. "If you need some alone time, I can find something to do—I can always see if Fawn wants to hang out."

Sofia was surprised by Nico's response. "Oh, now that's random."

"Well, I have something I want to ask her," Nico said.

With a hint of curiosity, Sofia asked, "Like what?"

As their two *cappuccinos* floated over to them, Nico grabbed his mid-air and replied, "I'm hoping she'll know if there's a fairy door near the mountain. That would make it easier for us to get there and rescue Flora from the efreeti."

"Good point—using a fairy door would be helpful," Sofia said, taking a sip of her cappuccino.

"And she's pretty good at coming up with plans," Nico added.

Sofia's excitement grew, though she wasn't sure if it was from the caffeine or memories of their last adventure. "You're right! Fawn was the one who came up with the plan to get into the mortuary—you couldn't have gotten in without her. We wouldn't have been able to stop the Oliveto Abductor without her help."

Nico set his cup down. "She also wouldn't have been rescued—she unknowingly was the key to saving herself!"

"You're right! I never looked at it that way. It's almost like she knew she was going to be the next to be abducted," Sofia said, speaking quickly. "Maybe she's a bit psychic or read her tea leaves—or has a crystal ball like your nonna!"

"I think you need some food. The little bit of caffeine in that cappuccino has really got you amped," Nico suggested.

"It's all this magic stuff—you know how it excites me," Sofia responded. "But you're right; I probably should eat something."

"OK, let's get ready and go downtown," Nico suggested. "I think a greasy spoon breakfast is in order—let's go to Doc's! A breakfast sandwich with extra bacon should hit the spot."

Sofia's mouth began to water. "That does sound good," she said. "Breakfast, then we'll visit Fawn and Sterling."

"Meet you in thirty?" Nico asked, bringing their empty cups and saucers to the sink.

"See you then," Sofia called as she passed through the short hallway on the way to her bedroom.

***

They returned to the foyer thirty minutes later. A fresh bouquet of roses from the garden, arranged in a pewter vase, filled the room with a lovely fragrance.

"This wasn't here before," Sofia noted. "And I recognize those roses! They're from that rosebush we brought back from the cemetery."

Nico leaned in to smell one of the blooms. "Intoxicating!" he remarked. "Glad to see the house is back to its usual routine."

Just as they were about to leave, Sofia rushed back to her bedroom and returned with her charm bracelet, quickly clasping it around her wrist.

"I see you didn't forget the ring and medallion," Nico teased.

Slightly embarrassed, Sofia confessed, "Well, I take off the charm bracelet when I go to bed—the other two I keep on. I tried wearing the bracelet to bed that first night, but I woke up with the charms tangled in my hair."

"Makes sense—let's go," Nico said, opening the front door. "House, please lock up."

As Nico closed the door, they waited to hear the click of the lock.

"A reassuring sound," Sofia remarked.

They drove downtown and found a parking spot right in front of Doc's Drugstore and Soda Shop. As they stepped out of the car, the smell of bacon and other delicious breakfast aromas filled the air, enticing them to enter.

"Ah, look, the guy you had a crush on last time is working today—let's sit at the counter," Nico said, leading them to two available seats.

"Hello, my name is Tomás, and I'll be your server today," the waiter greeted with a smile. "Oh, I remember you two! You came in for ice cream one evening back in the spring—your name is Sofia, if I'm not mistaken."

Sofia, flattered that the handsome server remembered her, smiled. "Excellent memory!"

"It's one of my gifts," Tomás whispered. "Besides, how could I forget such a beautiful face?"

Nico interrupted the flirtation, "Can we get two breakfast sandwiches with extra bacon and two coffees? I know Sofia is eager to see her *boyfriend*, so if you could put our order in now, I'm sure she'd appreciate it."

"Uh, yes, right away, Mr. Frantoio," Tomás replied and hurried off.

Sofia elbowed Nico. "You didn't have to be so blunt about it, Mr. Frantoio," she said, holding back a laugh. "It was just some harmless flirting."

"And should I tell Solomon?" Nico said with a grin.

"No. You're right," Sofia admitted. "I should be focusing on him and our next task."

"After breakfast, why don't you head over to see Solomon. I'll visit Fawn and Sterling—we'll kill two birds with one stone," Nico suggested.

"OK," Sofia agreed, looking up as Tomás placed their coffees down on the counter.

"Your breakfast sandwiches will be right up," Tomás announced.

"Thank you," Sofia said, trying to suppress a smile.

***

They finished their breakfast and then parted ways. Sofia headed to Schwartzman's Quality Clothing to see Solomon, and Nico crossed the street to the north side of the piazza.

Nico's family's business, S. Frantoio & Company Real Estate, was just a few doors down the block, so he decided to stop and peek inside. Several of the realtors waved to him from their desks as he entered, and he greeted each of them while making his way to the private office in the back, where his mother was busy typing up a contract.

"Hello, mother," Nico said.

Startled, Siena jumped in her seat, pressing multiple keys on the electric typewriter at once. "Nico!"

"Sorry. Is this a bad time?" Nico asked.

Siena yanked the paper from the typewriter, crumpled it up, and tossed it into the trash bin. "No, not at all. I'd just started typing and can easily start over."

Feeling guilty, Nico put his hands behind his back and concentrated on the bouquet of roses from the foyer of his home. "*Evocare Objectum*," he mumbled.

"What? Did you say something?" Siena asked.

Nico revealed his summoned gift and placed the vase of flowers on her desk. "Uh, I was just starting to say that I brought you something."

"Oh, they're so beautiful, Nico," Siena complimented. "I've only seen roses this red—"

Siena seemed to freeze, staring at the roses, deep in thought.

Nico walked over to her side and put his hand on her shoulder. "Mother, are you OK?" he asked.

Siena snapped out of her trance-like state. "I'm fine, Nico. I just thought I'd seen these roses before—they are very rare—but then my mind went blank."

"Well, I was just in the area and wanted to say hello to my favorite mother," Nico joked.

Siena quickly retorted, "I'm your only mother!"

"I know—it's a joke," Nico replied with a laugh, hugging her.

"Sorry, Nico. I guess I'm a little off today," Siena admitted.

"You're probably worried about my brother," Nico suggested.

"I am, and that's part of it," Siena said, taking a sip of her coffee. "But for the past two months, random images have been popping into my head when I'm here at the office—like unknown memories. And as soon as I try to focus on them, they disappear."

"Hmm, maybe you should see Dr. Matto," Nico suggested. "He might be able to help you make sense of them."

"Perhaps—but you didn't come here to listen to my worries," Siena said, taking another sip. "What brings you downtown on this hot day?"

"Sofia and I had breakfast, and now she's off doing some shopping, so I thought I'd stop by to say hello," Nico answered. "I'm supposed to meet her shortly, so I'll let you get back to work."

He hugged his mother again, and they said their goodbyes.

As Nico left the real estate office, he noticed workers going in and out of the building next door, The Griffon's Claw. Curious, he peered inside. *Ah, they must be preparing for their grand opening party this Saturday*, he thought.

"Nico? Nico Frantoio?" a voice called from further up the block.

"Yes," Nico answered, turning to see a woman approaching.

A woman with mousy brown hair pulled back into a messy bun stood before him, extending her hand. She wore a navy linen suit with the sleeves rolled up over a white halter top. Adjusting her tortoiseshell horn-rimmed glasses, she looked him up and down before smiling. "So good to finally meet you in person!"

Nico stood there, expressionless. "Might I know who you are?"

Embarrassed, the woman quickly introduced herself. "I'm sorry— you're probably thinking, 'Who's this crazy lady?' Let me introduce myself. My name is Renata Giornale, investigative reporter at *L'Essenziale*."

Nico extended his hand. "Nice to meet you."

"The pleasure is all mine!" she beamed. "I finally get to meet the one who stopped the Oliveto Abductor."

Flattered, Nico smiled. "Well, I did have some help—I couldn't have done it alone."

"Ah, yes, your college friend, Sofia Saggio," Renata said.

Nico's expression changed, irritation growing. "Wait—if you know all of this, and I'm assuming you're the one that wrote the article, then why was it all fabricated?"

Renata stood there silently and just nodded as Nico continued, "And if I recall, the article said that the missing girl had ridden her bike off an embankment, hit her head on a rock, and lay there unconscious until she was found the next day."

"It's true—that's what I wrote," Renata confessed. "But, full disclosure, that's my job. I report on the magical happenings in Oliveto and then cover them up, so *the regulars* never learn the hidden truths about this town."

"But aren't some of your regular readers already aware of what happens here?" Nico asked.

"When I refer to '*the regulars,*' I mean non-magical beings," Renata clarified.

"So, what does that make you?" Nico inquired.

"I'm a *regular*, which is why I'm able to twist stories into something believable for non-magical beings," Renata explained.

"OK, I think I'm following you," Nico replied, still curious. "But how did you learn about the 'non-*regulars*'?"

Renata smiled. "Well, when I first came to Oliveto over five years ago, I thought working at *L'Essenziale* would be an easy paycheck—small town, nothing ever happens. But I was wrong. The first time I stumbled upon something magical, my editor pulled me aside and revealed the town's secrets. I was immediately given a raise to keep me quiet and was tasked with hiding all magical events from *the regulars*."

"Does anyone else know you're aware of the truth?" Nico asked.

"Yes, my partner, Dorotea Macellaia, the town butcher—she's a Malandanti," Renata revealed. "Being an investigative reporter, it didn't take long for me to figure out her secret. One day, I caught her in the midst of casting a spell, and that's when I confronted her."

Intrigued, Nico pressed for more. "What kind of spell was she casting?"

"It was actually quite sweet—and I felt a little bad afterward," Renata recalled, pulling a fountain pen from her breast pocket. "She was in the kitchen enchanting this pen. She explained that as long as I keep it by my side, I cannot be harmed or influenced by basic spells."

Nico smiled. "Yeah, that *was* thoughtful of her." Wiping the sweat from his brow, he asked, "Say, is there a coverup related to this heatwave?"

"I've been investigating it, but I don't have any solid leads," Renata replied, stepping aside to let a woman with a stroller pass. "But I have found that the heat seems be coming from the mountain. Look."

Renata pointed to the mountain overlooking the town, where smoke seemed to be rising from its peak.

"In grade school, Sister Mary mentioned in science class that the mountain is actually a dormant volcano," Nico recalled. "Do you think it might be active again?"

Renata took out her notepad and jotted down Nico's comment. "That's a plausible cover story I hadn't considered."

"What else is happening in town that's being covered up?" Nico asked, hoping for some magical gossip to share with Sofia.

"There's been a string of deaths over the past few months," Renata shared. "Another happened last night—you probably heard Orla announce it."

"Orla?" Nico asked, confused.

Renata, noticing more people were now out and about, leaned in, whispering, "What we report as 'high winds,' is really Orla, the town banshee, howling to announce an impending death."

Nico's eyes widened in surprise. "Wow. I'm always learning something new about this town—even from a *regular*, and I mean that with all due respect."

Renata smiled. "Well, I haven't even mentioned the common link among the victims.

"There's more?" Nico asked, now anxious. "How did they die?"

"Exsanguination," Renata whispered. "Their bodies were completely drained of blood through two puncture marks on their necks,"

Nico's jaw dropped. "Sounds like a vampire might be in Oliveto. But you don't actually believe it could be a vampire, do you?"

"You're the one who said vampire," Renata teased. "Sounds like you might believe in them more than you care to admit." She nodded toward someone behind Nico. "Oh, here comes your friend Sofia."

Nico turned to see Sofia approaching with a smile.

"I'd thought you'd be at Indelible Delights by now, talking to Fawn," Sofia said, wiping beads of perspiration from her upper lip. "Who were you talking to?"

"Oh, this is—" Nico started, but when he turned back, Renata was gone. "She was right here—I swear!"

Sofia raised an eyebrow. "I believe you. She probably made a quick exit when she saw me." She pulled out a hand fan from her purse and fanned herself. "Ah much better."

"Her name is Renata Giornale, a reporter for *L'Essenziale*," Nico said, stepping closer to share some of her breeze. "I'll tell you more later— let's get out of this heat."

They made their way down the block and turned the corner. Ahead, on their left, was the entrance to Vicolo Fato / Fate Alley. As they walked down the shaded alley, grateful for the slight reprieve from the heat, they reminisced about their first visit to Indelible Delights.

"I still remember my first night in Oliveto and your brilliant idea to get tattoos," Sofia said. "Do you have any regrets?"

"Nah," Nico laughed. "I think after Sterling explained why he added the unsolicited mushroom next to my griffon tattoo, I felt much better about it—I mean, having the ability to travel via fairy door is pretty rad."

"Fairy door travel has come in handy," Sofia said, gazing down at the tiny fairy door beside the tattoo shop's entrance.

Nico tried to open the door to Indelible Delights, but it was locked. "They must be taking a lunch break," he guessed. "Hmm, how did I open the door last time?"

Sofia pointed to three tiny bells to the right of the door; they were barely visible in the shady alleyway.

"Ah, yes," Nico said, passing his hand through the three bells.
Click.

Sofia pushed the door inward, and they stepped over the threshold into the terracotta-tiled, patchouli-fragranced waiting area. The front door slowly closed behind them and locked. Nico sat down on a worn leather couch and thumbed through tattoo design albums.

Sofia looked down at Nico. "Are you ready for your next tattoo?"
Nico looked up and grinned. "You never know!"

Sofia turned to a large, paisley-patterned, floor-length curtain that covered the entrance to a backroom, and called out, "Fawn? Sterling? Anyone here?"

A gentle feminine voice soon answered, "Sofia, is that you?"

"Yes. Nico and I came to visit," Sofia answered.

"And we need your assistance," Nico added.

Fawn drew back the curtain and entered the room, a cheerful smile on her face. "So, you need my help with something?"

"Yes," Nico said, putting down the design album he had been browsing. "Sofia and I were just talking about how instrumental you were in formulating the plan to access the mortuary."

Fawn smiled. "Yeah, that plan worked out well. So, what do you need help with this time?"

"We need to get inside the mountain to confront Caleo and rescue Flora, the Light Dryad," Nico explained.

"Ah, so you were successful in finding her sister?" Fawn asked.

Sofia jumped in. "Yes, but we barely made it out of the subterrane alive!"

"Trolls?" Fawn guessed.

"Yep!" Nico replied, "Stinky things they are."

Fawn thought for a moment. "OK, for the task, you need to find Calypso, the river nymph. She can get you into the heart of the mountain where Caleo resides. But you'll need to bring a gift to offer him. If you don't, he'll likely destroy you on the spot. He's a collector of relics, artifacts, and other valuable treasures."

Nico recalled the treasures of the four founding families kept in the basement of the library, protected by Teresa Libretto. "I know where we might be able to find something of value."

"Good, but he's not likely going to release Flora as a trade for the object. You'll have to use the object as a way in—as a conversation starter of sorts—and then find a way to immobilize him," Fawn advised.

Sofia blurted out excitedly, "Like a sleep spell?"

"Unfortunately, efreeti are immune to most types of spells," said a male voice from behind the paisley curtain. Sterling pushed back the curtain and entered the room. "You'll likely have to trick him into drinking a sleeping draught or something similar."

Nico rose from his seat to greet Sterling. "Good to see you again!" he said, extending his hand.

"We're beyond handshakes, my boy," Sterling said, pulling Nico into a hug. "You two are like family to me. After all, you did rescue my daughter!"

Sofia went over to give Sterling a hug, and then they all sat down.

Nico turned to Sofia. "We'll have to check the grimoire for a sleeping potion—though I don't recall seeing one."

Fawn had a suggestion. "Try looking for Mad Honey. That sounds like something your nonna would have inscribed."

"Mad Honey—that does sound familiar," Sofia said. "I think I've seen it on the Malandanti side."

"Sofia's probably right," Nico said. "She's obsessed with the family grimoire and anything magical—I'm sure she knows that entire tome inside and out."

Curious, Sofia had to know more. "What does Mad Honey do?"

"It can have different effects depending on the amount ingested," Fawn explained. "Anything from temporary madness or delusion to paralysis, or even death."

Nico leaned in. "So, we're looking for a concentration strong enough to temporarily paralyze the efreeti?"

"Exactly," Fawn confirmed. "That should give you enough time to rescue Flora and escape before the effect wears off."

Sofia had an idea. "Nico, remember that pewter goblet in the dining room—the one your nonna used to serve you a special drink from when you weren't feeling well?"

"Yes!" Nico exclaimed, catching on. "It has those strange glyphs on it. We can totally use it to serve the Mad Honey and claim it's ancient nectar from the gods."

"Now you're thinking," Fawn cheered.

Sterling warned, "Make sure the backstory of the goblet and its contents is believable. Remember, Caleo has lived for centuries—he'll see through any weak story."

"Got it!" Nico affirmed.

Sofia turned to Fawn. "One more thing. Do you know of a fairy door close to the mountain? We're looking for a way to get there quickly."

Sterling answered, "There's one at Vino Vecchio Winery— near the gates at the beginning of the driveway. It'll take you to a large willow tree by the river's bend, where Calypso resides."

Fawn chimed in, "And you can take the fairy door by the utility shed in the piazza. It'll take you to Vino Vecchio. A couple of hops, but still faster than driving."

"Excellent," Nico and Sofia said simultaneously.

"Oh, I almost forgot," Fawn added. "Calypso collects shiny things, so bring a little trinket to offer her in exchange for her help."

Nico rose from the couch. "Thank you both for your guidance. You've been a big help—wish us luck!"

"Safe travels, you two," Sterling said.

"Drinks soon?" Sofia asked Fawn as she got up to leave.

Fawn smiled. "Most definitely, but make sure you come back safely."

Chapter 20: Prep Time

The two drove back home and rushed into the house, excited to put their plan into motion.

"Shall we work upstairs?" Nico suggested.

"Sure—I'll meet you there," Sofia answered, heading to her room. "I just want to freshen up a bit."

Nico made a quick stop in the kitchen to grab some snacks. As he entered, he noticed a serving tray with two drinks and some sliced focaccia waiting on the kitchen island.

Oh, what's this? Nico thought, picking up one of the glasses filled with fizzy brown liquid and taking a sip. "Yum! I'm not sure what this is, but I like it. Thank you, House."

He grabbed a couple of napkins and carried the tray to his nonna's bedroom. Entering the sunlit room, he went over to the closet. Balancing the tray on one hand, he opened the door with the other. The light filtering in from the bedroom windows provided just enough illumination for Nico to navigate to the door at the back of the closet. He quickly unlocked it with the Pick Lock spell and started to head up the stairs, but realized it was too dark to make his way safely to the top.

"Crap," he mumbled. "And I don't have any more dried leaves to cast the Fairy Fire spell."

He placed the serving tray on the first step and went back into the bedroom. Spotting his nonna's beloved candelabra on the nightstand, he thought, *Perfect*! He reached for the candelabra, then stopped. *Shoot, I've got nothing to light it with.*

Not wanting to go all the way back to the kitchen, Nico thought for a moment. *I guess I could summon some matches, or—*

Inspiration struck. He placed his finger on the only remaining candle's wick. "*Incen*—hmm, what's the word?" He wracked his brain,

trying to recall the word from his Latin 110a class. "Ah, yes—
Incendium!"

A small flame appeared at his fingertip, lighting the candle wick.
"Now that's what I'm talking about!" Nico said, proud of his ingenuity.
He took the candelabra and returned to the base of the stairs. Setting the
candelabra down, he picked up the tray, balanced it in his right hand,
grabbed the candelabra with the other, and headed up the stairs to the
door of the upstairs room.

Nico started laughing. *I'm batting a thousand*, he thought. *Sofia's
wearing the ring to open the door, unless—* He put down the candelabra
and looked at his nonno's signet ring on his left hand. *Maybe it'll work,*
he thought, touching the doorknob.

Click.

"Bingo!" Nico said triumphantly, opening the door. He set the tray
down on the table in the center of the room and returned to fetch the
candelabra. Once inside, he blew out the candle and placed the
candelabra next to the tray. He took his soda over to the seating area by
the bookcases and settled into the oversized pillows. A creaking sound
caught his attention. The door to the room slowly closed and locked on
its own.

Sofia, having freshened up, made her way to Chiara's bedroom. The
room was now stuffy and hot, so she walked through the open closet
door into the cool interior. She noticed the door in the back of the closet
was already open for her.

"That was nice of him," she mused. "But it would've been even nicer
if he'd left me a source of light!"

Reaching into her pocket, she felt a single piece of dried leaf but then
realized Nico wasn't there to touch, so she couldn't cast her most-used
Benandanti spell. As she pulled her hand out, the charms on her bracelet
jingled, and she had an idea. She looked through the charms, pulled off
the star charm, and tossed it onto the stairs. The charm transformed into
a three-dimensional light source, about the size of a tennis ball. Sofia
picked it up and climbed to the top of the stairs.

Hmm, the door is closed. I guess Nico couldn't get in, she thought. *I
wonder where he is*. Sofia touched the doorknob, and the lock clicked

open. As she stepped into the room, the star dimmed in the presence of the afternoon sunlight flooding through the clear magical dome ceiling.

"Oh, there you are," Nico greeted. "There's a soda for you on the table and some sliced focaccia. Not sure what kind of soda the house made for us, but it's really good."

Sofia placed the glowing star on the table, picked up her glass, and took a sip. "Delicious—it's *Chinotto*. When Paolo and I were kids, the monks at the orphanage would make it for us on hot days. The house must've used the myrtle-leafed oranges from the backyard to make a syrup and then mixed it with soda."

"I'm really liking it—reminds me of a non-alcoholic Campari," Nico remarked.

"So how did you get the door open? Was it the signet ring?" Sofia asked.

"Yup. Works just like your ruby ring," Nico replied, taking another sip of his drink. "Oh, by the way, the door closes and locks on its own after a while."

Sofia turned just in time to see the door slowly close and hear the lock click. "I was wondering why it was closed when you'd left the other door open for me," she said, grabbing a piece of focaccia. "I thought you couldn't get in and were somewhere else in the house."

"I had my struggles," Nico said with a laugh. "We definitely need to do something about that dark stairway—wait, how did you make it up in the dark?"

"I tested a theory—recognize this?" Sofia held up the magic star.

"Whoa! Is that one of the charms from your bracelet?" Nico asked, getting up to take a closer look.

Sofia smirked, clearly pleased.

"Nice!" Nico said, impressed. "I guess I should show you something new as well." He went to the candelabra, placed his finger in front of the unlit wick, and said, "*Incendium!*" A flame sparked to life, and Sofia, mid-bite, paused in amazement at his newly crafted spell.

"Wow, pretty ingenious!" she said. "While we're up here, we should add that spell and the Silence spell I came up with the other day to the grimoire before we forget."

"Great idea," Nico agreed. "But is *Silence* really the name you're going with? I feel like its needs more oomph to it—something like Silent Space, since it only affects a six-foot radius."

"Yeah, you're right," Sofia agreed as she walked over to Chiara's work desk and sat down. "So, what are you going to name your spell?"

"Let's keep it simple: Flame Finger. What do you think?"

"I like it—simple and to the point," Sofia said, dipping a quill into Chiara's inkwell and inscribing the spell name onto a sheet of parchment.

Nico hovered over her shoulder, watching. "I'm glad you're the one doing this. Your penmanship is way better than mine."

Sofia added the instructions and magic word, then blotted the ink dry. "One down. That sounds like a Benandanti spell, so I'll put it on that side of the grimoire. Now, the Silent Space spell definitely seems darker and should go on the Malandanti side."

"Yes, ma'am!" Nico joked, filing the parchment alphabetically between Fairy Fire and Fruit of the Vine.

"Here's the other one," Sofia called out, handing him the second spell, which he filed on the Malandanti.

Nico concentrated for a second, then invoked, *"Evocare Objectum!"*

Sofia watched as the pewter goblet from the dining room appeared in Nico's hands.

Nico moved the crystal ball aside as Sofia opened the grimoire. "OK, let me find the reference to Mad Honey," she said, thumbing through the Malandanti section. "Ah, here it is."

"What does it say?" Nico asked.

"Crap! Unless we're planning a trip to Turkey in the next twenty-four hours, I don't know how we'll get some."

Puzzled, Nico asked, "What do you mean? Can't we just make it with a few ingredients and an incantation?"

"There are two rhododendron species from Southeast Europe we could use, and I know one of them is in the backyard poison garden. But we need bees to make honey from its nectar. And the last time I checked, your nonna didn't have a hive."

"We could extract the nectar and mix it with some store-bought honey," Nico suggested.

"It's too risky—it might not be potent enough," Sofia warned. "And if Caleo realizes we're there to rescue Flora before he's immobilized, he'll kill us."

Nico grew frustrated, sitting in silence until an idea came to him. He took a deep breath, reached for the crystal ball, and focused. "Show us where we can obtain some Mad Honey," Nico commanded.

White smoke swirled inside the crystal ball before revealing a storefront with a sign that read: La Farmacista.

"That looks familiar," Sofia said. "I think I saw that store earlier today."

Nico grinned. "You're right—I know exactly where that is! It's across from the alley entrance near Indelible Delights."

Sofia looked up at the ceiling. "Judging by the position of the sun, it must be late afternoon. Most of the stores will be closing soon."

"Unfortunately, you're correct," Nico sighed.

Sofia had an idea, "Let's have another low-key evening and rest up. We'll get an early start tomorrow and try to knock everything out in one day."

"That sounds good. But are you sure you don't want to see Solomon tonight?" Nico asked.

"I'm good—I already saw him earlier," Sofia replied. "Besides, I want to make the garlic scape pesto I've been dying to prepare for you."

Nico's stomach growled. "Now you've made me hungry! You get started on dinner, and I'll clean up here and bring down the leftover focaccia and our empty glasses."

Sofia left the room, eager to harvest the garlic scapes from the garden and make the pesto recipe for Nico.

Nico gathered the pewter goblet, the focaccia, and the empty glasses, placing them on the serving tray. Balancing the tray in one hand and grabbing the candelabra with the other, he moved toward the door. With his hands full, he set the candelabra down to open the door, propped it open with his foot, and then picked the candelabra back up.

He looked down the long staircase; the room's natural light streamed down and illuminated the way. *If I'm quick, I can make it down the stairs before the door closes and locks on its own*, he thought. And he did just that.

Nico returned his nonna's candelabra to her nightstand and went to check on Sofia. Entering the kitchen, he placed the serving tray on the island and walked over to the counter, where Sofia was busy chopping the freshly cut garlic scapes.

"Wow, you harvested those quickly!" Nico remarked.

Sofia jumped, slightly startled. "I'm going to have to put a bell on you!" she said, resuming her chopping. "Somehow the garden gnomes must have known my plans. When I opened the back door, they were already cut and placed in this nice basket."

"Ah, see, they like you!" Nico said. "I'm still not sure why they scare you so much."

"They're growing on me," Sofia admitted. "I just don't like it when they sneak up on me."

***

After enjoying a meal of fusilli with garlic scape pesto, paired with a robust pinot grigio from Vino Vecchio Winery, they discussed their plans for the next day.

"So, once we get the Mad Honey, we can take the fairy door in the piazza," Nico suggested. "Sterling and Fawn said we'll need to take a second fairy door to the river, then search for Calypso. Now we just need to find something shiny to offer her for her help."

"I'll give her my old bracelet," Sofia suggested. "I probably won't wear it again now that I have Solomon's gift."

"OK, then that's settled," Nico said, pouring the last of the wine into their two glasses. Raising his glass, he added, "It might be a little late for a toast, but here's to a successful rescue—may we live to see another day!"

Sofia clinked her glass against Nico's. "I'll drink to that!" she said, taking a sip. Her expression grew serious. "But what if the Mad Honey doesn't work? Shouldn't we have a backup plan?"

Nico laughed. "The default backup plan is always to run."

Sofia joined in the laughter and got up to clear the plates.

Nico gestured for her to sit. "I'll take care of the dishes—you relax."

As he rinsed off the plates, he gazed out the window. "The sunset sure is beautiful tonight—just look at those red, orange, and yellow colors swirling together."

Intrigued, Sofia rose but suddenly stopped in her place. "Nico," she whispered, "quick, come here."

Nico turned off the faucet and joined Sofia. "What is it?" he whispered back.

"Listen," she urged. "Do you hear that?"

A clawing sound coming from the cabinet door that led to the basement grew more persistent.

"I hear it," Nico answered. "Sounds too light to be a troll."

"Could the Babau still be alive?" Sofia guessed.

"Not possible—it should be a frozen block by now," Nico said. "Even if it were, it couldn't get out of the freezer—it's latched shut."

Nico approached the cabinet door, Sofia shadowing him closely. He put his hand on the handle and slowly turned it. "Ready?" he whispered.

Sofia placed her hand on Nico's shoulder, preparing to cast the first spell she could think of if danger lurked behind the door.

Nico swung the door open. He saw nothing at first, but then felt soft fur brush against his leg and looked down.

"Ah," Sofia said, relieved. "It's just Negroni."

Nico picked up his feline companion, cuddling her in his arms. "So, have you been hiding in the basement all day?"

Negroni meowed, as if in response.

"You gave us a little fright, you cute little thing," Sofia cooed, caressing Negroni's head. Her charm bracelet jingled with each touch.

Negroni purred loudly, occasionally pawing at the charms. Then Nico witnessed something amazing. As Sofia continued petting her, her bracelet flashed and her star charm reappeared, reuniting to its link.

"Wow! Did you see that?" Nico exclaimed. "Your star charm is back. I left it upstairs as a test—to make sure it would return, like your beer stein charm did."

"I saw!" Sofia said, amazed. "So, if we activate a charm, it seems we have about an hour to use it before it returns to my bracelet."

"Kind of makes you want to test the unicorn charm, doesn't it?" Nico tempted.

Sofia pretended to reach for the unicorn but stopped. "All in good time—I'm sure it'll be useful when we need it."

Nico set Negroni down. "Hey, it's still too early for bed. Want to see what's on TV?" Nico asked.

"Yeah, I'm down," Sofia agreed.

"Pick a movie or something—I'm going to find something to feed Negroni—she must be starving," Nico said, grabbing a can of tuna from the pantry.

As Sofia settled in the living room, Nico plated the tuna and filled a bowl with water, placing them on the floor. But Negroni wasn't interested. Instead, she followed Nico to the living room, where the three of them watched TV until they decided it was time for bed.

Chapter 21: Mad Honey

The next morning, Nico woke early from a restful night's sleep and shuffled to the kitchen, following the aroma of freshly brewed coffee. Sofia sat at the kitchen island next to a pot of coffee, engrossed in reading the morning paper.

"Whatcha reading?" Nico asked, breezing past Sofia to grab a coffee cup from the cabinet.

Sofia peered over the top of the newspaper. "The obits—after you told me what Renata said about the mysterious deaths in town, I thought I'd check. Apparently, there's been another one."

"So, that wasn't the wind we heard howling last night—it was Orla!" Nico said, walking over to the island. He sat down, filled his cup with coffee, and then topped off Sofia's.

Sofia put the newspaper down. "So, are you ready for our big adventure?" she asked before taking a sip of her coffee.

"Actually, I am," Nico replied confidently. "A good night's sleep and now a great cup of coffee with my best friend—I'm totally ready! What about you?"

"I am, although I didn't sleep well," Sofia admitted. "I kept running different scenarios through my mind. I think I've thought of every possible outcome."

Concerned, Nico asked, "Are you worried, or just anxious?"

Sofia sighed. "A little bit of both, to be honest. And I've decided to leave my purse here—I don't want to risk losing it. So make sure to wear the shorts with the enchanted pocket; you're carrying the supplies this time."

"I can handle that," Nico said, taking another sip of coffee. He sighed contentedly. "This coffee is really good today. Did the house make it?"

"Nope, I made it the old-fashioned, non-magical way," Sofia said proudly.

"*Brava!*" Nico praised. "*Delizioso!*"

"Thank you. Shall we get ready?" Sofia asked, then had a thought. "Oh, and can we grab a bagel or two downtown—something simple to eat along the way?"

"A bagel sounds perfect," Nico agreed, grabbing the goblet to take with him. "And it'll be another hour before La Farmacista opens. It'll be a nice way to pass the time and fuel up."

***

Nico and Sofia got ready and drove downtown, parking in front of the Circle of Life Bagel Factory. Sofia was surprised to see a line out the door of the kosher eatery and hurried to join it. "I hope they don't run out of the cinnamon raisin ones—those are my favorite!"

Nico caught up and reassured her, "They're still baking fresh ones at this hour. We'll have plenty to choose from."

The wait was shorter than expected, and within six minutes, they had their order: a cinnamon-raisin bagel, an everything bagel, and two pizza bagels. They sat down on a nearby bench, and, after deciding which two bagels to eat first, Nico discreetly tucked the remaining bag into the enchanted pocket of his shorts.

Sofia stifled a yawn and took a bite of her bagel. "Yum! But it looks like I'll be needing more caffeine. Let's grab some coffee from Patisserie Angelique."

"Excellent idea," Nico agreed, finishing his first bite. "It's still pretty cool out, so let's leave the car here and walk."

They finished their bagels in silence, savoring every morsel as they watched the early-morning activity around them. Rising from the bench, they made their way to Patisserie Angelique.

"*Bonjour, mes amis!*" Lisette greeted as they entered.

"Good morning," Sofia replied as they approached the counter.

"What can I get for you?" Lisette asked.

"Two drip coffees, please," Nico said.

Lisette busied herself with their order while Sofia admired the various pastries in the display case. When Lisette handed them their coffees, she smiled and asked, "Any macarons today?"

"Not today, thank you," Nico said, taking the coffees and handing one to Sofia. "They wouldn't survive today's activities."

Sofia added, "But we'll be back soon to get some—Nico loves them!"

Lisette's face lit up. "Ah, I'm so happy to hear that. I still don't know many people in town, so I get excited when people around our age—who aren't tourists—come in."

Touched by her honesty, Sofia said, "Next time we go out with our friends, we'll invite you and introduce you to everyone."

"Oh, really? I'd love that," Lisette responded humbly.

Nico added, "And if you're free this Saturday, The Griffon's Claw is having an anniversary party. You should come with us!"

Lisette's eyes brightened. "I should be free, unless my boss keeps me late to prep for the morning baker."

"Hopefully, you'll be free," Nico said, remembering something. "Oh, by the way, are the crows still stealing your tips?"

Sofia chimed in, "Yeah, did that ever stop?"

"*Mon Dieu*," Lisette said. "Now that you mention it, I haven't seen a single crow around in days."

"Good to hear!" Nico said, smiling and dropping a few dollars into the tip jar. "I doubt they'll bother you again."

From a few blocks away, the church bells at St. Anthony's began to chime.

"Ah, it must be ten o'clock," Sofia noted, counting the gongs silently. "Nico, we should get going."

"Right!" Nico acknowledged. "Good to see you, Lisette—remember Saturday!"

They waved goodbye and headed to their next stop. Crossing the street to La Farmacista, they felt the cool morning giving way to a warm, humid breeze.

"There it is," Sofia said, pointing at the store. "It looks like a modern apothecary."

"They must have just opened. I don't remember it being here before—seems new," Nico observed.

As they approached, something strange from a neighboring store caught their attention. Nico and Sofia peered into the window of Petali Floral Design. Something was definitely off; all the flowers inside were dead, and the scent of decaying vegetation seeped through an open mail slot, assaulting their noses.

"Ugh, that smell is rank," Nico said, wrinkling his nose. "I wonder what happened here."

"The owner is probably out of town," Sofia speculated, noting the scattered mail on the floor inside.

"You're probably right," Nico agreed. "Onward we go."

They walked next door and entered La Farmacista, and a tall, well-dressed gentleman with slicked black hair welcomed them. "*Buongiorno*! Welcome to La Farmacista."

Sofia glanced at the grinning gentleman, his perfect, dazzling smile reminiscent of the Cheshire Cat from Alice in Wonderland. "*Buongiorno*," she replied.

"*Buongiorno*," Nico said, making his way to the back where the proprietor stood. A row of dark walnut bookcases lined the wall, each shelf filled with a variety of labeled apothecary jars. "Is your store a recent addition to Oliveto?"

"Yes, we opened last month," he answered. "Is there something specific I can help you find?"

"Actually, yes. Do you happen to sell honey?" Sofia asked.

The man led them to a table displaying an antique bee skep, a bouquet of dried lavender, and various jars of honey. "The orange blossom honey is our best seller, but I personally prefer the lavender," he said, picking a jar to show Sofia.

As Sofia took the jar from his hand, she noticed a large diamond ring on the man's finger. As it sparkled in the light, she became mesmerized. "Look! Did you ever? Anywhere, anything like it?"

Nico interrupted with a chuckle, "Please excuse her, she didn't sleep well last night—still waking up."

"Yes, I'm sorry," Sofia said, slightly embarrassed, and took a quick sip of her coffee. "Your ring is truly gorgeous."

The man smiled. "Thank you. And your ruby ring is quite extraordinary. A rare heirloom, perhaps?"

Sofia leaned into Nico. "It's from his nonna—an heirloom, indeed. Oh, and my name is Sofia."

"A pleasure," the man said. "I'm Manolo Ombra." Just then, the telephone rang. "Excuse me, I must get that."

While he was gone, Nico and Sofia searched the various jars for the Mad Honey.

"Acacia honey, clover honey, eucalyptus honey—" Nico quietly listed.

"It's not here," Sofia said, sounding disappointed. "Now what?"

Manolo returned to the table where they stood. "Did you not find what you were looking for? You two seem disappointed."

"Uh, well, we were looking for a rare honey," Nico admitted.

"Oh? And which type might that be?" Manolo asked.

"Mad honey," Sofia blurted out.

"Ah, you're not *regulars*," Manolo chuckled. "That explains it. Come with me—I keep the black market and specialty items in the back."

Manolo raised his ringed hand into the air and gave it a dramatic twirl. Nico and Sofia watched as the window blinds lowered and the sign on the door flipped to "Back in 10 Minutes."

He led them to a massive storeroom lined with rows of shelves, each meticulously organized in alphabetical order and filled with unique items.

"Wow, I could spend hours in here," Sofia marveled.

"Well, I'm hiring if you're ever looking for a job," Manolo suggested.

"We're still in college—and on the East Coast," Nico interrupted. "We're just visiting."

"Ah, too bad. I could use the help," Manolo sighed, continuing down the aisle of shelves until he stopped. "Here we are, Row M."

As they followed Manolo, they scanned the row of labeled oddities: Makapansgat Pebble, Mandrake Root, Mask of La Roche-Cotard, Mastic, Mercury, Minotaur Horn Shavings, Mistletoe Berry, Morning Dew, Moss, and Mummy Dust, among many others.

Manolo reached for a small jar on the top shelf. "Here we go—one jar of Mad Honey. You're in luck! It's my last one," he said, handing it to Sofia.

Nico asked, "What do we owe you?"

"For these specialty items, I usually require something magical in return," Manolo answered. "Let's go up front and we can discuss things further."

Back on the sales floor, Manolo gestured with his hand once more. The window blinds lifted in unison, letting sunlight flood the space, while the sign on the door flipped back to "Open."

"So, about the price—" Nico grinned. "Uh, well, we don't have anything magical on us to barter with, but perhaps I can make you something."

Manolo's interest piqued. "Do tell."

Sofia, unsure of what Nico was planning, stood there quietly.

"Do you have a briefcase or something similar?" Nico asked Manolo.

"I do," Manolo replied, disappearing into the back. He soon returned with a black Prada briefcase and placed it on the counter.

"Excellent taste!" Nico complimented, picking up the briefcase. He leaned in and whispered quietly, "*Fac Spatium*," before placing it back on the counter.

"Ah nice!" Sofia exclaimed. "You're going to love this."

Manolo looked unimpressed. "It seems unchanged. There's no value in that!"

"Ah, but it's not the same—watch!" Nico said. He scanned the sales floor, spotted a broom near one of the bookcases, and went over to retrieve it. "Open up your briefcase."

Manolo did as he was asked, but the look of impatience was visibly noticeable.

Nico handed the broom to Sofia. "And now, if my lovely assistant will place the broom into the briefcase—"

"That's going to ruin it!" Manolo protested, panicking as he watched Sofia slowly lower the broom handle into his prized Prada possession.

Amazed, Manolo watched in awe as the broom began to vanish, inch by inch, into the briefcase.

"Well done!" Manolo cheered. "This feat of magic is worth far more than the Mad Honey. Is there anything else you need?"

"Can we take a raincheck?" Sofia asked, slowly pulling the broom back out of the briefcase.

"Of course!" Manolo agreed. "That's some serious magic you have running through your veins."

Nico smiled smugly, then took the jar of Mad Honey from Sofia and, as Manolo watched, tucked it into the pocket of his shorts.

Manolo clapped. "Bravo! Truly amazing!"

"Well, thank you for helping us—you might have just saved our lives," Nico said. "And with that, we need to be on our way."

"Yes, thank you so much," Sofia added, following Nico to the door.

Manolo called out as they left, "Please come back soon!"

Now back into the heat of the morning sun, Nico and Sofia made their way to the utility shed in the Piazza, where the fairy door was located.

"I think it's in the southeast corner—over here," Nico said, leading Sofia to their destination.

"Good thing you remembered where it was," Sofia said. "It's really hidden among these bushes."

They circled the shed, searching for the fairy door, and Sofia spotted it first. "Here it is!"

The door was adorned with intricately carved grapevines heavy with fruit. Sofia took Nico's hand and held it tightly as they knelt down before the tiny portal. Nico gave her one last look to ensure she was ready, and when she nodded, he touched the door.

In the blink of an eye, they arrived. Before them stood two massive stone pillars, each topped with a sphinx statue and connected to a high stone wall encircling the property. Between the pillars loomed a large iron double gate, topped with a sign that read: Vino Vecchio Winery.

"Wow, this place looks beautiful," Sofia said, eyeing the cypress-lined driveway leading to the winery. "We'll have to come here for a tasting sometime!"

"Most definitely—we can bring your brother when he visits," Nico said. "Maybe we can set him up with Lisette?"

Sofia ignored his comment and began searching for the next fairy door. Nico joined in, but both were unable to locate it.

"Maybe it's on the other side of the gate?" Sofia suggested. "But how do we get past it?"

"We might have to wait until they open," Nico said. "Most tasting rooms around here open around eleven or eleven-thirty."

"Or—" a female voice interrupted.

Nico and Sofia looked up to see that one of the sphinxes, whose face resembled Madame de Pompadour, was looking down at them.

A second voice spoke. "I don't know, Agatha." Nico and Sofia turned to the other sphinx, whose face was modeled after Marie Antoinette.

"You two can talk?" Nico said, astonished.

The sphinx known as Agatha turned to her companion. "Emily, it's not often we get to speak with humans. Maybe we should help them."

"How can you help us?" Sofia asked.

"We are the guardians of the gate," Emily explained. "We can allow you passage, if—"

"If you can answer our riddle," Agatha interrupted.

"Very well ladies," Nico said flirtatiously, flashing his smile in an attempt to charm them. "What is your riddle?"

Emily nodded. "Agatha, go ahead and ask them one of your riddles."

Agatha thought for a moment, then cleared her throat. "You measure my life in hours, and I serve you by expiring. I'm quick when I'm thin and slow when I'm fat. The wind is my enemy. What am I?"

Nico and Sofia turned away to discuss.

"OK, let's think this through," Sofia said. "The last clue, 'The wind is my enemy,' seems the easiest."

"Wind blows…" Nico mumbled, closing his eyes and picturing what the wind could affect. Suddenly he remembered blowing out a candle from his nonna's candelabra. "Aha!"

"Did you figure it out?" Sofia whispered.

"I think so. Could it be a candle?" Nico said.

"A thin candle does burn quicker than a fat one," Sofia reasoned. "And the longer it burns, the shorter it gets. I think you've solved the riddle! Go ahead and tell them our answer."

They turned to face Agatha and Emily.

"We have our answer," Nico declared. "It's a candle."

The two sphinxes exchanged glances, impressed by how quickly their riddle had been solved.

"You are correct, young human," Emily declared.

"You may pass," Agatha said, and the gates slowly swung open.

"Thank you, ladies," Nico said as he and Sofia stepped through. They checked the back of each pillar for the next fairy door.

"Found it!" Sofia called out.

Nico rushed over, and they examined the door. This one had a mountain with a river carved into the wood.

"Nice job," Nico complimented. "This should take us to Calypso. Ready?"

Stefano A Giovannoni

Chapter 22: Into the Mountain

Nico and Sofia passed through the fairy door, landing on a mixture of sand and river stone at their final destination. About five hundred feet away stood the base of the mountain, Oliveto's familiar backdrop, which seemed far more ominous up close. Wisps of smoke rose lightly from its apex.

"Ouch, that wasn't a pleasant arrival," Nico said, brushing sand off his shorts as he stood up. He extended his hand to Sofia.

"Yeah, I won't forget this one anytime soon!" Sofia replied, grabbing Nico's hand and pulling herself up.

"So, any idea where Calypso might be?" Nico asked.

Sofia thought back, recalling what Mr. Pendolino had told them during their last visit to Oliveto. "Do you remember the story Mr. Pendolino told us about the founders and the thirteen Coins of Favor?"

Nico thought for a moment. "Ah, yes—vaguely."

Sofia shared what she remembered. "If I recall, he said that the founders sat by a large willow tree, and that's when Calypso first emerged from the water."

Nico looked around and spotted a willow tree about fifty feet downstream, near a bend in the river. "That must be it," he said, pointing.

The large willow tree grew at an angle from the embankment, its roots exposed and clinging to the earth as its long branches draped over the flowing water.

"What a majestic willow!" Sofia exclaimed. "Ooh, and here's the fairy door at its base."

They examined the miniature door, which had the image of a flexed bicep with a tattoo.

"Cool! This will take us back to Indelible Delights," Nico noted. "That'll make the return trip easier."

Behind them, they heard a splashing sound, followed by a soft female voice saying, "Greetings."

Nico and Sofia turned around to see a young woman who had just surfaced from the depths of the river. Her long, light brown hair, naturally highlighted by the sun, covered her upper body.

"You must be Calypso," Nico greeted. "I'm Nico, and this is my best friend, Sofia. We're here on official business for the Dark Dryad and could use your help."

Sofia dangled her old bracelet for Calypso to see. "And I can give you this."

The river nymph's emerald-green eyes lit up. She swam closer, beckoning, "Come closer and show me your shiny offering!"

Sofia approached and handed over the silver bracelet. Calypso became entranced, watching the sunlight bounce off its shiny links.

Nico looked over at Sofia and joked, "I think we've lost her."

"Hello? Earth to Calypso—anyone home?" Sofia asked, waving her hands to get the nymph's attention.

Calypso snapped out of her trance, embarrassed. "Right. How may I help you?"

"We need to reach the heart of the mountain," Sofia explained.

A serious look crossed Calypso's face. "Why go there? That's where the evil efreeti lives! He's bad news and up to something."

"We're here to rescue Flora, the Light Dryad," Nico said, anxious. "She's being held by Caleo."

Sofia chimed in, "We know you can safely guide us through the underwater passageways to mountain's center—you've done it before— many, many years ago."

"It wasn't *that* long ago," Calypso responded, admiring the bracelet now on her wrist. She looked up at the two and nodded. "I suppose I do owe you something. Grab your friend's hand and hold tightly onto mine. Remember: never break the link. If you lose your connection to me, your ability to breathe underwater will end abruptly, and you'll surely drown, as the only place to surface is at the end of the long swim."

162

Nico took Sofia's hand and stepped into the refreshingly cool water. "Such a relief from this heat," Sofia said as she waded deeper.

Calypso smiled at Nico. "Grab my hand, and don't let go!" She quickly dove in the water, jerking them forward into the river's depths.

Within seconds, they were thirteen feet underwater, nearing the riverbed. Ahead, Nico and Sofia saw a hole in the river's floor that led into the unknown. Calypso stopped, turned to them, and pointed downward, signaling where they were headed next.

She led them down into the depths of darkness, and as they descended further, the pressure of the water made Nico and Sofia's ears increasingly uncomfortable. Thankfully, Calypso eventually stopped her descent and began swimming forward. The water grew warmer and microscopic bioluminescent algae, disturbed by their movements, began to glow blue, illuminating the walls of a sunken cavern passage.

Are we there yet? Nico thought.

Calypso stopped again, pointing upward to a hole in the top of the cavern. They all swam upward, and Nico and Sofia soon saw the surface about ten feet above. Suddenly, Calypso let go of Nico's hand and waved goodbye as the high mineral content of the water buoyed Nico and Sofia, causing them to rise rapidly to the surface.

Once they broke through the surface, Nico and Sofia quickly climbed out of the water and into a small, dark cavern within the center of the mountain. Nico reached into his pocket and pulled out a candle. Holding his finger to the wick, he called out, "*Incendium*," and the candle began to glow.

The two looked around the cavern. Stalactites and stalagmites encircled the space, except for two passageways opposite each other, where warm air flowed into the room from one passage and out through the other.

"Well, that was a thrill ride," Sofia said. "I almost panicked when she let go."

"I think she did that on purpose, knowing that we'd safely rise to the top," Nico guessed.

Sofia wrung out her hair. "Or maybe she's afraid of Caleo and didn't want to go any further?"

"You know, you might be right," Nico said, peering down the hole they had just swum up from. Seeing no sign of Calypso in the water, he added, "She's gone!"

"Well, that blows! How will we get back?" Sofia said, a hint of concern in her voice. "I guess we'll deal with that later."

Nico affixed the candle to a nearby rock using some wax, then reached into his enchanted pocket and pulled out two beach towels, tossing one to Sofia.

"I'm surprised you remembered to bring towels!" Sofia said, unfolding hers and starting to dry off.

Nico joked back, "You know I wouldn't let my Calabrian princess down."

With the help of the warm air blowing through the cavern, they dried off quickly. Sofia folded the towels and handed them back to Nico, who tucked them into his pocket.

"Ready to do this?" Nico asked, retrieving the lit candle and shielding its flame from the breeze with his hand.

"Yup! Which way?" Sofia answered anxiously.

Nico looked to the left and then to the right. "I'm guessing the warm breeze is coming from the center of the mountain and then escapes to the top. So, let's take the right passage, against the airflow."

"Makes sense," Sofia agreed, following Nico into a winding, snake-like tunnel.

The once-comfortable breeze grew hotter with each step forward and carried with it a horrible stench. As the tunnel opened into a large cavern, they saw the ground littered with bat guano. Nico and Sofia covered their noses, trying not to gag from the strong scent of ammonia.

"Ugh, now we know the source of the smell," Sofia muttered, her voice slightly muffled by her hand.

Nico looked up at the ceiling of the cavern, which almost seemed to be shifting. Curious, he reached into his pocket, pulled out a dried leaf, crumpled it, and whispered, "*Lux Saltatio*." As he tossed the leaf bits upward, they transformed into dancing lights, illuminating what couldn't be seen by candlelight alone. The ceiling was home to a large number of roosting bats, now becoming agitated by the unexpected light.

"We better move quickly before they—" Sofia began quietly.

"*Revocare,*" Nico whispered, and the dancing lights faded away.

Sofia smiled at him. "Well, look at you, Mr. Wizard!"

Nico grinned back. "I came up with that one last night—figured at some point we might need a way to nullify a spell before it expires."

As the bats settled down, Sofia pointed to an opening in the cavern leading to another passageway. Nico followed her through the passage, which made a sharp left before continuing toward a light-filled opening. As they neared, they could hear the faint sound of snoring.

"We must be nearing the center of the mountain, which means Caleo should be close by," Nico whispered.

They peeked into the large cavern and took in their surroundings. At its center was a large pool of bubbling magma, and suspended above it hung a large, ornate iron cage. A female figure lay among a pile of pillows.

"That must be Flora," Sofia blurted excitedly.

Nico quickly put his finger to his lips, signaling her to be quiet, but it was too late. Flora stirred from her slumber, looked down at them, and waved to get their attention. She then pointed to their left.

Nico and Sofia looked over but saw that the area was obstructed by rocks. They snuck over, hiding behind and peering around a rock wall. There, lying on a bed of golden coins and other treasures, was Caleo, the efreeti, snoring heavily.

Caleo's nearly naked, muscular body was covered only by a leather loincloth. His fiery red skin contrasted with the brass jewelry he wore: a wrist cuff, an ankle cuff, a nose ring, a single hoop earring, and a large medallion necklace. Two horns protruded from his head, surrounded by flames resembling wisps of hair. With each exhale, smoke drifted from his nostrils and rose into the air.

Nico and Sofia ducked back to formulate a plan.

"Any thoughts?" Nico asked.

"Over there," Sofia said, pointing to a geared mechanical device connected to the chain suspending Flora's cage. "I see a lever."

"Good find, but it looks like it would only lower the cage into the magma—we don't want to harm her," Nico said, looking around. "But I think," he added, indicating a smaller lever on the opposite side of the pit, "I see a solution."

165

"What do you think it does?" Sofia asked.

"I honestly don't know," Nico admitted, wiping sweat from his forehead. "But it has to help somehow."

"Well, it's worth a try, but we need to hurry. It's getting hotter, and I don't know how much more of this heat I can take," Sofia said, then added, "Oh, and that gear mechanism will probably make noise, which could wake Caleo up."

Nico had an idea. "What about casting that Silent Space spell of yours? If I cast it around Caleo, he won't hear a thing."

Sofia's face brightened. "That's brilliant! Just be careful getting close."

"I will," Nico assured her. "What's the spell word again?"

"Silentium," Sofia answered, then glanced over at the magma pit. "Hmm, my ears must still be plugged with water," she thought, slightly confused. "I can't hear the sound of the gurgling magma anymore."

Nico carefully sneaked around the cluster of rocks toward Caleo. As he approached, his foot nudged a few stray coins, producing a low clinking sound. He immediately froze, his heart pounding as he watched as the efreeti stir, turning onto his side and now facing Nico.

Phew, that was close, Nico thought, *I'd better wait a minute to be sure he stays asleep.* As he waited, Nico surveyed the various treasures Caleo had collected over centuries. One item stood out: an animal tusk with an engraved silver cap, seemingly out of place among the gold. He ignored it and crept forward, careful to avoid more stray coins.

Nico was now in position, so close that he felt the warm smoke from Caleo's breath on his face, nearly causing him to cough. Thankfully, he managed to restrain himself. "*Silentium,*" he whispered, and the world fell silent within a six-foot radius. *It worked,* he thought. *Now to sneak back and rescue Flora.*

Nico returned to Sofia without waking the efreeti. "Ready for phase two?" he asked.

"You handle the chain lever; I'll take the smaller one," Sofia suggested. "That big one looks like it needs more strength."

Nico gave her a thumbs up and moved into position. Sofia, hearing the gurgling of the lava once more, shouted across the lava pit, "Hey—

remember, the Silent Space spell lasts about six minutes! We have to hurry!"

Nico gripped the lever with both hands and pulled. A loud click was followed by the sound of gears ratcheting, lowering the chained cage link by link. Sofia saw the cage descending and quickly pulled her lever, praying it would keep Flora dropping into the magma. The ground rumbled, and a metal plank extended from one side of the pit to the other, creating a platform for the cage to rest on.

Sofia ran to the edge of the pit as the cage settled onto the plank. Without hesitation, she ran to Flora, touched the padlock, and shouted, "*Resero!*" The lock immediately sprang open and dropped from the cage, clanging against the metal plank before falling into the magma. The plank heated rapidly, and Sofia felt the burn through her shoes. She grabbed Flora's hand, and they dashed to the other side where Nico was waiting.

Grateful for Sofia's safety, Nico grabbed her and gave her a hug.

"Thank you for rescuing me," Flora said.

Nico released Sofia from his embrace and turned to Flora. "You're welcome."

Sofia eyes suddenly widened. "Guys we need to split—the spell is about to wear—"

A deep, gruff voice echoed from within the chamber, "Who has disturbed my slumber?"

"—off," Sofia finished, her voice trembling as the beastly efreeti rose and advanced toward them.

"Phase three—Run!" Nico shouted.

Stefano A Giovannoni

Chapter 23: Escape to Normality

The three hurried out of Caleo's lair, navigating the narrow corridor that led into the darkness of the bat-guano-filled cave. Behind them, they could hear the maddened efreeti's voice echoing through the caverns.

"Fools!" Caleo called out, followed by a maniacal laugh. "You may think you've escaped to live another day, but your time's almost up. Soon, you and the rest of Oliveto will suffer for your transgressions!"

Nico retrieved the candle from his pocket and magically relit its wick, casting enough light to guide them through the serpentine passageway and back to the cavern where they had first entered the mountain.

Breaking the tense silence, Flora reassured them. "Don't worry, he won't come after us—we're safe now. He can't fit through the narrow passages."

Nico and Sofia sighed in relief and sat down on the cavern floor before Flora. Only now could they clearly see the woman they had rescued. She was unlike any other nymph and dryad they had encountered before. Instead of long flowing hair, her dark strawberry blonde hair was cut into a stylish bob with bangs, and her figure was more curvaceous than the slender forms typical of her kind.

Flora continued, "Thank you again for rescuing me—I never thought I'd be freed from that horrible cage."

"You must be hungry," Nico said, reaching into his pocket and offering her their bag of bagels. "Would you like one?"

Flora smiled. "How very kind of you, young man. It may be some time before my appetite returns—I'm still a bit shaken."

"I'll take one," Sofia interrupted, holding out her hand.

Nico handed a bagel to Sofia and took the remaining one for himself.

"Now, may I know the name of my two brave rescuers?" Flora asked.

Nico and Sofia, both mid-chew, scrambled to respond.

"My name is Sofia, and this is my friend Nico," Sofia managed, after quickly swallowing. "Nico is a descendant of one of the four town founders."

Flora's eyes widened in surprise. "Oh, I see. Then what I have to say may make more sense to you."

Nico and Sofia leaned in, anticipation written on their faces.

"While I was held captive, I overheard Caleo speaking to a mysterious man," Flora explained, pacing as she spoke. "He ranted about being wronged nearly a century ago by the town's founders. They had commissioned him to create thirteen magical coins. When his back was turned, they took the coins and fled his lair without paying the agreed upon price."

"Those must be the Coins of Favor Mr. Pendolino mentioned," Nico interrupted.

Flora's eyebrows arched. "So, you know of them."

"Yes," Sofia answered. "We have all thirteen in a safe deposit box at the bank."

"Then there's still hope," Flora said with relief. "Caleo mentioned giving the founders exactly one hundred years to return all thirteen coins, or the entire town would face his wrath."

"Wrath?" Nico asked. "What did he mean?"

"The total annihilation of Oliveto," Flora explained, "everything the founders built, gone."

A realization dawned on Sofia. "Nico, your nonna must have known."

"You're right—she must have foretold it in her crystal ball," Nico agreed.

"That's why she collected the coins," Sofia added. "She must have intended to return them to Caleo but was murdered before she could."

"One question remains." Nico turned to Flora. "Who was the mysterious stranger? Can you describe him?"

Flora stopped pacing and sat down. "To be honest, I was too high up in my cage to see clearly, but I could tell he was a muscular man with dark hair, and he sounded young."

"Well, it's something to go on," Sofia said, standing up to stretch. "I guess we should focus on getting out of here."

"Yes. Flora, you must be anxious to get back to your tree," Nico said.

"Tree?" Flora laughed. "I'm not like the others. Sure, I have a 'tree,' but I haven't lived in it for decades. I actually have a house and run a floral design business in town."

"My apologies," Nico said, looking embarrassed. "I didn't mean to offend you."

Flora's expression softened. "No offense taken. You saved my life, and I owe you a debt of gratitude. But how did you even know I was in danger?"

"Your raven Simone told us," Nico answered.

"That poor creature went through so much while you were gone but never gave up on finding help for you," Sofia added.

Flora beamed, "Ah, my beloved Simone! Not surprising."

Nico stood and dusted off his shorts. "Let's get out of here."

"Do you have a plan?" Sofia asked. "We can't make that long swim without Calypso's help."

"I have an idea—everyone in the water," Nico said.

The three dropped though the hole into the warm water.

"Now, hold onto my hands," Nico instructed. Flora and Sofia each took one, and Nico closed his eyes, concentrating.

He opened his eyes and spoke, "Hopefully this will work—*Respirare Aqua!*"

Treading water, they waited anxiously. Suddenly, Nico began choking, followed shortly by the other two. They exchanged panicked looks before watching in amazement as narrow slits opened on the sides of their necks—they had gills.

Nico immediately pulled them underwater, and their choking subsided. Now able to breathe in the water, they began the long swim though the sunken cavern's passageway. As they neared the end, Nico turned and gestured for them to swim forward into the darkness and then upward.

Flora and Sofia followed Nico's directions, swimming until the light of day shone through the river's surface. Breaking through, they gasped for air, only to find themselves unable to breathe.

Nico quickly grabbed both of them and croaked out the magical words, "*Respirare Aerem!*" The slits on their necks gradually sealed up, allowing them to breathe air once more.

Sofia inhaled deeply. "Ah, so good to breath fresh air again!"

Nico turned to Flora. "We're almost there. Just a little farther upstream is a willow tree with a fairy door that will teleport us back to town. But in the meantime, there's someone who will be happy to see you." He retrieved the whistle from around his neck and blew into it.

Within minutes a familiar kraa'ing sound announced Simone's arrival. The excited raven swooped down and landed on Nico's shoulder.

Flora rushed over to greet her corvine friend. "Simone, my dear, I've missed you so much," she gushed, then noticed something was off. "Oh my, what's happened to you? Your eyes—they're milky white!"

"While you were captive, Simone saved our lives more than once," Sofia said, walking over to pet the happy raven.

"And, unfortunately, died while saving us from being hit by an oncoming bus," Nico continued. "The local mortician used necromancy to bring Simone...."

Tears welled up in Flora's eyes. "It's all my fault. If I hadn't been abducted, you wouldn't have ended up like this."

Nico placed a comforting hand on her shoulder. "It's not your fault! You were taken against your will—please don't blame yourself."

Simone walked across Nico's arm and onto Flora's shoulder, nudging her tear-stained cheek.

Filled with emotions, Sofia spoke up, "I think Simone missed you greatly and is happy that you're back."

Nico turned to Sofia and grinned. "Maybe we should hear what Simone has to say."

He then reached out, and touching Simone, incanted, "*Do Vocem Meam!*"

Simone ruffled its feathers before speaking in Nico's voice. "Hello mistress!"

Flora's heart swelled with joy at Nico and Sofia's touching gesture, and tears streamed down her face once more.

"Don't worry about me," Simone said. "Life isn't so bad. I actually feel stronger!"

Flora stroked the raven's head as Simone continued. "I'll be OK—it's just a lot to process. I'm just glad you're back."

Nico suddenly kraa'd to get Flora's attention and handed her the silver whistle.

Sofia joked, "What Nico means is that he believes this belongs to you."

They all laughed, except for Nico, who managed a playful grin.

The raven ruffled its feathers once again, then spoke. "It's getting hot out here, let's head back to town."

"No thanks to the efreeti," Flora added. "He's the reason for this extreme heat. It was another thing I overheard him mention to the mysterious visitor. He said he would keep stoking the flames inside the mountain to make things unbearable to the townspeople."

Sofia spoke up, "Nico told me the newspaper reporter he'd met said the unseasonable heat was coming from the mountain—she was really onto something."

Nico walked in the direction of the willow tree, with the others following. Simone flew over and perched once more on his shoulder.

"Thank you for rescuing my mistress," Simone said. "I knew I chose well when I asked the two of you for help—I'll forever be in your debt."

Nico glanced at the raven and smiled, then pointed to a large willow tree.

"Simone, it's time we give Nico his voice back," Sofia said. She reached out, touched the both of them, and nullified the spell by saying, "*Revocare*!"

Nico cleared his throat and tried to speak. A *kraa* slipped out, followed by, "—not sure how safe it'll be for you, Simone, to use the fairy door with us. For your safety, you should fly back. Flora, hold onto Sofia's hand."

Simone took off from Nico's shoulder and headed toward town. Sofia reached for Nico's hand as he knelt in front of the tiny door engraved with an image of a tattooed bicep.

He looked back to make sure Flora was still holding onto Sofia's hand. "Ready? Here we go!" he said, then touched the fairy door.

The three appeared in Vicolo Fato, near the entrance to Indelible Delights.

"Ah, it's good to finally be back in town," Flora said, slightly dizzy from the brief journey.

"Don't worry; you get used to it," Sofia said.

"Oh, kudzu!" Flora cursed, seeing her store across the street.

Sofia rushed over. "What's the matter?"

"Are you OK?" Nico asked.

"I'm fine," Flora answered, pointing at Petali Floral Design, where Simone was waiting, perched on the store's awning. "Look at all the dead plants in my window display. I'll be cleaning up for days before I can reopen."

"Can't you bring them back to life?" Sofia asked.

Flora sighed. "Once they are dead, they join my sister's realm of decay. I can sprout new plants quickly from seeds, but it still takes time to gather the seeds and plant them."

"One of the town founders created a spell that works similarly," Nico said. "I just wish there was one to revive plants."

Sofia elbowed Nico and whispered, "Why don't you try making one up?"

Flora overheard and smiled. "Thank you, but you've done so much already. Besides, this gives me a chance to deep clean and reorganize the store."

Just then, the door to Indelible Delights opened, and Fawn stepped out. "I thought I heard talking—welcome back! It looks like the rescue mission was a success!" She waved to Flora. "Glad to see you back unharmed."

Flora greeted her. "Hello Fawn. I never thought I'd be found, but thanks to your two brave friends, I'm back."

Nico and Sofia stood quietly, humbled by the praise.

Fawn turned to them. "Why don't you come inside and tell me everything?"

"I think we need some rest first," Sofia said. "But we can meet for drinks later and tell you and Solomon everything."

"I should get going too," Flora added. "Thank you again. Please come by the store once I reopen."

"We certainly will," Nico said.

"Most definitely!" Sofia added.

Flora exited the alleyway and crossed the street. Nico, Sofia, and Fawn watched as she magically waved her hand over the front door of her shop, and it slowly opened. Before stepping inside, she turned, waved to them, and then disappeared through the door.

Fawn asked, "So, where do you want to meet tonight?"

"I'm craving those delicious *arancini* from Moraiolo's, if that's OK with the rest of you," Sofia answered.

"Sounds good to me," Nico said, then teased, "You just want Solomon to feed them to you."

A devilish grin formed on Sofia's face. "I do enjoy that!"

"Seven o'clock then?" Fawn suggested.

Nico checked his Swatch. "Wow, it's only 4:30! We made great time. Sorry, Fawn—yeah, seven o'clock sounds perfect."

Fawn smiled and hugged them goodbye before going back inside. As Nico and Sofia left the alley, they spotted the tan Mercedes idling by the curb, waiting for them.

"Now that's what I call service!" Sofia joked as they climbed into the car and headed home.

Stefano A Giovannoni

Chapter 24: Catch-Up

As the two entered the house, a delicious aroma greeted them from the kitchen.

"I wonder what surprise the house has concocted for us this time," Sofia said, making a beeline to the kitchen.

Nico followed, calling out, "Wait up!"

On the marble kitchen island, two orange-colored drinks served over ice awaited them next to a plate of *taralli*. Sofia reached for one of the freshly made Italian biscuits and held it up to her nose. She inhaled deeply. "Ah, the fragrance of fennel seed paired with cracked pepper, mixed with white wine and olive oil, baked into a crunchy little morsel."

"And the drink?" Nico asked.

"That's easy—Aperol spritz."

"I've never had one."

"It's like your favorite, Campari, but much sweeter and lighter in alcohol. It's mixed with Prosecco and a splash of soda water. Try it," Sofia said, handing one of the drinks to Nico.

Nico took a sip. "Oh, wow, this is good!"

They sat down at the island, enjoying the snacks the house had prepared for them and talking about their day.

"Sofia, there's something I've been meaning to ask you," Nico said after finishing a bite. "How did you cast the Pick Lock spell? You weren't even near me, let alone touching me."

Sofia took a sip of her spritz and laughed. "Adrenaline maybe? I don't really know. In the heat of the moment—no pun intended—I just cast it without thinking, and thankfully it worked."

Nico got up and rummaged through the junk drawer. Pulling out a padlock, he brought it over to Sofia. "Here, try unlocking this."

Sofia touched the lock and said, "Resero." The padlock popped open, and they exchanged smiles.

"Wow, you can cast spells now," Nico said. "OK, let's try locking it back up."

Sofia touched the padlock again. "Sero," she called out, but nothing happened.

"Hmm," Nico mumbled, touching the test object himself. "Sero." The shackle immediately clicked down into its locked position.

Sofia took another sip of her drink, recalling something. "Nico, remember when we were in the main cavern, and you asked me for the magic word for the Silent Space spell? Well, after I told you, everything went quiet. I thought my ears were still plugged with water, but maybe I really did cast the spell!"

"Only one way to find out," Nico said, moving to the other side of the kitchen, about six feet away. "Go ahead and cast it."

"Silentium."

"Can you hear me?"

"Yes," Sofia answered, disappointed.

"Maybe I'm not far enough away," Nico said, stepping back. "Can you hear me now?"

Sofia's face lit up. "Now I can't hear you!"

Nico returned to the island, passing through the spell's perimeter. "*Revocare*," he invoked, cancelling the spell. He sat down and had another *taralli*, pondering Sofia's new ability.

"So, both spells are from the Malandanti side of the book," Nico reasoned. "Maybe you can only cast Malandanti spells?"

"Yes, I think you're right! And I bet I know why." Sofia took off Chiara's medallion and placed it before them. She touched the padlock and spoke the magic word, but nothing happened.

Putting the medallion back on, she tried again. "Resero." The padlock popped open. "Chiara was right. She did leave me 'something special'—special in more ways than one."

Nico raised his glass in a toast, "To my magical bestie—welcome to my world."

***

Later, they got ready for their night out and headed downtown. The tan Mercedes circled the piazza, searching for a parking spot, and eventually found one.

"Looks like the tourists have arrived early for the weekend," Nico sighed. "The town is already bustling."

Sofia exited the car and took in the lively scene. "You're right. Look at all the people!"

"Hey, pretty lady," Solomon called out, approaching from down the street.

Recognizing the voice, Sofia spun around in excitement and ran to greet him with a big kiss. "Oh, how I've missed you."

"The feeling is mutual, my love."

"Cut that out, you two!" Fawn yelled from across the street as she crossed over to join them.

The four walked to the restaurant's entrance, and Solomon held the door open for them to enter.

A seemingly overwhelmed girl, about their age, stood behind the hostess stand, looking down at the reservation list and making notations with a pencil. Without looking up, she asked, "Do you have reservations?"

Nico stepped forward. "Aurora, is that you?"

The hostess, wearing a black miniskirt, starched white shirt, and a red bandana tied around her neck, looked up. Her highlighted blonde hair was pulled back, revealing dark roots, held in place with a rhinestone hairclip in the shape of a spider.

With a look of uncertainty, she asked, "Nico? Nico Frantoio— omigod, it's you!"

"I haven't seen you since graduation! How have you been?"

"Not bad," she answered. "I came up for summer break to help my mom with the restaurant."

"Oh, that's right! You're at Stanford. How are you liking it?"

"It's awesome," Aurora said, then glanced over at Nico's companions. "I see I've been replaced."

Nico laughed. "That's my friend Sofia. If you had come to Yale with me, like we planned, I might never have met her."

"I'm just teasing you," Aurora said as a group of five people entered the restaurant. "I'd better you a seat—it's starting to get busy."

Nico waved his friends over. Aurora took her pencil, waved it in the air, and then crossed off one of the reservations.

"You're in luck; we just had a cancellation," she said with a grin, just as the phone immediately rang. "Trattoria Moraiolo…oh, you can't make it? I see…well, thank you for letting us know."

Aurora grabbed four menus and led them to a table. "Tonight's appetizer special is roasted prosciutto-wrapped figs. Our *pizza del giorno* is spicy Italian sausage, caramelized onions, and burrata," she said, handing out menus. "Matteo will be by shortly for your drink order. *Buon Appetito!*"

Sofia, who was sandwiched between Nico and Solomon, elbowed Nico. "You two seemed chummy."

"We went to St. Anthony's and graduated together," Nico explained. "We were inseparable until we went off to college."

"So, I replaced her," Sofia joked. "Aside from the overly processed blonde hair, we could almost pass for sisters."

The waiter, Matteo, appeared. "*Ragazzi*, so good to see you again! Can I get you something to drink?"

"Hi Matteo," Fawn said, looking up from her menu. "Bring us your best bottle of wine—we're celebrating tonight!"

"*Subito*," Matteo said and hurried off.

Nico looked across the table at Fawn. "What are we celebrating?"

"That you two made it back alive!" Fawn shouted over restaurant chatter.

Solomon then put his arm around Sofia. "And in a few days, it'll be our three-month anniversary."

Nico rolled his eyes, and Fawn, having noticed, snickered.

"Oh, three months already?" Sofia asked, trying to do the math in her head.

"I guess I'll add one more thing to our celebration," Nico began but stopped abruptly. Looking around the restaurant, he continued, "Where's Matteo with our wine? We have so much to toast to, and nothing to toast with."

"It's a busy night," Fawn noted. "He's probably swamped with orders."

Nico leaned in. "Well, what I was about to say is that Sofia is now able to cast spells."

"Well, only the dark ones—the Malandanti spells," Sofia clarified.

Nico teased, "So, Solomon, you better treat her right. You wouldn't want to see what happens if she gets mad."

Matteo returned with the wine, opened the bottle, and poured each of them a glass. "I'll be right back to take your order."

Fawn raised her glass. "To my good friends who survived another adventure—"

"And to my beautiful girlfriend, who makes me happy to be alive," Solomon added.

Nico joined in, raising his glass. "To Sofia, my best friend and now magical companion—"

"Well, I guess I should say something, too," Sofia said, raising her glass. "To my incredible friend Nico and his family, who've embraced me as one of their own. Although I was adopted by a wonderful family— and I love them dearly—it's an amazing feeling to have the love of a second family."

They clinked their glasses together and cheered, "*Cin, cin!*"

Matteo returned, took their order, and soon after brought out their appetizers: *arancini* and roasted prosciutto-wrapped figs.

"So, tell us what happened inside the mountain," Fawn asked, reaching for an *arancini*. "Did the mad honey work?"

Sofia, busy being fed a fig by Solomon, had her mouth full, so Nico spoke up.

"Actually, after finally sourcing some, we didn't end up using it."

Fawn gave Nico her full attention, curious to hear more, and he began telling the story….

***

"…And then Calypso just left you there?" Solomon asked.

Sofia spoke up, "Yes. Once Flora was freed, we had to find another way to make it through the long underwater passage—but Nico will get to that part in a bit."

"OK, so now you're in the large cavern with Caleo," Fawn recapped. "If you didn't use the mad honey, how did you manage to subdue him?"

Nico gestured to Sofia. "She deserves all the credit for that one. Why don't you tell them this part?"

Sofia swallowed the last bite of her arancini and recounted how they had used the Silent Space spell to help keep Caleo asleep while freeing Flora from the suspended cage.

"…then the spell suddenly wore off, and Caleo woke up," Sofia finished.

Fawn's eyes widened. "I've heard stories about Caleo—he's a big guy, and I imagine quite frightening as well!"

"He was," Nico said. "Luckily, we managed to escape his lair, and he couldn't follow us through the narrow passageways because of his size."

Sofia put down her glass of wine and giggled. "Finally, an example of why bigger isn't always better."

Everyone at the table, except Solomon, burst out laughing.

"I don't get it," Solomon said, looking confused.

Sofia leaned in and whispered to her boyfriend, "Don't worry, I'll explain later."

Once Nico regained his composure, he continued the rest of their adventure story, finishing just as their food arrived.

"Matteo—another bottle of this excellent wine, *per favore*," Nico requested just before the busy waiter rushed off.

The food was delicious as always, and while they shared a classic Margharita Pizza and the pizza del giorno, Aurora returned to their table.

"How's everything tonight?" she asked. "I see you ordered the special pizza—that *burrata* is to die for."

Sofia looked up, wiping her mouth with a napkin. "It's absolutely delicious—everything is!"

"Yes," Nico added. "Even on a busy night, the food quality is still top-notch. Your family has done an incredible job running this restaurant all these years."

"*Grazie mille*," Aurora said, smiling. "Remember when we used to come here after school and share a pizza while doing our homework?"

"Yeah, those were the days," Nico said, smiling as happy memories filled his head.

Aurora started, "And then there was that time you—" but she was interrupted by Matteo.

"They need you up front."

"OK, I'll be right there," she answered, turning back to the table. "Another time then—duty calls."

Once Aurora was out of earshot, Solomon turned to Nico. "I think she has the hots for you. Maybe we should plan a double date?"

"She's not really my type—uh, I mean she's more like a sister to me—like Sofia," Nico said.

"Yes, like a sister," Sofia added, stepping in to ease the awkwardness. "Besides, Sol, I'd rather have more time alone with you before I leave."

Matteo returned to clear their plates. "Is there anything else I can bring you?"

"Just the check, Matteo," Nico replied.

"No check. Your meal is on the house—Aurora took care of it," Matteo said with a smile before heading off to another table.

"That was nice of her," Sofia said.

Solomon immediately blurted out, "See, I told you she likes Nico!"

Sofia whispered to Solomon, "Let it go—it's never going to happen. Trust me."

Before leaving, the four stopped by the hostess stand to thank Aurora for her generosity.

"It was great to see you again, and thank you for the delicious dinner—you didn't have to do that," Nico said, giving her a hug.

"You're quite welcome," Aurora replied. "Please come back soon, even if it's just to say hello! I can't wait to tell my mom you're back in town."

The others also expressed their appreciation for the comped meal before stepping out into the warm night air.

"Hey, I almost forgot to ask," Nico said. "Are you guys going to the grand opening party at The Griffon's Claw this Saturday?"

"I almost forgot," Fawn said. "Thanks for the reminder—I'll be there."

"Count me in, too," Solomon added.

"By the way, have you met Lisette, the girl from Martinique who works at Patisserie Angelique?" Nico asked.

Fawn yawned and then covered her mouth. "Sorry, all that good food and wine is making me sleepy. But yes, I've seen her around. She's very pretty, but seems aloof, so I've never introduced myself."

"Oh, yeah, she seems nice. She's come into the store a few times," Solomon added. "But I've never had the chance to talk to her since I'm always busy *working*."

They all laughed.

"Good one, Mr. Mannequin," Nico said. "Anyway, the reason I mentioned her is that she doesn't know many people our age here in town. I felt bad and invited her to join us on Saturday at The Griffon's Claw. I hope that's OK."

"The more the merrier," Fawn said with a smile.

"I'm cool with that," Solomon agreed.

Sofia walked up to Nico and whispered, "I'm going to spend some quality time with Sol; is that OK?"

"Sure—I'm beat and will probably fall asleep as soon as I get home. Should I send the car back for you?"

"No, that's OK. Solomon will take me home."

"All right, you two have a good night," Nico said, turning to Fawn. "Do you want me to walk you back to Indelible Delights or drive you somewhere?"

"Thanks," Fawn replied, yawning again. "I'll be fine. The Oliveto Abductor is no longer a threat, so all I have to worry about are drunken tourists," she joked before hugging everyone goodbye.

A few parking spaces away, they noticed the tan Mercedes headlights switch on, and the engine start.

"I guess the car is telling me that it's time to go home," Nico said lightheartedly. "Sofia, I'll see you tomorrow."

Nico arrived home safely, greeted by Negroni as he walked through the door.

"Hello, my little friend. I'm beat—off to bed I go," Nico said, trudging off to his bedroom.

Negroni followed and then jumped onto the bed, staying close to him throughout the night.

Chapter 25: That Darn Cat

Nico was awakened by the rising sun streaming into his bedroom. As he sat up in his bed, he realized that Negroni had left his side. *Hmm, I wonder where she went—probably roaming around the house*, he thought, stretching his arms. *And I wonder what time Sofia got in.*

He got out of bed and headed toward the kitchen, but stopped short in the dining room. *Odd*, he thought. *Usually, I can smell the fragrance of something delicious being prepared or, at the very least, freshly brewed coffee.*

Deciding to check on Sofia, Nico went into her bedroom, only to find that she wasn't there. Her bed hadn't been slept in. Nico felt a wave of panic but reasoned that Sofia had probably spent the night with Solomon and was still there, safe. *She's a big girl*, he reassured himself. *I shouldn't be worried—after all, she could probably spell her way out of a paper bag if she needed to. Time to get some food—I'm starving.*

Nico called out his breakfast order. "House, please make me a double *cappuccino* and some scrambled eggs." As he passed through the short hallway, the bust of his nonna turned and smiled. "*Buongiorno*," she said. "Word on the other side is that you and Sofia had a run-in with Caleo."

"Yeah, while rescuing one of the town dryads," Nico replied. "And while I have you here, I wanted to ask you about the thirteen Coins of Favor. You collected them all to return to Caleo, right?"

"Yes," Chiara said, "but as you know, I met my unfortunate demise before I could return them. It should be straightforward now—all thirteen coins are in my safe deposit box. You just need to retrieve them and deliver them to Caleo before the Founders' Day Celebration."

"Well, I'm not sure it's going to be *that* easy. He was pretty upset when we left with his captive, and I'm sure he'll want to kill us the next time he sees us."

Nico heard the front door open. "Sounds like Sofia's back—excuse me while I check on her." The animated bust smiled once more, then closed its eyes and became still.

Sofia, carrying the morning paper to the kitchen, nearly collided with Nico as they met in the dining room.

"Well, look what the cat dragged in!" Nico teased. Sofia stood before him, looking as if she'd done the walk of shame, wearing yesterday's clothes and with her hair disheveled.

"Stop—just get me some coffee, STAT."

"House, pot of coffee for Sofia, please." They went into the kitchen and took their usual seats; Nico's double *cappuccino* was already waiting.

Sofia opened the morning edition of *L'Essenziale* and placed it between them; the headline read: *Can Oliveto Beat This Heat?*

Nico turned to Sofia, studying her face. "You were a naughty girl last night, weren't you?"

Sofia just grinned but said nothing.

"Come on, tell me!" Nico begged.

"Yes," Sofia finally admitted, "I was a little naughty, but still very much a lady."

A pot of coffee and a cup floated over to the kitchen island and lowered in front of them. Nico reached for the pot and filled Sofia's cup.

"Oh, before I forget, I talked to my nonna, and she confirmed what we suspected about the thirteen Coins of Favor."

A plate of scrambled eggs floated over and landed in front of Nico.

"Oh, those look so good!" Sofia said, her stomach growling with hunger.

Nico slid the plate over to her. "Here, take mine—I'll ask the house to make more."

"Thanks," Sofia said, bringing a forkful of fluffy eggs to her mouth.

Nico requested another plate of eggs and continued, "So, my nonna said we need to return the coins before Founders' Day, and all should be good." He took a sip of his *cappuccino* before adding, "But I told her

Caleo wasn't happy with our last visit and would likely kill us if we returned."

"Yeah, we'll have to figure something out," Sofia said, more focused on eating than discussing plans.

Nico's new plate of eggs arrived, and, after finishing breakfast, they decided to spend a quiet day at home. They ended up spending hours in Chiara's secret attic room, exploring the many books and familiarizing themselves with their content.

Later that evening, Nico surprised Sofia by making her dinner: a simple *Caprese* salad made with fresh tomatoes and basil from the garden, followed by a delicious *Bistecca alla Fiorentina*, cooked blood rare. For dessert, they enjoyed a light lemon sorbet. Afterward, they retreated to the living room, watching back-to-back episodes of "Kolchak: The Night Stalker" late into the evening before heading to bed.

***

Saturday morning soon arrived, and the two well-rested friends met in the kitchen for their morning ritual.

"Are you excited about tonight?" Nico asked. "It's been a while since we've gone to a party or a club."

"I know," Sofia sighed. "I'm really looking forward to the trifecta: good cocktails, good music, and good friends."

"Hey, by the way, did you see Negroni this morning?" Nico asked

"No, why?"

"Well, she's been sleeping with me at night, but by morning, she always disappears—"

Sofia interrupted, "Maybe she's in the basement with Buddy?"

"I hadn't thought of that—makes sense. I'll check after this coffee kicks in," Nico said, yawning. "Sorry. It was so hot last night, I barely slept."

Sofia yawned, covering her mouth. "Looks like we need extra fuel this morning," she said, refilling both their cups. "I'll go downstairs with you and help you search."

"Thanks," Nico said. "I'm a little worried. Ever since she reappeared, she hasn't touched the food I've put out for her—even her water bowl is untouched."

After finishing their coffee, Nico opened the cabinet door to the basement. A horrible stench filled the kitchen.

"Omigod, what's that awful smell?" Sofia gasped.

"Something must have died down there—I hope it's not her."

"I doubt it. If you just saw her last night, there hasn't been enough time for the body to decay that much," Sofia reasoned.

"True," Nico agreed. "Maybe another gourd rotted from the heat?"

"It's not a gourd—I'll never forget that horrid smell!"

They covered their noses and continued down the stairs.

"Negroni, are you down here?" Nico called, his voice slightly muffled by his hand.

"Here, kitty, kitty," Sofia called, peeking into the wine cellar. "Well, she's not in here."

They passed the laundry area, nearing the entrance to the secret room.

"Buddy, are you around?" Nico called, and Buddy emerged from a dark corner moments later.

"Hey friend," Sofia said. "Have you seen Negroni?"

The winged construct jumped up and down, flapping his wings, and then pointed to a back corner of the basement.

"That's where we found the Babau," Nico said, turning to Sofia. "Could it be back?"

"We won't know until we look," Sofia said, yanking the star charm off her bracelet and holding it in her palm. The star began to glow, expanding to the size of a softball and illuminating the back half of the basement.

Together, they ventured further and stepped onto the raised cement area, where the stench intensified. They quickly retreated, trying to avoid gagging.

"I have an idea," Sofia said. "Come with me."

She led Nico to the entrance of the secret room, handing him her glowing star charm. She pressed the skull carving on the picture frame, causing the wall to slide open.

Nico watched as Sofia went to the sink in the corner of the room, where several shelves were lined with uniquely shaped apothecary jars. "What are you looking for?" he asked.

"This," Sofia said, retrieving a jar and opening it, releasing the fresh, camphoraceous scent of eucalyptus. She handed Nico two leaves. "Roll these up and put them in your nostrils, like this," she said, demonstrating.

Nico laughed at how silly she looked but complied. "You laugh now, but it'll help with the smell," Sofia insisted.

Back in the raised area, they found overturned boxes and the remains of dead mice and rats, some fresh and others desiccated. Sofia held up the light, revealing Negroni lying where the Babau had once rested.

"Looks like she's claimed her turf and has been feeding on a constant supply of rodents." Sofia said.

"But if she's been eating, there wouldn't be all these carcasses," Nico reasoned. He knelt beside Negroni. "Sofia, she doesn't seem to be breathing."

Sofia rushed over. "Maybe it's just the lighting—try picking her up," she urged.

Nico reached out, and as he touched her velvety fur, Negroni opened her eyes and meowed.

"Phew!" Nico exclaimed. "I'm so glad you're alive and OK, but I'm still going to keep my eye on you."

"Yes, kitty, you had Nico quite worried," Sofia said, pretending to scold the feline.

Negroni meowed again before settling back to sleep. As they exited the area, Buddy was waiting for them.

"Hey Buddy," Sofia said. "Are you up for a task?"

Nico gave her a confused look but stayed silent, curious to see what she had planned for the winged construct. Buddy's face lit up with a smile, and he jumped up and down, signaling that he was eager for the job.

"Great!" Sofia said, then turned to Nico. "Can you grab a garbage bag from the kitchen? I'm going to ask Buddy to collect the dead rodents."

Nico laughed. "You're giving him chores now?"

"Why not?" Sofia replied. "It'll make him feel valued."

Nico knelt near Buddy, who jumped up, flapping his wings, and plucked one of the rolled eucalyptus leaves from Nico's nose. As Buddy landed, he snickered.

Nico burst into laughter, removing the other leaf from his nose. "So, you think they look silly too?"

Buddy nodded.

Closing his eyes, Nico focused and summoned a garbage bag from upstairs. He handed a corner of it to Buddy, who looked amazed, trying to figure out how Nico had made the bag appear.

"OK, we'll leave you to collect the dead rodents," Nico said. "Make sure to tie up the bag so the odor doesn't escape."

"Now that this mini mystery is solved, let's head back upstairs," Sofia suggested. "I want to lay out my outfit for tonight."

Chapter 26: Grand Opening

Later that day, as the sun set, Nico and Sofia got ready for The Griffon's Claw Grand Opening Party. Nico, dressed in black shorts, a crisp white button-down shirt with black bow tie, and a festive vest, waited in the foyer for Sofia.

After about ten minutes, Sofia sauntered into the room, wearing a form-fitting black and white vertically striped dress and a red bolero jacket. She spun around, awaiting Nico's approval.

"Wow! I must say, you look really hot—you're definitely going to turn some heads tonight," Nico remarked. He then spun around, bracing himself for Sofia's critique of his outfit.

Sofia scanned his attire. "That vest is everything," she said, grinning. "You look incredibly sharp, Mr. Frantoio."

"Well, now that we've passed each other's inspections, shall we head out?"

"Oh, wait! Let me get my purse."

"Really? Just take your ID and maybe some cash," Nico suggested, then joked, "I doubt we'll need spell components while on the dance floor."

"You're right, but I still need my ID," Sofia said, dashing off to grab it. She returned moments later, tucking her ID into her bra. "OK, now I'm ready!"

They drove down to the piazza, where the bustling Saturday night crowd made parking a challenge. After a few loops, they managed to find a spot two blocks from The Griffon's Claw.

As they made their way to the piazza, they spotted Fawn walking down the street with Solomon. He had just picked her up at Indelible Delights and was escorting her to the bar.

"Hey, you two!" Nico called out from across the street.

Fawn and Solomon turned and waved, waiting for them to catch up. "Wow, you two look so fancy!" Fawn gushed. "So, this is how they dress on the East Coast."

Solomon's eyes widened upon seeing Sofia. "East Coast, West Coast—either coast, my girl is looking mighty fine."

Sofia rushed into Solomon's arms, planting a kiss on his lips. "Happy Anniversary Sol!"

Nico turned to Fawn. "Looks like there's a line in front of The Griffon's Claw. Why don't you three get in line while I pick up Lisette? Hopefully, she's still able to come."

Fawn gave him a thumbs up, and they continued down the street together. As they passed Patisserie Angelique, Nico stayed behind, watching his friends head to the bar.

Peering through the bakery's glass door, Nico saw Lisette shutting off the lights. As she turned to approach the door, she jumped slightly when she noticed Nico pressed against the glass.

"*Mon Dieu!*" she exclaimed, clutching her chest as she unlocked the door.

"Sorry, I didn't mean to scare you," Nico said as she stepped outside. "You look lovely—ready to have some fun?"

"*Merci, mon ami,*" she replied, locking up. "OK, let's go—I've been looking forward to this."

They strolled toward The Griffon's Claw, where Nico spotted Sofia and the others waiting in line. The bar's exterior was decked out with balloons and ribbons, signaling the night's celebration.

"Hey guys," Nico greeted. "This is Lisette. Lisette, you already know Sofia. And this is her boyfriend, Solomon, and our good friend Fawn, who's an amazing tattoo artist."

Lisette gave a polite smile to Solomon before turning to Fawn, who had already extended her hand. "*Enchantée,*" Lisette said, beaming as she eagerly shook Fawn's petite hand.

Before Fawn could reply, a deep, masculine voice boomed from the bar entrance. "Please have your IDs and invitations ready."

Nico looked over and saw that the voice came from a familiar face they'd encountered during their last visit. It was Baron, the bouncer, who stood about six and a half feet tall, with a solid, muscular build and a stern expression.

After the brief interruption, Fawn looked up at Lisette, whose hand she was still holding, and said, "The pleasure is all mine."

Baron's eyes scanned the line, which now extended down the block and around the corner. He eyed Nico and called out, "Frantoio, you and your party, step forward."

Nico and his friends bypassed the line and approached the burly bouncer, who informed them they could go inside.

"Ooh, VIP status," Sofia joked as they entered the bar.

The interior was lavishly decorated. Near the back, a cover band was warming up on a stage, performing their final mic checks. Behind the bar, a familiar face waved to them, beckoning them over.

"Isn't that the owner?" Sofia asked. "I can't remember his name."

"I've never seen him before," Fawn added.

Lisette leaned in, whispering, "There's something about him—"

Nico's eyes locked on the gentleman with pale skin, dark red lips, and shiny black hair pulled back into a ponytail. "Vincenzo—it's Vincenzo," Nico remembered.

They approached, and Vincenzo greeted them warmly. "I'm so glad you could make it, Nico—and you brought Sofia! And friends, I see."

"The more, the merrier," Sofia said as Solomon put his arm around her and pulled her close.

"Vincenzo," Nico said, "this is Fawn, Solomon, and Lisette."

"Nice to meet you all, and welcome to The Griffon's Claw," Vincenzo announced. "Your drinks are on the house, so enjoy! There's also a variety of delicious appetizers at the end of the bar—please help yourself."

"Wow, free drinks and food," Fawn marveled. "Thank you so much!"

"So, what would you like to drink?" Vincenzo asked.

"A Negroni, please," Nico answered.

"And for you, Sofia, what are you in the mood for?" Vincenzo asked.

Sofia grinned and chose the strongest drink she could think of. "A Long Island Iced Tea, please."

"Yum, that sounds good." Fawn said. "I'll have one too."

"When in Rome..." Lisette added. "Make that three."

Vincenzo then turned to Solomon. "And for you?"

"Just a beer—a Rolling Rock, thanks," Solomon answered.

Sofia turned to her boyfriend. "Really? Just a beer?"

Solomon, slightly embarrassed by his drink choice, whispered to Sofia, "To be honest, I don't really like hard liquor."

"Oh, I didn't know that. I guess there's still a lot more about you that I need to learn," Sofia whispered back, then looked up at Vincenzo. "Alrighty then, just the beer for my man."

As Vincenzo prepared their drinks, they noticed the venue was now nearly full. A keyboard began playing, soon followed by drumming, as the band kicked off their first song, a cover of "Cry Wolf" by A-ha.

People started crowding the bar to order cocktails, and three employees emerged from a door at the back of the room to join Vincenzo, assisting with the flood of drink orders from the thirsty patrons.

Sofia turned back to the bar and saw her drink waiting for her. She quickly grabbed it and took a sip. "Oh yes, this is going to be a fun night—I can already tell."

Vincenzo personally handed Nico his Negroni as the others collected their drinks from the bar and began to sip. "I must take my leave and help with the festivities, but I've instructed my staff to take good care of you and that your drinks are on the house," Vincenzo said. He then left the bar and disappeared through a door at the back of the room.

Fawn took another sip of her drink and began dancing in place. "I really love this song—let's hit the dance floor!"

The group waded through the throngs of people, making their way to the center of the dance floor, beneath a giant mirrored ball.

As they danced, Nico noticed Dino off to the side, moving sloppily with two unknown girls. Nico's nemesis appeared completely out of it, enjoying the moment as his companions danced seductively around him.

While Dino continued his awkward dancing, a brass medallion hanging from a chain around his neck slipped out from beneath his unbuttoned shirt. The medallion bore a raised image of a flame, which looked strikingly familiar to Nico. He stared intensely at it, trying to recall where he had seen a similar symbol before. Dino's eyes locked onto Nico's, and he shot him a dirty look, promptly followed by a raised middle finger.

Embarrassed, Nico quickly turned back to his friends. *Where have I seen that medallion before?* he wondered, moving to the beat of the music. Then it hit him. *Ah, now I remember! Caleo was wearing a similar one...and that's the same flame that's on the Coins of Favor as well.*

Nico continued dancing with his friends, and by the end of the fourth song, most of their glasses were nearly empty, with just a diluted mixture of alcohol and melted ice remaining. He offered to get the second round and left the dance floor.

At the bar, Nico waited his turn to place his order. Once the drinks were ready, he carefully balanced all five drinks between his hands. As he turned to head back to the dance floor, he accidentally bumped into the person behind him, causing a splash of Negroni, Long Island Iced Tea, and beer to soak his vest.

"I'm so sorry," said a voice said through loud music. "It's my fault—I should have given you more space."

Nico looked up and there stood Gino, his light gray eyes meeting Nico's.

A wave of awkwardness washed over Nico, and he mumbled, "Uh, it's OK," looking down at the floor.

"Can I at least help you carry the drinks?" Gino offered.

Nico kept his head down and mumbled once more, "No, thank you," then moved past Gino and back to the dance floor.

As he handed everyone their drinks, Sofia noticed something was off. "Are you OK? You suddenly seem withdrawn."

"Nothing another drink can't fix," Nico replied, raising his glass to clink it against Sofia's before taking a big gulp.

As they continued drinking and dancing, Nico started to feel like he was a fifth wheel. Sofia and Solomon, who couldn't keep their eyes off each other, had been dancing closely the entire time, while Fawn and Lisette were hitting it off, creating their own dance space. Nico found himself alone on the perimeter.

When the band began playing its next song, Nico perked up, instantly recognizing the first few notes of his favorite: Whitney Houston's "I

Wanna Dance with Somebody." Determined to shake off his insecurities about dancing alone, he gazed at the spinning disco ball above and mouthed the lyrics.

The music lifted his spirits, and soon Nico was fully committed to enjoying the moment, dancing freely with random people around him. As he spun around, he was surprised to see Gino nearby, his previously slicked back ash blond hair now hanging loose and swaying with his dance moves, beads of sweat dripping down his face.

Gino caught Nico's eyes and smiled. Nico, choosing to enjoy the moment, took a sip of his drink, let his guard down, and smiled back.

"Hey," Gino said. "It's nice to see you smiling and having fun."

"It's my favorite song," Nico admitted, taking the last sip of his cocktail and placing the empty glass on a nearby table.

"I thought you were mad at me," Gino said as they continued dancing.

Nico's smile faded slightly. "It's complicated," he replied, then did a double take as he glanced over at the bar. *Is that my dad in line?* he wondered. *What's he doing here?*

Gino moved closer and pressed further. "What's complicated?"

Feeling emboldened by the alcohol, Nico confessed, "I'm uncomfortable around you—I mean, I essentially killed your father."

Gino put his hand on Nico's shoulder and looked directly into his eyes. "My father was an evil man who did terrible things. You shouldn't feel guilty. And besides, that night when you showed up at the door glamoured as him, I realized pretty quickly it was you."

Surprised, Nico slowed his dancing. "You did?"

"Yes," Gino replied, taking a quick sip of his drink before continuing. "I first knew something was off because you weren't wearing the shoes my father had on when he left. I almost believed your excuse, but then you said something that gave you away."

"What did I say?" Nico asked, now barely moving.

Gino's expression softened. "I remember it clearly. When you brought us the pizza, you said you'd gotten 'an extra for my boys.' My heartless father never referred to us as his boys—so you see, I knew, and I didn't try to stop you. If anything, I'm just as guilty."

Nico felt a sense of relief wash over him, and the guilt he'd carried for months began to fade.

"Nico, can I get you another drink?" Gino asked as the band began their next cover: "Summer of Love" by the B-52's.

But before Nico could answer, a shout for help pierced the air, and the music abruptly stopped.

Everyone stopped dancing and turned toward the commotion. Through the crowd, Nico could make out the back of a man with a familiar black ponytail, hunched over a woman lying on the floor. *That must be Vincenzo*, Nico thought as he pushed through the crowd to get closer. As Nico drew near, a man rushed past, bumping into him and calling out in a familiar voice, "Siena, I'm coming."

That's my dad's voice, Nico realized, dread pooling in his stomach. *So that was him earlier, which means my mother is here—omigod, that must be her!*

Nico approached, confirming his fears. It was his mother; she lay unconscious, with Vincenzo leaning over her, holding her hand. Nico's dad, Dr. Pétros Kynigós, was now on the other side of Siena. "Get away from her," Pétros commanded, pushing Vincenzo back before addressing the crowd. "Please, give her some space."

As Vincenzo got up and walked away, Nico knelt next to his dad. "Mother, are you OK? It's me Nico."

In a faint voice, Siena murmured, "Luna...I miss the moon."

"Siena, don't speak—save your strength," Pétros said, scooping her into his arms. "She'll be fine," he assured Nico. "She probably didn't eat much today, and the alcohol must have gotten to her. I'll take her home and have her call you in the morning."

"Are you sure?" Nico asked. "Is there anything I can do—anything to help?"

"No," his dad responded sternly. "Thank you, she just needs rest. Go back and enjoy your night with your friends—I promise she'll be OK."

The crowd parted as Pétros carried Siena outside into the warm night air and took her home.

Things calmed down and the band started back up. Sofia and the others, including Gino, approached Nico.

"What happened?" Sofia asked. "Is your mom OK?"

"Is there anything we can do?" Fawn added.

"My dad says she'll be fine," Nico reassured them. "He thinks she didn't eat much today and got light-headed, though I'm not sure I believe it. My mother isn't one to skip meals."

Sofia gently rubbed Nico's back. "Maybe she was busy with clients—showing properties back-to-back—and just didn't have time to eat."

"Maybe," Nico replied. "She did seem swamped when I saw her the other day."

"Come on, let's dance," Sofia suggested.

"I will," Nico said, while looking around. "But first, I need to do something. Did anyone see where Vincenzo went?"

Lisette pointed. "He went through that door back there."

"Thanks Lisette," Nico said. "Oh, and this is Gino. Gino this is Lisette, and I think you already know Fawn, Sofia and Solomon."

Sofia gave Nico a knowing smile. As the others returned to dancing, Nico made his way across the dance floor to the closed door at the back of the room.

Must be a back office or a storage room, he thought as he reached for the doorknob. He tried to open it, but it was locked. "*Resero*," he whispered, and the lock clicked open.

Inside, the room was small, lined with stainless-steel racks stocked with liquor and supplies. Against one wall sat a desk, a ledger embossed "Vincenzo Alessandro Luna" resting on it, along with a calculator and a few other office supplies. A door stood to the side.

Great, another door! Nico thought, frustrated. He tried the doorknob, and it opened to a set of stairs leading down into darkness.

"Hello?" Nico called out, searching for a light switch. "Anyone down there? Vincenzo?"

"Nico, stay there—I'll be right up!" a voice called out from below.

As Nico stood there peering into the darkness, he heard the creak of footsteps on the stairs; someone was coming up. As the sound grew nearer, a face emerged from the shadows—it was Vincenzo.

"Nico, is everything OK?" Vincenzo asked. "How's Siena?"

"She'll be fine," Nico answered. "My dad took her home. But I'd like to know what happened."

"What do you mean?" Vincenzo asked, his expression serious.

"I saw you with her," Nico said, his voice tense. "You were holding her hand."

Vincenzo placed his hands on Nico's shoulders and looked deep into his eyes. "I was making my rounds, as any good host would, when I noticed her standing there alone," he explained. "I asked if she was OK, and she said she was, just waiting for your stepfather, who had gone to get them another drink. We chatted briefly, and then she suddenly collapsed."

Nico considered his words, then nodded. "It still seems odd to me that my mother would just collapse, but...I believe you."

"Good," Vincenzo said gently. "Now that that's settled, go and have fun. The night is still young!"

Nico returned to the dance floor, letting the music sweep him away. Despite the brief interruption, it had been a long time since he and Sofia had enjoyed themselves so much.

When the bar closed, the group said their goodbyes, each heading their separate ways—except this time, Sofia went home with Nico.

Stefano A Giovannoni

Chapter 27: Summer Solstice '87

Extremely hungover, Nico and Sofia slept late into the morning. It was nearly noon when a knock sounded at Nico's bedroom door. "Ugh," Nico moaned, pulling the covers over his head.

The door creaked open, and Sofia burst into the room, jumping onto Nico's bed and bouncing up and down. "Happy Summer Solstice!"

"Oh, my head—stop moving around," groaned Nico, wincing. "Of course, on the longest day of the year, I have to be hungover."

Sofia went over to open the French doors, hoping for a breeze to air out the stuffy room, but was met with warm, still air.

"Yuck! Another hot day," she said, stepping onto the patio. "I'm going to pick some oranges to juice—be right back."

"Take your time," Nico muttered, rolling over and quickly drifting back to sleep.

As Sofia approached the two orange trees, she noticed something hanging on the one with the fairy door. Rubbing her eyes, she blinked to bring it into focus—about twenty garlic bulbs were tied together and dangling from one of the branches. After realizing that the gnomes had probably harvested the garlic that morning, she began picking oranges.

Sofia carried her bounty back to Nico's bedroom and dumped the oranges onto his bed.

Nico pulled the covers off his head and sat up. "You're not going to let me rest, are you?"

"It's better if you get up now," Sofia replied. "The longer you sleep, the groggier you'll feel. Besides, some food might help."

Sofia went to close the French doors, and Nico, still half asleep with his hair sticking up in every direction, reluctantly climbed out of bed.

Sofia grabbed an orange and tossed it to him. "Think fast!"

Nico's reflexes kicked in, and he caught the orange with a quick, firm grip.

"Amazing," Sofia marveled. "How did you do that? I didn't think you'd catch it—you're still half asleep."

"How should I know?" Nico quipped, as he started helping Sofia gather the remaining oranges to take to the kitchen.

As they passed through the short hallway, Chiara's bust animated. "Nico, put some clothes on."

"Nonna, you're so old-fashioned—wearing just boxers still counts as dressed," Nico joked, entering the kitchen where a treat awaited them.

"Ooh, look!" Sofia exclaimed, pointing to a bundt-style cake on the kitchen island, paired with two double *espressos*.

They sat down, and Nico cut into the cake. "Wow, this smells amazing," he said, plating slices for both of them.

"I know this cake—the fragrance of orange and Grand Marnier is unmistakable," Sofia said, holding a forkful up to her nose and savoring the scent. "It's Italian Hangover Cake—the house must have known we'd need a little *richiamino*, or 'hair of the dog,' to get us back on track."

"There's something in the espresso, too!" Nico remarked, tasting the added flavor of Fernet Branca.

"A much-needed *caffè corretto*," Sofia said, taking a sip of her espresso.

As they enjoyed the treat, a now-alert Nico recalled fragments from the previous night.

"Sofia, there are a few things from last night I forgot to tell you."

"Like what?"

"First, I saw Dino. He was wearing a chain with a brass medallion engraved with a flame—the same style of flame as on the Coins of Favor."

"And like the one Caleo wore?" Sofia asked quickly, her eye widening.

"Exactly. I'm not sure if it means anything, but it might not be a coincidence." Nico hesitated before continuing. "Also, when I was at my mother's side, she started to come to. Her voice was faint, but I heard her say, 'Luna...I miss the moon.'"

"Well, *luna* is Italian for moon," Sofia noted. "It could be a clue."

Another flashback struck Nico. "There's something else."

"Tell me."

"When I went looking for Vincenzo, I went to the back room—it was locked but of course I got in—"

"And?" Sofia prompted.

"It was a small storage room with a desk and another door leading down to an unlit area—probably more storage."

"And?" Sofia asked again, anxious for him to get to the point.

Nico took a sip of his espresso, and continued, "I noticed a ledger on the desk."

"Typical for any business."

"I know I'm a bit slow this morning, but could you stop interrupting me?" Nico replied, half-serious.

"Sorry."

"I said stop interrupting me," Nico teased this time, smiling to show he was joking.

Sofia remained quiet but smiled, signaling all was good.

Nico continued. "So, at the time it seemed insignificant, but the ledger was embossed with Vincenzo's full name—Vincenzo Alessandro Luna."

"Wait!" Sofia exclaimed, dropping her fork. "We've seen that name before!"

"Have we?"

"Yes, at Olive Tree Hill Cemetery! Remember that rose bush growing from a crack in a grave? You went over to pick a rose from it and ended up grabbing a huge thorn that caused you to bleed everywhere?"

"How could I ever forget that painful experience!" Nico groaned.

"That grave had a simple headstone with just the name: Vincenzo Luna."

"It can't be the same person," Nico said, running a hand through his hair. "That grave was old, and the Vincenzo we know is around our age."

"What if he's a vampire?"

"Nah, those don't really exist."

Sofia raised her eyebrows. "Or do they? That might explain why your nonna kept garlic bulbs on every windowsill. Plus, we already deduced that the mysterious 'V' on her animal control chart in the grimoire stood for Vampire."

"True," Nico said, then recalled his conversation with the newspaper reporter. "And Renata from *L'Essenziale* mentioned that the recent town deaths were due to exsanguination—you might be onto something."

Sofia grinned with satisfaction. "Looks like you're finally awake."

Nico laughed. "I guess it's time to head to the library and get some answers. We'll ask Teresa to unlock the Founder's Treasure Room."

"Exactly! We can use the Books of Knowledge there to uncover the truth about the enigmatic Vincenzo Luna."

"All right, let's get ready and head out," Nico said, clearing their plates.

***

The tan Mercedes drove them down to the library and parked in front of its grand entrance.

"Can we use the side entrance, like last time?" Sofia asked, eyeing the long flight of steps leading to the second-floor main entrance. "I don't quite have the energy to climb them yet."

"I hear you—come on," Nico replied, leading them to the ground-level side entrance.

As they entered the library, the familiar scent of old books mingled with lemon oil used to polish the wood bookshelves brought back memories of their last visit. They passed through the periodicals section and into the heart of the library.

"Nico. Sofia. Welcome back," Teresa's voice called from above. She stood on a library ladder, returning books to a high shelf.

"Hi, Teresa," they replied in unison.

Teresa climbed down, turning to them. "To what do I owe the pleasure of this visit?"

"We need access to the Books of Knowledge again—there's something we need to know that only they can tell us," Nico explained.

"Very well. Let me lock up the library, and I'll unlock the Founder's Treasure Room door downstairs for you," Teresa offered.

"No need," Sofia said. "I remember the sequence you used to unlock the door last time—I should be able to do it myself, if you'd rather stay up here."

Teresa raised an eyebrow. "Well, I do have a lot to do, but are you certain? Choosing the wrong glyph could have…unpleasant consequences. I'd hate for either of you to be injured—or worse."

"I appreciate your concern, but I'm pretty confident I can get us in safely," Sofia reassured her.

"Very well, you know the way," Teresa said with a smile. "Oh, and Sofia, I love your earrings."

"Thank you," Sofia replied. "I had those beautiful pearls you let me keep last time made into earrings."

"Those pearls are the only reason I'm allowing you to open the door on your own," Teresa said with a knowing smile. "By wearing them, the door will think you're me and respond when the correct glyph sequence is pressed. Without them, even entering the right sequence would trigger the door's security measures."

"Then I'll be sure not to let Nico," Sofia teased, glancing at him. "Unless you want to wear my earrings?"

"Uh, no," Nico answered. "I'm good."

Teresa chuckled. "Well, be careful, and call out if you need anything." She returned to her ladder, balancing a stack of books as she climbed up.

Nico and Sofia made their way back through the periodicals room and took the staircase down to the lower level. The landing opened into a small room with a large, oversized door constructed of reclaimed driftwood. A salty tang filled the air as seawater trickled from the bottom of the door's frame, forming large puddles on the floor.

Nico and Sofia approached, gazing at the intricate maritime glyphs carved into the door. As they got closer, the glyphs began to glow with increasing intensity.

"Are you sure you know how to unlock the door?" Nico asked with uncertainty.

"It's easy once you figure out the pattern—watch," Sofia said confidently. She pressed the first glyph. "This one is a Unicorn fish. The second is a Narwhal."

Nico looked puzzled, clearly not making the connection.

Sofia continued, pressing four more glyphs in sequence: Lamprey, Octopus, Conch shell, and finally, Kelp.

Suddenly, the water on the floor receded into the door, evaporating as it went. The swollen wood dried, creating a visible gap between the door and its frame; the door was now unsealed.

"I still don't get how you did that," Nico admitted.

"I just chose the glyphs whose initials spell—"

"UNLOCK!" Nico blurted, smacking his forehead. "Brilliant—I get it now."

Nico pulled open the door, revealing a flooded cavern. Above the water, four platforms—one in each corner—held various valuables. In the center of the room was a circular dais with three pedestals, each holding a thick leather-bound book. They watched as the seawater slowly drained into a large fountain shaped like a hippocampus at the back of the room.

With the room now dry, they carefully crossed the slippery stone floor, stepping over the occasional starfish or wandering crab, until they reached the dais. Climbing onto it, they stood before the three Books of Knowledge.

Chapter 28: Who Is Vincenzo Luna?

Nico approached the book titled *Persons* and placed his hand on its damp leather cover. "Book, tell me about Vincenzo Luna," he commanded, then stepped back.

The book suddenly rocked back and forth, lifting slightly off its pedestal before settling back down and opening, revealing freshly written pages of text.

Vincenzo Alessandro Lunati was born in Venice, Italy, on March 6th, 1326, to Maria Isabella Lunati and Marco Armando Lunati, the reigning Doge of Venice. As an only child for thirteen years, Vincenzo enjoyed his parents' undivided attention. However, on June 13th, 1339, his mother gave birth to his first sibling, Orlando Antonio Lunati, and suddenly, that precious attention became something he had to compete for.

The following year, the Doge's Palace was completed, and the family moved in. Bound by duty, Vincenzo's father could seldom leave, except on official business, which required special permission. Feeling like a prisoner in the palace, Vincenzo found solace in a deck of cards. After his daily tutoring, he would sit on a balcony overlooking the lagoon, shuffling and playing with his cards.

One afternoon, a gray pigeon landed nearby and approached him, tugging a card from his deck and dropping it onto the marble balustrade. Vincenzo returned the card to his deck, but the pigeon repeated the action. Amused, he decided to test the bird's intelligence. The next time the pigeon drew a card, Vincenzo pretended to return it to the deck but instead palmed the card and dropped it onto his lap. The pigeon looked on, puzzled, as the deck continued to shrink with each round.

Vincenzo repeated this trick until only one card remained for the bird to pick. When he made the last card vanish, the pigeon, as if understanding the game had ended, fluffed its feathers and flew away.

From then on, Vincenzo returned to his new sanctuary each day, bringing bread secretly stolen from the dinner table to offer the pigeon. Before long, more and more pigeons flocked to the spot for the free food, becoming his private audience. Over time, Vincenzo perfected his sleight-of-hand skills, his tricks taking on an almost magical quality. His audience gradually expanded from pigeons to palace staff, and eventually to noble guests attending the elegant parties hosted at the palace.

Guests frequently asked the Doge about Vincenzo, hoping that he would be invited to entertain them. Vincenzo enjoyed this newfound attention—something he had missed in his early youth.

As Vincenzo grew older, his tutoring became more intense, preparing him to eventually assume his father's role as Doge. However, Vincenzo couldn't have cared less; he grew more and more rebellious. He befriended noble teens his age whose parents came to visit. During their stay, the troublesome teens would sneak in and out of the palace, causing mischief wherever they went. Before long, they began daring each other to perform increasingly inappropriate and scandalous acts, pushing the limits of what was acceptable for children of noble families.

One night, during the Venetian Carnival, a masquerade ball was held at the palace. Because of his latest antics, Vincenzo was forbidden to attend, but he knew his friends would be there. Disobeying his father's orders, he sneaked down from his room. Hiding in the shadows, he made his way to a table near the entrance to the grand ballroom, where an array of elegantly crafted masks awaited the guests. He quickly grabbed the nearest one and tied its strings behind his head.

Vincenzo entered the grand ballroom, confident he wouldn't be recognized as long as he wore the detailed papier mâché mask. He mingled with the guests, eventually locating a group of his friends near the punch bowl and revealing himself to them. After a while, the group grew bored of idle chatter. Looking to liven things up, they began daring one another to perform various tasks. When it was Vincenzo's turn, they goaded him into stealing something valuable from one of the female guests.

Vincenzo set off to complete the challenge. He moved among the attendees, searching for an object that would impress his friends, and eventually found his mark. Dancing in the center of the room was a masked woman, her gloved hand adorned with a flawless ten-carat diamond ring that sparkled in the light as her dance partner twirled her around the ballroom floor.

Vincenzo waited for the music to end, and as the mysterious lady was leaving the dance floor, he approached and asked her for the next dance. She stared at him intently, looking him up and down, and then agreed. Vincenzo took her hand and guided her back to the dance floor. With her mask in place, he couldn't see much of her face, though he noticed her décolletage was pale and smooth, without a blemish. Her reddish-brown hair was pulled back, except for a few wisps framing her decorative mask. The most distinctive thing about her, however, was her scent; she smelled of violets.

While Vincenzo guided his partner smoothly across the floor, he discreetly worked the ring off her unsuspecting finger. By the time the dance ended, Vincenzo had secured the ring in his palm, and as he bowed to his dance partner, he slipped it into his coat pocket.

As Vincenzo returned to his friends, relishing his successful dare, he heard a woman's outraged yell from behind him. Before he could turn around, he felt someone tugging at the strings of his mask, and his disguise fell to the floor.

The Doge, hearing the commotion and seeing his son's involvement, quickly dispatched the palace guards to bring all involved in the disturbance to a private room, where he intended to address the issue.

Upon learning that his firstborn son had been accused of theft and recognizing the potential for scandal to spread throughout the region, the Doge quietly settled the matter with the guest, promising it would never happen again. To keep his word, he had Vincenzo removed from the palace and stripped of all entitlements.

Now a commoner, Vincenzo was forced to fend for himself in Venice's maze of streets and canals. But it didn't take long before he found refuge among society's outcasts, joining a band of thieves in the Castello district, one of Venice's sestieri.

In 1348, during Vincenzo's twenty-second year, the Black Death swept through Venice. Seizing the opportunity created by the chaos, he and his gang devised a plan to rob the homes of plague victims after they were removed and taken to the neighboring island, now known as Lazzaretto Vecchio, for quarantine.

Aware of the risks, the gang formulated a protective vinegar solution, hoping it would shield them from the plague. Each thief collected a single ingredient believed to have medical properties: rosemary, sage flowers, lavender flowers, rue, camphor, garlic, and cloves. Under the light of the next full moon, they gathered on the rooftop of their hideout, adding each ingredient to a jar of vinegar before sealing it tightly. For the next seven days, they took turns shaking the mixture. On the eighth day, they were ready to test their concoction.

They poured the jar into seven individual vials, one for each thief. Before entering the marked home of a plague victim, they would douse themselves with their secret formula and proceed to loot the home.

After several weeks, over half of Venice's population had either perished or been quarantined, yet the seven thieves remained healthy and had amassed a small fortune in valuables.

One night, Vincenzo decided to take a high-stakes gamble by breaking into the Doge's Palace. It was an easy feat for him, given his familiarity with the routines of the servants, which allowed him to evade detection.

Vincenzo made his way to the upper floors of the palace. As he passed by his former bedroom, he heard persistent moaning from the adjacent room. Remembering that it was his younger brother Orlando's bedroom, he grew concerned and curious. Vincenzo quietly opened the door and approached the bed, where his nine-year-old brother lay, tossing and turning in discomfort. The tip of Orlando's nose and fingertips were covered in black patches, and three boils oozing a mixture of pus and blood, marked his face—clear signs of the plague that Vincenzo had seen many times before.

Even though this was the closest he had come to a plague victim, he believed the thieves' vinegar mixture would protect him. Spotting a pitcher of water on the bedside table, he filled a glass and sat beside his brother. Orlando, appearing to recognize him, reached out for the water. Vincenzo held the glass to his brother's parched lips, but as Orlando took his first sip, he coughed violently, spraying a mixture of water and phlegm onto Vincenzo's face.

Palace servants, alerted by the sounds of coughing, rushed down the hallway to check on Orlando. Before the door opened, Vincenzo quickly hid behind it and then quietly slipped out as the servants focused on attending to his brother.

Vincenzo felt a deep sense of sadness and dread as he left the palace. He wandered the winding streets of Venice for hours, trying to banish the image of his dying brother from his mind. As the sun rose, he returned to the thieves' hideout.

Within days, Vincenzo developed a high fever, and his body ached all over. The other six thieves, alarmed by his symptoms, alerted the authorities, and he was taken away to be quarantined.

In the weeks that followed, as Vincenzo lay in a large room filled with hundreds of others suffering the same fate, he noticed the same symptoms his brother had exhibited. He knew he wouldn't survive much longer.

Late one night, Vincenzo awoke to the scent of violets. Barely able to rise, he turned his head and saw a woman standing beside his bed. Assuming she was a night nurse, he watched as she knelt close and whispered, "Would my handsome dance partner grant me the pleasure of your last dance?"

Somewhat delirious, Vincenzo wondered if this might be a dream but extended his hand, nonetheless. As it touched the icy flesh of the visitor's hand, he recognized the familiar diamond ring she wore. "Arise and dance with me," she commanded.

It soon became clear to Vincenzo that his maskless dance partner was the very woman he had once stolen from. Suddenly energized, he managed to rise from the bed on his own. He spun her around in the darkness, and the moans and groans of the dying surrounding them, creating a haunting melody for their dance.

"Vincenzo, would you like to dance with me forever?" she tempted.

Anything seemed better than the horrible death he faced, so he answered, "Yes."

Shortly after, he felt the woman's lips touch his neck, and a chill spread through his body as his life drained away. His legs buckled, and he fell onto the damp stone floor as everything went black.

The next thing he remembered was waking up in one of the island's plague pits, surrounded by dozens of decomposing bodies. His body felt stronger, and he noticed that his fingertips were no longer blackened. Looking up, he saw his sire sitting on a nearby rock, beckoning him over.

"Sire?" said Nico. "Does it mean his father, the Doge?"

"I don't think so," opined Sofia. "A sire, to a vampire, is the person who brought you into the community of the undead."

"But that was a woman. Minerva Falcone."

"That's right. A sire can be a female in the world of vampires."

"The things I still have to learn!" said Nico, shaking his head as he returned to the text of the Book of Knowledge.

He rushed to her with questions. "Who are you? And what am I?"

"My name is Minerva Falcone, and like me, you are one of the living dead—a vampire," she said, then whispered, "and now, you're mine forever."

"But why me?" Vincenzo asked.

"Partially because I was drawn to you ever since that first dance...." She paused to run her fingers through Vincenzo's hair before continuing. "And partially to punish you for stealing my ring."

Anger filled Vincenzo. "But my father returned your ring that very night," he protested.

"No bad deed goes unpunished by me," she replied with a devilish grin.

After those chilling words, any attraction Vincenzo might have felt for her vanished, replaced by contempt and hatred.

For the next six centuries, Vincenzo endured Minerva's company as they traveled the world, amassing great wealth. As he grew stronger and learned all he could about their kind, he began to plot his escape.

In the early spring of 1948, while they were staying in the English countryside, Vincenzo went for a walk along a lonely moonlit road, contemplating how to free himself from Minerva. He came across a local couple with a flat tire. Instead of feeding on them, he felt compelled to help. The lady, remaining in the car, rolled down her window and struck up a conversation with Vincenzo as he and her husband worked on the tire.

"You look like a man with the weight of the world on his shoulders," she said. "We'd like to repay your kindness and help you, especially since you chose to help us rather than harm us."

Confused, Vincenzo asked, "What makes you think I would harm you?"

Her husband joined in, "You're a vampire, are you not?"

Vincenzo hesitated. "That I am," he replied reluctantly.

"Not to worry, we've helped your kind before," the woman said. "My name is Agnes Hornsby, and this is my husband, Edgar."

For the first time in centuries, Vincenzo felt a glimmer of hope. He smiled and responded, "A pleasure to meet you both. My name is Vincenzo Lunati."

Edgar removed the damaged tire from the car and dropped it onto the ground. He looked over at Vincenzo and asked, "So, my boy, what's troubling you?"

"I need to get away from her—my sire," he answered. "She's heartless and cruel, and I want nothing to do with her. Other than being a vampire, I am nothing like her."

"I can sense your goodness," Mrs. Hornsby replied gently. "And we know just the place to send you, where, hopefully, she'll never find you."

As Vincenzo placed the spare tire on the car, Edgar tightened the lug nuts.

"Looks like the sun will be up soon," Mrs. Hornby cautioned. "Meet us here tomorrow at midnight. Bring any valuables you don't wish to leave behind."

"And don't worry about a coffin," Edgar added, lowering the car from its jack. "We'll take care of that."

They then parted ways.

***

The next evening, Vincenzo sneaked away from Minerva and met his new benefactors at the agreed time and place.

They drove him to the Port of Whitby, a seaside town in northern England, where they met with the captain of a large cargo ship. Mr. Hornsby handed him a substantial sum of money and instructed him to change Vincenzo's surname on the manifest to: Luna.

Vincenzo turned to Mrs. Hornsby. "Agnes, I can't thank you enough for what you're doing. I don't know if I'll ever be able to repay your kindness."

"There's no need," Mrs. Hornsby replied with a smile. "This is what we do."

Mr. Hornsby shook Vincenzo's hand and said, "Take good care of yourself. Go with the captain. He's already loaded your coffin and will take you to it in the cargo hold. In less than two weeks, you'll be in your new hometown."

More than a week had passed when the captain entered the dark cargo hold and knocked on Vincenzo's coffin. He informed Vincenzo that the coffin would be unloaded later that morning and advised him to remain inside, as the coffin would be transported by train to its destination: Oliveto. There, it would be buried atop Olive Tree Hill Cemetery, marked by a simple headstone.

Once Vincenzo arrived at his destination and freed himself from his coffin, it didn't take long for him to adapt to the nightlife of the sleepy northern California village. Within a few weeks, he met someone special—an eighteen-year-old named Siena Frantoio. Smitten, he introduced himself one night as she and her friends sat in the piazza enjoying gelato.

The two became inseparable, and after numerous nightly encounters, Siena deduced that Vincenzo was not human but a vampire. They spoke at length about his past, and Siena was both intrigued and deeply saddened by his story, which only strengthened her feeling for him....

Stefano A Giovannoni

Chapter 29: Nonna, You Got Some Splainin' To Do

Nico angrily slammed the book shut. "Vincenzo was the one who raped my mother!" Nico fumed, his blood boiling as he jumped down off the dais and raced to the door.

"Nico, stop!" Sofia called out. "Where are you going?"

"I'm going to kill him," Nico yelled back as Sofia frantically tried to catch up.

"I know I shouldn't do this," she muttered, and just as Nico passed through the treasure room's door, she called out, "*Ligare* Nico!"

A thick rope suddenly appeared in front of Nico, startling him and halting him in his tracks. The magical rope wound around his legs like a boa constrictor, quickly working its way up his body and securing his hands by his side.

Now fully bound, Nico lost his balance. As he was falling backward, Sofia ran up just in time to catch him. But the unexpected weight from Nico's body caused Sofia's legs to buckle, and they both fell to the ground, with Nico in her arms.

"What did you do that for?" Nico shouted.

"What? Catch you or bind you?" Sofia responded sharply. "Either way, it was for your own good—and because I care."

The sound of rapid footsteps echoed down the stairs. Nico and Sofia looked over to see an irritated Teresa standing at the landing.

"What's going on down here?" Teresa scolded. "This is a library! You're supposed to keep quiet!"

"Says the librarian who's now yelling at us," Nico snapped.

Sensing the tension, Sofia interceded. "Nico was reacting to some unsettling news—we're really sorry about the outburst."

"Very well, but please keep it down. I have *regulars* upstairs," Teresa said sternly. "And if you're done in the treasure room, please seal it back up!"

With that, Teresa turned and marched back up the stairs.

"I'm sorry, Nico—I had to do something," Sofia said, untying the rope. "I've never seen you so enraged, and I panicked."

Nico took a deep breath and exhaled. Turning to Sofia, he said, "Thank you."

"There has to be more to the story," Sofia replied, removing the last bit of rope, which disappeared as its target was freed. "We should ask your nonna what she knows about Vincenzo and your mother—she has to know something."

"As usual, you're right," Nico agreed, standing up and brushing himself off. "Let's close up here and apologize again to Teresa."

They pushed the door shut and immediately heard the sound of seawater rushing out of the fountain's basin toward the back of the closed door. As the water hit the wood, the door and its frame began to swell until it was tightly sealed once more.

"Are you OK?" Nico asked Sofia. "You landed pretty hard when you caught me."

"There might be a few bruises," Sofia said, rubbing her backside, "but I'll be fine."

"Nice spell, by the way."

"Thanks! That Bind Object spell really came in handy—I've memorized almost all of the Malandanti spells now."

"I'll have to learn that one," Nico said as they climbed the stairs back to the library's main level.

Teresa was waiting for them at the top, keeping an eye on them while ensuring none of the *regulars* wandered downstairs out of curiosity.

"Oh, hello," Nico said, slightly embarrassed.

"Have you two calmed down?" Teresa asked.

Nico flushed, and noticing the bouquet of roses charm on Sofia's bracelet, he quickly yanked it off, jerking Sofia slightly toward him. Holding the charm behind his back, he could feel it transforming.

"Much better," Sofia said, trying to cover for whatever Nico was attempting.

Pulling the transformed bouquet of roses from behind his back, Nico smiled. "Here! These are for you. We're truly sorry about all the ruckus."

"Oh, thank you," Teresa said, smelling the bouquet of perfect red roses. "I'm just protective of the library and its contents—books, people, or what have you—I was just concerned about you two."

"And we greatly appreciate it," Sofia said warmly.

"Did you find the answers you needed?" Teresa inquired.

"Not all of them," Nico replied, then turned to Sofia. "We should get going."

"Good to see you again," Sofia said. "We'll drop by soon for a visit."

"Well, you know where to find me," Teresa said with a slight laugh as she waved goodbye.

The tan Mercedes drove them home, and as soon as they crossed the threshold, they hurried down the short hallway to speak with Chiara.

"What's with the stampede?" Chiara asked as the two stopped before her. "You almost knocked me over with your running about."

"Nonna, we've met Vincenzo Luna—and I know he knew my mother!" Nico asserted, his temper flaring once more.

Chiara replied calmly, "Now that my prophecy has been fulfilled, what would you like to know?"

Nico was thrown off by his nonna's first words. "Prophecy?" he asked, puzzled.

Suddenly, it all became clear to Sofia. "It's the cryptic one she wrote in the grimoire:"

> *When the blood of the sun meets the moon,*
> *The bound one shall be released from its tomb.*

"It all makes sense now!" Sofia blurted out. "You represent the 'sun,' but spelled S-O-N, and Vincenzo's last name means 'moon'. When you injured your hand trying to get the rose from his grave, your blood must have dripped down through the crack in the cement covering, releasing him."

Nico thought for a moment and then turned to Sofia. "That would explain why, when we returned to his grave, it had been disturbed."

"You kids are catching on—" Chiara said before being interrupted.

"So did you curse him for raping my mother?" Nico asked, his anger intensifying. "Were you afraid he'd come back for revenge? Is that why there are garlic bulbs on all the windowsills?"

"My dear Nico, Vincenzo did not rape your mother," Chiara answered calmly.

Relieved, Nico sighed. "Phew, I feel much better knowing that he's not my father."

Chiara clarified. "Nico, he is your father—and he's not a bad person. He loved your mother deeply, and she loved him. The curse I placed on him was only to spare his life."

Nico sat down on the floor, trying to collect his thoughts.

"It's time we told Nico everything, Benito," Chiara said, and the bust of Benito opened its eyes. "I'm getting weaker, so I'll let your nonno take over and explain further." Chiara closed her eyes, and her bust became still.

"Nonno, what really happened to my mother?" Nico asked.

"Unbeknownst to me, your mother had been secretly dating Vincenzo for quite some time," Benito began. "Eventually, your nonna found out and insisted on meeting him, keeping everything hidden from me."

Sofia sat down next to Nico, anxious to hear more.

Benito continued, "After meeting Vincenzo and seeing how much he cared for your mother, your nonna approved of him, even knowing he was a vampire. She kept this secret from me and even crafted a special ring that allowed Vincenzo to be human for a day, but only during each of the four primary phases of the moon."

"Ah—that must be the moon ring we found upstairs," Sofia added.

"In gratitude for your nonna's approval and the enchanted ring, he gave her the antique candelabra that she kept on her nightstand—it's supposedly linked to him magically."

Nico needed more answers. "So, if Nonna approved of their relationship, why did she end up placing a curse on him?"

Sofia added, "Yeah, she mentioned something about sparing his life."

Benito hesitated, a look of regret on his marble face. Finally, he revealed his actions. "After a few months of your mother and Vincenzo's secret relationship, I began hearing gossip. People told me they'd seen her out at night with a stranger who wasn't from Oliveto.

"One night, your mother told us she was going to the Harvest Carnival with friends. After she left, I secretly followed her and saw Vincenzo for the first time. I quickly deduced he was a vampire, and my concern for her safety grew. So, I gathered four townsmen, including Deacon Servitore, and we followed them."

Nico interrupted. "Let me guess—you confronted them at Dead Man's Path, by the cemetery?"

"Yes," Benito answered. "Your mother defended Vincenzo, standing between him and us. During the attempt to restrain Vincenzo, Siena was knocked to the ground, unconscious. Your nonna must have sensed she was in danger and arrived soon after to intercede.

"Chiara pleaded with me and the others to let Vincenzo go, but our anger and ignorance about vampires clouded our judgment. Deacon Servitore used his crucifix to weaken Vincenzo as we carried him into the cemetery and up the hill. We quickly carved a stake from an olive branch, and just as I was about to pierce his undead heart, I felt myself bound by a thick rope. I looked around and saw that the others—except Deacon Servitore—were similarly restrained—" Benito's eyes suddenly closed.

"Great, it's like reaching the climax of a TV movie and then the power goes out," Nico chuckled, shaking his head.

Sofia didn't respond; she seemed deep in thought. Nico waved his hand before Sofia's expressionless face. "Anyone home in there?"

Sofia shook herself out of it. "What?" she responded. "I'm sorry. I was just thinking. I myself used the Bind Object spell earlier today—it's a Malandanti spell, so Chiara must have cast it."

"Welcome back," Nico teased. "Well, at least now we know more of the story."

"Sounds like you were conceived out of love, not some horrible tragedy," Sofia said, "but there are still questions left unanswered."

"Definitely," Nico agreed, standing and stretching. "Like what happened to my mother after that."

"I've only known Solomon for a few months, but I can't imagine being ripped away from him, and never seeing him again," Sofia said, imagining what Siena must have endured. "Oh wow!" she said abruptly as a thought struck her.

"What?" Nico asked, curious.

"That means you are not only part-Benandanti and part-Malandanti, but also part—"

"Vampire!" Nico said, finishing her thought. "Which means the animals under the 'V' column in the grimoire are also ones that I can control."

Sofia smiled as the pieces fell into place. "The bat that got caught in my hair when we were in the subterrane—it listened to you, and so did the rats in the basement when we were here in the spring."

"So, what was the third animal on the list?" Nico asked. "I don't remember."

"Hey, let's grab something to drink—I'm a bit parched," Sofia suggested. "Then we can check the grimoire."

"Good idea—another Chinotto sounds great," Nico said. "And before I forget, I need to inscribe those spells I created during Flora's rescue!"

The two took their drinks upstairs to Chiara's attic room. At the table, Nico moved the crystal ball aside so Sofia could open the grimoire.

"Here we go," Sofia said, finding Chiara's cryptic chart. "Column one for Malandanti: ravens, lizards, and spiders; column two for Benandanti: hummingbirds, bees, and frogs; column three for Vampires: bats, rats, and wolves."

"Ooh, wolves—that could be useful!" Nico said, excited.

"Really?" Sofia scoffed. "And when have you seen a wolf in Oliveto?"

"I haven't, but there were paw prints outside of Remus's window," Nico answered.

Sofia set her drink down. "Omigod, I totally forgot."

Nico was about to bring the grimoire to the desk when he noticed Sofia's charm bracelet flash.

"I hope Teresa wasn't fond of those roses," he snickered.

Sofia looked down and saw the bouquet of roses charm had returned. "We really do need to find a way to help her gain her freedom."

"At least she has the enchanted nautilus brooch my nonna made, allowing her to leave the library for short periods," Nico said, sitting down at the desk.

"True, but it's not enough," Sofia replied. "She's helped us twice with important information."

"You're right," Nico agreed, inscribing the three new spells into the grimoire. When he finished, an idea popped into his head. "Since this room is turning into our magical headquarters, maybe we should redecorate. I wish there was a spell to create a giant chalkboard or whiteboard to keep track of everything."

"Could you bring me a piece of paper?" Sofia asked. "And a pen."

Nico took a blank sheet from the desk drawer. "Here you go—I just need to summon a pen from downstairs, unless you want to write with a quill?"

"Pen, please," Sofia replied, holding out her hand.

Nico summoned a pen from Sofia's purse and handed it to her.

"This looks familiar," Sofia said, inspecting the pen.

"It's yours—it's from your purse," Nico explained. "The spell only works if I've seen the object before and can visualize it in its current location. Your pen is the only one that I recall seeing."

"Oh, right," Sofia responded and titled the top of the page: *Magical To-Do List* and continued aloud, "Number One—save the town from Caleo's wrath; Number Two—finish hearing the rest of Chiara and Benito's story about Siena and Vincenzo; Number Three—find a way to free Teresa."

"We might be able to finish Number Two in a couple of hours," Nico suggested.

Sofia put her hand on Nico's shoulder, while touching their newly written list, and said, "*Excresco!*" The paper enlarged to the size of a refrigerator.

"Check the drawers for some thumbtacks so we can pin this to the wall," she directed.

Nico found the tacks, and they secured the giant paper to the wall, stepping back to admire it.

"Well done," Nico commended. "Very clever."

They spent the next few hours reorganizing the room. Nico summoned extra chairs from the kitchen and a small sofa that had previously been stored in the basement.

"Much better," Sofia said, while eyeing their work.

"I like it—now we can have Fawn and Solomon over next time we brainstorm."

Sofia turned to Nico. "You read my mind."

Nico raised his hands to his temples in mock concentration. "I'm sensing…you're hungry."

Sofia's stomach began to rumble loudly, making them both laugh.

"My stomach doesn't lie," Sofia said. "How about I make us *spaghetti aglio e olio*? The gnomes just harvested fresh garlic from the garden."

"Perfect—you know it's my favorite!" Nico said, and they headed to the kitchen.

After a simple yet delicious meal, they returned to the short hallway, waiting by the Mirror of the Dead. Chiara's eyes opened, and she let out a yawn.

"You're back—where did your nonno leave off?"

Nico recapped, "He was about to stake Vincenzo when thick ropes appeared around everyone except Deacon Servitore."

Chiara smirked. "Ah yes, such a handy spell," she said, then continued. "I arrived just in time to prevent a grave mistake. I confessed that I'd known about Siena and Vincenzo's relationship all along and warned your nonno that it would break your mother's heart if she ever found out her own father had destroyed the man she loved so deeply."

Sofia interrupted, "So, you made a deal and bound Vincenzo in a grave?"

"Exactly," Chiara answered. "Your nonno understood that I was right about one thing: killing Vincenzo would also destroy the relationship he had with Siena. So, I proposed placing Vincenzo in a state of torpor, bound to his coffin. The men believed that I meant forever, but I secretly added the caveat to my spell, allowing a way for Vincenzo to be set free—thus, the prophecy. I also discretely removed his moon ring, so that he wouldn't become human during the four primary phases of the moon and suffocate while buried."

"Clever," Sofia whispered to Nico. "I like how she thinks."

"But what about my mother?" Nico asked. "Why doesn't she remember?"

Chiara explained, "Deacon Servitore brought her back to the house, and I ordered him to remain silent. But over time, rumors spread, twisting the story into the version you must have heard. I couldn't bear to see her heartbroken, so I gave her the Tea of Forgetfulness to wipe away her memories."

"Nonna, she's starting to remember things," Nico shared. "I think Vincenzo sent her flowers on Mother's Day, and that's when things began to resurface. The other day, when I visited her at the real estate office, she recognized the roses I gave her—they came from the bush that had originally grown out of Vincenzo's grave. She also mentioned that images, like 'unknown memories,' as she called them, have been popping into her head the last two months."

Sofia quickly added, "And don't forget that night at The Griffon's Paw's grand opening when Vincenzo approached her, and she fainted."

"True love can overcome many things, even the power of the Tea of Forgetfulness—you can't repress memories of the heart forever," Chiara said with a smile before closing her eyes and falling silent once more.

Nico sighed. "Now we finally know the whole story."

"Don't you feel better knowing the truth?" Sofia asked. "At one point, you were determined to kill your father."

"Thank you for being the voice of reason," Nico acknowledged. "That could have turned into an awful mess."

"And now we know why you heal from wounds so quickly—it's the vampire blood in your veins," Sofia added, focusing on the positive as more realizations dawned on her. "Oh, and didn't you say that when Negroni scratched you, she drank some of your blood? That would explain how she returned from her grave—"

"So then my vampire kitty has been surviving off of rodent's blood...it all makes sense now," Nico interrupted. "But why don't I crave blood?"

"You haven't died yet," Sofia suggested. "Maybe that's why?"

"I guess that's another mystery to add to our list for later. Let's go watch TV." Nico said with a grin.

Stefano A Giovannoni

Chapter 30: Happy Birthday?

The following week, Nico and Sofia transformed the upstairs attic into their own cozy clubhouse, adding more furniture, a large chalkboard, and even a mini fridge for cold drinks. Each afternoon, they gathered around the circular table to strategize their plan to return the thirteen Coins of Favor to Caleo while minimizing any risks to their lives. Using the chalkboard, they diagrammed various options, carefully considering each possible outcome, preparing themselves for whatever challenges might come their way.

Most evenings were spent with Solomon and Fawn, out and about, until someone suggested going to The Griffon's Claw. At that point, Nico would excuse himself and head home.

One evening, Nico had a brilliant idea to host an open house for his friends. Before the evening's impressive formal dinner, prepared and served by the house, Nico gave Solomon and Fawn a tour of his home. In the basement, they finally met Negroni and Buddy, whom Nico and Sofia had often mentioned. Buddy, thrilled to meet a fellow construct in Solomon, followed him around like a little puppy. As the tour ended, Buddy seemed almost sad to see Solomon leave the basement.

As the days drew closer to his and his mother's joint birthday party, Nico confided in Sofia and revealed his unease. "I'm still trying to come to terms about Vincenzo," he admitted.

"You mean your father?" Sofia asked gently.

"I can hardly bring myself to call him that," Nico answered. "I mean, he looks like he should be in college with us."

Sofia placed a comforting hand on his shoulder. "Remember, he's over six hundred years old. Try to see beyond appearances."

Nico gave a small smile. "Yeah, you have a point. But I'm not sure how to start."

"Baby steps, Nico," Sofia advised. "You have plenty of time to get to know each other—well, he does, anyway!"

"Thank you," Nico said, chuckling at Sofia's attempt to cheer him up with humor.

***

The morning of the birthday celebration finally arrived. Sofia had spent the night with Solomon, while Nico enjoyed a quiet, restful night alone in the house.

Nico awoke to a thud at the front door. Assuming it was the morning paper, he got out of bed and went to retrieve it. But as he opened the door, he was startled to find Sofia standing there, holding the latest edition of *L'Essenziale*.

"Well, good morning," Sofia greeted cheerfully. "Are you going to let me by?"

"Oh, right," Nico said, taking the newspaper from her and stepping back into the foyer to let her in. "Would you like some breakfast? I was craving a *frittata* this morning."

"Thanks, but I already ate with Solomon and his parents," Sofia answered. "I'm going to shower, then I'll join you for a cappuccino—see you in a bit."

Nico went to the kitchen and asked the house to make him breakfast and a *cappuccino*. He removed the rubber band from the newspaper and unfolded it. Today's headline read:

Husband of Founding Family Member Dies Tragically.

A chill ran through him. *Who could it have been?* he thought. *What if it was my dad?*

Delaying the inevitable, he waited for his cappuccino to arrive before reading. Just then, the phone rang, startling him. "Hello?" he answered, his voice shaky.

"Nico, it's your mother." Siena said calmly.

"Is…Dad OK?" he stammered.

"Of course. Why wouldn't he be?" She paused. "Are you all right? You sound like you're about to have a panic attack."

228

Nico exhaled in relief. "I'm OK—I just saw the headline in the paper and was worried."

"Yes, very sad news," she replied. "It was Vanda Moraiolo's husband, Giovanni."

"Oh, no!" Nico gasped.

"I think you went to school with their daughter, Aurora. She was a year younger than you but quite bright and skipped a grade."

"I just saw her recently too! She came home from college for the summer to help her mother at the restaurant."

Changing the subject, Siena reminded him about their party that evening. "Your dad and I have gone all out for this celebration—I even invited all of your friends."

Nico was quiet for a moment before saying, "Mother, aside from Sofia, you don't really know any of my friends."

"I had some help from Sofia. She seems to know everyone," Siena laughed.

"Oh, OK," Nico said, deciding not to delve into what Sofia may or may not have told his mother. "What time should we arrive?"

"Anytime between six-thirty and seven."

"Got it. See you then." Nico said, hanging up.

As he returned to his seat, a plated *frittata* floated over, accompanied by silverware and a napkin, landing neatly in front of him.

Just then, Sofia entered the kitchen, her hair wrapped up in a towel, and sat down beside Nico. She noticed the newspaper's front page and, with a look of panic, turned to him.

Anticipating her concern, Nico quickly reassured her, "It wasn't my dad—it was Aurora's."

Sofia read the article. "How terrible—what a horrible way to die!" she exclaimed.

"I haven't read it yet—how did it happen?"

"It says he died from multiple spider bites."

"Really? What kind of spider?" Nico asked.

"*Latrodectus tredecimguttatus*, which is strange," Sofia said, puzzled by the species of Black Widow mentioned in the article.

"That's a black widow, right?"

"It is, but that species is from Europe," Sofia explained. "The only species here in California is *Latrodectus hesperus*."

"Ew!" Nico shivered. "Even though I can control spiders, black widows are still the one kind that creeps me out."

Sofia asked the house for a cappuccino and continued reading while Nico ate his breakfast.

"By the way," Sofia said as she finished the article, "did I hear the phone ring earlier?"

"Yes, it was my mother," Nico answered. "She just wanted to remind us of tonight's party and said to be there between six-thirty and seven."

"Cool. I'm looking forward to it," Sofia said, taking a sip of her *cappuccino*.

After Nico finished breakfast, they spent the rest of the morning and afternoon being lazy, staying indoors to avoid the day's intense heat, until evening arrived. They dressed up for the party, met in the foyer as usual, and then drove to Siena's home.

As the tan Mercedes climbed the hill to the party location, they were surprised to see how many cars lined the street and cul-de-sac; the guest list appeared to be larger than Nico had anticipated. With no close parking available, Nico asked the car to drop them off in front of the Kynigos's home. The birthday boy and his best friend exited the car and walked down the lit pathway, passing by cypress trees and neatly trimmed boxwoods, until they reached the front door.

All seemed to be quiet, and Nico noticed the front door was slightly ajar. *Hmm, this is odd*, he thought as they entered the foyer.

"Surprise!" shouted over fifty guests, including Fawn, Sterling, Lisette, Mr. and Mrs. Schwartzman, and Solomon. Nico looked around the room and noticed Gino among the crowd. Although Gino had his back turned, Nico recognized him instantly by his stature and ash-blond hair.

"I'm going to kill you," he half-jokingly whispered to Sofia, pinching her side. "You told my mother to invite *him*, too?"

"Easy there, tiger," Sofia said. "This is partly a celebration of you, and your mother and I wanted to make sure you were surrounded by people who care about you—I believe Gino is one of those people."

Siena rushed over to Nico. "*Buon Compleanno!*" she exclaimed, hugging her son.

"*Buon Compleanno*, mother," Nico responded half-heartedly, still distracted by Gino's unexpected presence.

Various townspeople, mostly Siena's friends celebrating her birthday, approached Nico to offer their well wishes. Seizing the moment, Siena slipped away to turn on some music and get the party started.

Once Nico finished greeting everyone, he realized Sofia had long left his side. Scanning the room, he noticed her with Solomon, Fawn, and Lisette in the formal living room.

"There you all are," Nico said, relieved to be back with people near his own age.

"Happy Birthday!" Solomon exclaimed, patting him on the back.

Lisette and Fawn approached Nico together, each kissing one of his cheeks and wishing him a happy birthday.

"Thank you," Nico said. "It means a lot that you're here. Can I get you all something to drink? Beer, soda, wine?"

Solomon, of course, asked for a beer, as did Fawn and Lisette, who now seemed inseparable.

"If it's not too much trouble," a voice behind Nico said, "I'd like a beer as well."

Nico turned and saw Gino standing there, smiling.

"Uh, yes," Nico said awkwardly, then composed himself. "Of course. I'll be right back—Sofia, could you help me with the drinks?"

Sofia stood close to Solomon, staring dreamily into his eyes, and didn't hear Nico.

Solomon whispered to her, "I think Nico needs your help."

"Oh, sorry! Yes, let me help," Sofia said, quickly giving Solomon a kiss before heading off with Nico to the kitchen.

Siena, making her rounds, noticed Nico and Sofia heading to the kitchen. She stopped them, asking, "Nico, are you enjoying everything?"

"Yes mother—it's quite the party," Nico answered. "But where's Remus?"

"He's upstairs resting," Siena explained. "The new medication Dr. Matto prescribed for his anxiety made him drowsy, so Gigi is watching over him."

Sofia went to the kitchen island where the drinks were kept, searching for beer.

"Is there something you're looking for, dear?" Siena asked.

"Do you have any beer?" Sofia said as she looked over the drink selection.

Siena checked the drink station. "Looks like someone took the last one," she said, then turned to Nico. "There's more in the garage—Nico will show you where. Oh, and I forgot to mention, Aurora called to say she couldn't make it—for obvious reasons—and she asked me to wish you a happy birthday."

"Thank you for letting me know," Nico replied, then turned to Sofia. "Come with me."

Nico led Sofia through a door off the kitchen and into the garage.

"Wow, this is a large garage," Sofia marveled, looking around.

Nico walked over to a spare refrigerator and opened it. "Ah, jackpot—more beer!"

Sofia was on the other side of the garage near Pétros's work bench. "Hey Nico, come here."

Nico closed the refrigerator door and went over. "What is it?"

Sofia pointed to a shelf above a pegboard filled with various tools. Lined up on the shelf were mason jars of different sizes, each containing what appeared to be teeth.

"I've never noticed these before," Nico said, astonished.

Sofia took down a jar labeled: λύκος and handed it to Nico, then grabbed another labeled: βρυκόλακας.

"Do you know what the labels mean?" Sofia asked.

"It's all Greek to me—literally," Nico joked. "All I can tell is that each jar holds the canine teeth of a different animal."

Sofia looked around and noticed a locked rack against one wall containing a rifle, a shotgun, a revolver, and a crossbow.

"Is your dad a hunter?" Sofia asked.

Nico saw what she meant. "Yes, but I don't think he hunts anymore. He doesn't like leaving my mother and Remus alone at home."

Sofia walked over to the weapon rack. "These look very old."

"They are—they belonged to his father."

"I see the connection now," Sofia reasoned. "A dentist who hunts—he must be keeping the canines as souvenirs."

"I guess it's better than taxidermy," Nico said.

Suddenly, a wailing sound coming from outside startled them, sending chills down their spines.

Sofia put her hand on Nico's forearm and squeezed. "I hope that was just a strong gust of wind."

"I don't think it was," Nico said quietly, moving to a side door. He unlocked and opened it, poking his head out to check, but everything was calm. "I heard that exact same sound last night—I think it was Orla, the town Banshee, announcing that another will die tonight."

"That would make two deaths in such a short time," Sofia mused.

Not wanting to dwell on the inevitable, Nico changed the subject. "Come on, let's get those beers and rejoin the party."

"Yeah, don't want to keep Gino waiting," Sofia teased.

They returned to the kitchen, popped the beer caps off, and rejoined their friends.

"Welcome back, pretty lady," Solomon greeted Sofia as she handed him a beer.

"Fawn, Lisette, here you go," Nico said, passing them their drinks, then looking around. "Where did Gino go?"

"He got a page and had to go back to the mortuary—someone must have died," Fawn said, handing Nico a colorful envelope from Gino. "But he wanted you to have this."

"That was kind of him—I'll open it later," Nico said and slipped the card into his pocket.

"Nico, *excusez-moi*, is there any food?" Lisette asked, slightly shaky. "It was busy today at work, and I didn't have time to eat—I'm feeling a bit peckish."

"Yes, of course. Let's head to the kitchen—there's plenty of food there," Nico suggested. "We definitely don't want you drinking on an empty stomach."

The group moved to the kitchen, chatting with other guests as they passed.

"Wow, look at all that yummy food!" Lisette exclaimed to Fawn.

Fawn grabbed a plate for Lisette and began adding items. "Here, you have to try one of these," she said, adding a meatball, "and this prosciutto-wrapped melon looks amazing!"

Nico whispered to Sofia, "I didn't expect that to happen so quickly—they act like a married couple already."

"Another perfect match," Sofia said, turning to Solomon. "Just like Sol and me."

"Guess I'm destined to be a lonely cat dad," Nico joked.

Suddenly, a crash sounded from the garage, causing everyone nearby to turn.

Nico's dad rushed in. "Nothing to worry about—probably just a fallen box," Pétros announced, raising the stereo volume. "Please go back to enjoying yourselves."

"You know, I think I left the side door open," Nico whispered to Sofia as he watched his dad enter the garage. "Hopefully, a raccoon or something didn't wander in looking for food."

A tipsy Sofia joked, "Maybe whatever left those paw prints outside Remus' bedroom is back—"

"That's not even funny," Nico snapped, growing increasingly worried about his dad's safety.

With the music turned up, Nico and his friends joined the guests in dancing.

Then came another loud thud, followed by shouting from the garage. No one but Nico seemed to notice. Overcome by a sense of dread, he quickly bolted into the garage to check on his dad.

Inside, he found Pétros pointing a loaded crossbow at Vincenzo. Nico shut the door behind him, hoping to keep others unaware of the confrontation.

"I already warned you to stay away from my wife," Pétros said, releasing the trigger.

Nico watched in terror as the bolt sped toward Vincenzo's heart, only for him to catch it mid-flight. Enraged, Vincenzo redirected the bolt at Pétros. Nico leapt in front of Pétros, shouting, "Father, no!"

But his warning was in vain. Vincenzo had already released the bolt from his grip, hurling it toward Pétros, but missing his mark. The projectile pierced Nico's shoulder, and he collapsed into his dad's arms.

"Nico, my boy, you're going to be OK—just stay calm," Pétros said as he gently lowered his son to the ground. Nico's vision blurred as he started losing consciousness. Just before everything faded, he saw Vincenzo transform into a wolf and escape through the open side door.

Pétros hurried to one of the cabinets, retrieving a worn leather medicine bag. Kneeling beside Nico, he opened it and took out a small vial of ochre-colored liquid. He opened it and poured a single drop of the strange fluid directly onto the embedded crossbow bolt. The bolt began to dissolve, leaving only the open wound in Nico's shoulder.

Nico started to come to, his vision slightly blurry, as he watched his dad soak a handkerchief with another mysterious liquid and press it to the wound. Seeing that Nico was alert, Pétros asked, "Are you OK?"

With his dad's help, Nico attempted to sit up. "I'm OK," he said, looking around for signs of Vincenzo. "Dad, is he gone?"

"Yes," Pétros answered, still visibly upset. "That coward ran as soon as you were hit."

"We should get back inside before people start wondering where we went," Nico suggested.

"You're in no shape to return to the party," Pétros said, removing the handkerchief to examine Nico's wound. "What is this?"

"I don't know Dad, I can't see," Nico replied, trying to view his wound. "What's wrong?"

"The wound…it's already closed and starting to scab over," Pétros remarked in amazement.

"The bolt probably didn't penetrate that deeply," Nico speculated, standing up slowly. "I'll be fine. Do you have a T-shirt I can borrow? I can't go back in there with a bloody hole in my shirt."

Pétros quickly went back into the house, grabbed one of his T-shirts from the laundry room, and returned. Sofia, having noticed the comings and goings of Nico's dad, came into the garage to check on them.

Hearing the door open again, Nico turned, still in the process of wiping dried blood from his bare torso. Sofia hurried over and asked Pétros, "What happened here?"

Pétros hesitated until Nico said, "It's OK, Dad. You can tell her."

As Nico slipped on the borrowed T-shirt, Pétros recounted the events to Sofia.

"OK, go back inside—Siena is probably looking for you by now," Sofia instructed Pétros. "Nico and I will be in shortly."

As Pétros left, Sofia turned to Nico, "Are you OK?"

"I'm fine," Nico replied with a reassuring smile as he ran a hand through his hair. "But that was a close call. Vincenzo almost killed my dad."

"How much do you think your dad knows?" Sofia asked.

Nico chuckled. "Oh, he knows something, all right," he said. "I think he has a few secrets of his own, too!"

"Well, we'll worry about that later. If you're OK, then we should get back inside—I think your mother's about to bring out the cake."

"And knowing her, she probably got my favorite—Italian Rum Cake." Nico said, his spirits lifting as they returned to rejoin their friends.

After several birthday toasts, Nico and his mother blew out the candles on their cake and cut slices for their remaining guests.

As the evening wound down and the guests began to leave, Siena came over and gave Nico a big hug and kiss on the cheek.

"Ouch!" Nico exclaimed.

"Are you OK?" Siena asked.

"Oh, yeah—I just strained my shoulder lifting some boxes earlier today. It's still a bit sore," Nico said.

"Well, I hope it feels better soon." Siena said. "I'm so glad you made it to the party. I rarely get to spend time with you anymore. I miss the days before you went off to college, when we'd go downtown for breakfast or lunch together during the week."

"Those will always be some of my favorite memories," Nico responded, slightly teary-eyed. "Well, we should get going. If you need help cleaning up tomorrow, just let me know."

"Thank you, but we'll manage," Siena said. "Besides, you should rest that shoulder."

Sofia hugged Siena goodbye. "Thank you for inviting me, and *buon compleanno a te!*"

"*Grazie,*" Siena responded, then walked Nico and his friends to the door.

After the rest said their goodbyes to their hostess, they met up with Nico and Sofia, who were waiting for them on the sidewalk.

"Is everyone OK to drive?" Nico asked. "If not, let me know and I'll make sure you get home safely."

Solomon chimed in, "I didn't drink much and am totally sober now—I can take the girls home."

"Perfect," Nico said. "Sofia, are you coming with me, or going with him?"

"I think I should go home with you tonight," Sofia answered, reflecting on the evening's events. She gave Solomon a goodnight kiss. "Sol, I'll see you tomorrow."

Stefano A Giovannoni

Chapter 31: Breakfast with Dad

The next morning, Sofia was up early, enjoying her *cappuccino*, when the phone rang precisely at 8:30 a.m.

"Hello?" she answered.

"Good morning, Sofia, it's Pétros."

"Good morning. Is everything OK?"

"Yes, everything's fine," Pétros replied. "Is my son up? I was hoping he's free for coffee."

"He's still asleep, but I can wake him."

"No, that's OK. He probably needs his rest after last night's incident. Just have him call me when he's up."

"Will do!" Sofia said, hanging up the phone. She returned to her coffee, debating whether to wake Nico but decided to let him sleep a bit longer.

She opened the morning paper, and the headline caught her eye.

"Wow!" Sofia exclaimed.

"Wow, what?" Nico asked as he entered the kitchen.

"Good, you're finally up. Your dad called," Sofia said.

"Thanks, I'll give him a call after I have some caffeine," Nico replied, asking the house for coffee and toast with orange marmalade. "So, what were you 'wowing' about?"

Sofia slid the newspaper over to him. The headline read:

Another Death Adds to Record Total.

"So, it really was Orla's wail we heard last night."

"Oh. Well, we kind of already knew someone would die last night," Nico said.

"True, but read on," Sofia directed. "Wait until you see who it was."

Nico rubbed his eyes and focused on the small print. When he reached the paragraph revealing the name of the deceased, he gulped and looked at Sofia in silence.

"I know, right?" Sofia said, recognizing his disbelief.

Nico read aloud, "Santo Servitore, beloved deacon of St. Anthony's Catholic Church, died early last evening. The deacon, a known hemophiliac, apparently slipped while getting out of the bathtub, striking his head and losing consciousness as he bled out. Father Michael, of the same parish, discovered the body shortly after…."

"What a horrible way to die," Sofia said, after a moment's silence. "I wonder how much of that narrative is a cover-up for what really happened?"

"And to think he was partially involved in the cover-up about my mother," Nico added. "Want my other piece of toast? I've kind of lost my appetite."

"Sure, I'll take it," Sofia said, reaching for it. "And remember to call your dad back now that you're up."

"Right, I better do that now—he doesn't like to be kept waiting." Nico rose to make the call.

"Hello?"

"Dad, it's Nico. You called?"

"Yes. Can you meet me for breakfast downtown in fifteen minutes?" Pétros asked. "We need to talk about last night."

"All right," Nico agreed. "Where should I meet you?"

"How about Enchanted Doughnuts? I remember you used to love their maple buttermilk bars."

At the mention of his favorite doughnut, Nico's appetite returned. "Sure! I'll see you there in fifteen."

"Sofia, I won't be gone long," Nico called while rushing out of the kitchen to get dressed.

"OK!" Sofia replied.

***

Nico parked a few doors down from Enchanted Doughnuts, spotting his dad waiting for him.

"Good morning, Sport," Pétros said, holding the door open.

240

"Hey, Dad."

"Hi, Dr. Kynigos," the young hostess greeted giddily. "Table for two? Or would you prefer to sit at the counter?"

"Good morning, Gracie," Pétros answered. "A table in the back, please."

"Certainly. Please follow me."

Once seated, Gracie started to hand them menus, but Pétros declined. "We already know what we want. Two coffees, a maple buttermilk bar for my son—"

"—and a blueberry corn muffin for my dad," Nico finished.

"Right away," Gracie said, leaving to get them coffee.

"Ah, you remembered my order!" Pétros said to Nico. "It's been a long time since we've had breakfast together."

"How could I forget? Those mornings were special."

Gracie returned with two cups of piping hot coffee, along with cream and sugar, and set them on the table. "I'll be back shortly with your two pastries."

As she walked away, Pétros leaned in. "So, about last night—I thought we should talk. I'm sure you have questions, as do I."

"I have a few—" Nico began, but Gracie returned, placing their pastries before them.

"Can I get you anything else?"

"No," both Nico and his dad said in unison.

As Gracie left, Nico continued, "I have a few questions, mainly about how much you seem to know. You didn't seem fazed when confronting Vincenzo in the garage."

"True. I've dealt with his kind before—or creatures like him," Pétros explained. "I suppose it's time you knew what I am?"

"You mean you're not a *regular*?"

Pétros chuckled. "A '*regular*'? What does that mean?"

"It's what certain townspeople call non-magical humans," Nico said, wincing as he burned his tongue on the hot coffee. "Damn, that's hot!"

"Have a piece of your doughnut; the sugar will help ease the pain."

Nico broke off a piece of his doughnut and took a bite. *Omigod, I forgot how delicious their doughnuts are*, he thought.

"To be clear, I'm not quite a *regular* but not exactly magical either," Pétros explained. "I come from a long line of Hunters."

"Hunters?" Nico asked, intrigued. "I've never heard of them."

"In Greece, my father and grandfather taught me their skills, training me to become a Vrykolakas hunter, just like them."

"OK, let's take a step back," Nico said, totally engrossed in the conversation. "What's a Vrykolakas?"

Pétros looked around, then lowered his voice. "It's similar to a vampire, but craves flesh—mainly the liver of their victims—instead of blood."

"So, like a mix of a vampire and a ghoul?" Nico asked, trying to get clarification.

"Yeah," Pétros replied, buttering his muffin.

Nico blew on his coffee before taking another careful sip, his mind swirling with what felt like a million questions.

"Honestly, I came to America to leave those old-world traditions behind," Pétros said. "I settled in Southern California, worked my way through dental school, and eventually graduated at the top of my class."

"How did you end up in Oliveto?" Nico asked.

"An older dentist here needed a successor," Pétros explained. "He spoke with our dean, who recommended me. He offered me the job and a place to live, so I jumped at the opportunity."

"And then eventually you met my mother?"

"Yes, and soon after, Chiara and Benito as well," Pétros answered.

"And my nonna approved?"

"Well," Pétros replied, "one day, she asked to meet with me privately. Somehow, she already knew I was planning to propose to your mother in the coming days. She then set me down and asked what felt like a hundred questions to make sure I was the right one for her daughter."

Nico was about to take another piece of his doughnut but stopped, anxious to keep the conversation going. "And you obviously passed."

"I did," Pétros replied, taking another bite of his muffin. "That's when she told me about Oliveto's magical inhabitants and its history."

"So, then you've known about me all this time?" Nico asked.

"Yes. Your nonna gave me a vague explanation of your family's mixed magical bloodlines and what happened to your mother, but she left out details about who—or what—your father was. She told me she'd erased part of your mother's memory to protect her and made me promise never to speak about her magical past, for fear it might trigger memories of your father."

Nico felt a mix of emotions. "So, you live as *regulars* to protect my mother from her past?"

"Exactly," Pétros replied. "That was the promise I made to your nonna so I could marry your mother—and I'd do it all over again to keep her safe."

"That's very commendable," Nico complimented. "Thank you for taking such good care of her—and me—all of these years."

Gracie returned with the check and topped off their coffees. "No rush, just pay up front when you're ready to leave."

"Thank you, Gracie," Pétros said, then turned to his son. "So, if Vincenzo's a vampire, you must have vampire blood, which explains a lot."

"You must think I'm a monster," Nico said, worried about what his dad might think of him.

"A monster? No. A remarkable son? Yes." Nico eyes teared up as Pétros continued. "Nothing will ever change that."

"Thank you. That means a lot," Nico said, holding back his emotions.

"Now, as I was saying, your vampire blood explains how you healed quickly from the crossbow bolt and why Remus has been acting out."

Nico pondered. "How would this affect my brother?"

Pétros took the last bite of his muffin, washed it down with coffee, and continued. "Well, Remus just became a teenager, and aside from the surge of hormones, that's usually when a hunter's instincts start to kick in."

"So, you think that's why he's been aggressive toward me—because he sensed my vampire blood and saw me as a threat?" Nico asked.

"I'd say that explains his erratic behavior as of late," Pétros said.

"Hmm. And if the wolf prints Sofia and I found outside the house were from Vincenzo in wolf form, then it would explain why Remus has been having trouble sleeping and says he's been seeing things outside his window—poor kid." Nico felt a pang of guilt. "It's all my fault!" he murmured, lowering his head.

Pétros, concerned, reached over. "How could any of this be your fault?"

"I'm the one who freed Vincenzo—it was my blood that broke the spell binding him!"

"I'm sure you didn't do it knowingly. You can't blame yourself," Pétros assured him, touching Nico's shoulder. "Now stop thinking such nonsense."

Nico looked up. "But I've disrupted our family—my poor brother unknowingly wants to kill me!"

"Nico, there's no need to worry," Pétros said comfortingly. "I'll explain everything to Remus and help him learn to control his feelings. We just need to keep Vincenzo away from your mother. I fear if her memories come back, it may end our marriage."

Nico wiped his eyes. "What you and my mother share is true love— I'll make sure Vincenzo doesn't destroy it!"

"Just be careful," Pétros advised. "You're an adult now, living on your own, so I can't protect you like I do your mother and brother."

Nico tried to hold back a smile. "Dad, if you only knew what I've experienced in the past few months, you'd know I'll be OK. So please don't worry about me—just keep my mother and Remus safe."

"Speaking of which, I should get back home and check on them," Pétros said, reaching for the check. "Ready to go?"

"Yeah," Nico said, standing.

They approached the cashier, and as Pétros paid, Nico eyed the case of delectable doughnuts.

"Thank you for breakfast, Dad. I'll talk to you later—I'm going to get a couple of doughnuts for Sofia."

"You're welcome," Pétros said, patting Nico's back. "I'll tell your mother and brother you said hello."

"Thanks," Nico replied, then turned to Gracie, choosing two apple fritter doughnuts to take home.

***

Nico returned home and called out to Sofia, but the house was quiet.

Hmm, where could she be, Nico wondered, then had an idea. "House, where's Sofia?"

244

The hallway lights to *la stanza naturale* flickered, and he guessed she was upstairs. He made his way to the hidden room, and at the top of the stairs, he thought he heard talking. Putting his ear to the door, he could just barely make out Sofia's voice—it sounded like she was speaking Latin.

Nico quickly opened the door, startling Sofia, who quickly raised her hands and shouted, *"Aranea!"*

Strands of spider silk shot from Sofia's palms toward Nico, who dodged just in time to avoid being cocooned.

"I'm so sorry!" Sofia gasped, lowering her hands. "You scared me!"

Nico looked over at the now-webbed door. "That was a close one!" he said. "What's going on? Are you OK?"

"I've just been so engrossed in learning Malandanti spells that I didn't hear you come home," Sofia admitted.

"You make it sound like this isn't the first time you've been up here alone."

"Truth be told, it's not," Sofia confessed. "I've been coming up here nightly to study the Malandanti side of the grimoire. I think I almost have all the spells memorized."

"Don't you think you're becoming a little obsessed?" Nico teased. "If could take you to Dr. Matto for some therapy sessions."

Sofia shook her head with a smirk.

"Here, these are for you," Nico said, holding out the bag of doughnuts.

Sofia took the bag and looked inside. "Ah thanks! These look and smell amazing—and you got my favorite!"

"Of course. I know how much you love apple fritter doughnuts, and Enchanted Doughnuts make the best."

Sofia took a bite and moaned. "Oh, this is so good."

"Other than a slice of toast, did you skip breakfast?" Nico asked, amused.

"I wasn't hungry earlier. The toast and *cappuccino* seemed enough—but enough about me, how was breakfast with your dad?"

"I learned a lot!"

Sofia went over to the sofa and sat down. "Come sit, and tell me everything."

"Well, my dad already knew a lot, except that Vincenzo is a vampire."

"After last night, I bet he figured it out pretty quickly," Sofia joked, taking another bite.

Nico chuckled. "Now, here's what I found out: my dad is a Vrykolakas hunter."

"A what?" Sofia asked, licking glaze off her fingers.

"I wondered the same thing. Apparently, all the men in his family back in Greece are trained to hunt and eliminate all Vrykolakas—they're like vampires but feed on flesh instead of blood."

"Ew!" Sofia interrupted. "I'll take a classic vampire, thank you."

"Thanks," Nico joked. "I feel special now that I'm at least partially included in that category."

Sofia finished her doughnut. "You know, we could really use an espresso machine up here—I really need something to wash down all this sugary goodness."

"Let's go downstairs and talk there," Nico suggested, rising from the sofa.

"Good idea, but we'll need to clear the webs off the door first—the spell said they'd be strong."

Nico walked over and pulled one of the silken strands; it had impressive tensile strength. He tried the Revoke Spell. "*Revocare,*" he commanded, but nothing happened. "Strange, that didn't work."

"Maybe there's a limited window of time to revoke spells before they become permanent or fade on their own?" Sofia suggested. "Those spider webs have been there for at least ten minutes now."

"I think you're on to something," Nico agreed. "The other times we used the spell, it was within five or six minutes of casting the original spell—I should note that in the grimoire." Nico took the grimoire over to the desk and added the observation to the spell's page.

"Sofia," Nico called. "Since you now know the Malandanti side of the book by heart, is there a spell that might help?"

Sofia shook her head. "I can't think of one."

Nico flipped through the grimoire, stopping when he saw his nonna's folded note. *That's it*, he thought, then closed the grimoire.

"Did you find something useful?" Sofia asked.

Nico got up and approached the webbed door. "I think I have the solution," he said, concentrating.

Sofia watched patiently, but nothing seemed to happen at first.

Then Nico spoke. "Come to our aid and free this door."

Sofia continued watching, playfully pretending to yawn and check her Swatch for the time.

But soon, something happened. From beneath the door, a spider crept through a small gap and climbed onto the web. Sofia, not fond of spiders, backed away and suddenly let out a shriek.

Nico quickly turned to see her stepping onto a chair in panic as spiders emerged from every corner of the room, crawling toward the door to join the first one. They watched as the obedient spiders quickly dismantled the web, rolled the filaments into a large ball, and retreated to where they'd come from, allowing Nico to open the door freely.

"Good work, my friends."

Sofia stepped down from the chair, grabbed her bag of doughnuts, and followed Nico downstairs to the kitchen.

Stefano A Giovannoni

Chapter 32: Dinner with Father

Sofia sat down at the kitchen island and pulled out the remaining apple fritter doughnut.

"Do you want another *cappuccino*, or maybe some coffee this time?" Nico asked.

"Coffee—it goes better with doughnuts," Sofia answered. So Nico ground some beans and started brewing a pot of coffee, the non-magical way.

Ring, ring.

"I'll get it," Sofia said, heading over to answer the phone. "Hello?"

"Is Nico Frantoio there?" an unfamiliar female voice asked.

"Yes, one moment—let me get him for you," Sofia replied. She put her hand over the receiver and whispered, "Nico, it's for you."

"Who is it?" he asked softly.

"I don't know—some chick," Sofia teased. "You sure are popular today!"

Nico went over and took the handset from Sofia. "Hello, this is Nico."

"Nico, this is Payton—I work at The Griffon's Claw," the bartender said.

"OK," Nico responded, puzzled as to why she'd be calling.

"I know this is out of the blue, but Vincenzo would like to have dinner with you tonight. He said he wants to explain things."

Nico covered the receiver and quickly called over to Sofia. "Hey—my father wants to have dinner with me tonight 'to explain things.' What should I do?"

Sofia, mid-bite of doughnut, nearly choked on it before blurting out, "Go!"

Nico uncovered the receiver and replied to Payton, "All right, where should I meet him?"

"Reservations for two have already been made at Trattoria Moraiolo for 9:00 p.m."

"OK, Trattoria Moraiolo—I'll be there," he agreed, then hung up.

Nico brought over the fresh pot of coffee and two cups, setting them on the counter in front of Sofia. As he poured, he commented, "Wow, dinner at 9:00 p.m.—I don't think I've ever eaten that late."

"Well, sundown isn't until around 8:40 p.m.," Sofia reasoned. "That's probably the earliest he could make it. Plus, with all the tourists, most restaurants are likely booked."

Nico's anxiety crept in, and he began doubting his decision. "Are you sure I should go?"

"Of course," Sofia reassured him. "You need answers, and if nothing else, you'll either get to know your biological father or finally get some closure."

Nico closed his eyes, concentrating. "*Evocare Objectum*," he whispered, and the moon ring appeared in his palm. "And what should I do about this?"

Sofia put down her coffee cup. "Simple. Return it to him, like your nonna advised. She made the ring for him, and it does belong to him."

"You're right. It's the right thing to do," Nico said, slipping the ring into his pocket.

"If it'd make you feel better, Solomon and I could sit at the bar," Sofia suggested, "for a little moral support from a distance, just in case it doesn't go well."

"Thanks, but I should handle this on my own."

"All right then, but if you change your mind, just let me know. Oh, and I'll probably spend the night with Solomon—unless you'd rather I come home in case you need someone to talk to."

Nico smiled, touched by her thoughtfulness. "No, you spend time with your man—I'll be fine."

***

Later that evening, Solomon picked up Sofia, leaving a nervous Nico pacing around the house, constantly checking his Swatch. He peered out the living room window and watched as the sun began to set.

Meow, meow.

250

Negroni must be up, he thought, heading to the kitchen. He opened the hidden basement door and let Negroni in.

"Hey, friend," Nico said, picking her up and bringing her to the living room. Sitting on the couch, he held Negroni, who purred loudly, bringing him some comfort and easing his anxiety.

"Ah, such a good kitty," Nico murmured, scratching under her chin.

The grandfather clock chimed the quarter-hour—it was now 8:45 p.m. Nico gently put Negroni down and stood up. "Well, my friend, it's time for me to get going—wish me luck!"

"Meow," Negroni responded as Nico grabbed his car keys and headed to the restaurant.

He was fortunate to find a parking spot right in front. *Luck must be on my side tonight*, he thought, turning off the engine and stepping out of the car.

Inside the restaurant, he saw Aurora at the hostess stand, her eyes on the reservation list.

"I'm so sorry to hear about your father's passing," he said as he approached.

Aurora looked up, comforted to see Nico. "Thank you. It's been a rough week."

"If there's anything I can do for you or your mother, please don't hesitate to ask."

"I kind of expected it, to be honest," she revealed quietly.

Nico was taken aback. "Expected it? What do you mean?"

"I think our family is cursed," Aurora explained. "Remember in school when Sister Monica had us diagram our family trees?"

"Oh yeah, I almost forgot—that was actually kind of fun."

"Well, I noticed something odd in mine. Every Moraiolo woman had only one child, always a girl."

"Nothing too sinister about that," Nico reasoned.

"But there's more," she continued. "The father of each daughter meets a tragic end within six days of her twenty-first birthday."

Nico's own dinner plans suddenly felt less daunting. "Yikes! I see what you mean."

"Sorry, I didn't mean to unload all of this on you. Are you here for a late dinner?"

"Yes," Nico answered. "I believe the reservation is under Vincenzo Luna."

Aurora scanned the list. "Yes, here it is—table for two, 9:00 p.m. Come with me."

Once seated, Nico checked his Swatch—8:58 p.m. Still feeling anxious, he distracted himself by reading the menu.

Moments later, he sensed someone standing nearby and looked up.

"*Buona sera*, Nico," Vincenzo greeted. "I'm so glad you accepted my offer to have dinner."

"Hello...father," Nico said, stumbling over the last word.

Just then, Matteo arrived. "*Buona sera, ragazzi!*"

Before Matteo could say more, Vincenzo dismissed him with a simple command, "A bottle of Vino Vecchio Zinfandel."

Matteo left without a word.

Nico was confused by the bizarre interaction. "Did you just...compel him? I think that's what it's called."

"Smart boy—you're correct," Vincenzo answered. "You must've done your homework, as they say."

"I did a lot of 'homework,'" Nico shot back. "I know your entire history up until you met my mother."

A pensive look came over Vincenzo. "Knowledge can sometimes be a dangerous thing, but from what I've heard, you handle it well."

"Since my nonna's death, I've had to learn a lot in a short time."

"Your nonna was a wonderful, kind woman—I was deeply saddened the night she died."

"How? You weren't even there."

"True, I was entombed by your nonna's spell, but that night, for a brief second, she sent me a sign."

"How?"

At that moment, Matteo returned, uncorked the wine, and filled their glasses before departing.

"So, how?" Nico repeated.

"I had given Chiara—your nonna—an enchanted Venetian candelabra as a thank-you for allowing me to date your mother and for creating the moon ring."

"The one on her nightstand—I know the one," Nico said. "My mother found it on the floor the next morning, after…."

Vincenzo nodded. "I told her that if she were ever in danger, she could touch it, and I'd come to help."

Nico felt a surge of emotion and took a big gulp of wine. "That explains why it was on the floor—she must have been reaching for it during the struggle."

"She did touch it, just long enough for me to feel her fear and see a shadowy figure over her."

Seeing his father's sadness, Nico softened. "I can't imagine how hard that must've been—trapped in a coffin, knowing that someone you cared about was in danger and being powerless to help."

"Thank you for understanding," Vincenzo said. "I've felt guilty every night since."

"I believe you would have saved her if you could," Nico said, reaching into his pocket and retrieving the moon ring. "Here, this belongs to you."

Vincenzo's face lit up. "My moon ring! I thought I'd never see it again. How can I ever repay you?"

Feeling more comfortable, mostly due to the wine, Nico blurted, "Stay away from my mother."

The joy faded from Vincenzo's face. "Firstly, I would never hurt the only woman I've ever loved. Secondly, I don't intend to interfere—I can see she's happy now."

"Then why have you been stalking her house?" Nico demanded.

"Last night was the first time," Vincenzo replied defensively. "I just wanted to leave her a birthday present, but was interrupted."

"And what about the peonies on Mother's Day? And the wolf paw prints outside of my brother's window?" Nico volleyed back.

"The flowers, I had delivered," Vincenzo answered. "After all, she is the mother of my child. I wanted to show my gratitude, nothing more."

"Well, she didn't even know who they were from—she thought they might've been from me," Nico said, his tone a bit combative. "What you don't know is that my nonna erased her memories of you. But the flowers, you being next door to the real estate office, and talking to her at your grand opening event seem to have stirred some vague memories."

"Having her memories wiped was probably for the best, then. Look, I don't want to interfere; I promise to avoid contact with her," Vincenzo said, then paused as he remembered something. "Wait—you mentioned paw prints outside your mother's home?"

"Yes. I assumed they were made by you."

"They weren't mine. And, like I said, last night was the first time I'd ever been to her home," Vincenzo said, a concerned look on his face.

"What's with that look?" Nico asked. "I can tell something's bothering you."

"The paw prints, along with the unusually high number of deaths in town these past few months, confirm my suspicion—she may be in danger."

"What kind of danger could she possibly be in?" Nico asked. "I mean, you've met my dad—he'd do anything to protect her and my brother. I think she's quite safe."

Matteo arrived with an appetizer of *arancini* and an *insalata mista*.

"I figured you'd be hungry, so—"

"So you compelled him with your order while we were talking?" Nico asked.

Vincenzo grinned. "Yes—I think it's what you kids call multi-tasking."

"Well, thank you," Nico said. "Truthfully, I don't eat this late and was famished."

"Eat up—more can be brought, if you so desire." Vincenzo offered.

"I'll let you know—so, back to my mother and this impending danger," Nico said, taking a bite of his salad.

Lowering his voice, Vincenzo said, "I believe there's another vampire in town."

"Another vampire? So you're only partially responsible for the recent deaths?" Nico asked. "I spoke with a reporter, and she said all the deceased had been drained of blood—except for Aurora's father. But that's another topic."

"I don't drink the blood of humans," Vincenzo replied. "Remember the night of the grand opening, when you came into my office looking for me, and I came up from the basement to greet you?"

Nico nodded his head while chewing a mouthful of lettuce.

"Well, I was down there feeding on vermin."

Just like Negroni, Nico thought, stifling a laugh.

Nico finished his bite and composed himself. "Then my nonna must have known another vampire was coming," he said. "She kept garlic on every windowsill—she wouldn't have done that if you were the threat."

"She was wise—always planning ahead," Vincenzo agreed.

"So then, who did you think the other vampire is?" Nico asked.

"You said you did your homework?" Vincenzo ribbed.

Confused for a moment, Nico thought back to what he had read in the Founder's Treasure Room. "Minerva?" he guessed.

"Yes. After all these centuries, she's finally come looking for me," Vincenzo sighed, shaking his head in dismay.

"But why now?" Nico asked.

"I think wearing the moon ring, which made me human four times a month, broke our connection. And then, being under your nonna's spell and buried for twenty or so years—"

Nico interrupted, "And now that I've fulfilled my nonna's prophecy by releasing you, Minerva probably sensed your presence again and has tracked you down to Oliveto."

"At least now I have the moon ring back," Vincenzo said, looking down at it on his finger. "It should throw her off for a while, but it's likely too late. She must already know my whereabouts—the town isn't that big, and you know how people talk. That's why I'm worried she's found out about you and your mother—she'll punish me for leaving her by hurting the ones I love."

"Come to think of it, I think she already knows about me," Nico said, recalling the night he first visited The Griffon's Claw last spring. "The night when Sofia and I first met you at your bar, something happened after we went home."

Vincenzo leaned in. "Do tell."

"The house—my nonna enchanted it, by the way, probably sometime after my nonno died, to help her with small chores and things. Anyway, it seemed to sense that something had followed us home from the bar. As we approached the front door, it opened on its own, then slammed shut and locked once we were inside. At the time we didn't think much of it."

"Interesting. Please continue."

"A little later, Sofia was in the kitchen and noticed my nonna's frog figurines moving—they're enchanted to act like little security guards. They all turned toward the street and started croaking. Sofia peered out the window and saw a shadowy, misshapen figure approaching the house."

"That sounds like Minerva," Vincenzo said with a chuckle. "She always liked using mist form to move about."

Now that the *arancini* had cooled down, Nico took a bite, "Yum! You've got to try—oh sorry, maybe we can have dinner again, during one of the cycles of the moon when you can enjoy food as a human."

"That would be nice," Vincenzo said, "but for you and your mother's safety, I think you should leave town. At least until we come up with a plan on how to deal with Minerva."

"I can't. There's something important I need to do."

Curious, Vincenzo asked, "More important than your mother's safety?"

"Yes—the town's safety," Nico explained. "An efreeti named Caleo plans to destroy Oliveto—utterly destroy it—if I don't return the thirteen Coins of Favor stolen from him."

"And do you even have all of the coins?"

"Yes," Nico answered. "Thankfully, my nonna saw the future and collected them before she passed—I found them in her safe deposit box."

"Is there anything I can do to help?"

"No. Sofia and I have a plan," Nico assured. "But Caleo isn't too pleased with us, so we're hoping he'll accept the coins and allow us to leave in one piece."

Vincenzo waved his hand in the air and Matteo brought the check and a to-go container.

"Maybe I'm not done eating?" Nico stated.

"You are—I can tell you're already full and not a big eater." Vincenzo said with a smirk. "In the to-go container, you'll find two *cannoli*, in case you and Sofia crave dessert later."

"Thank you—I guess," Nico said, a bit confused by his gesture.

"It's been wonderful clearing the air, and I hope you have a better understanding of who I am." Vincenzo said as he stood up, placing two one-hundred-dollar bills into the check billfold. "I need to head over to the bar before it gets busy—stop by for a drink if you want."

"Thanks for dinner," Nico said as his father left.

He picked up the to-go container and stopped at the hostess stand to say goodnight to Aurora.

"Did you two have a nice dinner?" Aurora asked.

"The food was delicious, as always," Nico replied. "And thank you for the birthday wishes—my mother passed along your message. I'm just so sorry you couldn't make it to the party, but even more sorry for the reason why."

"It's fine. I hope you enjoyed your night."

Nico chuckled. "Well, let's just say it got a little crazy at one point. Anyway, maybe we can get together sometime—I'd love to take you out for a belated birthday meal or drink."

Aurora blushed. "I'd like that."

"Great," Nico said. "Well, I should let you get back to work—I can't believe the restaurant's still packed at this hour."

Aurora shrugged. "It's tourist season—what can you do?"

Nico smiled and waved goodbye as he headed out of the restaurant to go home.

Stefano A Giovannoni

Chapter 33: The End?

The next morning, Nico was awakened by the sound of the front door slamming shut. He sat up abruptly and glanced at his alarm clock: it read 6:30 a.m.

He listened intently for any further activity within the house. At first, there was only silence, but soon he heard faint footsteps approaching, growing louder as they neared his room.

Nico jumped out of bed and reached for the door, but as he looked down, he saw the doorknob begin to turn. Acting quickly, he took hold of it and pulled the door open.

"Oh, good morning!" Sofia greeted him cheerfully. "I didn't think you'd be up this early—I was going to surprise you."

"And that you did!" Nico replied, taking a deep breath to calm his nerves. "But what are you doing up so early?"

"I didn't really sleep much last night—" she started.

Nico smirked, cutting her off. "You little minx!"

Sofia laughed. "No! I couldn't sleep because I was worried about you. I tossed and turned all night, and Sol suggested I come back sooner so that I could check on how things went with you and Vincenzo."

Nico returned to his bed, gesturing for Sofia to join him. "Come sit with me; I'll tell you everything."

Once they were situated, Nico began recounting his evening, but stopped abruptly when he noticed Sofia nodding off.

"House, please bring us two cups of coffee," he called out, causing Sofia to stir and open her eyes.

"Sorry. Was I asleep?"

"Afraid so," Nico said with a grin. "But don't worry—coffee's on its way."

"Oh, thank goodness," Sofia said, yawning. "Please, start from the beginning again."

"OK, but try to stay awake this time!" Nico teased. "So, I met him at the restaurant. Aside from some intense emotions and a few awkward moments, things went well."

"And? Do you think he's involved in any of the nefarious things happening around town?" Sofia asked.

"You know, I don't think he is," Nico answered. "At first, I had my doubts, but after he answered my questions, I really think he was being sincere—"

"Unless he compelled you!" Sofia interrupted.

"While there was a little compulsion used on the waiter, I don't think he'd try that with me—or even that he could. For all I know, I might be immune to it." Nico said, just as a tray with two cups of coffee floated into the room and settled on his bed.

Sofia sat up, reaching for a cup and holding it in both hands. "OK, go on."

"First, we talked about my nonna. They were actually close, and he's the one who gave her that antique candelabra in her bedroom."

"A man who gives gifts—I'm liking him already," Sofia said, sipping her coffee with interest.

"And get this," Nico continued, "the candelabra is enchanted!"

Sofia leaned in. "Enchanted? How?"

"He told my nonna that if she were ever in danger, she could hold the candelabra, and he would sense her fear, even see through her eyes, and come to her aid."

"Wow."

"And apparently, when he was buried underground, he caught a brief glimpse of her last moments," Nico said, his voice catching. "In the midst of her struggle, she managed to touch the candelabra for just a few seconds before it was knocked to the floor."

"That's heartbreaking," Sofia said softly. "To witness someone you care about in danger but being powerless to help."

Nico took another sip of coffee and asked the house to bring them the *cannoli* from last night.

"And where did you get those?" Sofia asked, her mouth watering.

"My father—I mean Vincenzo—ordered them for me to share with you."

"Maybe he's a good guy after all," Sofia said with a smile. "And thoughtful, too!"

"Oh, and I returned his moon ring," Nico remembered suddenly.

Sofia smiled. "I'm glad you followed your nonna's advice. I bet he was happy to see it."

"He was—and he even offered to repay me!"

"What did you say?"

"I told him to stay away from my mother."

"That was a bit harsh," Sofia said, half-joking.

"I know. Between my anxiety, emotions, and the wine, I just blurted it out," Nico admitted. "Though, in retrospect, I think it was mostly due to my dad's concern that my mother's memories might be returning. He's worried she might leave him for Vincenzo if they do."

"Do you really think she would?"

"I hope not, but Vincenzo was her first love. Sometimes that's a powerful thing—"

"Well, no one forgets their first love," Sofia interrupted. "One day, she'll remember."

"Well, I promised my dad that I'd try to prevent that. And Vincenzo even promised to stay away from her."

"So, he's fallen out of love after being buried for over twenty years?"

"On the contrary," Nico corrected. "He told me my mother was the only woman he'd ever loved and that he'd never want to disrupt her happiness."

"Do you trust Vincenzo?"

"Actually, I do," Nico answered assuredly. "He even said the only time he's ever been to my mother's home was on the night of the party. So, the wolf paw prints we found outside of Remus's room weren't his."

"Then whose were they?

"We concluded they were likely made by Minerva," Nico answered, looking toward the door just as a plate with two *cannoli* floated over and lowered onto the tray.

"His sire?" Sofia asked, reaching for a *cannolo* and taking a bite.

"Yes. He thinks she's come for revenge—to make him pay for leaving her side centuries ago."

"And I suppose you and Siena are her prime targets!"

"Exactly," Nico agreed. "He also suspects she's the one draining the townspeople's blood."

"So, he doesn't drink blood?"

"Oh, he does, just not from humans," Nico explained, taking a bite of his *cannolo*. "Wow, these are really good!"

"I know—so yummy," Sofia agreed before pivoting back to their conversation. "So, what does he feed on?"

"Well, remember the night of the grand opening party when I went to speak with him in his office?"

"Yes."

"He'd been in the basement—feeding on rodents."

"Just like Negroni!" Sofia joked.

Nico laughed. "Omigod, I thought the same thing!"

They finished their *cannoli*, and Nico continued, "Oh, and he wants me to leave town."

"What? Why?" Sofia exclaimed, nearly spilling her coffee on Nico's duvet.

"He thinks that by doing so, Minerva won't be able to harm me. We even think she's the misshapen figure you saw outside the window that spring night—"

"That night still haunts me," Sofia interrupted. "To this day, I avoid looking out those kitchen windows at night."

"I think she was already in town then and followed us home from The Griffon's Claw."

"Did you tell him you'd leave?"

Nico was getting a cramp in his leg and changed positions. "I said we had things to finish first. I told him about Caleo and that we need to return the coins before the July 7th centennial celebration."

"Nico—"

"What?"

"Today's July 6th!" Sofia exclaimed. "We need to put Project: Snuff out the Fire into action."

Nico jumped off the bed. "Oh crap! We'd better grab our supplies and head out."

"More coffee first," Sofia persuaded.

"Yeah, that might be wise," Nico agreed. "We'll need to stay alert in case he tries anything unexpected."

***

An hour passed quickly, and the caffeinated duo met in the foyer.

"Do you have everything we agreed on?" Sofia asked.

Nico double-checked his pocket. "Yup," he confirmed. Then he noticed her charm bracelet. "Hey, why are you wearing that? I hope you weren't thinking of offering it to Calypso—we don't need her help this time. I'm planning to cast the Breathe Water spell so we can make the swim ourselves."

"I figured as much," Sofia answered. "I just thought if worst comes to worst, one of the charms might come in handy."

"I doubt Caleo would be pacified by a stein of beer or a dozen roses, but hey—better safe than sorry," Nico said, opening the door for her. "House, if we don't make it back, thanks for looking after us."

"Such a drama queen," Sofia ribbed. "House, we'll be back later."

Their first stop was the bank to retrieve the thirteen coins from the safe deposit box. Once acquired and placed in Nico's enchanted pocket, they decided to drive to the river to save time instead of using the fairy doors.

Once they arrived, Nico and Sofia carefully scaled down the rocky embankment to the riverbed.

"There's the willow tree with the fairy door," Nico said, pointing.

Sofia briskly walked toward the flowing water, wiping sweat from her brow. "So, the entrance to the underwater passageway should be right about here. Come on, let's hurry—I'm roasting in this heat."

"Agreed," Nico responded, following her across the sand and stones, into the water.

Together, they waded into the cool water. Once they were submerged up to their necks, Nico placed his hand on Sofia's shoulder and whispered the spell, *"Respirare Aqua."*

As narrow slits opened on the sides of their necks, they dropped into the river's depths and made the long swim to the underwater entrance of the mountain.

Eventually, they reached the end of the passageway and surfaced in the dark inner cavern. As they broke the water's surface, Nico quickly touched Sofia's shoulder and croaked out the counterspell, "*Respirare Aerem*!" The slits on their necks sealed, and they were able to breathe air again.

They climbed out of the water, and Nico reached into his pocket, but then paused. "Damn, I must've forgotten the candle," he muttered. "Oh well—*Incendium*."

With the small amount of light coming from his enchanted fingertip, he saw Sofia smiling at him.

"Let me handle this," she said, placing her hand on his shoulder. "*Visio Nocturna*."

Nico blinked in surprise as his vision adjusted to the cavern's darkness. "Nice work! Is that one of the Malandanti spells you learned?"

Sofia blew out the flame on his finger. "Yep! Pretty good, huh?"

Nico grinned at his friend's stroke of brilliance. "Agreed. Let's rest a bit and dry off," he suggested, pulling two beach towels from his pocket and handing one to Sofia.

"I can't wait to get this over with," Sofia said, toweling her hair dry.

"Same. I'm not looking forward to this encounter," Nico replied.

As the warm breeze from Caleo's inner sanctum dried their clothes, they noticed it felt noticeably warmer than the last time. Sofia folded her towel and handed it back. Nico tucked both towels into his pocket and asked, "OK, ready?"

"Yes," Sofia answered, following him into the serpentine tunnel. They moved swiftly through the guano-filled bat cave and into the passageway leading to Caleo's lair.

Ahead, they could hear voices. Silently, they crept closer to listen as Caleo spoke to an unknown man.

"—you've been a loyal ally, bringing me the town relics I requested for my treasure horde," the efrecti said. "And for that, I'll give you the chance to save yourself—for tomorrow, I'm going to destroy the town."

"But why would you do that?" the stranger asked.

Nico turned to Sofia and whispered, "That voice sounds familiar, but I can't seem to place it."

"Nearly a hundred years ago to this day, the town's founders betrayed me by refusing to pay for the thirteen magical coins I forged for them," Caleo explained. "They and all their descendants have failed to return the coins within the time given. So, take my advice—leave town, or share their fate."

"But—" that stranger started, but Caleo suddenly turned toward the entrance of his lair.

"Who's there? Come inside and face me!" he commanded.

Nico turned to Sofia. "We've been spotted—it's time."

They stepped into the cavern's expanse, and Sofia caught a quick glimpse of the mysterious visitor clutching something near his chest before he vanished without a trace.

Caleo looked down at the two intruders. "Ah, you meddlesome kids are back. Here to meet your doom?" he said, ending with a maniacal laugh.

"Wait!" Nico held up a purple satin sack by its gold drawstring. "We've collected the Coins of Favor and brought them back to you."

"Ah, just in time," Caleo sneered. "Come, bring them here, and we shall talk."

Reluctantly, the two approached Caleo, who sat on a gem-encrusted throne near his mound of gold coins and other various treasures. Nico, unwilling to get too close, tossed the sack over to him. The efreeti rose, catching it with one taloned hand. "Let's make sure this isn't a trick."

Caleo poured out the coins into his palm and counted, "...twelve, thirteen! Well done," he said, smiling grotesquely.

Nico looked up at the terrifying creature, carefully avoiding his gaze. "So, you'll keep your promise not to destroy Oliveto, right?"

"Yeah, you have the coins back—that was the deal," Sofia added.

But instead of responding, Caleo moved to the cavern's entrance, blocking their escape. As he turned to face them, smoke began to billow from his nostrils.

Knowing this was not a scenario they had planned for, Nico quickly positioned himself in front of Sofia, shielding her from whatever may come.

Stefano A Giovannoni

The efreeti lumbered toward them, his large, clawed hands outstretched. Trapped between Caleo and the pool of molten lava where Flora had once been caged, they began to back away.

Suddenly, Sofia's foot rolled on a loose piece of volcanic rock, causing her to fall. Her charm bracelet jingled as she hit the ground, reminding her of its hidden potential. She quickly scanned the charms. "Beer, no; roses, no; unicorn—no chance on horseback. But the fairy door—that might just work," she thought.

Yanking the charm off, she threw it to the ground. The charm transformed from metal into wood and began stretching in every direction until it was the size of a regular fairy door.

"Caleo, we returned the coins before the hundred years were up—you promised—" Nico pleaded, feeling Sofia grip his hand.

The furious efreeti loomed closer. "I reserve the right to change my mind—and I never promised to spare your lives!" He raised his hand to strike. "You took Flora from me, and now I shall take your lives," he snarled, his talons descending.

Just as Caleo's claws began tearing into Nico's flesh, everything went dark, and bone-chilling cold enveloped him.

Chapter 34: Ice, Ice, Baby

Nico opened his eyes, finding himself lying on a bed of snow. Beside him, Sofia was leaning over, applying pressure to his bleeding wound.

"Where are we?" he asked, voice weak.

"I don't know," Sofia replied, her teeth chattering from the cold. "But thankfully, that fairy door worked."

Nico sat up, looking around. They were in a clearing within a snow-laden forest. About twenty-five feet away, nearly blending into the snowy backdrop, a majestic white stag stood observing them.

The distant crunch of approaching footsteps shattered the silence, and the stag darted off, vanishing into the trees.

"Do you hear that?" he whispered.

Sofia grabbed Nico's hand, and placed it against his chest. "Keep pressure here," she directed before rising to survey their surroundings. From the north, a small army of beings, armed and battle-ready, was coming into view.

"Nico, how are you feeling?" Sofia asked, slightly panicked. "We might need to run—can you stand?"

Nico struggled to rise but stumbled back into the snow.

"Halt!" a commanding voice called out.

Five figures approached, clad in leather armor trimmed with fur and wielding halberds. They were thin with pale, blue-tinged skin, reminiscent of Sterling. Beside them, a female fairy hovered, scribbling notes with quill on parchment.

"Intruders, come with us!" the leader barked, pointing his halberd's tip at Nico.

The fairy fluttered over to the commander. "Eldon, the human male is injured—force isn't necessary."

Eldon lowered his halberd, directing Humphrey, his second-in-command, to assist Nico.

Realizing they had no choice, Nico and Sofia complied, following their captors deeper into the forest. After a lengthy hike, they arrived at a clearing where a castle, shrouded in snow and ice, loomed before them.

Sofia's bracelet flashed as the fairy door charm returned, catching Eldon's attention.

"What's going on?" Eldon demanded. "Are you attempting to escape with magic?"

"No, nothing of the sort," Sofia replied quickly.

"Well, stop dawdling!" Eldon snapped. "The queen is waiting. Move!"

The fairy scribe hovered beside them, whispering, "Don't mind him; he takes his job way too seriously," followed by a faint giggle.

The castle gate creaked open, allowing them into the courtyard. A servant approached Eldon, whispering urgently. After a brief exchange, Eldon announced, "We're to bring the intruders to the queen—let's go!"

The servant led them swiftly through the castle to the throne room. Nico, weak and now tired from walking in the snow, struggled to keep pace.

"Move it! Mustn't keep the queen waiting," a guard barked, shoving Nico forward.

At the throne room's end, the queen sat regally, observing them as Nico collapsed to the floor from fatigue.

"Nico!" Sofia cried, kneeling beside him, trying to revive him.

The queen rose, advancing toward them.

"My queen, please stay back—these are intruders to our realm," Eldon cautioned. "They may be dangerous!"

"Fool! Can't you see the poor boy is injured and weak?" she reprimanded, directing the royal attendant to summon the court physician.

"Right away, Your Majesty," the attendant replied, quickly leaving the room.

"Stand back! Give them space," the queen commanded, surprising her court as she knelt beside Nico and Sofia. "I am Queen Anneliese, ruler of the Snow Fairy Realm. May I know your names?"

Sofia bowed her head respectfully. "My name is Sofia Saggio, and this is Nico Frantoio."

At the sound of his name, Nico opened his eyes, seeing Sofia and the snow fairy queen gazing down at him. "Hello," he murmured, managing a faint smile.

"Nico, are you OK?" Sofia asked, concerned.

"I think so—I guess I don't heal as quickly in this realm," Nico replied.

Upon seeing her attendant enter the room with the court physician, the queen stood up, pointed to Nico, and returned to her throne.

The physician, an elder with a mane of wiry gray hair, knelt beside Nico, pressing a stethoscope-like instrument to his chest.

"Hmm, very strange," he remarked, glancing up at the queen. "Your Majesty, I've had the rare chance to study humans before, and his heart rate is unusually low for one of his kind." Turning to Nico, he asked, "How are you feeling? Can you sit up?"

With Sofia's help, Nico sat up as the physician inspected the gash on his chest. Opening his medical bag, the physician pulled out an ochre-color salve and gently applied it to the wounds.

Sofia gasped in amazement as the deep claw marks began to close up and heal before her eyes.

"That salve looks a lot like the one my dad used on me, but it never worked this well!" Nico remarked. "I wonder why?"

"Magic works differently across realms," the physician explained. "What works quickly here, may also work in another realm but not as fast, and vice versa."

"That makes sense," Sofia said. "And Nico isn't entirely human; maybe that's why his heart beats differently. He's part—"

Nico quickly interrupted Sofia, standing up before she could divulge his magical background. "I'm feeling much better now. Thank you."

The guards, startled by Nico's sudden movement, tightened their grip on their weapons and stepped forward, leveling the tips of their halberds at him.

"Enough! Stand down," the queen commanded sharply. "Nico and Sofia, please approach me."

Sofia stood, and together they approached the throne. Nico bowed, and Sofia curtsied.

"Gale," the queen called to her royal scribe, who fluttered over with her quill and parchment. "Document my words."

"Yes, your majesty," Gale acknowledged, smiling at Nico and Sofia as if she already knew what the queen would say.

"Due to acts of extreme heroism, I hereby recognize Nico Frantoio and Sofia Saggio as friends of the court. They are to be treated as my royal guests, with unrestricted travel to and from this realm," the queen proclaimed to all present.

Sofia looked at Nico and whispered from the corner of her mouth, "What did we do to earn such recognition?"

"Young lady, speak up," the queen commanded. "No whispering in my presence."

Sofia curtsied. "Your majesty, we're honored, but we're unsure as to why you grant us such recognition."

The queen smiled. "Your names are known across the fairy realms. We've heard of your bravery in rescuing one of our kind, namely Fawn Argento, from certain death, and preventing future abductions."

Sofia exchanged a smile with Nico.

Queen Anneliese continued, "If Eldon and his men only had the sense of mind to ask your names, they would have treated you better—I shall deal with them later."

"Your Majesty, we weren't treated poorly," Nico said, downplaying his experience while glancing at Eldon. "Please forgive them."

"Very well. It seems I do owe you a favor," the queen acknowledged. "Now, the question on the entire court's mind is, how did you come to be in our realm?"

Nico explained, "Your Majesty, to put it simply, we were about to be killed by an efreeti, so Sofia used the fairy door charm from her enchanted bracelet."

Sofia raised her wrist, pointing to the charm. "It teleported us to your realm and saved our lives."

Gale leaned in to whisper something to the queen, who nodded thoughtfully before asking, "Why would you confront such a fearsome creature? May I assume it was another act of bravery to save someone?"

"Well, not only someone, but our entire town as well," Nico began.

"Go on," the queen urged, leaning forward.

"We first rescued Flora, the Light Dryad, who was held captive by Caleo, the mountain efreeti," Nico said. "Flora then warned us that Caleo planned on destroying the entire town."

The queen raised an eyebrow, interrupting. "And what would prompt him to do such a thing?"

"Nearly a hundred years ago, our town founders took thirteen magical coins from him," Nico explained. "He gave the town exactly a century to return them, or he'd destroy our realm—I mean town."

Sofia chimed in. "We returned all thirteen coins, but Caleo, still angry over Flora's rescue, reneged on his promise to spare us. We barely escaped."

Nico jumped in, urgency in his voice. "Your Majesty, we desperately need to return and stop him before it's too late."

The queen frowned. "Hmm. News of Flora's return hasn't reached us yet." She turned to Gale, who was hovering nearby, and instructed, "Look into why we weren't informed."

After Gale made a note, the queen asked, "How do you intend to stop him?"

Nico hesitated. "We hoped returning the coins would settle the debt, but now...we're not sure."

"An interesting dilemma," the queen responded, sitting in contemplation for a moment before calling Eldon over and whispering something to him. Eldon bowed and rushed out of the room.

"I believe I might be able to help," the queen said at last. "I've sent Eldon to retrieve the Gauntlet of Frost from the royal treasure chamber. While wearing it, your hand will be immune to all forms of fire and heat. You should then be able to touch Caleo and bring him through the fairy door to our realm."

"Your Majesty, then what?" Nico asked.

"Once out of his element and in our realm's cold, he'll be weakened. Eldon and his men will take it from there," the queen replied.

"Thank you, Your Majesty," Sofia said, bowing.

Eldon returned, carrying a red pillow upon which rested a silver gauntlet that seemed to deepen the chill of the already frigid room. The gauntlet was adorned with three striking sky-blue topazes, and its surface was intricately etched with delicate snowflake patterns.

"Nico, come forward," the queen instructed, handing him the gauntlet. "Take this and follow Eldon back to your realm. Safe travels, brave humans."

Nico accepted the silver gauntlet, an icy tingle running through his body as he held it. He quickly tucked it into his enchanted pocket, then bowed while Sofia curtsied. Together, they left the room with Eldon.

Eldon led them down a long, portrait-lined hallway, stopping halfway. "Thank you for speaking up on my behalf, though the queen was right— I should have asked your names and treated you with more respect."

Sofia smiled. "You were only protecting your realm, as any good commander would."

A faint reddish glow warmed Eldon's icy-blue cheeks. "You're very kind," he said, humbled.

He then continued to the end of the hallway, where an oversized portrait of the king hung. Raising his hand, he waved it in front of the painting. Nico and Sofia watched as the portrait's image gradually faded, revealing an entrance to a hidden room. Eldon stepped through without hesitation.

"Must be an illusory doorway," Nico noted, admiring the magic.

Sofia whispered, "Think we could recreate this at your house?"

"Are you coming?" Eldon called.

Sofia nudged Nico, and they passed through the portrait's frame into a small, unfurnished room lined with miniature paintings.

Curious, they turned back, watching in amazement as the hallway they had just walked down faded away, replaced by a blank canvas where the entryway had once been.

"Stop dawdling and come help me," Eldon called out.

Nico and Sofia surveyed the multitude of framed paintings lining the walls. Most depicted landscapes, while a few were of town settings.

Sofia pointed to one in particular. "That one looks like the monastery in Italy where Paolo and I lived until we were adopted."

Another painting caught Nico's eye. "Hey, a look at this one! It's the backyard of Hornsby Manor—right by that large sugar maple!" He glanced down at the frame's label, reading aloud, "Hornsby Manor,

Connecticut. Sofia, check the label on yours. It might confirm your suspicions."

Sofia looked down at the tiny label, slightly covered in dust, and tried to read it.

"Stand back!" Eldon warned suddenly.

Startled, they jumped back from the paintings.

"This is the Portal Room," Eldon explained. "We use it to travel to different realms or locations within our own."

"Ah," Sofia said, turning to Nico. "These must work like the fairy doors in Oliveto. Good thing I didn't touch the frame, though—Italy does sound tempting right about now."

"Correct," Eldon affirmed. "They work the same way as your fairy doors. Now, let's find the one for your town."

After a about ten minutes of searching, Sofia called out, "Here! This one is of the fairy door by Indelible Delights."

Nico and Eldon joined her, checking the label: *Oliveto, California.*

"This is it," Nico confirmed. "Do we just touch the frame?"

"Yes, it's that simple," Eldon said with a chuckle. "That's why we store all the paintings in this hidden room now. They used to hang in the royal bedrooms, but quite a few chambermaids went missing while dusting their frames."

"Oh, that's terrible," Sofia gasped.

"Not to worry, they were all safely returned to the castle," Eldon assured them. "OK, now let's get you back to your realm."

Nico and Sofia reached out and touched the wooden frame. Everything went dark, and suddenly, they found themselves in Vicolo Fato with Fawn standing over them.

"Welcome back, you two!" Fawn greeted them. "My father and I just received word that you'd be returning."

As the warm weather eased their chilled bones, they stood, grateful to be back, and hugged Fawn.

"Whoa!" Fawn laughed. "What's with all this love?"

"I think I can speak for the both of us—we're so glad to be back," Sofia said.

"Yeah," Nico added. "It was a close call. Caleo wasn't happy to see us and tried to kill us."

"Fortunately, we escaped to the Ice Fairy Realm using one of the charms on my enchanted bracelet," Sofia explained.

"Lucky you," Fawn sighed. "I've never been allowed to visit the other realms, let alone other towns, especially after having been abducted."

"We could take you to Connecticut for the day sometime—" Nico began to offer, but Sofia interrupted.

"Right now, we need to figure out a way to save the town."

Fawn looked confused. "But didn't you return the coins to Caleo?"

"We did," Nico answered, "but Caleo was so furious over Flora's rescue that he's moving forward with his plans to destroy Oliveto."

"We didn't anticipate this," Sofia added with a sigh. "Now we've less than six hours to come up with a solution."

Anxiety gripped Nico as he realized how little time they had. He started pacing, trying to think of a way to save his beloved town. Then he noticed the fairy door next to the entrance of Indelible Delights. The image of the church's cross and steeple carved into it sparked an idea.

"Fawn, we'll catch up with you later," Nico said abruptly, turning to Sofia. "I have an idea. Come with me."

Chapter 35: Talking to Myself

Sofia followed Nico out of the alleyway and asked, "Where are we going?"

"To Saint Anthony's. I have a feeling we'll find some answers there," Nico answered, quickening his pace. "Father Michael might know something. He and my nonna were very close, so he must know all about the town's magic and secrets."

When they arrived at the church, they climbed the steps leading to its front entrance. Nico pulled at one of the doors, but it was locked. Knowing the church was warded against dark magic, which rendered the Pick Lock spell useless, he moved to the next door, but it was also locked. Sofia joined in, testing the remaining doors—all locked.

"Good grief!" Sofia exclaimed. "This isn't a good sign."

"There's a side door by the rectory—it might still be open," Nico suggested, heading down the stairs.

Sofia followed him around to the side entrance, and fortunately, the door was unlocked. They entered the dimly lit church, which was filled with the lingering scent of incense from a funeral earlier in the day. It was silent, and only one person appeared to be inside.

"Hey Nico," Sofia whispered. "Is that the guy we saw last time—the one in the sixth row? The one you said is always here praying the rosary?"

Nico looked over at the kneeling parishioner, who unexpectedly looked up at them.

"Finally!" the stranger uttered. "Nico. Sofia. Come quickly!"

They approached cautiously, meeting the gaze of the man, who appeared to be in his forties, rosary beads dangling from his hand.

"Nico, he looks vaguely familiar," Sofia murmured quietly.

"Probably because you remember him from last time we were here," Nico whispered back.

"No, it's more than that—he just reminds me of someone I know."

The stranger invited them to sit, and they obliged.

"You don't have much time," he said. "I know why you're here—you have less than six hours to stop Caleo from destroying our town."

"But how do you know that? And who are you?" Nico asked. "All I know is that I've seen you in that exact spot ever since I was a kid."

"I am you," the stranger answered. "I'm from the future—and it's not a happy one."

Sofia's eyes widened. "How is that possible?"

"I'll explain," the stranger said. "But first, to prove I am who I say I am, let me show you something."

He pulled up his right T-shirt sleeve, revealing a griffon tattoo with a small mushroom beside it—the same one Nico had.

Sofia gasped. "Now I know why I felt I knew you!"

"So, you really are me? Wow, we didn't age well," Nico joked, trying to lighten the mood.

The elder Nico from the future gave a faint smile. "It's been a hard life, but I'm here to hopefully spare you from all I've endured." He took a deep breath. "Twenty-five years ago, I sat in this very seat with Sofia. We ran out of time and tried to warn as many townspeople as we could to evacuate. Many thought it was a prank and didn't heed our warning."

"So, Oliveto no longer exists in your timeline?" Sofia asked.

"Correct. And…you didn't make it out in time." His voice shook as he continued. "You were my best friend. I couldn't save you."

Nico clenched his fists. "How could you leave her behind?"

"As soon as Caleo triggered the eruption, the town was in chaos. Lava flowed down the mountain, annihilating everything in its path, while volcanic bombs rained from the sky. As we tried to escape through the fairy door in the backyard, a molten fragment landed nearby, engulfing Sofia before she could make it through."

The elder Nico paused, visibly pained. "Mrs. Hornsby found me in my closet the next day. I was incoherent, banging my head against the wall. The trauma of losing my family, my best friend, and my hometown must have caused a complete mental breakdown. Mrs. Hornsby kindly looked after me while I recovered, though somehow the trauma had suppressed most of my past memories.

"Eventually, I left Connecticut and moved to San Francisco, where I became a monk. I took a vow of silence and spent my days alone, immersed in prayer and deep meditation.

"Then, on the twenty-fifth anniversary of this day, during a meditation session, my memories returned. Suddenly, I remembered everything—my family, Sofia, the secrets of this town, and even many of the spells from the grimoire. That's when I knew I had to find a way to return and try to save the town."

Sofia interrupted. "So, you created a spell to take you back in time?"

"Yes, but unfortunately, I couldn't control the exact day or time I'd return. So, I kept recasting it each time it wore off, which is why Nico saw me here at different points in his life."

Finally, Nico understood why the man had always looked the same over the years.

"Now, if you're going to save the town, you must use The Grand Reversal spell from the grimoire," the elder Nico instructed.

"That's the one in the middle of the grimoire, right?" Sofia asked. "We've been wondering what it's for—there's no real description of what it does, only how to cast it."

"The spell is a bit complex," the elder Nico explained. "You'll need seven people—three Benandanti and three Malandanti—to join hands and form a hexagram, with the seventh person standing in the center. Once the spell is cast, time will roll back twelve hours for everyone, but that individual in the center will retain all of their current memories and any possessions they have with them. That's why it's crucial for that person to hold the gauntlet; otherwise, it will disappear, since they didn't possess it twelve hours earlier."

"Where will we find enough people to perform the spell?" Nico asked.

"Thankfully, we can take the place of either a Benandanti or Malandanti, as the blood of both runs in our veins," the elder Nico explained.

Sofia turned to the elder Nico. "Thank you. This gives us hope."

"Time's wasting! Now go and save—" he said, just as his spell ended, causing him to vanish suddenly before them.

"Well, you heard me," Nico said with a snicker. "Let's get going."

"Can we first stop by Schwartzman's?" Sofia asked. "I want to see Solomon, just in case…well, you know."

"Of course," Nico answered, with a reassuring smile. "But, as my nonna wrote, 'never give up on hope.' We've got this!"

They headed to Schwartzman's Quality Clothing, but the window blinds were already down; the store was closed. Sofia knocked repeatedly, hoping someone would answer. Finally, the door unlocked, and Mrs. Schwartzman opened it.

"Hello, you two," she greeted. "What brings you by at this hour?"

"I need to speak with Solomon," Sofia replied, her voice slightly anxious.

"And may I use your phone?" Nico asked.

"Of course. Please come in," Mrs. Schwartzman said, stepping aside. "Solomon will be right up—he's downstairs gathering more shirts for the sales floor. And, Nico, you know where the phone is, please help yourself."

Nico went over to the register area. He paused before picking up the phone, reached into his pocket, and pulled out a piece of paper. Looking down at the handwritten number, he dialed: 555-3323.

"Thank you for calling P. Cadaveri and Sons Mortuary, this is Gino. How may I help you?"

"Gino, it's Nico."

"Oh, hello! I was wondering when you'd get up the nerve to call me," Gino teased.

Nico fell silent, feeling a bit awkward.

"Nico? Are you there? I was just joking."

"Uh, yeah, I'm still here." Nico finally responded. "Sorry to bother you, but I need your help."

"Of course," Gino said. "How can I be of assistance?"

"Can you meet me in the piazza in about ten minutes—oh, and bring your brother, too!"

"Sure, I'll be there, but I'm not sure where my brother is," Gino answered. "He left a few hours ago, and I don't know when he'll be back—he seemed in a hurry."

"Damn!" Nico said in frustration, trying to figure out where he'd find a replacement Malandanti to complete the spell. "OK, never mind. Just promise me you'll be there—it's a matter of life and death."

"Don't worry, I'll be there—I promise."

"Thank you," Nico said, hanging up the phone. He walked over to where Sofia and Solomon were talking.

"Hey, Nico," Solomon said. "Sofia filled me in. Is there anything I can do to help?"

"Here's the plan," Nico explained. "Sofia, you go to La Farmacista—hopefully it's still open. Persuade Manolo to come to the piazza—I need him to be the third Malandanti for the spell."

Nico then turned to Solomon. "Please go to the bank and find Mr. Pendolino and—"

"The bank's already closed," Solomon interrupted, "but I know where Mr. Pendolino lives; it's only a few blocks away."

"Phew!" Nico said, relieved. "As soon as you find him, bring him to the piazza. I'll go to Trattoria Moraiolo and get Aurora and her mother, Vanda—they'll be our last two Benandanti needed for the spell."

"Got it!" Sofia and Solomon said in unison.

The three left Schwartzman's and went their separate ways.

Nico hurried to Trattoria Moraiolo, went inside, and rushed up to the hostess stand where Aurora was standing.

"Nico, you look flustered," she remarked.

"I don't have much time," he said, looking around. "Is your mother here?"

"Yes, she's in the kitchen."

"Please get her—the town's in danger." Nico's tone was urgent. "I need you both to help me cast a spell."

"You're actually serious?" Aurora asked in disbelief. "This isn't a prank, is it?"

"I would never joke about something like this," Nico answered with a serious expression. "Please get her and meet me in the piazza, beneath the Founders' Tree."

As Aurora went to the kitchen, Nico left the restaurant and crossed the street to the piazza. Sofia and Manolo were already there, waiting for him.

"Hi Manolo," Nico greeted. "Has Sofia filled you in?"

"Yes," Manolo replied with a nod.

"Oh, Sofia, before I forget, I'd better give you this," Nico said, pulling out the Gauntlet of Frost from his enchanted pocket and handing it to her.

"Thanks!" Sofia said. "Glad you remembered, I almost forgot."

"I'm here," a voice called out from behind Nico.

Nico turned around to see Gino standing there, smiling.

"Thank you for taking me seriously and helping us out," Nico said, looking around nervously to see if the others were coming.

"There's Solomon." Sofia pointed toward the west side of the piazza. "And it looks like he found Mr. Pendolino, too!"

"OK, we're just waiting for Aurora and Mrs. Moraiolo," Nico said, closing his eyes and concentrating.

As Solomon and Mr. Pendolino joined the group, Nico muttered, "*Evocare Objectum*," and his family's grimoire appeared in his hands, to the amazement of the others.

"Well done!" Mr. Pendolino commended him. "Looks like you've made good use of the spell I taught you."

Nico smiled. "Yes, it's come in handy more than once."

Aurora and her mother finally arrived, and awaited Nico's instructions.

Nico opened the grimoire to its center, where The Grand Reversal spell was inscribed, half on the Benandanti side and half on the Malandanti side. He read the first part of the spell, then flipped the book over and read the rest.

"OK, Sofia, you stand here with the gauntlet," Nico directed. "Mr. Pendolino, Aurora, and Mrs. Moraiolo, please join hands around Sofia, forming a triangle."

As the three Benandanti took their places, Nico turned to Gino and Manolo. "The three of us create a Malandanti triangle around Sofia, completing the hexagram."

Nico reviewed the spell once more, then placed the grimoire on the ground. Checking his Swatch, he noted it was now 6:28 p.m. He joined hands with Gino and Manolo.

"All right. We'll need to say the incantation twice to complete the spell and roll back time twelve hours," Nico said to the group. "Is everyone ready?"

"Yes," they replied in unison.

"OK, repeat these words after me:

Through the veil of hours past,
By the echoes of shadows cast,
We summon forth the threads of fate,
To turn back time, before it's too late."

After the first recitation, they watched as Sofia's body began to tremble, fading in and out.

"It's working," Nico said. "Now, one more time."

The group focused and, following Nico's lead, repeated the incantation a second time.

Stefano A Giovannoni

Chapter 36: Groundhog Day

The next morning, Nico was awakened by the sound of the front door slamming shut. He sat up abruptly and glanced at his alarm clock: it read 6:30 a.m.

He listened intently for any further activity within the house. At first, there was only silence, but soon he heard footsteps rapidly approaching, growing louder as they neared his room.

Nico jumped out of bed, standing ready as the door swung open.

"Oh, it's you—you scared me," he said, as Sofia entered the room.

"Nico, we need to talk."

Nico returned to his bed, gesturing for Sofia to join him. "Come on up—and what's that metal, glove-like thing you're holding?"

"OK, listen to me; this is important."

"House, please bring us two cups of coffee," Nico called, settling in. "OK, I'm listening. What's got you so worked up?"

"I've just come from the future."

Nico laughed. "Did someone have a little too much to drink last night? Are you still drunk?"

"No, I'm serious," Sofia implored. "You used The Grand Reversal spell to roll back time so we could save the town."

"Why would we need to do that? Oh, right, today's the last day to return the Coins of Favor to Caleo."

"We already returned them—well, in a future instance we did," Sofia explained, frustrated. "But Caleo took them back, reneged on his promise to spare the town, and even tried to kill us."

Nico looked into her eyes, sensing the intensity in her gaze. "Wait…you're serious."

"I am. And this gauntlet is proof!" Sofia declared, just as a tray with two cups of coffee floated into the room and settled on the bed.

"All right," Nico said, "catch me up on everything over coffee."

As they sipped, Sofia recounted the events.

"Wow!" Nico murmured, amazed as she finished. "So, I really came back from the future to save us?"

"Yes," Sofia confirmed. "It sounds incredible, but it's true. And now you know where this gauntlet came from."

Nico finished his coffee and hopped off the bed. "OK, time to put Project: Snuff out the Fire into action."

"Shall we meet in the foyer in about an hour?"

"Sounds good—see you shortly."

***

An hour later, they reconvened in the foyer.

"Do you have everything we agreed on?" Sofia asked, handing the Gauntlet of Frost to Nico.

Nico double-checked his pocket, then tucked the gauntlet inside. "Yup," Nico confirmed. Then he noticed her charm bracelet. "Hey, why are you wearing that? I hope you weren't thinking of offering it to Calypso—we don't need her help this time. I'm planning to cast the Breathe Water spell so we can make the swim ourselves."

"Yes, I know," Sofia answered. "The fairy door charm is our escape plan, remember?"

"Oh, right," Nico said, opening the door for her. "House, if we don't make it back, thanks for us."

"House, we'll actually be back this time," Sofia added.

***

Just like before, they first stopped at the bank to retrieve the thirteen coins from the safe deposit box. Then the tan Mercedes drove them to the river.

Once they arrived, Nico and Sofia carefully scaled down the rocky embankment to the riverbed.

"There's the willow—" Nico said, pointing, but Sofia was already headed toward the river's edge.

Stepping into the cool water, she urged, "Come on, let's hurry. The heat's already getting to me."

"Agreed," Nico responded, following her across the sand and stones, into the water.

Once they were submerged up to their necks, Nico placed his hand on Sofia's shoulder and whispered the spell, "*Respirare Aqua.*"

As narrow slits opened on the sides of their necks, they dropped into the river's depths and made the long swim to the underwater entrance of the mountain.

Eventually, they reached the end of the passageway and surfaced in the dark inner cavern. As they broke the water's surface, Nico quickly touched Sofia and croaked out the counter spell, "*Respirare Aerem!*" The slits on their necks sealed, and they were able to breathe air again.

They climbed out of the water and into the dark cavern. Nico reached into his pocket for a candle, but Sofia had already placed her hand on Nico's shoulder.

"*Visio Nocturna*," she whispered, granting them night vision.

"Nice one!" Nico complimented, pulling two beach towels from his pocket and handing one to Sofia.

"I can't wait to get this over with," Sofia said, toweling her hair dry.

"Yeah, this is your second time doing it—I don't envy you at all."

Once dry, Sofia folded her towel and handed it back. Nico tucked both towels into his pocket and asked, "OK, ready?"

"Yes," Sofia answered, following Nico through the serpentine tunnel and into the guano-filled bat cave, where Nico suddenly stopped midway.

"Why are you stopping?" Sofia asked.

"We might need a little help," Nico answered, looking up at the colony of bats hanging from the cavern's ceiling. "Hey, little guys," he called. "If you hear me yell, 'Now!' come help us in the next cavern by swarming around Caleo."

"Good thinking!" Sofia commended. "I'm surprised we didn't think of that last time."

They advanced into the passageway leading to Caleo's lair, where Sofia heard his familiar conversation with the mysterious guest. She gestured for Nico to stay still.

"—you've been a loyal ally, bringing me the town relics I requested for my treasure horde," the efreeti said. "And for that, I'll give you the chance to save yourself—for tomorrow, I'm going to destroy the town."

"But why would you do that?" the stranger asked.

"That voice sounds familiar," Nico whispered to Sofia, "but I can't seem to place it."

Sofia had an idea and pulled out her compact. She opened it and angled its mirror carefully, allowing her to glimpse the unknown guest's face.

"Omigod, that's Dino!" Sofia blurted out to Nico.

Caleo turned toward the entrance, grumbling, "Who's there? Come inside and face me!"

"It's time," Sofia said, turning to Nico. "Put on the gauntlet and be ready."

As they entered the cavern, Sofia caught sight of Dino just in time to see him vanish, clutching a brass medallion hanging from his neck. Caleo looked down at the two intruders. "Ah, you meddlesome kids are back. Here to meet your doom?" he said, ending with a maniacal laugh.

"Wait!" Nico held up a purple satin sack by its gold drawstring. "We've collected the Coins of Favor—"

"Ah, just in time," Caleo interrupted, sneering. "Come, bring them here, and we shall talk."

Nico looked up at the terrifying creature, avoiding its gaze, and finished his sentence, "—but we're not giving them back!"

"Insolent fools," Caleo snarled, and moved to the cavern's entrance, blocking their escape. "Your town will surely perish because of your actions. In the meantime, you'll make a fine meal."

Nico quickly positioned himself in front of Sofia, shielding her as the efreeti lumbered toward them, his large, clawed hands outstretched.

Remembering their plan, Sofia fumbled for the fairy door charm on her bracelet, pulled it off, and tossed it onto the ground behind her. "Nico, get ready to grab hold of him."

As Caleo drew near, Nico felt Sofia grip his unadorned hand, and he called out, "Now!"

Caleo raised his clawed hand to strike. "It's been nice knowing you two," he jeered. But just as his hand was about to swoop down, a cloud of bats flooded into the room, swarming around the efreeti exactly as Nico had planned.

While Caleo swatted frantically at the bats, struggling to clear his view, Nico seized the moment and grabbed on to the efreeti's leg with his gauntleted hand. Caleo's movements began to slow as the two watched his fiery red skin turn pale pink, ice crystals forming and spreading across his body.

"What have you done!" Caleo roared.

"It's time you cooled off," Nico snapped back. "Sofia, go for it!"

Still clutching Nico's free hand, Sofia reached out and touched the fairy door, plunging them into a brief moment of darkness. Within seconds, they found themselves in the Snow Fairy Realm, the welcoming crunch of Eldon's men's boots on the snow filling them with relief. They were now safe.

They looked over at Caleo, whose skin was now a light shade of blue; all traces of fire within him appeared to be extinguished, rendering him helpless.

"Nico! Sofia!" Eldon called out to them. "Are you both OK?"

"Yes!" Sofia replied. "All is well—no injuries this time around."

"Wow, so this is the Snow Fairy Realm," Nico remarked, looking around in awe. "Your description didn't do it justice."

"Wait until you see the castle—it's beyond words," Sofia said, distracted by the sound of approaching horses.

They both turned to see an elegant crystal carriage with silver accents drawing near. Eldon directed his men to stand at attention and then addressed Nico and Sofia, "OK, you two, please stand up. The queen is coming to survey the situation."

They brushed the snow off themselves as the royal coach pulled up next to them.

"Whoa!" the coachman commanded, bringing the horses to a halt. He then jumped down and opened the coach's door.

"It is good to see you both again," Queen Anneliese greeted, extending her hand to the coachman for assistance out of the carriage.

"This time went much smoother," Sofia said with a smile, curtseying as Nico bowed before the queen.

The queen inspected the frozen efreeti. "I assume this is the troublemaker you called Caleo? Not so much trouble now," she said with a chortle. "Eldon, transfer this beast to the royal dungeon."

"Yes, Your Majesty," Eldon replied. "Right away."

Turning to Nico and Sofia, the queen continued, "Please, ride with me back to the castle so we can ensure your safe return to your realm."

Nico and Sofia followed the queen into the royal coach, settling into its plush seats as they enjoyed a swift ride through the frozen forest to the castle's courtyard.

As they disembarked, a host of royal attendants gathered to assist the queen, guiding her into the castle. Once in the throne room, Nico approached her. "Your Majesty, I don't remember having been here before, but Sofia has spoken of your hospitality and the use of this gauntlet, which I now return to you with deep gratitude."

The queen's attendant, carrying a red pillow, approached, and Nico carefully placed the Gauntlet of Frost onto it before bowing to the queen.

"I am glad it was helpful and that you were successful in saving your town," the queen replied. "For humans, you are both quite brave—in fact, the court may find it necessary to summon you in the future."

"Thank you, Your Majesty," Nico said. "We're just a realm away should you require our services."

The queen smiled and turned her attention to her scribe. "Gale, come here," she commanded, and the fairy fluttered over to her side.

"Yes, my queen?" Gale responded, awaiting instructions.

"Please escort our adventurers to the Portal Room so that they may return home."

"Right away," Gale nodded. "All right, you two, please follow me."

Nico and Sofia said their goodbyes and followed Gale to the hallway of portraits. When they reached the end, they stopped, standing before the oversized portrait of the king.

"Now that we're alone," Gale began, "I wanted to thank you for having saved my grandniece."

Nico and Sofia exchanged confused glances.

"From your expressions, I suppose I should elaborate," Gale continued. "Fawn is my grandniece."

"Oh—you're welcome!" Nico said, smiling.

"We're close friends—she even created this tattoo," Sofia added, showing her wrist with the hummingbird tattoo.

Gale fluttered closer to inspect it. "Lovely work. Fawn definitely inherited her talent from me, though as the queen's scribe, my skills are now limited to quill and parchment."

"Would you like us to pass a message along to her?" Nico asked.

Gale pulled a tiny, feathered quill from her pocket. "Just give her this," she said, dropping it into Nico's outstretched hand. As the quill touched his palm, it expanded to a human-sized version, much like the one in Chiara's secret attic.

"We'll make sure she gets it," Sofia promised.

"Now, I have delayed your return long enough," Gale said, waving her hand in front of the portrait. The image of the king faded, revealing an entrance through which they could step into the Portal Room.

"I believe you know how to find your way back from here," Gale said. "It was an honor to meet you both—safe travels."

The two waved goodbye, watching as she fluttered back toward the queen's throne room.

Nico turned to Sofia, laughing. "I don't even remember how to get out of here."

"Oh, that's right—it's essentially your first time here," Sofia replied. "I totally forgot to tell you about this part. The pictures work like our fairy doors—we just need to find the one we want and touch its frame."

Nico marveled at the countless framed locations lining the walls. "If we ever want to go to Europe or anywhere, all we have to do is come here for a free trip," he joked.

"The last time we were here, I found a picture that reminded me of the monastery where Paolo and I stayed before being adopted," Sofia mused. "It makes me want to go back to Italy."

"Someday!" Nico replied, spotting the picture of Oliveto. "Ah, here it is—"

Stefano A Giovannoni

Chapter 37: Recap with Friends

Nico and Sofia arrived once again at the door of Indelible Delights, with Fawn standing over them.

"Welcome back, you two!" Fawn greeted them. "My father and I just received word that you'd be returning."

Sofia felt a wave of relief, noticing the temperature was significantly cooler than before. Curious, she looked up at the distant mountain; smoke was no longer billowing from its peak.

"Ah, thank God!" Sofia exclaimed, standing up with Nico to give Fawn a big group hug.

"Whoa!" Fawn laughed, "what's with all this love?"

"I think I can speak for the both of us—we're so glad to be back," Sofia said.

"Yeah—it was a close call…" Nico said, trailing off.

"Nico, what's the matter?" Fawn asked.

"Just a moment of *déjà vu*, I guess," Nico answered.

"Fawn, how about we meet up with you and Solomon later at The Griffon's Claw for drinks?" Sofia suggested. "I think Nico needs a little rest for now."

"Sounds good," Fawn replied. "I'll let Solomon know, and we'll meet you there around eight?"

"Perfect," Nico said. "See you guys then."

Nico and Sofia left the alleyway, noticing the tan Mercedes waiting there for them.

"What a welcoming sight!" Nico said, exhausted. "I don't think I have the energy to walk another block."

Sofia noticed long rows of folding chairs lining the sidewalks on both sides of the street. "Hey, Nico, what are all these chairs for? I don't remember them being here before."

Nico looked down the chair-lined sidewalks and laughed. "Every year, people claim their spots two to three days before Founders' Day to ensure they have a place to sit for the parade."

"Really?"

"Really," Nico confirmed. "It's almost as much of a tradition as Founders' Day itself."

The tired twosome got into the car and drove home. After resting for a bit, they got ready for their night out and headed back to the piazza to meet their friends at The Griffon's Claw.

Over a round of drinks, courtesy of Vincenzo, Sofia recounted the events of the past twelve hours, explaining how they'd met Nico's future self, who had outlined what would happen to the town unless they followed his advice.

"So, the Nico from the future tells us about The Grand Reversal spell in the grimoire—" Sofia began, before Nico cut in.

"And so, we gathered enough people to cast the spell, rewinding time by twelve hours while allowing Sofia to retain all her memories. That was the only way we could have a second chance at saving Oliveto from annihilation," Nico explained. "At first, I didn't believe her when she said she'd already lived this day; I thought she was joking."

Sofia jumped back in. "But when I showed him the Gauntlet of Frost, there was no denying that I was telling the truth."

"And that gauntlet was the one from your first visit to the Snow Fairy Realm, right?" Fawn asked.

"Yes," Sofia confirmed. "Oh, and speaking of that realm, we met a relative of yours!"

"Really?" Fawn asked excitedly. "I didn't know I had family there."

Nico took a sip of his Negroni, then reached into his pocket, pulling out a quill. "Here, this is for you," he said, handing it to Fawn. "It's from your great-aunt Gale. She wanted me to give it to you."

"Cool. Literally!" Fawn examined the chilly quill. "Do you think it has any magical properties?"

"It might," Sofia suggested. "Your aunt didn't really say—she just asked us to give it to you. She's the queen's royal scribe, documenting everything for her."

A little tipsy, Fawn waved the quill around like a magic wand. Pretending to cast a spell, she touched it to her glass, and condensation on the outside began to crystallize.

"Whoa, little lady," Solomon chuckled, moving Fawn's hand away. "Maybe explore its powers once you've sobered up."

The friends laughed, and Fawn, heeding Solomon's advice, tucked the quill into her bun.

Vincenzo came over to check on them and asked, "Another round for my son and his friends?"

"Not for me, thanks," Nico answered. "It's going to be an early night for me, but the others might like one."

"I probably shouldn't," Fawn said. "I need to be up early to help my dad with our float. You two are coming to the Founders' Day Parade, right?"

"Of course!" Sofia said. "Especially now—the town has even more reason to celebrate. It almost didn't exist!"

Nico leaned into Sofia, whispering, "Are you sleeping at the house tonight or staying the night with your man?"

"Since there's no impending doom, I think I'll spend our last night here with him," she whispered back.

Vincenzo, with his enhanced hearing, caught their private conversation and, without thinking, asked, "Oh, are you two heading back to Connecticut tomorrow after the celebration?"

Slightly annoyed, Nico looked up at his father. "As if you didn't know."

Sofia added, "Yes. After all, wasn't it your suggestion to Nico?"

"Yes," Vincenzo said, addressing the group before turning to Fawn and Solomon. "I'm not sure how much Nico has told you, but my sire, Minerva, has come to Oliveto. I suspect she's behind the recent string of deaths in town over the past few months."

"Oh, that's dreadful," Fawn shivered.

Vincenzo continued, "Knowing her, she's probably in hiding, plotting revenge for my having deserted her centuries ago. I think she's realized Nico is my son and will likely try to harm him and his family."

Nico added, "We've already found signs she's been casing my mother's house, and likely mine as well."

A thought struck Sofia. "Vincenzo, can Minerva perform magic?"

"Thankfully, no," he answered, though concern filled his eyes. "Why do you ask? Did something happen?"

Nico turned to Sofia. "Do you think the Babau—"

"Exactly," Sofia interrupted.

"But my father said she can't do magic."

Vincenzo piped in, "But that doesn't mean she couldn't get help from one of the Malandanti witches in town."

"Well, if that's the case," Nico started, "we made sure she won't know we're onto her."

Fawn's curiosity was piqued. "How so?"

"We never banished the Babau," Sofia explained. "Nico's nonna told us that banishing a Babau would alert whoever summoned it."

Nico added, "So, after Negroni had her revenge by killing it, we put it in the freezer instead."

"Brilliant," Vincenzo praised. "That buys us all more time to figure out a plan. But in the meantime, you two should leave town as soon as possible."

"Ah, I'm just getting used to having my girl around," Solomon sighed. "I'm not looking forward to going back to nightly phone calls."

"Well, if either of you can get some time off," Nico suggested, "I can always return to Oliveto and take you with me through the fairy door."

"Yeah," Sofia said. "Then you could spend some time with us in Connecticut."

Fawn and Solomon's faces lit up at the idea.

"Well, if you're not having more drinks, I'll excuse myself to check on the other customers," Vincenzo said. "Please enjoy the rest of your evening."

The group thanked Vincenzo and eventually parted ways for the night. Solomon left with Sofia, escorting her back to his place, while Fawn accepted Nico's offer to drive her home. Afterward, he returned to his own home, eager for a good night's sleep.

Chapter 38: Happy Founders' Day?

The next morning, Nico woke up feeling refreshed; it was the first good night's sleep he'd had since returning to Oliveto.

He went over to the French doors, opened them, and took a deep breath of the cool morning air. "Ah," he sighed, "it's so nice to have the temperature back to normal."

Surprisingly, the air was a little too chilly, so Nico grabbed his sweatshirt and pulled it over his head before stepping outside. As he walked toward the bubbling fountain, a hummingbird appeared, hovering before him and staring intently. Nico nodded in acknowledgment, smiling at the tiny creature.

Out of the corner of his eye, he noticed the garden gnomes standing in a circle under one of the orange trees. "What's going on over here, guys?" he asked, knowing they wouldn't answer.

He strolled over to the gnomes, and the friendly hummingbird followed close by, hovering at his shoulder. "Hmm, I wonder what they're trying to tell me?" he mused, turning to the hummingbird. "Any ideas?"

The hummingbird darted over to the group of gnomes, then flew upward, circling around the garlic they'd previously harvested and hung to dry.

"Ah, yes," Nico acknowledged. "I almost forgot. I still need to replace the old bulbs on the windowsills before I leave town."

Thanking the gnomes for the reminder, he took down the cured garlic bulbs, then headed back to the house. The hummingbird fluttered in front of him, bouncing up and down.

"Oh, yes—thank you, too," Nico said to the tiny bird, which appeared to nod before zooming off.

Back in the kitchen, Nico trimmed the garlic's roots and leaves, then called out, "House, please make me a double *cappuccino*." With the prepared bulbs in hand, he walked around the house, replacing the old ones on each windowsill. *This should at least keep Minerva out while I'm away*, he thought.

On his way back to the kitchen, Nico grabbed the morning paper from the front door and sat at the kitchen island with his *cappuccino*. He unfolded the newspaper and read the headline: *Cooler Temperatures Arrive Just in Time for Oliveto's Founders' Day Celebration!*

Flipping through the pages, he found the parade details. "Ah, here it is," he muttered. "'Parade starts at noon, followed by food and festivities in the piazza.' Plenty of time to get ready."

It was 10:00 a.m., and after finishing his *cappuccino*, he stopped in front of the Mirror of the Dead to update his nonna and nonno on recent events.

"We're so proud of you," Chiara praised. "Your nonno and I knew you'd find a way to save the town."

"I couldn't have done it alone," Nico replied. "Sofia's quick thinking saved me more than once."

"And how is she doing?" Chiara asked. "Is she enjoying my gift?"

"She's happy with her boyfriend, Solomon," Nico answered. "But when it comes to your medallion, she's grown quite fond of casting Malandanti spells—perhaps a bit too fond."

"Well, just make sure…" Chiara began, before her eyes suddenly closed, and she fell silent.

Oh, well, it probably wasn't anything important, Nico thought, leaving the short hallway to make one last stop at the attic.

Nico went up to the secret room, sat at Chiara's desk, and pulled out a piece of stationery. After writing a short note, he slipped it into an envelope and reached for sealing wax.

"*Incendium*," he intoned and held his lit finger up to the wax, letting it drip onto the envelope flap. Once a nice pool had formed, Nico removed his nonno's signet ring and pressed it into the wax. He then placed the sealed envelope into his pocket, replaced the ring on his finger, and headed downstairs.

After a shower and getting dressed, Nico left the house, choosing to walk to the piazza. He took the same scenic route he and Sofia had used on her first visit to Oliveto. Seeing the folding chairs lined up along the sidewalks reminded him how much he cherished his town. Many cheerful townspeople greeted him as he strolled down toward the piazza, and Nico smiled at each of them, aware that this moment had nearly been lost.

As he passed Vicolo Fato, he thought, I could use more coffee—I'll stop by Patisserie Angelique.

Turning the corner, he spotted Lisette clearing off one of the café tables. "*Bonjour*, Nico," she called out. "Are you here to watch the parade?"

"Good morning, Lisette," Nico greeted. "Yes, and I thought I'd grab a coffee and maybe a snack beforehand."

"Well, take a seat before they're all gone—this is a prime spot to watch the parade."

"Good idea," Nico said, sitting at an empty table. "Sofia and Solomon are supposed to join me."

"I'll be right back with some coffee."

"And a *pain au chocolat* too, please," Nico called out as she walked away.

"*Tout de suite!*" she replied.

As Nico looked out at the many townspeople taking their spots on the sidewalk, he was startled by a tap on his shoulder and quickly turned around.

"Hey, friend," Sofia greeted, with Solomon by her side.

"So glad you made it," Nico said with relief. "I was hoping I wasn't going to have to sit here by myself."

Solomon pulled out a chair for Sofia and then took a seat himself.

"Looks like you wouldn't have been alone for long," Sofia teased, waving to Nico's family across the street.

"I didn't even see them there—they must've just arrived," Nico said, waving to them. "Let me know if you want some coffee or anything; Lisette will be back out shortly, and she said we could sit here for the parade."

"Oh good, I seemed to have worked up an appetite this morning," Solomon said, causing Sofia to blush.

Lisette returned with Nico's order. "*Bonjour*—coffee for you two as well?"

"Yes, please," Solomon said, "and whatever he's having."

The sound of a loud whistle signaled the start of the parade. Nico checked his Swatch; it was noon on the dot. "Looks like they're on time as usual."

Lisette soon returned with their order and asked, "Would it be all right if I take my break at your table?"

"Of course!" Sofia answered, and Solomon pulled out the remaining chair for her. "Are you excited to see Fawn on their float?"

"Yes! And it's my first time watching an American parade!" Lisette said eagerly.

A marching band led the parade, followed by the Oliveto Fire Department, who tossed candy to the crowd from their shiny new fire engine.

Suddenly, a few groans from the crowd caught Nico and his friends' attention. They watched as a fashionably dressed woman pushed her way through, stopping about twenty-five feet ahead with her back to them.

"*Mon Dieu*! Who is that rude woman?" Lisette asked.

"I'd recognize that old harpy from any angle," Solomon grumbled. "That's Malvina Falena. She's one of our competitors—own's Falena's Fine Wares."

Sofia's eyes widened. "This town has harpies, too?"

Solomon laughed. "Sorry, I shouldn't call her that—it's an insult to harpies. But she just makes my sap boil."

Just then, Lisette jumped up from her seat. "Here comes Fawn's float!"

"Wow, that's impressive!" Nico said, standing to see over the crowd.

Indelible Delights' horse-drawn float was styled like a circus sideshow, with vintage, hand-painted canvases depicting various attractions: the Sword Swallower, the Fire Eater, the World's Skinniest Man, and the Tattooed Girl.

"That's Sterling as the World's Skinniest Man," Sofia called out.

"And of course, that's Fawn as the Tattooed Girl!" Nico said. "I don't recognize the others."

"They're probably other members of the fey community," Solomon suggested.

As the float drew closer, Sofia noticed Malvina's bandaged arm reaching into her purse and pulling out a woolen scarf. Her lips seemed to be moving as she shook the scarf out. "Guys, something's up," Sofia warned.

The horse pulling the float suddenly became agitated as winged insects swarmed around its head, obscuring its vision. It started backing toward the crowd, where Nico spotted Remus's frightened face across the street.

"Sofia, I think you're right," Nico confirmed. "The horse is getting closer to Remus and my parents."

Sofia stood up and hurried toward the float.

"Stay here, guys," Nico told the others. "I'm going with Sofia to make sure nothing happens to my brother."

Sofia stopped, positioning herself behind Malvina, who seemed to be snickering. "That witch is up to something," she said to Nico. "I'll put a stop to her."

Nico paused, stunned, and watched his best friend point a finger at Malvina's legs and silently mouth a few words, causing Malvina to collapse to the ground.

As Malvina cried out in pain, the horse reared, its front legs poised to come down on Remus. Sofia quickly pointed her finger at the horse and mouthed a few more words.

One of the horse's back legs suddenly buckled, causing it to fall safely into the center of the street, away from Remus and Mr. and Mrs. Kynigós.

Nico rushed over to his brother. "Are you guys OK?" he asked.

"We're fine, Nico," Siena answered.

"Something must have spooked the horse," Pétros added.

"You OK, Remus?" Nico asked, noticing his brother's tearful nod.

Turning to the injured horse, Nico cautiously approached it, joined by Sterling, who had jumped down from the float. The horse was in severe pain, and with closer examination, Nico noticed that its left hind leg was broken, with the cannon bone protruding through the skin. He knelt beside the horse, pointed to its leg, and whispered, "*Sarcio Ossum.*" Nico and Sterling watched as the bone slipped back under the skin and the wound closed.

The horse looked up at Nico, almost as if to thank him. Nico smiled, and Sterling helped the horse off the ground. As it rose, Nico noticed a pile of dead Death's-head moths on the ground. *That must be what agitated the poor horse*, Nico thought.

Sterling addressed the crowd, "Everything's fine! Let the parade resume!"

Nico waded through the cheering townspeople to rejoin Sofia and the others.

"Sofia, can I talk to you for a minute?" Nico asked.

"Sure," Sofa answered, stepping a few feet aside with Nico.

"What happened to Malvina?" he asked.

"I don't know. She just shot me a wicked stare before hobbling off into the crowd."

"You seem to have no remorse—I saw what you did. Are you OK?" Nico asked, concerned.

"I'm fine," Sofia replied, a slight smirk forming on her lips. "I did what I had to do to protect the people I care about. Besides, she's probably the one who sent the Babau!"

Nico stayed silent for a moment, thinking. "If she sent the Babau, then she's probably working with Minerva—"

"Which means your family was targeted today and is in danger," Sofia said, finishing his thought.

Nico shook his head. "I guess we really need to heed my father's warning and leave town today."

"Sad but true," Sofia acknowledged. "Until we can come up with a plan, it's probably for the best. But for now, let's rejoin our friends and enjoy the time we have left."

The two rejoined their friends and sat down to watch the rest of the parade. About ten minutes after the last participants had passed, Fawn came from around the corner and hurried over to them.

"Fawn, your float was stunning," Lisette said, beaming. "And you were amazing!"

Solomon stood and offered his seat to Fawn, who sat down and took a deep breath. "Aside from the brief scare, I think it went pretty well," she said with a relieved smile.

"You must be starving," Sofia said.

"You bet I am. I've been up all morning and didn't even have breakfast," Fawn replied.

Nico stood up. "Should we head over to the piazza and check out the food booths and activities?"

Fawn looked over at Lisette. "I wish you could come with us. When do you get off work?"

"Surprisingly, the owner decided to close early today—at 1 p.m.," Lisette said with a smile. "So, I'll join you all shortly."

The four of them headed to the piazza, spending the rest of the afternoon sampling different foods and playing carnival-style games. Solomon even won a stuffed animal for Sofia, which she proudly carried around.

As the day wound down and the townspeople dispersed, Nico and Sofia began saying their goodbyes to their friends.

"Fawn, can you do me a favor?" Nico whispered as he hugged her.

"Of course," Fawn whispered back.

Nico discreetly pulled the sealed envelope from his pocket and handed it to her. "Please give this to Gino," he said softly.

Fawn smiled, took the envelope, and quickly slipped it into her pocket before anyone could notice.

As Nico and Sofia left the piazza and headed toward the house, Nico couldn't shake the thought of how easily Sofia had cast such a harmful spell.

"Sofia, what made you choose to cast the *Break Bone* spell—not once, but twice today?"

"I don't know," she snapped, then immediately softened her tone. "Sorry. I'm still trying to make sense of it myself. One moment, we were all talking, and when I saw Malvina, I just knew she was up to something bad. I was filled will malice. In that moment, I just wanted to hurt her."

"Well, you succeeded," Nico replied. "As for the horse, I suppose that was the only way to keep it from falling on Remus. Thank you for keeping my brother safe."

Sofia just smiled but remained silent for the rest of the walk home.

As they entered the front door, a tray with two Aperol spritzes awaited them on the entry table.

"Ah, perfect! Thank you, House." Sofia said, picking up one of the drinks.

Nico took the other glass and raised it in a toast. "To us—and to surviving another adventurous stay."

"*Cin cin!*" they both said, clinking glasses before taking a sip.

"Well, let's gather anything we want to take back to Hornsby Manor and meet in the backyard in fifteen minutes," Nico suggested.

Sofia nodded, took a sip of her drink, and then went to her bedroom.

Knowing he could summon anything he left behind, Nico used the time to call his mother to say goodbye and to visit Negroni before making his way to the backyard. There, the gnomes had gathered by the fairy door, as if they sensed that he and Sofia were leaving.

"Hi, guys," Nico greeted them warmly. "Please take care of things, and just knock on the fairy door if you need me."

"Goodbye, House," Sofia said, opening the door to the backyard. "Thank you for everything."

"There she is," Nico said to the gnomes, then turned to Sofia. "Your buddies are here, waiting to send you off."

Sofia laughed. "I'm already missing them," she said, extending her hand to Nico. "Shall we?"

"Yep," Nico answered, and then touched the fairy door.

***

A few months passed without incident; even the deaths in Oliveto seemed to decrease in frequency, at least according to Fawn and Solomon's reports during their visits. Nico also made frequent calls to his family to make sure they were all right.

As the fall semester approached, Nico and Sofia registered for their courses and purchased all their supplies. Their days settled into a routine of school, sleep, rinse, and repeat—until one particular Wednesday night. It was October 7th and the moon was full.

Exhausted from an evening cram session, they retired early. Sofia tried to fall asleep, but the moonlight streaming through the window kept her awake.

"Uh!" came a groan.

Sofia sat up and glanced at the clock; it was 11:59 p.m. She got up to investigate, thinking it sounded like Nico. She slowly opened their adjoining door and saw Nico tossing and turning in his bed.

"No!" he said, his voice growing louder.

Sofia cautiously approached. His body glistened with perspiration as he rocked back and forth, gripped by some kind of nightmare. As she sat on the edge of the bed, the grandfather clock in the hallway chimed, counting up to midnight.

Suddenly, Nico sat up, terror in his eyes, startling Sofia so much that she fell off the bed. She scrambled to her feet and rushed to his side. Nico stared blankly ahead.

"Nico, are you OK?" she asked, placing her hands on his sweaty shoulders.

"He's returned!" Nico cried out before collapsing back onto the bed and drifting back into sleep. Sofia watched him with concern, feeling a sense of foreboding. But what could it mean?

"And so, another adventure begins," she muttered to herself with a smirk, shaking her head.

Made in the USA
Middletown, DE
23 June 2025

77377791R00184